THE GiFT HORSE

THE GIFT HORSE

A novel by
Leslie Silton

The New Atlantian Library

For my dad.

"... sing of the building of the horse of wood, which Epeius made with Athena's help, the horse which once Odysseus led up into the citadel as a thing of guile, when he had filled it with the men who sacked Ilium"

- Samuel Butler

PART ONE:

New York City

CHAPTER ONE

"Yikes!" Maggie and Parker shrieked in unison. Maggie cast a look over her shoulder at the nearly horizontal scarves and coattails of pedestrians hurrying down the street. She decided she wouldn't have been surprised if dogsleds mushed by men with frozen beards suddenly came racing by. For sure The Montreal Express was out in full force, pushing normally winter-hardened New Yorkers into any available doorway or building for shelter. The girls hurried under the portico, in through the revolving door to the cavernous foyer. At least she and Parker would be inside for a few hours while the battering ram of bitter cold continued to hammer down on the city outside.

They joined the lineup of ex-pedestrians. Parker huddled close behind Maggie still pulling off her mittens, stuffing them into the deep pockets of her down-filled duffle coat.

"This is ridiculous," Maggie said to no one in particular.

Others were welcome to comment or not. After all, this was New York City. A brief monologue by a disgruntled citizen was considered normal. The main branch of the library was one of her favorite places on any day. The bitter cold had merely hurried their arrival because the girls had already planned to spend several hours working on homework assignments anyway.

"Hey!" Maggie yelped when someone bumped her. Turning around to glare at the offender, she heard a muffled, "Sorry." The unidentified Someone was swathed in a large, second-hand army coat, their face hidden by a wolf fur-edged hood tied up like a funnel. Maggie sized him up. She was pretty sure it was a 'he'. Obviously on the way to some remote location in the arctic, making a last quick pit stop in civilization to borrow some good reading material. A red scarf peeked through at the throat. (Useful for waving at search-and-rescue planes.)

His hooded face was looking down at the floor. She looked down, too. His footgear was sneakers and heavy gym socks. Ah. A Tourist.

"It's all right," Maggie offered diplomatically. "Everyone wants to get inside." With that she turned away.

Now that they were indoors, talking was a lot easier because *the* wind would not be ripping her words right out of her mouth. Being in the queue meant they would all be shuffling forward like prisoners on a chain gang for the next little while. Parker was first to pick up their discussion where they last left off.

"Remember: it was *war*," she said while unwinding a six-foot-long scarf.

Maggie got down to business unbuttoning the top of her coat, pulling open the knot of her own scarf – a mere five-foot wonder. Her response to Parker's argument was violent shakes of her head.

"Listen, babe," said Parker. "A lot of people think it's hip to mock the idea."

Maggie replied, lowering her voice to a husky whisper, "Yeah, some people also think everyone is out to screw them." Raising the volume back to normal, she said, "What's that about, huh?"

While waiting for Parker to top that, she lost focus as the image of Leonardo da Vinci's extraordinary "Il Cavallo" crossed her mind. She had been making copies of this and his other equine drawings for the past month. Too bad they couldn't go to Milan for the unveiling of the real thing. Maggie knew that all things Italian could send Parker over the moon. As for Maggie, she was blissed out just considering the monumental sculpture ... until Parker tapped her on the shoulder. What's this? Parker was smirking at her.

"No, listen," Maggie said picking up where she left off. "You simply can't walk around thinking everyone has a hidden motive. You just can't live your life that way."

Parker shrugged. "Well, of course, not *everyone* is dangerous and untrustworthy. But when are you going to get it through your head that there are some bad hats out there. The trick is to be able to recognize who they are."

"Oh, phooey," said Maggie. Signaling a time-out, she wiped the smile off her face. This particular ongoing discussion tended to be fairly intense so entertainment breaks were a necessity. Maggie had it down to a science. She launched into her favorite gag: a pantomime of Simon Legree. Just a few deft motions. Twisting the ends of long (imaginary) mustache ends while silently demanding The Rent, she quickly morphed into Poor Thing begging piteously. Then Maggie mouthed in silence the famous, *"But I can't pay the rent!"* As Legree, again, she strangled Poor Thing, which was Maggie energetically throttling herself, gurgling dramatically. But she couldn't keep a straight face and burst out laughing.

Parker laughed, too. It might be an old chestnut but it was still very funny. Even The Tourist just behind Maggie horse-laughed except that when she turned around, she saw that his face was still covered. She shrugged. The lady standing in front of Parker, however, a proper uptown matron, definitely disapproved of their hi-jinks and aimed a frown at them both.

"Excuse me, but we're not in church," Parker replied in a loud whisper, thereby partially disproving the notion. However, all around the lobby there was plenty of low-volume chatter, foot stamping, hand-warming activity echoing. Also every time someone new entered, the wind would whistle loudly through the revolving door, announcing a new escapee had arrived.

The girls smiled at each other. And rolled their eyes. The long queue was growing longer as more people hurried in. The security checker was falling way behind.

Parker pushed Maggie on the shoulder. "You're such a goof. Hey, maybe they'll set up sleeping cots. We won't have to go back out there at all," she replied, half-seriously and they both giggled.

The rigid shoulders of the lady in front continued to demonstrate how thoroughly she disapproved, but The Tourist behind them apparently did because there was chortling coming from deep inside the fur-edged funnel. Maggie turned around a third time to have a friendly word but whoever he was, he was still turtled in his coat, so she gave it up. Well, it was that cold. She could still feel it in her bones, too, so she gave her hands another blood-stirring shake.

Meanwhile, the funny had worn off. Parker was ready to enter the fray of their long-running discourse again. She tapped Maggie on the arm.

"Listen, missy. People with bad intentions don't wear long, greasy mustachios and twist the ends while leering."

"You think?" Maggie replied, then executed a reprise of her favorite moment – Poor Thing getting strangled by Legree (another fun self-throttling).

Both girls laughed out loud. As it happened, they had also finally reached the front of the line. Their backpacks, having been inspected and found innocent of weapons, drugs or liquids that could spill, they headed for the stairs. The affronted matron ahead of them took a final moment to harrumph loudly, turned left, heading for the elevator.

"Oh, geez. I don't think she's here to borrow books," Parker whispered, nudging Maggie's arm. "That's the way to the Trustee's Room on the second floor."

"You know this because?"

"Richard and Emily took me to an event there once. Very luxurious."

"Naturally," Maggie said. "Anyway, laughing isn't a shooting offense ... yet," and they both laughed again.

Reaching the long stairway, Parker guided Maggie to one side, allowing people to pass. "Stand still," she ordered. "My question remains: so, do you know what to look for?" Leaning in very closely, she finished off with a determined, "Hmmm?"

Maggie didn't like the way this was going. "I know enough," she said, angling away. "Anyway, would you be willing to turn down the very thing you want more than anything?" She let that sink in. She was sure she had Parker pinned down at last.

"Listen closely," Parker answered back. "You know what happened. The Trojans were total suckers for a tribute. The Greeks were their *enemy*. Hello? Look at me. E-n-e-m-y? Had they not been waging war against the Trojans for nine years? Why are the Trojans suddenly giving gifts? Come on already. I understand the Greeks were pretty sick of the fighting. Nine years is a long time ... *but see? That's how you do it*. You work on your enemy – you work on them – on and on – until they let down their guard. They shouldn't, but they do! When it comes to freedom, you can never let down your guard.

"Listen, Maggs, people never give up on something once they set their mind to it. Some dictator thinks he has it all sewed up. What about Hitler? If he hadn't gone on vacation during the Battle of Britain, we might all be speaking German and '*heiling*' each other. But he screwed up. He even screwed up again. D-Day even started without him! He was off having nookie with Eva when he should have been paying close attention. What about the White Russians? Huh? They were the descendants of Swedish mercenaries – hired by the Russian nobles a long time back. I mean, I'm sorry for Nicholas and Anastasia and the royal family getting slaughtered ..." (she shuddered) "... but that's the thing. The Russian people never agreed to be ruled by a bunch of ..."

"Oh, no, no. That's just too long a time to be carrying a grudge," Maggie interrupted

"What?! What's the matter with you? Of course it's not! Listen. Those Swedish mercenaries were brought in like ... enforcers ... see? You're a peasant. You've got no rights and no way to fight back. But you can bide your time. Injustice can really fester. Of course, the czar thinks it's all forgotten. But it's not! So what if it takes a few generations? Peasants have nothing but time, starvation and backbreaking work, of course. Finally, the Bolshies come along and they have the perfect solution ..." Parker here aimed an imaginary gun and pulled the trigger. "*Pi-chew! Pi-chew!* End of *uninvited family dynasty.*"

Maggie shook her head. "But what if you can show the other person something they didn't know ... like how Nicholas totally felt he was Russian ... like ... he was their king and he had devoted his life to them. He built schools and hospitals. He did lots of good."

"Except that it wasn't really his money to spend! It was the wealth of his country," Parker reminded her. "All those tiaras, Fabergé eggs, furs and jewels. Think, Maggs: tapestries, gilded furniture, chandeliers the size of a baby elephants – ohmygod ... all that *stuff.* The whole royal family and all the hangers-on, just making out like bandits while everyone suffered. It was plunder! Remember: it wasn't his money. No wonder they had a revolution. *Pi-chew, pi-chew* ..." She blew away the imaginary smoke from the barrel of her imaginary gun with a grim smile.

"Maybe he could have done what we did after the Civil War. You know – forty acres and a mule." It was a weak comeback. In fact, she felt like she was sliding towards a rift in the earth.

"Sure. Go forth, peasant. Take this brace of oxen and make a living. Now you've got a chunk of forest. You're free now. Hmmm? I don't think so. Anyway, they got Communism instead," and here she shrugged, a smug smile on her face.

Maggie had to admit Parker was getting the upper hand, but she still wasn't willing to concede. "So, okay. Nicholas should have made it be known that his allegiance was to the Russian people, that he had foresworn his Swedish heritage."

"Well, we don't know if he thought about it or not. But the fact is he didn't say it. Maybe it would have saved their lives ... maybe. But I don't think so. The only thing to do would have been to pack up the royal luggage, leaving behind all the jewels and painted eggs, furs, silk gowns – all their ill-gotten gain – and take the cheapest way home – *rapido*. Of course that takes a lot of personal integrity. Of course it requires some serious moral courage ... I guess it could be done. Except that *some people are not up to the challenge*. Like the Romanoffs." She pointed her finger and fired off another round. *"Pi-chew."*

"God knows you've had my back for years ..."

Suddenly there was a different inflection in Parker's voice that Maggie recognized all too well. Parker was no longer talking about the Russian Revolution.

"... I mean, your parents are more like real parents to me than ... Richard should be paying Evan for foster child support, for god's sake ..."

Maggie fumed. Richard. Of course. The royal stinker himself. No hump. Not much of a kingdom, but still ... a stinker ... and of course there was no use looking for help from The Adored Emily (as her mother was disrespectfully referred to by Parker). Obviously Richard, the paternal rat, had committed some new sin.

"What did he do this time?"

Parker's face crumpled.

"Oh, god," Maggie demanded. "What! Tell me right now!"

"They're closing the apartment …"

"But we're supposed to be moving in there in June!"

"Tell me about it. I am so seriously disgusted … Richard says they don't need the apartment anymore, now that I'm graduating. I'm sorry, Maggs. This is just the shits. We had everything planned …"

"Not to mention that's your home, for god's sake. What's the matter with that man? Is he totally devoid of human feeling?!" Maggie growled.

But Parker didn't notice. "He says – get this – they are going to stay in a hotel when they're in town. Right. Some hotel. It's *The Pierre*. He makes it sound as though they're staying in a log cabin with an outhouse. Anyway, he says it's more convenient and cost-efficient. Oh, sure. Like the man knows anything about economic restraint. He knew we were counting on living there. The creep. Do you understand? My father is a freakin' creep. That's what." She sat down on a wide marble step. "Well, we technically have ten months. Until Christmas. We were going to get place of our own anyway …" She closed her eyes.

"Hey," Maggie said, tapping her on the shoulder.

Parker opened her eyes.

"See these?" Maggie said as she held up her hands. "These are not broken. Plus, I've got a little money saved.

Plus Gramma Nonie is going to give me some graduation moola. I can cash in the Certificates of Deposit that Grandpa Brendan left me ... you know Evan and Barbara will help us. Besides, it's not like Richard and Emily can actually leave you high and dry ..."

The truth was Richard could – legally speaking. Her list of resources had dried up. She looked at Parker, whose eyes were now closed. Right then Maggie wanted to strangle Richard. Really strangle him. Really. *Really.*

"Yeah, I guess ... anyway, Emily did tell me that she's been siphoning off money that Richard doesn't know anything about ... oh, sure. Like that's possible. He knows. He just likes making her sneak ... I'd feel sorry for her if I wasn't her daughter."

Unlikely starvation was never the point. Of course they were welcome to live with Evan and Barbara – actually it was a really nice room – but what kind of life would that be? What was the good of graduating from college, only to go on living with your parents?

"I think Evan and Richard should duel! Meet up at 5 a.m. in the meadow over in Central Park. Barbara and Emily can be their seconds. I can see it now. Rolled-up New York Times Financial Section for weapons. Well?" Maggie really was angry.

Parker smiled wanly. "No. It wouldn't work. Richard would die clueless. A total waste of a good newspaper. I'm sorry I got you all riled up." She was feeling contrite. "We've still got ten months officially. Okay? Right?" She nudged Maggie. "Right?"

Maggie nodded. "Sure." She was still focused on Richard. Richard The Detestable. Her own father would never do anything so low. She was so lucky, it was disgusting.

"I had to tell you," Parker said. "I thought I would explode. He called this morning ... oh, never mind. I'm not starting again." She held up her hands. "See, I'm done."

Maggie grabbed her by the shoulders. "Of course you have to tell me. That goes without saying." Holding up her index finger for the 'one minute time out'. "I say we get a place of our own as soon as we graduate. Serve Richard right. I say we stuff his apartment."

Parker stood up. "Yes!" and she punched the air. "Serfs of Russia arise! What's the Russian National Anthem? *Allons enfants de la patrie* ... oh, that's *Le Marseillaise*. Well, never mind. But that reminds me. Back to business: The Trojans versus the Greeks ..." She looked around. Below her, the foyer was still busy with foot traffic. "So listen, Maggs. You can argue that Nicholas was clueless. And I do mean Nicholas. Just a big warm, fuzzy, benevolent dear of a king but ..." Here her voice softened to a whisper, "Oh, who knows what he knew."

Back to Richard again. Maggie jiggled Parker's coat sleeve. "The way I look at it ... this trouble is mainly your fault."

Parker gasped. "Me!?"

Maggie continued: "Of course. *You've spoiled us.* Richard and Emily are fools to waste a great person like you ... so I say phooey on them. I always think we're getting the best end of this deal."

The affinity card. Maggie could play it like a master at these moments, when Parker thought she just might succumb to her father's tyranny. There was no discounting the fact that affinity of the Malone Family was a powerful force. Take that *King* Richard. The only thing missing is your hump, you rat!

Parker looked at Maggie. "You win. The Chair recognizes the Malone Family." Sweeping her arm up the stairs, she said, "Onward, Noble Artist."

Maggie savored the exultation that temporarily banishing Richard always provided. Having reached the top landing, they walked through the Catalog Room into the main reading room. Fortunately their favorite spot was unoccupied. Dumping her things on a corner chair, Maggie sat down.

"Oh, no, you don't. Come along, Rembrandt," ordered Parker. "Get up. Go ... research. Remember?" She had finally calmed down and was back in control.

Conversation lapsed while the end of the long table was covered with pens, notebooks, laptops and other paraphernalia. Maggie walked down to the Reference Desk.

"I need a little help," she said to a familiar face focused at a computer terminal. "This time it's Paul Gauguin."

The face replied with a show of mild amusement. Ms. Browning was a very good Reference Librarian. Over the last couple of years Maggie had discovered that the woman was more than capable of sussing out especially good material when it came to the subjects of art history and artists.

"I need to explain why an artist who didn't care about being famous, who kept trying to leave civilization behind, was also almost completely obsessed with what people thought about him."

The librarian's eyes glittered with interest. "I'll see what I've got. You've read his letters, if memory serves me?"

"Yes, last fall. It was a good start. But I want to do more about this. If I can."

Ms. Browning turned to her computer terminal again, ran competent fingers rapidly over the keys. She scanned the results. "I'll be back," she said and hurried away.

From her seat Parker watched the librarian. She noted as a colleague stopped her to exchange a few words. From this distance she couldn't hear what they were saying, only the librarian's surprising laugh – silvery and clever. Probably a Wellesley grad, Parker thought ungraciously as she aimed a frown in that direction. That charm is strictly manufactured. I can practically guarantee it. Parker knew a phony when she met one. Maggie, she reminded herself, did not. That was the main difference between them. Parker really did not like Ms. Browning. She added to her disapproval: probably rents romance movies and eats unbuttered popcorn to keep her figure.

She flicked an eye at the clock, reminding herself that she had a paper to finish so she quelled her disapproval. What she really needed was to write one more mind-blowing paper. Either she would stagger her instructors with her scholarly brilliance or she could kiss a long goodbye to any hope of winning the one remaining full-year scholarship to study abroad. Parker wanted to go to Italy so badly she ached. What Richard would not provide, Parker would get anyway – somehow! Poor little rich girl. The joke was on her. No one would believe it. No one ever does. But eat your heart out, Richard Feldman. The Malones love me. She opened her laptop and got busy.

Maggie walked back to their table, sat down and got to work. At four o'clock she was ready to wrap up for the day. Her search had rewarded her with some useful tidbits, the sort that always earned extra points from instructors. She looked up to see Ms. Browning standing there.

"May I?" she asked. Turning Maggie's laptop around, she tapped the keys in quick succession, bringing up a web page. "Take a look at that ... also I have a couple of books from the stacks coming up shortly. Here's a list – some resources you might want to check out." She left the handwritten list on the table and walked away..

"Thanks," Maggie called out while peering at the monitor. "She's right. Look, Parker. We all forget that Gauguin lived in Peru as a young child ..." her voice drifting into silence as she read the contents of the screen, tapped into the search box, following to a link.

Parker nodded and went back to work on her own report.

Maggie's attention re-surfaced. She checked the clock on the wall. "As long as we've got five minutes, why not take a quick peek," she muttered to herself, reading down the hand-written list left by Ms. Browning. Finding an interesting item, she tapped it into the search box. "Oh, this is pretty good ..." as she lapsed into silence again, absorbed. After scanning the home page, she started following various links again, now ignoring stomach growls, pushing on.

Parker heard Maggie's stomach gurgling and laughed a couple of times.

"Okay. That's it. I'm *so* hungry. Parker?" She bookmarked the page and exiting the Internet, looked up.

"How's it going?" It was Ms. Browning. In her hands were three books.

"It's good. I'm done. I've been to this site already," she replied pointing to the list, "and I bookmarked that one." "I'll do the rest at home. Thanks. It's very interesting. Too bad they had to close everything down ..."

Ms. Browning looked at her with curiosity for a few seconds. "Oh, you found that artist colony I told you about ..."

"Right," Maggie replied. Ms. Browning nodded. Maggie continued, "But hey, who wants their DNA nuked. Spoils the spermatozoa." Ms. Browning didn't smile back. Okay, so they weren't all that close. Obviously didn't share the same sense of humor. "So, let's see what else is on this list ... um ... I read that one. It's already part of my bibliography. This one – about the Salons des Refuses – and this one about the Salon des Independents ... yup. I have that covered. But this one about Caillebotte looks good. "That'll work. Thanks for your help," Maggie said. closing the lid on her laptop.

When she looked up, the librarian had left. Where was Parker? Okay. On the other side of the table, as it turned out, sitting down but ready to go, waiting for Maggie. What was she doing? Maggie looked where Parker was looking. Having followed Ms. Browning's line of progress back to her station as she returned to her work diligently addressing her computer terminal, Parker was glaring warily in the librarian's direction.

The rather elegant librarian was wearing a trim navy blue suit consisting of a short pencil skirt, a jacket with a pert little peplum, her slender neck adorned with a single strand of very small pearls. The fine ash blonde hair was sleeked back in a tiny bun like a ballerina. On her it looks good, Maggie thought to herself. With my curls, it would look like I was wearing a fur pompom on the back of my head. Maybe Parker should try her hair that way ... I'll bet Emily would really like it. It's very fashionable ... er ... or not. Maggie remembered that Parker did not like the librarian and made no bones about it. Besides, pleasing Emily was not Parker's favorite pastime, either. Better skip the hairstyling suggestions altogether. We've had as much drama as we can take for one day.

Parker looked at Maggie. "Done?"

"Yup," but Maggie procrastinated by looking up intently at the murals filling the ceiling. Just one more quick gander.

Parker looked up, too. "Boy, that sure is one hell of a ceiling."

"Yup," Maggie agreed. She stood up and hoisted her backpack with a grunt. "It's time to giddy-up out of Dodge."

"Yup," Parker mimicked. With that they headed out of the room towards the long staircase leading back down to the foyer.

At her station, Elizabeth Browning was facing the computer monitor but her unseen hands were at rest. Mentally reviewing the plan she was focused on, she decided they were making good progress. It was unfortunate that human pleasure signals tripped a particular hormonal wire in the pituitary, causing a flow which would inevitably bring a smile to her face. Even after all this time, the feeling of her facial skin being stretched still didn't feel very comfortable. If Elizabeth had had her way, she would have disabled those muscles a long time ago. But of course that would have been a grave tactical mistake. Humans set enormous store by these smiles. Never mind. It was a small price to pay.

Vig hanish dal. (*Never forget.)* The reason for being here preceded all. *Vig hanish dal.*

She did miss being able to speak Minda more often. That was the one real drawback about being here. Human language couldn't hold a candle to their own. For that thought she was rewarded by a pleasure sensation emanating from the gills hidden behind her ear coverings that required no engagement of her human parts. The tantalizing flutter which turned on her internal sensors continued flowing. Mutely she received her reward. Her way was better, she concluded. No fuss. No smiles. In the meantime, there was a pile of special requests to be logged before her workday was over. She hurried back to her duties.

Standing by the top of the stairs, Parker whispered to Maggie, "Don't look now but I think there's a man is looking at us."

Maggie looked in the direction of Parker's slight nod. Deep inside the room she saw a man standing near Ms. Browning. It looked like he was patting her arm. Oh, look at that. Ms. Browning, always the cool customer, has a friend. Or a honey. Well, well. She's human after all. But now he was looking their way. It was an intrusive look for

17

someone who was an utter stranger. Parker didn't like it and made a show by putting her arm through Maggie's. That's how they warded off bounders. Show of force. Or let them think we're lesbians. It didn't matter. Either way, it worked.

Parker scowled at the man. "I don't think he likes me," she said.

"Like you? He doesn't know you," Maggie noted with a small chortle.

The man continued looking at Parker in a decidedly interested way. Parker reminded herself *she* was a New Yorker. She knew how to handle his kind. She would not look away. She would not knuckle.

"Let him look. I'll tell our Daddy on him," Maggie whispered   with   an   impish   smile. "Right ..." and they both laughed.

Enough was enough. Parker did look away. He didn't win anything anyway. They both decided he would have to enjoy the sight of their backs as they departed; that little would have to suffice. In fact they both agreed they would never even deign to speak to a person of his ilk, (whatever that ilk was) and had another good laugh.

Walking down the stairs felt good to their legs after all that sitting, until Parker reminded them with a dramatic moan, "Oh, god, we have to go outside again."

"Can't be helped," Maggie replied as she tied on a fur hood while Parker deftly twisted her long blond hair into a knot on top of her head and stuffed it inside a knit ski cap. Wrapping her scarf around and around her neck, she made sure to cover her mouth as well. With a mutual nod, they each took a breath as they pushed through the exit. The cold wind hit them broadside.

"Ridiculous," said Parker, her mouth well muffled. "But hey. It's New York."

Huddling at the corner of the street with their backs to the wind, Maggie asked Parker, "Are you coming to dinner? Barbara's making brisket."

"No, I can't."

"She's also making home-made biscuits even as we speak ..."

"Shut up. I can't. I have to finish this paper. I typed everything into the computer in the den the last time we were there, remember? I should have put it on my laptop but I didn't. And they aren't networked ... so I can't. Anyway, now there's just this last bit. I'll meet you in the morning. Bring me a sandwich? ... Besides, Richard said he might call again. End of the night here is morning there." She didn't dare miss his calls.

Maggie felt herself biting her lip. As if Richard would inconvenience himself to work out the 5-hour difference between London and New York. That man really really *really* irked her. Well, that was nothing new.

Parker punched her lightly on the shoulder. "I'd better be there to take the call."

(*If he calls.* Richard was pathetic. His promises were unreliable.) "Okay. Love you. See you tomorrow."

Parker grabbed the sleeve of her friend's coat. "Please don't say anything to Evan. Not yet. Okay? I know you. But this is my fight. I have to learn to stand up to him ... what's the use of graduating from college if I still can't deal with my own father."

"Okay." (*Grrrr.*)

Maggie turned east, Parker headed downtown.

Back inside the reading room, Arthur's hand was still resting on Elizabeth Browning's arm, albeit discretely. He liked the feel of her cool, humanoid skin. Just touching it made the fluid deep inside the small pockets within his shoulder blades quiver with pleasure. The brief caress also stirred the corresponding fluid in the wells behind his ears, making them fibrillate silently. It was very erotic. Too bad there was no place to go – and no time.

As much as he liked life on this planet, he had to agree with Elizabeth. The fake skin covering their ear valleys was a nuisance. On the other hand, any discovery of the extra ear holes would constitute a dead give-away and ruin decades of hard-won ground. The anomalies between their divergent races would have to continue to be tolerated. For now.

"Well, I must be going. Oscar is waiting. The man simply can't do a thing unless I am there to direct him. Have Nick keep an eye on our prospect. She's coming along very nicely." With that Arthur swept grandly out the door.

Once gone Elizabeth hurried through her work. She had no intention of leaving things to Nick. How many times had she explained to Arthur that Nick could not carry a firearm without a permit, but he just brushed it off. One of these days, Nick would use that stupid thing – and then what? Oh, no. She didn't like Nick one bit. It was just that he had certain skills and some necessary brawn. But she didn't have to like him. He had been an unsatisfactory but necessary replacement for James. Which mention of the long-departed defector was still disconcerting, even after all this time. Elizabeth simply didn't care to follow where those thoughts would lead. On this Mission she had seniority over Nick He would do as he was told. After she logged off the computer, she retrieved her coat from the employee closet. Downstairs she paused at the entrance, checking to make sure Arthur's limousine was already gone. He was. Good. Sometimes he liked to sit there, like some foreign diplomat, flaunting the no-double-parking law, just to enjoy the effect. Foreign? Oh, definitely. Except that no one would recognize Mindar's symbol anyway, so he used Oscar's Venezuelan special visitor status and flag instead.

Outside it was incredibly cold. No extra bits of warmth even though the sun was sending long shafts of light flaring dramatically down the street. Elizabeth noted again that her back itched. She was going to have to find somewhere safe to shed – soon.

In the meantime, she wanted to find out if their little Earth Girl was still really worth all the effort. If not, they could end this now. Personally she didn't care a hill of beans one way or the other, but Elizabeth needed to see for herself, again, to be sure. She would have no qualms about shutting down the Maggie Malone Project even though Arthur would have to be convinced. If Maggie was as good as he thought, the girl could make them a fortune. Elizabeth had no qualms about making a fortune at the expense of one human being. Even after her decades here, she felt no loyalty to the human race whatsoever. Their only value was their usefulness. Those not useful were open to discard.

Blending with the other pedestrians, bending into the wind to allay the worst of its effects, Elizabeth was an expert in knowing how to be comfortably overlooked. She could easily be just one more attractive woman wearing the upscale 'uniform' of good, grey herringbone wool coat with the black velvet collar fashionably turned up, a pair of Jackie O-dark glasses and high black suede boots. Over her hair was a baby-soft black pashmina tied with the ends wrapped around and around and knotted in the back, her chin and throat well protected. It wasn't enough to really keep out the cold but it would have to do.

Following Maggie was easy since she knew exactly where the girl was going. Therefore, Elizabeth could afford to reflect, even as she walked along as a fair clip. The winter months of cold here were abominable. There were times when she thought she couldn't wait anymore to get home and stretch out her natural length on a large, flat, warm rock in a desert region: The Noave Coalition would be quite perfect right about now. They gave very good service. As a less expensive alternative, there was always the Juno Sanitation Waste Region. Much more economical. Not as service-minded and often littered with useless but attractive lay-abouts … still, one could manage to come across the occasional fellow reptile worthy of coiling with – which thought produced a well-hidden blue mottling on her chest and a kind of hormonal vibration. It was nearly her favorite sensation and even the biting cold couldn't dampen the effect it was having. Elizabeth recognized she was having a moment of happy self-gratification.

A few yards further on, she picked up the dropped thread of thoughts that had brought it on. She knew the scenario only too well: you go to Juno because you have to; you go to the Noave because you can. Naturally the itching and the molting is never anything to write home about, but if you need to save money, you go to Juno and sometimes ... just sometimes ... you unexpectedly meet someone that maybe you can nest with. That's Juno for you. After all, an egg is an egg ...

By now the blue mottling with its sensual vibration had descended to her torso, circling her thighs. It paused, climbed back up to her waistline and paused again. Which handsome reveler had she coiled with who had reminded her of this lovely reward? Ven-deeth? No. He had annoyed her with his fawning. Ky-phan? No. Not him, either ... although he had managed to hold her attention longer than usual. But when he told her he planned to eat their egg, that truly disgusted her. An egg-eater. Meaning: a baby-killer. Remembering that made the pleasurable buzz begin to fade. A picture came to mind. Far-jhan. That's right. Far-jhan. Young and muscular. He knew how to coil. And squeeze. Too bad there hadn't been enough time to make an egg with Far-jhan. She had quite fancied him.

A gust of wind reminded Elizabeth she was catching up to Maggie too quickly, so she slowed down. The sensory recall of that languid coiling under the warm comfort of the twin red suns of Mindar caused the mottle to blaze again. Elizabeth stopped. Closing her eyes, she felt like she was at the center of a storm. She waited. In a minute or so the storm was over.

She knew the mottling was gone. She could afford to be flexible about such matters, as long as she could stand being Elizabeth, that is – wearing this humanoid skin. This was the real work that counted. Not the library. Because of the real work, she could practically hear the credits accruing in her home planet account. Day by day. *Ca-ching. Ca-ching.* No, she wouldn't be stuck here forever. That was the thing to remember. If she couldn't find Far-jhan again, she'd find someone else. Since we live a very long time, even one more decade is acceptable. In fact, by her calculations, one more decade and she would have enough set aside for a proper retirement. By Earth standards she would be filthy rich. By Mindarian standards, she could enjoy a reasonable life of moderate leisure for decades thereafter. In the meantime, there was Arthur.

Arthur. Most of the time, she was satisfied with their relationship. He really could provide a most satisfying squeeze, but whatever he might promise in the heat of the moment, she was pretty sure Arthur knew very little about nesting.

Her musings were interrupted when Elizabeth saw Maggie enter the Park and head purposely down a familiar path. Actually she was glad when Maggie finally sat down on a nearby bench. Walking was so uneconomical. Slithering never tired one out. She picked a bench on the other side of the path, took a book out of her tote bag and opened it. It would allow her to continue her observation, herself unobserved.

Suddenly, miraculously, the brute force of The Montreal Express subsided. It sometimes happened that way, for reasons best explained only by meteorologists. The world seemed to quiet itself and come to rest.

Sitting on her own favorite bench, Maggie looked around. She could imagine the whole city was sighing with relief. Little remained of the intense blowing. It felt like the mercury was actually climbing. The cloud cover had been torn to small pieces even as the last bit of good light turned the underside of those same clouds a celestial pink and gold.

On a bench some yards away, Elizabeth was reminded that at home on Mindar no one ever had to suffer through these inopportune seasons. That's when she felt another pang of loss for her home planet shear through her because, in its own stark way, it was quite beautiful. Well, well, she thought. That would be the feeling of ... never mind. She had no heart. Literally. Her body looked authentic. Naturally. She had certainly paid enough. Her cheek muscles gave way because her endocrine system worked quite well and she felt a momentary, ruthless sneer spread itself on her face as a *frisson* of hate shot through. Now *that* wasn't an entirely objectionable sensation as she thought: let's just see what our Maggie is doing these days,

CHAPTER TWO

William ambled over carrying a pail of duck feed. Leaning towards Maggie, he said, "One of your fans is back," as he unbuttoned his heavy khaki work jacket, seeing as how the temperature gauge at his work station announced itself as a toasty 28 degrees, now that the wind had quieted down to a barely noticeable thrum.

Maggie knew how brief such respites could be; she needed to take advantage of the miraculous warm snap to diligently apply herself to the drawing in progress. Pulling off her mittens, she got started. There was just enough residual heat in her hands for a few minutes of work.

"What do you mean, William?" she asked without looking up because she was sinking into that zone, the one that enveloped her as she concentrated on the grey paper stump in her hand that she was going to use to soften some of the lines.

"Do you not see her?"

She looked up and around. "Who?"

On one bench some man in a long overcoat was reading a newspaper in the fading light. On the other side of the path was a Jackie-O wannabe looking in her pocketbook. No one was looking at Maggie. "No."

Maggie squinted in the direction of the sun, gauging her time. Very little natural light was left. This day was definitely over. Her pencil danced over the drawing. A mark here, a dab there with her kneaded eraser. A judicious motion or two using the stump. That was it. The light was gone. Time to pack up. Still, it was worth it. It was always worth it. Checking her watch and noting again the grumble in her stomach, she knew she was hungry. The policy was firm: never work when she was hungry or tired. She especially didn't want to ruin this drawing. She would have to come back tomorrow, school work permitting. The thing was: with this drawing she believed she had finally moved her work into a new realm by taking some chances. She had changed the way she organized the image on the page. Studying the Impressionists and the Fauves had done that for her. More snapshot, less classical. It gave the work an extra life-like touch that she really liked.

After sorting her tools into her kit, Maggie eased the drawing, still in the confines of the long, wide rubber bands holding it in place, into her portfolio. Luckily the wind had died down and she didn't have to wrestle for control.

Strange how the cold could make one dreamy ... she paused to consider some of great artists who had elevated the creatures of the earth to serious greatness by their exquisite rendering ... da Vinci, Delacroix, Tintoretto, Courbet ... Claude Loraine ... Oudrey. Maggie had recently discovered Jean-Baptiste Oudrey, a slightly obscure 17th-century Baroque painter of animals. Of course there was George Stubbs. She had done her last big paper on George Stubbs. That should net her an Honors when it was time to hand out the grades.

"People are always having a look over your shoulder," remarked William coming back up the path without the inevitable pail. He stopped by her bench. "'Tis a good drawing, that one," he remarked, pointing to the portfolio. "Looks like it might walk right off the paper."

"Thank you, William. That means a lot to me." They smiled at each other, old friends that they were. The city was going quickly dark. She had to go. Pulling her mittens back on, she noticed even William had buttoned up his work coat against the cold that was inching back. "You're a good friend." She gave him the last good smile left. "What a day. I'm bushed."

Maggie had a plan. Maybe there was greatness in her. Maybe not. She could always hope. Surely one had to be able to think these thoughts, even if only to oneself. She felt sure she had to think this way before anyone else would, but even without reaching that oxygen-thin height, she had long ago decided there was to be none of that noble, starving martyrdom for her. No garret. No living on rice and beans ... she wanted it all. The whole package, as she called it. The top of the mountain. It's where I belong.

She didn't understand why Parker kept reminding her to watch out, watch her back, keep an eye peeled ... for who? *Who??* Who am I supposed to looking for? It didn't make any sense. It wasn't like there was a whole pack of Richards out there. That was his game with Parker. It had nothing to do with her. Parker was wrong. She wasn't some kind of fortress – metaphorically speaking. There were no "Greeks" working out how to storm her gates or infiltrate. Anyway, there was no such thing as a real Trojan horse. It was just a legend. A myth. Pah. Which reminded her, she had to get home.

"I'll be grand to all my loyal followers," she promised William.

"Give my best to Evan and Barbara. And Nonie. Tell them all that I saw you."

"I will," she promised as he walked her partway up the path. William, Maeve and their whole clan had been friends with her family for ages, since way before Maggie was born. They had history together. All the way back to their days in Ireland.

Maggie shivered. The wind was working itself into a drama again, so she wrapped the scarf another turn around her neck and covered her nose as well. Of course the temperature was falling. Why have any consideration for us humans, huh? She looked up at the sky. When she looked back, William was still there, coiling a hose. The man on the bench was folding up his newspaper. The Jackie-O wannabe was gone. Good. You have to be nuts to be outside on a day like this. Well, she had made good use of that 15-minute window of decreased bitter cold and now it was time to go home. Warm up. Chow down on her mother's divine brisket. And remember to make a sandwich for Parker.

"My duckies are waiting on me," William called with a wave. Somehow he absorbed bad weather – rain, snow, wind. It just didn't bother him. He treated the elements like a naughty child. Maggie thought there was a lesson there. William was a dear. When she looked back to tell him so, he was gone.

CHAPTER THREE

Before dinner that night Maggie handed over the new drawing to Evan. Rarely did she consider a piece finished until it had been reviewed by her father.

"So, what do you think, Daddy?" she asked swallowing hard.

Untying the black ribbons, he opened the left flap of the big cardboard portfolio. Next he turned back the right one. He always treated her portfolio like a religious object, like he was unveiling the Torah in Shul. He was already a fan, if for no other reason than this was the work of his daughter. But he had also been looking at her work for a long time; he had no choice but to mark her ascent from a child who loved to draw animals to an artist who was capable, almost like a god, of breathing life into her creations. Her work was uncanny. He didn't tell her he had made it his business to see what those who came before her in this genre were doing that established their greatness. As far as he could tell, she was getting very close to the mountaintop. Not that she would believe him. This night as he scanned the drawing carefully, his hand reached out involuntarily. The drawing was so lifelike and inviting, it startled him.

"Come on. Is it better? Because I think it's almost done, really ..."

"Maggie. I'm speechless."

"... so, it's good?"

"It's better than good. It's wonderful."

That was too much praise for Maggie. She reached over hurriedly to close the flap. "Thanks. Well, you know. It's not finished. I just wanted you to see it ..."

"No, Maggie, I really mean it ..." He put his hands out to stop her but Barbara had just come sailing through the pantry door carrying a platter of savory, roasted meat and vegetables steaming deliciously so Maggie took advantage of the diversion to close up her portfolio quickly. Her mother took a victory lap around the table, finishing her final turn around the table by placing it next to a silver tray with filled just-made biscuits piled on a snowy napkin.

"You're a wonderful artist, my dear," she murmured to Maggie while executing a smooth landing into her seat.

"Your mother is right ... my god, Barbara, but that smells fantastic."

The telephone rang . "Don't answer it," Evan ordered as he began carving but Maggie was at the phone in the instant and picked up anyway.

"Hi ... uh-huh, yeah ... Oh, god. Well, that was to be expected. All right. He did? Oh, lordy ... ask Randall to save a piece for me. Beg, if you have to ... yuh, I will."

Maggie came back and sat down. "Randall made carrot cake for dessert. His cream cheese frosting is so good, it ought to be outlawed. She is going to save a piece for me. I'm going to trade it for a brisket sandwich tomorrow. Please?"

She had to report that Richard and Emily were leaving for Switzerland to get tummy tucks. "This is their version of a good reason not to be in New York for Spring Break. Can you believe it? Daddy: why did God give those two boneheads so much money?" She needed to deflect their attention from her drawing. She didn't want to talk about her drawing. Anything but that.

Of course his daughter's strategy was quite transparent. But he would honor it. "Good question, Maggs ... I just don't have an answer. I'll be in *shul* on Friday night. I'll ask Him."

"Let me know if God answers ..." she replied moodily. She wasn't a good Jew. Barely a High Holidays Jew. Still, Jewish was Jewish, whether she went to Temple or not. Which jogged her memory – that site that Ms. Browning had showed her.

"Listen. Do you remember anything about a meteorite that crashed into a town on Long Island years ago?"

"Seems like I do remember hearing something about that. Terrible how something the size of a baseball could make a hole that size. Isn't that right, Barbara? Left a long scar on the ground, too. All very exciting. Of course everyone who lived around the crash site had to evacuate. All kinds of government people running around, taking pictures, checking the radiation levels. There was so much radiation the whole town was shut down. Everyone had to leave. What a *'tsimis'*. Let me see. What was the name of that place? ... uh ... oh, something-'foot'. Something like that. Barbara, do you remember?"

"Is that near the place where we ran out of gas and I got home past my curfew and my parents banned you for a month?" His wife asked. She was smiling mischievously.

"Might have been," Evan replied assuming a neutral tone as he buttered a biscuit. "Daughter, do not give me that look. *We were well-behaved young people.*" He put down the biscuit and cut a bite of meat. It sat on the fork, now pointing at his wife. "Your mother wants to imply some hanky-panky was going on ... don't pay any attention to her, Maggs."

"This is a new story. I want to hear it."

"Nothing happed except that we ran out of gas."

"Poor planning on my part ... a simple miscalculation, nothing more."

"Your father flagged down a highway patrol officer ... he helped us get some gas."

"Oh, Daddy. For shame," Maggie grinned.

"Mother, stop that smirking. Nothing happened."

But Maggie noted her mother was smiling as she served her husband another slice of brisket and lovingly spooned some of the juice over it. He was smiling, too. Well, something had happened.

"Could it have been Copper Springs, dear?" Barbara asked.

"No, I think it was some kind of Indian name ... hmmm. I'll think of it later. Anyway," he continued, "the crash site is just an old pasture now. Quite safe. Since all the half-lifes have been exhausted, it's all back, just about the way it used to be. Traveling entertainment companies used it for outdoor plays in the old days. They've had Scottish games there and pow-wows. I like the pow-wow. Maybe we'll all drive out and visit it one of these days. If the quarantine sign is still there, that would be an interesting artifact." He picked up the forgotten biscuit.

They lapsed into a happy, quiet rhythm for the rest of dinner. Maggie was in some kind of reverie and said nothing for the rest of the meal, but eating slowly in starts and stops as she imagined not for the first time what a coffee table book filled with color plates of her work would look like. Naturally there would be a big stack of them in the window of Barnes & Noble; she would do a book signing.

The quiet gave Evan time to reflect as well. When he first understood that his daughter had decided to specialize in animal drawings, he had misgivings. As long as she was going to be an artist, he thought she should pick subject matter a little less esoteric. Several times he'd risked voicing his concern to her, albeit as delicately as possible. Her replies had been adamant and vociferous. "Daddy, I've told you! There is a market. And not just in the United States. Overseas, in the Far East, the market is huge. Prints and paintings. Collector's plates, books, illustration jobs. You'll see." Now, he rather thought he would. Maggie was turning into a fine artist.

As he buttered yet another flaky, fragrant rosemary biscuit, he considered the news about Richard and Emily. Tummy tucks? Well, no one was coming near his wife with any nonsense like that. Evan considered his wife to be a goddess. In fact, all the Malone women were beauties and his Barbara outdistanced them all. He was perfectly happy with her womanly figure. In the case of his daughter, he was lucky there, too, as the various fads of one kind of drama queen or another had passed by the Malones with hardly a hiccup. Maggie was smart, loyal, incredibly talented, persistent ... she had that tidy, huggable figure so appealing to the male population and he just hoped she would soon bring some nice-looking, intelligent, ambitious, decent young man home to meet the parents.

Poor Emily Feldman. There was nothing wrong with her figure either, if you liked the idea of sleeping with an ironing board. Maggie was right. Richard was nuts. He ran that family like ... like something out of Charles Dickens. What was that book he wrote? Oh, yes. "Dombey & Son". Poor Emily, my foot. Poor Parker was more like it.

Looking across the table at his wife, he acknowledged that on rare occasions when did they cross swords, his arguments had to be very very good, because his wife was one smart cookie. It was just a good thing this wasn't the 'old country,' he reminded himself, because otherwise she would have no qualms about braining him with the hot brisket pan. As it was, this was America and her best weapon was not to make a dessert. And that was punishment enough. Mainly he had to be careful about the company they kept because Barbara was a woman who did not suffer fools lightly. Evan was a bit more democratic; Barbara had her standards. Well, that was all right. Those he didn't bring home, he met at the club to play tennis with or ping-pong or even chess. It all worked out.

He always knew the way to his wife's heart: keep making her number one and never flag in his affections. Oh, yes. He adored The Mighty Barbara. From the tippy-top of her Irish red hair to the bottom of her feet. A *bracha,* she was. A blessing. And God forbid the words 'tummy tuck' should ever pass her lips.

As for Richard, he may love his wife, but it was to the exclusion of just about everything else, including his lovely daughter. Stupid man. As far as Evan was concerned, Parker had come into their lives when their daughter really needed a friend. To say that they loved Parker

Feldman to pieces was an understatement. Your loss, jerk ... and Evan took another bite of the biscuit still sitting in his hand.

CHAPTER FOUR

Come the following week the girls made another visit to the main branch of the library. To their surprise, this time Ms. Browning wasn't there. When they were told she was on some kind of leave, Parker became distinctly happy. For whatever reason and no matter how long, having 'that woman' out of their hair pleased her.

On the other hand, the same somewhat sullen, pale, thirty-something fellow of medium height and brown hair unmemorably dressed in a plaid work shirt and blue jeans was still there shunting books around on a three-shelf truck. Normally Maggie and Parker enjoyed being friendly with the library staff but he wasn't what they would call a 'fun person', so they left him alone. On this particular day he was standing near the girls' table when he overheard Parker saying she needed to do more research for her "Doges of Venice" paper. He left the floor and returned shortly thereafter with a small pile of books and set them down.

"Maybe these will help."

Parker looked up. Was this a peace offering? She was a bit flummoxed. "Thanks, uh …?"

"The name is Nick. I forget to wear my name tag."

"Thank you, Nick. That's very nice of you."

"It's okay," he said as he walked away.

Maggie leaned over and whispered to Parker. "Now that was weird. Why is he being nice to you? I think he's a strange guy."

"He is strange, without question. Still, those books he pulled might be useful ... god, I want to finish this paper," she groaned dramatically.

Maggie looked around until she spotted him. "Nick, hmmm." His back was turned, busy sorting books on top shelf of his truck. "I don't know as I trust him."

Parker nodded in agreement but she knew she needed the help. This last paper was crucial. Maybe one of the books he had pulled would help her clinch the scholarship.

"It's all right, Parkie," Maggie added in her best library voice whisper. "It's not like your dating him."

"God forbid," Parker replied and both girls laughed quietly.

At the end of the afternoon, Nick's peace offering was placed at the end of the table, waiting for pick-up. A smattering of historical data had been gleaned. She would add these into her paper. Anything was better than nothing. Parker scanned the room looking for Nick. She planned to thank him but he was nowhere to be seen, so she shrugged it off. Maybe next time. They packed up and walked downstairs to the door. It was still cold but today it was bearable.

"Richard called again last night. Two in one week. It might be some kind of record. Anyway, my parents have now decided we need to spend time together. They have figured out that there's enough time to recovery from the surgeries, then come to New York ... can you believe it? This will be like General Sherman's famous march. Except that we will be burning our way through Manhattan for two weeks, after which they leave for Paris. You know, Maggs, I don't know whom they talk to or where they get their ideas about child raising. I mean, they are missing my graduation, so, really, who cares?"

Taking a moment, Maggie considered her friend. "Yup. You look raised to me. Richard is always a couple of years behind when it comes to you," she quipped. "By the way, is this their version of a graduation present?"

"I would say so but I don't think actually Richard knows for sure. He just expects that when time comes, whenever that is, I will magically matriculate. He lives in his own time-warp." She pushed her way through the revolving door and Maggie followed just behind. They stood on the pavement. "Beam him up, Scotty, will you?" which request Parker aimed at the sky overhead. "Anyway, we'll be dining out at every seriously expensive place they missed since the last time we did this. At least it's a vacation for Randall and Cook. The last time we did this it was my sophomore year. We saw all the best plays and ballet. Remember? At least Richard always gets great seats. I'll give him that. So, as of right now, I'm on Clothes-And-Hair Watch. Have to look gorgeous for two – possibly three – meals a day for the next two weeks. Heaven forefend that there should be a hair out of place or an imperfections in wardrobe! Gotta go ... please tell Evan and Barbara. I've got a hair appointment." She gave Maggie a mock scowl, which was followed by a quick kiss on the cheek.

She headed south on Fifth Avenue. Maggie watched her. She turned north. It was just warm enough to walk home. She really wanted the exercise after all the sitting she did.

Meanwhile Parker wormed her way to the front of the curb amongst the crowd of pedestrians. She was feeling just a little frantic. Oh, hurry, people ... her appointment was for 4:30 sharp. Jacopo waited for no one.

Her thoughts were filled with the do's and don'ts of being with her parents when someone bumped her so hard she yelped in sharp, surprised fear as she started falling toward the cars still whipping right turns around the corner. In that very instant, a man in an overcoat took her arm and pulled her back. Instead of being a smear on the street, she was still alive!

"Oh, God, that was close! I ... I wasn't paying attention ... thank you! Thank you so much ..." She wanted to get a good look at her rescuer but except that he was very tall and bundled up like everyone else, there weren't many details to get.

"Not at all," the man said politely disengaging his hand from her arm. He stepped back.

"Thank you," she called out. He just waved a backwards hand and kept walking. Everyone else was crossing the street and he was gone, having turned the other way. The only memorable feature was a fur hat with flaps hanging loose over his ears. Did Parker detect an accent? She wasn't sure. But he had kind eyes. She was pretty sure about that. Dark brown and ... something ... anyway. She was alive!

What a hero! Ohmygod. She couldn't suppress the shakes. So that's how it happens – *snap!* Just like that. Poof! Then it's, "Mr. and Mrs. Feldman? So sorry but your daughter is ..." Parker, get a hold of yourself. She would have to pay attention to the traffic. There was no 'phoning it in.' None of her plans included accidental death or a long, agonizing stay in the hospital as a medical miracle.

At the next corner she stood well back while waiting for the light to change, prepared to cross with new vigilance. Even though she arrived on time at Jacopo & Company and tried to look as though nothing had happened, the receptionist was sharp. One look told her something had upset their customer. In short order, Parker was settled into a comfortable chair surrounded by two idle hair washers, plus Jacopo himself and Jackie, the Receptionist. A decaf café au lait with two raw sugars was handed to her as well as a plate of yummy madeleines to soothe her rattled nerves.

"I'm okay now. Really I am," and she made to get up.

Jacopo pushed her back into the chair. "Lissen to me. If you don' show up, I take everyone from the shop an' look for you myself! We are a posse!" Jacopo exclaimed, nodding his head to include everyone in the room. "We don' going to let you not to come. Is your hair. Is must be perfect!" and everyone laughed, including Jacopo, until he realized they were all looking at him. "What? You don' believe? I do the hair of Parker for all the times her mama and papa want her to look be-oo-tiful, is this not so?"

It was so.

Parker knew how close she had come to losing her life. The surrounding glow of affection had pulled her back from that precipice helped enormously. "You are right. In two days from now my parents will be expecting me to look perfect. You must do my hair."

So Parker drank her decaf while they stood there and watched. Apparently a near-death experience also made a person hungry; she ate the whole plateful of cookies as well. The end result was a comfortably stuffed, gurgling tummy. She looked around with a smile. Satisfied that Parker was all right, Jacopo clapped his hands with authority and sent everyone scurrying back to their stations. The crisis was over.

More than a few blocks back, a thirty-something man in a denim jacket with a dark plaid scarf wrapped around his neck who had nearly successfully bumped Parker into the frenzied traffic was himself caught striding down the street when he was grabbed by the same tall man wearing a long overcoat and a fur hat with loose ear flaps.

"Hey! Let me go!" Nick snarled in a not-so-low voice as he was pulled in close and anchored fast by a strong grip. He wished he knew enough bad words so he could say something that would really sink Oscar. That man needed to be 'broken' and Nick really wanted to be the one to do it. If this was Mindar ... but it wasn't.

"*We do not murder*," Oscar replied very softly, his own voice well under control. "You have overstepped your Mission authority."

"Hah. A lot you know. Interfere with me again and it might be you next time, under a car, getting squashed ... you ... *shen-fee trin-dach!*" he hissed. (*Eggless bottom-feeder!*)

The taller man remained unfazed. "Threaten either of them again and it'll be you under the wheels, I promise you. Threaten me again and I'll stuff you in a Transport Locker personally – without food or water. Do you understand me? You'll be lucky to shed, if you're still alive. Think about that. It's a long way home, laddie." His mouth was firm. His ear fluids were stable and he knew it. Oscar released him and walked away.

Nick looked around but sensible New Yorkers didn't care much about two men having brief, if unpleasant, discourse. Under his denim pants the gills behind his knees flared. "This isn't over," he growled. When he was safely several blocks distant he said it again. "It isn't over."

Oscar understood that the girls had to be watched. The plan was at a critical point. He would hereafter make sure there was no more such aggressive shadowing or near-accidents. Personally. That was the least he could do. Murder would not be tolerated.

* * *

Parker decided to tell no one about the close call – not even Maggie. The chances of Maggie ever coming to Jacopo & Company for a haircut were nil, therefore, she would never hear how Parker had arrived in such a state. Parker wanted to forget it ever happened. But as a consequence, rather than squirm or disagree or think critical thoughts, she determined she was going to do her best to ensure that her parents enjoyed their visit by being on her best behavior. Richard would appreciate that ... well, as much as he ever noticed her at all, even during these mad visits. He seemed to look everywhere but at Parker. She had learned just to be gorgeous and enjoy his largess. As it turned out, the visit was indeed jam-packed and left little time for any such concerns. The two friends had to make due with quick catch-ups between classes and several hurried phone calls of "Tell Evan and Barbara that I'm fine."

Two weeks later Richard and Emily were gone. The quiet after their departure was palpable. Parker was totally thankful she could go home again to the people she had more or less lived with steadily for the past nearly thirteen years. Her first evening back Barbara served a delicious dinner of roast chicken and fresh vegetables, which Parker said rivaled anything the four-star restaurants were serving up. Evan nodded with approval. After all, it was true.

The girls spent a decent time at the dinner table dawdling over coffee and dessert. After that they bolted for the den with a plate of extra slices of cake.

"Okay, spill," Maggie ordered from the comfort of a big club chair.

Parker started off by saying she had actually ... kind of ... really .... almost enjoyed the two-week blowout.

This isn't what Maggie had expected to hear. Or liked much hearing, either. Putting down an unfinished slice of cake, she asked half-seriously if Parker had 'gone over to the dark side'.

"Did you guys rent *Star Wars* and root for Darth Vader?"

"No, of course not. And don't be nasty. I just decided not to resent my parents flying to a Swiss clinic for tummy tucks or the six weeks of leisurely recovery taken at a lovely mountain resort in the Austrian Alps. Or to hold it against them because they are flying to Paris where Emily will happily ravage the racks of several of the most select, couture designers because she has a divine new figure.

Obviously fitting her will be a pleasure. I've also decided I'm okay that they're scheduled to improve their physical fitness at a spa in Arizona. It's their post-shopping recovery protocol. You've heard it all before. Of course they will need a rest after all that, so that by year's end they will be ready to vacate the old homestead. Fa-la-la-la-la ... la-la ... la-la."

"And this rant is supposed to be reassuring? Who are you? Did they hit you over the head? Does it hurt? Did you have neurosurgery?? Maybe you need a nap after all that exhausting entertainment, hmmm?"

Parker sat back. Maggie was pretty angry with her. Parker knew her 'détente' with her parents seemed like a betrayal, but Parker could absolutely not tell Maggie about the near-death thing the day she went to have her hair done. "I know. I know ... it's a change. Wait. Peace. Listen. I have a question for you. Is there such a thing as the empty-nest syndrome in reverse? Like when the child is all done with being <u>not</u> looked after and she moves on – and doesn't mind it so much?"

Maggie knew Parker to her core. It was difficult for her best friend to stay on an even keel after these infrequent parental blowouts. "Sure. It's called Growing Up And Leaving Home." She sounded pretty cynical. On the other hand, that pretty much summed it up, too.

Parker ignored her. "I can't explain it. I just decided to have a good time and let myself be spoiled. And let Richard and Emily be ... well, whoever it is they think they are."

"Are you ill?"

"Maggie. That's not nice. Come on. Can't a daughter have a good time with her parents?"

"Please. We're talking about Richard and Emily. I ask you once again: did you get hit on the head or something? Maybe a big dictionary fell off the shelf in the library and you were concussed?"

Maggie was getting too close to the truth. Parker really didn't want to tell her that she nearly got herself killed in traffic. Maggie could be unmanageable when Parker was in danger. There were lots of times when Parker was so grateful to have Maggie in her corner. She was fierce in battle. But Parker just couldn't tell her about this. It was hard keeping a secret. She just felt sure it was the right thing to do. This one time. "Sure. Big book fell down and conked me. Can't I be tired of being at war with them and just go with the flow for a change?"

"Yes, but that's not you. So something happened and you aren't telling. I suppose there are some very teensy-weensy, itsy-bitsy, ultra-miniscule parts of your life that I don't know about, but just remember: *all the rest belongs to me!*"

"I love you, too."

There was a pause.

"Okay ... so the food was <u>that</u> good?" Maggie asked. "Oh, yeah," Parker replied with great relief. That was Maggie's version of a peace offering. "It was awesome ..." Parker said, as she proceeded to give a blow-by-blow description of the past two weeks – every overindulgent, ultra-expensive minute of it. Maggie finally had to admit – right or wrong, albeit it was 'selling out' – it sounded pretty damn great.

CHAPTER FIVE

Over the next few months, whenever the girls weren't around, Evan remarked to Barbara on at least several more occasions, until the joke wore out, that God continued to remain silent on the matter of the Feldmans' jet setting ways. Each time his wife knew better than to answer.

Graduation arrived. Parker was frankly relieved that Richard and Emily were out of country. Therefore, the moment of disappointment when neither called to wish her well didn't last long. It was a great day anyway and the girls were determined to savor it. They both did their stroll across the stage to receive classy-looking parchment diplomas in the moiré silk-covered folders. It was fun to move their tassels from one side of the mortarboard hats to the other while Barbara and Evan looked on, proud as two peacocks. At least no one tripped while walking across the stage or got the giggles when the Dean shook hands with the graduates.

A UN diplomat from Hungary gave a satisfactory graduation speech about freedom in the arts that was delivered in very careful English. In the end, the mortar board hats were flung into the air with wild and partially lethal abandon, after which everyone immediately ran to get out of the way as they came back down, sometimes landing en pointe or in inconvenient places. There was a lot of mildly hysterical laughter. College was over. For better or worse. It was nearly summer. Their day was wrapped up with a first-class dinner at a great fish place down on Jane Street. Hugs and kisses were served all around followed by Maggie and Parker going home to their newly rented, very modest, shabby-chic-decorated apartment.

Two freshly-minted and framed diplomas were hung on the wall in the tiny foyer. Their decision to 'stuff' Richard and Emily's apartment had been carried out.

That Richard and Emily refused to be ruffled by this act of rebellion was also not surprising. Some things just didn't change. The girls celebrated with movie rentals, "Stand By Me" and "The Color of Money," noshing until they were almost sick. Randall had baked a carrot cake for them while Barbara had provided a picnic basket full of enough good food to last a week. Therefore, all in all, it was considered a successful rebellion.

As it turned out, their new routine was not so different than the old one. Having both applied for jobs at the same non-profit organization, they both got hired – on the promise that they didn't spend all day chit-chatting together. That was easy to promise. Instead of 8 a.m. class, they got to punch in at 9. How cool was that?

Maggie signed up for life drawing classes at Art Students' League's evening program. Things were a bit harder for Parker. For whatever reason, her scholarly brilliance had failed to astonish her instructors. Some other worthy had claimed the remaining one-year scholarship to be awarded.

"Richard could have just given me the damn trip for a graduation present," she nattered, breaking her usual silence about such things. Maggie didn't answer. She wasn't expected to. Parker took 'the hit' by signing up for night school, too. Another literature class. In Italian, of course. She was determined that her Italian would be beyond flawless in every way.

"That would have made you happy? If Richard came through for a change?" Maggie asked at last. She'd been saving up this question for awhile. It was a gorgeous Saturday afternoon. They were lounging on the steps of The Met. All around them were fellow city dwellers and day-trippers alike, also enjoying the sunshine.

"No," Parker admitted. She was leaning back on her elbows, contemplating the sky, which was deeply blue. The sky was a very satisfying place to look. Maggie patted Parker on the shoulder and nodded towards the jingle of the ice cream cart parked at the bottom.

"You need one of those," she said. "Doctor's orders."

"Of course I do."

While the canvassing jobs meant their income was sufficient for each to cover their share of the bills and put a little aside, no one was going to get rich very fast – unless Maggie sold a lot of drawings and paintings for really good prices soon. They refused almost all monetary handouts from Evan and Barbara. As a matter of pride. Dinner with family? Sure. Even bringing their laundry home once in awhile was no problem. Movies tickets taken care of when the four of them went to see something? That was okay, too. Brown bags with Barbara's famous sandwiches and homemade cookies – absolutely. But actual money for rent and bills? No. They would have to be seriously desperate, and have seriously screwed up. Which the girls wouldn't permit.

At least Maggie now felt she was painting as if her life depended on it – which it did. Persistence in making the rounds with her portfolio finally yielded an offer from a small gallery for a two-person show. She contacted her painting buddy, Denny Jennings, immediately. The manager liked Denny's work equally well. He did still lifes glorious enough to rival the Dutch masters. They visited the gallery, checked out the exhibition space and made their plans. At that point Maggie dived into production mode. She needed at least six new pieces to make sure her participation in the show looked fresh.

Their September opening went well. She knew she was slightly frazzled by all the excitement, but what the hell, she said to herself. Did I go through all this to behave as though it's not wonderful? She sold two pieces and felt herself to be quite The Artist. Denny trounced her in number of sales and total money earned but it didn't matter. She was off and running. Besides, there were worse things than being trounced by Denny.

By Halloween she was hard at work on her Big Cat series again for the next show when the gallery owner broke the news that it would be at least a year before he could give her a one or two-man show again. Her sales didn't warrant it. It was a blow Maggie hadn't expected. But Denny was there with a good suggestion: join the same artists' co-op he was a member of. That meant she was welcome to put at least a couple of pieces in any show the co-op did. And it would be a matter of 4-6 months, not a year, until she got up a show of her own again. Maggie took his advice. Furthermore, she liked the idea of being in a group. In the meantime, she was plumbing the depths of a new series that would uniquely celebrate cheetahs and snow leopards. Surely exquisite art highlighting these special creatures would the draw the crowds she needed. There were many people who believed as she did that these marvelous creatures must be celebrated, treasured and saved visually as well as for real.

If that following winter was a repeat of the interminably invasive, frigid weather of the year before, it was no surprise. The Montreal Express roared in, dumping its freezing blasts with cheerful vengeance. On the very coldest days, the friends found refuge at an inside table at their favorite café at Rockefeller Plaza. They would drink hot chocolates, watch the skaters outside (dressed half-naked, Maggie said) and continue planning and dreaming.

In February Maggie got good news. She was in the pipeline for a two-person show for April. These deadlines were invigorating. There was nothing she liked so much as a good fight, which is what a show was. The reality was that her chosen subject was going to make breaking into the Big Time harder than she had believed, but she was unwilling to give up. When Denny said he wasn't going to be ready to show with her, she was sorry but it turned out that Martha was willing to step into the breach. This was good because Maggie really liked Martha. She was fun to be around and Maggie really admired her unique, splotchy portraits of people. They captured people's attention. Maggie knew her own work wasn't everyone's cup of tea, but for those who loved animals, the admiration was vast and comforting. She had always understood it was a special public that she was painting for.

In the weeks before the show went up, Maggie would saunter into the living room while Parker was practicing her Italian diction and ask: "Shouldn't one of my baby giraffe pastels be able to beat one of Martha's double portraits?" Which was funny because Parker knew that Maggie wasn't going to show any of her baby giraffe pastels.

"Oh, you really are not going to make me to pick sides. Bad Maggie. Martha is my friend, too," Parker said with a mock scowl and the girls laughed.

This next show Maggie did much better, selling three of her big canvases and several drawings picked out from her portfolio which wasn't even officially part of the show. Also the fashion season was again favoring Big Cat fur patterns. Her paintings had pulled interest and appointments at the gallery which resulted in another two sales. Several fashion magazine editors were talking about using several of the big cat paintings for a fashion layout. Maggie was elated. She did several victory dances at the apartment – because dancing like a happy maniac in front of customers was absolutely *verboten*, even though it was exactly what she wanted to do each time she made a sale.

Still, it was Martha who had sold more pieces, made more money, including a commission for a family portrait. That meant she was elected to pony up for the post-opening movie treat. It was a tradition among the friends. They all went to see, "Crouching Tiger, Hidden Dragon."

Standing in line, waiting for the theatre door to open, Parker marveled to Martha that their respective parents were actually acquainted, which information had somehow bubbled to the surface unexpectedly as they shuffled towards the entrance. Maggie held her breath for an instant, but when it was evident Parker was not going to speculate aloud on the diversity of parenting behavior, she whispered, "Good girl," in Parker's ear.

A few days later, in a moment of mischief, Maggie not only framed the photocopied checks from her sales and a tiny mention in the paper, she also framed the tiny movie ticket stub as well and these took places of honor next to their diplomas on the living room wall. She decided that a ceremonial hanging of these objects was necessary to her morale. She would see it every day upon leaving and every night arriving home. It said: people will pay good money for your art. *And don't you forget it.*

Thereafter, copies of checks for sold work were likewise framed and hung.

"Uh, isn't it supposed to be the first dollar bill that a restaurant earns?" Parker asked while standing in front of the sofa, examining the wall, which was sprouting very small frames like mushrooms after a rain storm.

"Usually."

"Just thought I'd ask."

Silence from Maggie. That was a scowl on her face? Parker wondered if it was worth the effort Maggie was putting herself through – practically killing herself on these shows. Was this what it meant – being a professional artist?

"Okay, you: back to the trenches ..." she said and Maggie did go back, working fiercely on a canvas she wouldn't even show Parker.

But the truth was a tiny crack had presented itself in Maggie's armor. She had begun to doubt her future as an artist. The first sales had been exhilarating, naturally. The first glorious flurries of interest kept waning in a worrisome way. Yes, there were still sales, but was there also something wrong? She seemed to forge ahead and but there was also this unaccountable 'slippage'. Of course not every interested person became a buyer. She knew that. But there was something she just couldn't put her finger on. Considering the volume of her sales per show, and her Emerging Artist status, she knew she was looking down the barrel of an awful gun: at the rate she was going, she would have to make peace with always having a separate full-time job, taking classes at night and a show – when she could get one. It meant admitting she might have been all wrong from the beginning.

Standing at the kitchen sink one night, she swished a stiff boar bristle paintbrush on the large bar of soap, followed by a thorough rinse. Checking the base of the ferule for specks of paint, she repeated the lathering, using her thumbnails to dig down deep. She rinsed again. A third lather. A thought formed: if this was a race, she was hardly getting out of the gate. It's like a doping scandal but there's no one to report it to or even to be silently outraged. I'll just get scratched off. They won't even know I'm gone. It wasn't a good thought.

After work a few days later, she walked over to the co-op gallery, hung up her coat and pasted a smile on her face. There was paperwork to do. Keeping an eye on the foot traffic into the gallery, she answered questions from those who showed interest in the various pieces, handed out brochures, answered the telephone. After all, the show must go on. She felt a modicum better when some dull hope was raised by two extremely polite Japanese gentlemen who stopped in to make some inquiries about one of her paintings. Their English was so bad, Maggie wasn't sure they knew she was the artist. In any case, Maggie worried that they would want to dicker about prices and she didn't know what she would do if push came to shove. The whole worry turned into a non-starter because while they looked at her work, the discussion remained between themselves in the rapid-fire of their language. But that was it. They bowed, thanked her and left.

"So, that was that," she reported to Martha, Denny and Parker. They were all sitting together on the steps of The Met. It was a Sunday afternoon. "That was the only nibble. It's like eating one potato chip. I want a plateful."

The sky was clouded over but no threat of rain, so an hour out of doors was always worth the effort.

She looked over at Denny. "So?"

"You know me. I paint at the pace of a snail."

"Martha?"

"The public hated the purple splotches of shadow that Monet painted on Aline's face. They said she looked diseased. I always thought it looked fine." Martha's answers were sometimes obscure in an art-history sort of way.

"Parkie?"

"I'm practically a foster child. I rely on the kindness of strangers."

Maggie nodded. Great. A human sloth, an art historian and a Tennessee Williams escapee. But they meant well and she knew that, too.

Therefore, nothing could have surprised her more than when the same ultra-polite Japanese gentlemen showed up again after the next group show in September. But it was the same thing. Lots more incomprehensible Japanese language back and forth, with no one asking questions of Maggie.

"Oh, well, at least the admiration is nice," was all she could think of to say in her report to her posse as Denny, Martha and Parker sunned themselves on the stairs of The Met like the seasoned Manhattanites that they were. All she knew was that the honorable Japanese gentlemen had smiled in her direction ... but so what?

Then miracle of miracle. The day the latest show was due to come down, the polite Japanese men came back with a third man, who was also Japanese, but spoke English. He asked the co-op member manning the desk to please ring Maggie on the telephone and have her to come over to the gallery.

It was a Saturday morning and Maggie was still in her pajamas when she got the call. She had never dressed so fast in her life. Since she didn't have time to dress up, she put on her painting togs, added an oversized sweater with some paint daubs that wouldn't wash out and hurried off. It would have to do.

Feeling frantic, she had to promise herself she wouldn't salivate or humble herself or behave like a cretin. Walking through the gallery door, she was determined not to let them hear her knees were knocking. As it was, a mild breeze could have knocked her over when she found out, due to their careful translator's halting English, the two men represented a Japanese publishing house. They wanted to discuss a limited-run print series of her baby giraffe drawings. If that went well, it would be possible to renew the contract for several of her Big Cat drawings. Each piece would, of course, be hand-signed; she would 'touch up' each print – adding to the individuality and authenticity ... and they were offering her an advance. That meant they were very certain the print run would sell.

Maggie was so thrilled she could hardly speak. After the meeting, she knew she wasn't ready to go home. Her legs were wobbly with excitement. Pretty much floating down the street, she assumed this was what was meant by an out-of-body experience. Large orange and gold oak leaves leaving the trees landed with a soft *'skitch'*. She picked out one to watch it while it descended. That's me. One leaf among many. She, too, was letting go of the branch, finally able to stand on her own. She had a thought: I need to thank God, personally. So she went to Temple. Not their temple but no one would care. It was enough just drop in and sit. She watched several men going about the room, putting things in order, touching this, arranging that. She didn't need the service. She just needed to be under God's watchful eye for awhile. It worked. She let the calm wash over her.

Walking home later on, she took the better part of an hour strolling cross town and over to the Malone family pile – one side of the first floor of a brownstone. Not ready to go indoors, she sat on the stairs and counted the pointy maple leaves spontaneously quitting the several trees in front of their apartment building and lazing onto the sidewalk. She was being a kid again, just for a little while, and she knew it. Maggie was on top of the world. She felt hardly tethered to the earth. Luckily there was such a thing as gravity. Finally it was time to go in and share the news and enjoy the pandemonium.

The next week there was a meeting with everyone concerned at Evan's lawyer's office where the publishing house contract was double-checked under a magnifying glass. Maggie was proud of herself, if for no other reason than she was able to suppress the urge to scream uncontrollably. She had no idea success could be this exhilarating. She always imagined herself as cool and calm. Mistress of her emotions. But the truth was different: it was a wild roller-coaster ride. It was all so vivid. So immediate.

It turned out that the company was well-heeled, had contacts everywhere.

"Bank the check and let's see if it clears," said Evan wisely.

Maggie banked it and two weeks later it cleared. The money was hers. That weekend the whole posse was sitting on the sun-washed stairs at The Met when Maggie told them the money was burning a hole in her pocket.

"Ah so," said Martha bowing to Denny. "Honorable Sister want to take Honorable Fliends for velly expensive lunch."

Parker giggled.

A suitably expensive dining establishment was selected and off they went. The huge smile glued to Maggie's face wouldn't quit. Right after she told the waiter to bring her the check, she smiled at them so brilliantly, no one knew what to say. So they didn't say anything. Next up was a movie. They picked one out and roamed down the street languorously, having an hour to waste until the movie started.

"Having to paying for this lunch and the movies is better than sex," Maggie whispered to Martha while they stood in line to go in.

"Have some sex and we'll compare," was the wise Martha's reply. Even in the dark, Maggie kept smiling her million-watt, glazed-eye, happy to the nth degree smile throughout the whole movie.

"Dinner?" Maggie asked when they emerged from the movie theatre. "My treat. I can't go home yet. I would drive Parker crazy."

Parker nodded in agreement. "This is true. Come on. Let the poor slob spend her hard-earned gelt. I'm hungry," so they picked out a steak house two blocks away and headed down the street.

"How does it feel?" Parker asked as they sat down.

"Helium," Maggie grinned as the group toasted their various successes. "Pure helium," she said to the faces at the table: Denny, Martha and Parker.

The raised glasses (ice water – since no one in the group was a drinker) were clinked. They were sitting in Tobey's Bistro, her favorite. Maggie was overcome by the wonderfulness of it all. Naturally she planned to frame both the check from the publishing house, the restaurant receipts and the movie tickets stubs.

It had already been explained to her that she would have to wait her turn to see the first print run but she didn't mind. All Maggie had to do was buckle down to her day job again and keep painting. In honor of all this wonderfulness, she decided to let Parker see the new painting, which she had been hiding. It was a cheetah. The pose was majestic.

"It's gorgeous," Parker said and she meant it.

Nights passed when Maggie could hardly sleep. This was the toehold she had been looking for. The strange feelings and doubts she'd been dealing with had been vanquished. Of course the exultation of it all made it hard to settle down. But Maggie had her plan. She would consolidate her gain and keep going. It was going to be a good Christmas. She was smiling so much these days her cheeks sometimes ached. That was how she fell asleep each night.

CHAPTER SIX

One Tuesday morning in the middle of following February, Parker gave Maggie a shake. It was still early and Parker was in a hurry. She wanted Maggie to know she was meeting a night school classmate for breakfast. They were going to talk Italian. Maggie nodded 'fine' and turned over.

About a half-hour later the phone rang. It was from Japan. The caller, a Mr. Jiro Nakamura, had news for her. The son of the publishing house owner, with the aid of their top sales rep, had successfully absconded with the entire contents of the company's reserve account. Every penny they still had needed to be used to pay their current bills. Then they would have to figure out if they could go forward or if they would have to close down altogether. Her series was cancelled. It was 'most regrettable". They were "velly solly". She staggered so hard she would have fallen down. It was a good thing she was still in bed.

Mr. Nakamura spoke English fairly well so Maggie could understand what he was saying. He explained that they were liquidating the assets still left. It was decided that Maggie did not have to return the good faith payment but, of course, there would be no further payments. The company now had many bills, many creditors to sort out. Print runs had been interrupted. The whole situation was a mess. A formal letter of apology was already on its way by overnight mail.

She had hardly hung up the phone when the doorbell rang. Their mailman was outside and he needed her to sign for a letter. She walked down to the landing at the front door, signed for the item and climbed the two flights of stairs. Her legs felt like ingots of pig iron. It was a wonder that she managed to get inside and close the door. With her heart beating that fast and loud, she thought maybe she was having a heart attack. Bad news could do that. She read the letter twice. It was from the publishing house in Japan. Boy, international mail sure moved fast.

She scanned it for any sign of a reprieve. A line in the last paragraph said it all: "Please go forward with any other plans, any other offers." Another words, 'don't call us, we'll call you.' Yeah, right.

Maggie could hardly find fault. It wasn't as though as someone had targeted her. A number of artists were being similarly disappointed by this devastating news. At least I'm not broke, she reasoned. I mean, the advance is still mine. That was something. She opened the drawer in her desk, filed the letter along with the contract and closed it all up.

So much for that.

She had been standing but she felt wobbly. Sitting down with a thud, she moaned out loud. "Why did this have to happen?" She had been on her way to Paradise, bags packed, ticket waiting at the station and what?! She was cut loose and she hated it. Maggie had never guessed that wealth (moderate as hers was, comparatively) could turn to ashes in the mouth. She had been all dressed up for the party and it was called off! Who cares about the damn dress? Why did the money suddenly mean nothing?

A searing pain exploded in the back her head. Managing to reach her bed, she lay down and pulled the covers up close. The thing throbbed and throbbed miserably before it decided it had punished her enough and finally subsided. She called her supervisor at work. Explaining that she was sick, he asked if she wanted to talk to Parker. She said, 'No, thanks,' and hung up. All she wanted was quiet and darkness and an end to the pain. Near the end of the afternoon she took a comforting shower. Drying off, she sat in dimmed living room light wrapped in a comforter and drank some tea. All she wanted was to crawl back to bed and sleep. It was early evening when Parker came home and got the news.

"Missed you at work," she said.

"I know."

Standing at the doorway to Maggie's darkened bedroom, she said "I'm sorry about this," softly. She closed the door quietly, shutting out the light from the living room. Standing in front of the couch, Parker surveyed The Wall of Honor. All Maggie's framed stuff – all that trying, trying ... and it made her think: what about herself? One college diploma. Not much to show for nearly a year and a half, she thought. We have to do better. I'll think about this tomorrow. Tomorrow something will happen. Time for bed.

Maggie stayed home a few more days. It was as though someone important in her family had died. Mostly she took to walking around the apartment carefully – fearful that the pain would come back, but when it didn't she considered the episode over. Lots of people have setbacks. It knocks them down but they get up on their hind legs again. You learn to walk tall, no matter what, she reminded herself. And that's what she would do.

Of course she called Denny and Martha. After going over it all in miserable, revolting detail and coming to the conclusion that there was nothing she could do, it was just rotten luck, she was willing to be coddled a little, which included them getting her to join a new artists' co-op. Thank god she was needed three evenings a week helping in the gallery or office doing mailings, making calls, tagging artwork when it came in. Maggie was determined to give a good account of herself, paying sharp attention to the many details of helping prepare for an upcoming group show in March. She was going to unveil the cheetah painting. It was only one piece but an important painting, nevertheless.

"Get rid of those dark circles under your eyes. Way too Goth," Denny said, as they stood in his studio, doing a review of the work he would show. He could talk her out of almost any dark mood. He made Maggie smile. She was glad to have him for a friend.

She nodded. "I will."

Her own solo show would come later in the following spring. That was going to work better for her anyway because she was in no condition to handle an event of that significance right now. She needed a lot more new work completed to support a solo show anyway.

In the meantime, attendance at the Friday night opening was decent. Various artists sold their work; a few of those few got mentioned in the Arts Calendar including M. Malone's gorgeous cheetah painting, "Out for a Stroll". One store decorator came by and sniffed around the painting and left a card for Maggie to call. Maggie called. It was iffy. She should call again in about six weeks. Maggie said she would call. Did the decorator wonder at the lack of enthusiasm in her voice? She wasn't sure. The painting didn't sell, which was okay with Maggie, but at least she got mentioned by name. That made for some happiness. She knew she wasn't ready to part with the painting itself yet anyway. Thank the gods, the reviewer didn't mention the failed print contract. At least that was old news by now.

On the following Sunday, Maggie helped take down the show. Parker came, too. They ambled over to a coffee shop, ordered toast and coffee and generally ignored the whole proceedings in favor of reading the funnies out loud, an old pleasure they had recently revived.

"Something else will come along," said Parker, looking up from "Brenda Starr"..

Maggie munched her toast. "I know," she replied dully.

They all knew the waiting list for co-op member solo shows was a long one. Maggie would push on. Her turn was months away yet. On the other hand, one new painting wasn't enough. She had to get back to work. The truth was: she was miserable even though she refused to cry. Bottling it in seemed right. Someday some journalist would interview her about this challenging period in her career and she was damned if she was going to say she had spent it heartbroken. Nothing was on her easel yet. That was the next major barrier to overcome.

Meanwhile, she spent Saturday afternoons checking out every gallery and every decorator, trying every way she knew to get a foot in the door again. The potential window placement of her Cheetah painting dead-ended. The senior decorator was off on another trail-- flimsy eveningwear and a bikini shoot in the Bahamas.

April arrived. She noted a certain crankiness was beginning to inform her every thought, which she was intelligent enough to realize in a moment of useful self-criticism. An instance of a smile grazed her mouth but then it was over. The moment of self-awareness sank out of sight. Now she was Sisyphus and the rock which she had so triumphantly slaved to get to the top of the mountain was on its way, rolling back down to the bottom. There was no stopping it. The gods had arranged it that way. I think the Greeks gods were rotten, she thought reasonably as the bus she was riding worked its way downtown. Sitting next to her was Maggie. It was the second Sunday in April. Slush still narrowed portions of the sidewalks but it was Sale Month. She and Parker always went down in The Village for this event. They hadn't missed Sale Month since 7th grade.

The girls were careful to tiptoe past any possibly icy patches as they crunched on down the street. Their routine was to start on MacDougal Street, at the end closest to Washington Square, and proceed forward. Each store was crawling with like-minded shoppers foraging through every rack and basket of discounted goods. Maggie's shopping style was harsh this year. With a take-no-prisoners grimace, she snapped each dress or t-shirt with a hard shake-out-the-wrinkles and reviewed its merits. An instant later it rejoined the pile of rejects.

"You see?" Maggie asked frowning at the basket in front of her. "Salon des Refusés, eh? That's how the Monet and Cezanne felt. Rejected," she muttered to the pile of t-shirts.

Parker stopped checking out the baby doll dress she was holding up to look at Maggie. "Do you need a food break? It's okay if you do. We've got a long way to go."

Maggie shook her head. "No. I'll put a lid on it." She turned away to closely examine a bin of bugle-bead encrusted evening bags, the likes of which she had never owned in her life, and never would.

Watching Maggie for a few seconds more, Parker went back to her review of the baby doll dress, which actually had possibilities.

The next crack in Maggie's militant façade came to light at about three o'clock when they stopped for coffee. "You'd think I was being blackballed, for god's sake! I was hot. Well, semi-hot. Okay ... beginner-hot ... oh, some kind of really warm ... it just doesn't make any sense."

Parker kept silent.

"It's just downright weird, that's what it is." Her brief tirade ended.

Parker nodded. "You're right. It is weird," she agreed. Personally she didn't actually think there was anything weird going on, but why antagonize the situation? They were sitting in Rienzi's friendly gloom.

Parker waited while Maggie looked in her coffee cup as the waitress refilled it. *There should be more to this. It's been two months. There's got to be more to this. I know her.* She felt her own mouth to be a thin, hard, line of tension. It was the only way to hold back the words of comfort that Maggie so obviously didn't want to hear. Whatever had uncorked, Maggie had obviously plugged back up again. Parker didn't feel she had anything constructive to say, so she left the matter alone. They finished their snack and the shopping expedition was resumed.

At 6:00 p.m. they agreed to end their shopping expedition, even though daylight lingered. Six hours had netted them each exactly two pairs of tights. All the way home on the bus Maggie gave the city streets, the pedestrians and the traffic her main interest. She had been slightly mean to Parker and for this she thought she would be sick even though she was sure Parker had already forgiven her. They said goodbye at the corner of 57th and 5th. "See you later," and with that Parker got off the bus. Richard and Emily were in town. She had promised to see them – a sleepover, in fact. The apartment had not been sold after all. Maggie and Parker didn't care. They had already self-administered their anti-Richard and Emily inoculation shots.

A few days later Emily even took the absolutely audacious step of calling to ask the girls to reconsider. They could give up their little apartment. "Come live in the lap of luxury," she offered. Of course Randall and Cook were still in service. "You're missed," she said. Parker found Emily's offer almost unreal.

"Maybe Emily got hit on the head? I don't get it."

"Are you tempted?" Maggie asked.

"Why, are you?"

"I asked first."

"All right. Well, I suppose I was – for about 15 seconds."

"We would live to regret it, Randall and Cook not withstanding. Right?"

"Right. There is no way Richard would not end up doing *something* unforgivable. Believe it. Emily cannot control him. Granted she managed to sneak me $2,000. It was all in small bills. I felt so sorry for her. It was like she had embezzled funds from a children's orphanage or something. She is so completely in his thrall, it's unreal."

"I hear you. Well, we'll go see Randall and Cook. That will make them happy. I like those people."

"Imagine how I felt before I met you and Evan and Barbara, because Randall and Cook *were* my family."

That Friday night, the girls went to dinner at Evan and Barbara's. During coffee and dessert they revealed the offer and their decision.

"You're right," Evan remarked. "The time to have made the offer has passed. I agree with our gal Parker here. Richard can't be trusted."

He took a bite of the brownie he was holding and let the rich chocolate taste melt slowly on his palette. He washed it down with a sip of coffee. Evan nodded. Coffee and one of Barbara's brownies. God was good. *L'chaim.*

They finished dessert and moved into the den. Barbara took the corner of the couch and picked up her knitting. Someone would be getting a handsome scarf for Chanukah. The oversized wood needles clicked and clacked with steady speed. Pausing in the middle of a row to count stitches, she said, "You can always come here when you need to take a break. I know your new place is kind of small. Places like this are hard to fine. It's so big. High ceilings, sliding doors, those built-in's that I won't let Evan

71

get rid of. I think it's modern enough. We have a great view."

No one said anything.

Barbara started again. "We got this apartment right after the War ended. Brendan had a friend who was a painting contractor. This building was one of his jobs. I love it," she said looking around the den. "Well, of course it's too big for us without you two but we are never going to leave it. It can be yours someday, Maggs." She smiled at the girls, returned to her knitting and re-counted the stitches on her needle one more time.

The evening came to a pleasant end and the girls took the bus downtown, got off early, having decided to walk the rest of the way.

A week later Emily called again. Twice in one week? It was unheard of. This time she suggested that if her offer was too easy, she'd ask for modest rent. "I know you two want to be self-sufficient," Emily said, but the girls were adamant.

They thanked Emily anyway. That one could never be sure of Richard's rare largess went unmentioned. Emily let the matter go, too. She never mentioned it again. The girls wondered what Richard knew or thought about her offer. It was mighty weird, whatever it was. It creeped out Parker because her mother – although it was hard to really consider Emily as her mother – had actually showed some interest in her, however brief. The whole thing was suspect. Had Emily suddenly realized she had a daughter – that she had missed the boat – by almost 15 years? Hard to say. Parker shrugged and let it go. It was way beyond too late.

Evan and Barbara were her real parents, all things considered.

After that, however, Parker usually spent one night over at the old apartment. It allowed Randall and Cook to make a fuss over her; Maggie got to have the little apartment all to herself. When necessary, Parker would time her weekly sleepovers so that when Richard and Emily came into town, they could have dinner together. Not entirely relaxing, but being able to stand on her own helped Parker's outlook.

At the end of April, Parker found herself sitting in the Feldman family room, a mostly un-used den, with the two new pairs of opaque tights resting in her lap. Richard and Emily were home as well, if they still called it home. Parker wasn't sure about that anymore. She felt she should talk with Maggie first but when she called, the answering machine picked up, so Parker figured that Maggie had probably turned off the ringer. All right. She would do this without talking with Maggie first. It might be just as well. Parker decided she could handle a conversation with her father. After all, she was a college graduate.

Picking up the extension, she rang the bedroom down the hall six rooms away. Richard didn't like to be approached physically unless he initiated the contact. Parker had learned this a long time ago. To Richard the sound of little feet padding down the hall had been an annoyance. Therefore Emily had showed a 3-year old Parker how to use the intercom. "This helps Daddy," she had explained. Presenting oneself unannounced, unless conditions were dire, was against family policy. Parker rang and Emily answered but she had her own news to share first. They were leaving for Paris on Thursday. "I simply must sort out my spring wardrobe."

"That's great. But, Mom ... what about all that stuff you got last year? I mean, it's gorgeous ... and practically new ..."

Emily took a measured breath. "That was last year, Parker. The world has moved on. Misoni, Chanel, St. Laurent ... one must keep up."

Emily sounded as if she actually believed this nonsense, Parker thought.

"Absolutely, Em."

Keep up with who? Parker knew she would never be in sync with her parents. At least the fashionistas in Paris were ready to remedy the wardrobe flaws of their faithful client. There was always that. "Listen, Em, can you put Richard on the phone?" Parker thought she was calm – it was the only way to successfully negotiate a communication with Richard.

Unfortunately, Parker was upset – both on her own account and for Maggie – so when Richard picked up, against her own better judgment, when he simply didn't seem to understand the situation, she reverted to her old ways: "Can't you do something, Daddy? Don't you have friends?" It was blurted out so quickly she didn't have time to prevent its issuance. Misspoken after all, and tactless, Parker had meant to ask (politely): don't you have contacts in the art publishing world? Richard knew many people but he didn't often share them with others. Ignoring the gaff, misspoken or not, as he always did when he was talking to his daughter, he nevertheless sniffed at the hint of imposition.

"Maggie is perfectly capable of solving her own career problems. It's something we all have to deal with."

Parker could kick herself. She had just violated her NEVER ASK RICHARD FOR ANYTHING RULE. NEVER. (As in 'absolutely, may I die and go to hell first' never.) She had been so very good on this point for such an extremely long time but her worry about Maggie was so severe ... Richard must know that she would never ask for herself. What did Richard have to deal with besides hotel reservations, dinner reservations, haircut appointments – the logistics of the next vacation? His money seemed to work all by itself, like rabbits on a baby-making spree. How did he do it? The man didn't know what struggle and accomplishment were about. It made her sizzle. As far as she knew, nothing dented her father's selfish hide. "Well, thanks anyway ... Goodnight, Richard."

So, it was "Richard" again, he noted. But she didn't hang up.

"We'll call you June 3rd. In fact, plan on it." (Emily's birthday, in fact). If it was his idea of a peace offering, his daughter's lack of reply indicated she wasn't interested. He tried once more. "Maybe you'll have some good news for us about Maggie's career by our next chat." Parker didn't answer. She hung up the receiver. His daughter was not notably an impolite young woman so he decided he would forgive her momentary lapse.

Parker considered the totality of the conversation. Her mother was a decent, if slightly foolish woman, about everything but her ironclad grip on her husband's attentions. There was not and would never be another important person in his life. Richard's world began and ended with Emily. Amazing. And strange. Such loyalty. Lucky Emily. Which was, parenthetically speaking, why Parker always got short shrift.

From his comfortable spot on the chaise lounge Richard announced: "I just promised Parker we'd call her on June 3rd. You'd better put that in the appointment book."

"Why, darling. How sweet of you. But tell me, why did you promise that?"

"Parker is worried about Maggie. Her print contract fell through and Maggie feels she's being manipulated by outside forces so that no other gallery will take her."

"Really?" Emily put down the silk nightie she was folding. "Do gallery people indulge in such politicking?"

"Possibly, but Maggie is an unknown. Why would anyone bother? No, I don't think so. She's not successful and she wants to be and ... we don't know any gallery people to speak of, anyway."

Emily picked up the silk nightie again. She unfolded it thoughtfully. "No, Bill Jackson and his lot are investment counseling. Not the same thing. Did you pack your slippers?"

He 'uh-hummed' but inwardly Richard was wondering if he was getting 'soft', promising to call his grown daughter on June 3rd all the way from Paris. I suppose she'll expect a call for some occasion every year hereafter ... wherever we are. How inconvenient. Still, the promise was made so there was no getting out of it now. I tell myself I will not get involved in these dramas and yet ... why do I do it? Unfortunately, Richard's inquiry of his inner-self had been sadly neglected for such a long time, there was little inner-self to contact. Therefore, getting no reply did not present a problem. The momentary self-review was over and not being deep enough to repeat the effort, he let the whole matter go.

The week completed itself and the friends were walking in the West Village again, nosing around the funky shops they hadn't visited the previous weekend. Maggie's attitude had marginally improved. She wasn't savaging innocent t-shirts and lush, hand-knitted socks. But Parker was on edge because she knew the storm clouds were brewing. How could she deflect the worst of it?

"My father must be having a mid-life crisis," Parker remarked dryly.

She explained this as they examined a window display full of Doc Martens. She liked the dark green ones and said so.

"Why?"

"Because he actually expressed the remotest iota of knowledge about your career – which is to say, he told me that he didn't know any 'gallery people'."

"Why are you talking to Richard about my career?" Maggie asked cautiously.

"Oh, well ... I mean, I keep them posted ... about ... things ... we have to talk about something." Oh, this was so lame.

"What did you say?" Maggie asked, flushing. The heat of suppressed emotion, which had been intently looking for the smallest opportunity to vent, had finally found a fissure. Now that it had launched itself, it was now hell-bent on wending its dangerous way to the surface.

Parker couldn't look Maggie in the face.

"Oh, Parker! Tell me you didn't! First of all, you know better than to ask Richard for anything. And second, just leave it alone! I had no business ranting like I did last weekend. I told you I was sorry. Of course no one is responsible for my lack of success but me. Please, you must leave this alone ..."

The instant of shouting subsided to a whisper. But Maggie's face was wet with silent tears. She turned to the store window they were stopped in front of. Still full of Doc Martens.

"I ... like ... the ... red ... ones," she said. Tears ran. Her nose was filling with snot. It was disgusting. She didn't have a handkerchief so she snuffled.

Parker heard her and found a yellow bandana scarf in the recesses of a pocket and passed it over. A vast amount of wet blowing and wiping followed. She patted Maggie's shoulder, pulled a mitten off Maggie's hand, taking it into her own, which was also uncovered. Moments like this required 'a little skin', as Parker described it, even though the temperature had dropped again. A mean, chilly anvil had clanged down on the city that morning with a smirk, blotting out the soothing spring warm-up. Still, there were more important issues than personal comfort.

"Yeah," Maggie said quietly, finally, by way of thanks.

"Yeah," said Parker. She handed the mitten back to Maggie and put back on her own as well. Taking back the bandana back, she folded it small. "I'll wash it in the sink – separately," and they both smiled. It was a house rule. Snotty hankies were to be segregated.

After that emotional blowout, Parker reasonably assumed that Maggie's festering wound of disappointment had been at least partially lanced. As if to prove Parker was right, they came home from this shopping trip with a few goodies including the baby doll dress Parker had visited twice – like a puppy seen at the pound that was too dear to leave behind. A warming trend further helped to kick this latent vestige of cold weather back where it belonged (somewhere north of the border) allowing the remainder of April to continue forward towards the spring that everyone was looking for.

To all her friends Maggie seemed measurably happier. New York during a good month like April was not to be denied. Piercing blue skies filled in all the negative space amongst the towering buildings. Crocuses were breaking ground on tiny vestiges of front yards. Window boxes were filling with color, shouting the arrival of spring with fresh verve. Up and down the streets vivacious plantings of impatiens around trees trunks were blooming. Overhead bright green buds exploded from the multitude of trees branches. The change of season was there to greet the people with that exhilarating tang that says the air is deliciously breathable. It filled the many eager lungs. Cheeriness was rampant. Parker decided it was safe to stop holding her breath every time she saw Maggie sitting quietly. It didn't have to signify depression. The shock and loss that had consumed February, March and half of April was done with. Her period of mourning had ended.

Maggie also considered that she had improved. In honor of it, she inaugurated her 'Brittle English Period" beginning with her invention of "The Tomb of The Unknown Artist". It was supposed to be funny. Consisting of laying on their living couch in the lozenge of sun that filled that end of the room for an hour or so in the afternoon, on Sundays, after reading the funnies, she would hold a limp flower in one hand, assume a beatific smile and read something from Oscar Wilde, beginning with "The Importance of Being Earnest." It was funny at first, but when she was still doing it the following autumn it wasn't funny anymore. Parker did not want to hear even brief installments of "The Portrait of Dorian Gray."

When Maggie graduated from the bracing wit Oscar Wilde to the more acid comments of Dorothy Parker, her roommate shook her head in mock indulgence. Maggie wasn't doing any art. She was working, of course, and going to all the museums on Museum Mile over and over again, but deliberately staying away from the galleries and shows unless she absolutely had to, to retain the loyalty of an acquaintance. Evan and Barbara had the girls to Friday night dinner almost every week, and Randall and Cook saw them roughly once a week as well when they would all eat in the kitchen. The friends went to the movies, had their Sunday snack at Rockefeller Center Café, and sat on the steps at The Met when the day was sunny and warm. It seemed that Maggie had softened a fraction in her strike on making art. She now carried a small drawing notebook and a small cartridge of pencils. Occasionally she read aloud some of the funny parts of P.G. Wodehouse's antic adventures of Bertie Wooster, the silliest of men, which Parker had to admit, was an improvement over Dorothy Parker ... but when Parker sneaked an occasional peek in Maggie's drawing notebook, she was saddened. It was empty.

For the first time ever, Parker wasn't sure she could live in the same apartment with Maggie. Nothing in their lives as friends pretty much joined at the hip had prepared her for this.

Even Richard decided a mote of concern would not be out of place when his daughter was politely disinterested on all fronts during their irregular telephone calls, which despite Parker's very sour attitude, did occur at Richard's pleasure and convenience. Therefore, he called Evan, who made him wait until two messages were left before he deigned to call back. Richard supremely, truly, did not care about the attitude of others where it concerned him.

"Are the girls there?" Richard asked mildly. He had to be sure he wasn't found out.

"No. The coast is clear. Saturday nights are movie night out. Preferably something with sub-titles, in black-and-white if possible, and nothing made after 1941."

"I thought they went on Friday nights." That should show the philistine.

"That's our family dinner night," Evan replied. "Saturday night is movie night." The subtext however was clear. But, if you were a real parent, Richard, you would know this.

"Well, that's nice," Richard replied. This data was of no interest, his tone informed.

Now certain neither girl would barge into the room at Evan's end of the line, he moved on to find out how the waters stood. That Evan didn't approve of his life mattered not at all.

"We're going to Sardinia," he offered with a certain amount of sunniness. It was draining to talk this way, but necessary. "Should be marvelous." Evan barely grunted. Well, that was better than nothing. Richard shot his next bolt. "I asked Parker if she'd like to come and she said she was busy. I was quite surprised. Emily and I thought it would make a nice graduation gift."

"It would ... but they graduated in 1999, Richard, old man. This is 2002. Also they are working." He knew his reply was way too hearty-old-school-pal but it was the only way Evan could bear to deal with the other man's ultra-urbane sideways communications.

Not a person to be thwarted, Richard executed his version of getting right to the point. "I asked Parker how her studies were going and she said they were fine. She thinks I don't keep track," letting an ounce of complaint color his voice to prove that he had parenting skills. "And by the way, I hear that Maggie is still trying to get ahead with her art thing ..."

Art thing? Ah, well. So that's what's up. Evan finally understood what had driven Richard to call him. Evan knew his daughter was fairly unhappy, all assertions aside. He was keeping watch. Parker must have said something despite her firm policy not to talk to Richard about anything of substance. Well, Richard could vacation on Mars for all Evan cared. He didn't know what contacts Richard had, but if Evan knew anything for sure, it was that Richard didn't share. End of story.

But Richard was still talking. "... I asked Emily. She agrees with me. We don't know any gallery-people. It's what I told Parker just before we went to Paris because Emily needed a wardrobe update. The wife of a man in my business has to look right and Emily is very conscientious about these matters."

Evan still found the man's attitude unreal after all these years. The only possibly mitigating factor in Evan's massive intolerance towards Richard was that he actually shopped with wife, taking as much interest in all the details as she did. Schlepping the woman to Paris and Milan yearly. Spending a fortune on her. Not many husbands do that. But was it enough to get Richard into Heaven? God knows when Richard had last, if ever, attended the High Holidays. Evan had stopped inviting the Feldmans years ago. Also, he was of the consideration that in the case of the Feldmans, Moses would have called the Red Sea down on Richard, leaving him to drown with the Egyptian army while the rest of the tribes of Israel went forward to find the Promised Land.

Evan decided to take a chance. One last reprieve, Richard. "What Parker really wants is to go to Italy. She's been obsessed with the place – well, the idea of the place, for years. Anyway, we can only hope that the real thing matches her expectations." Evan had chosen his words with care, he being more father to Parker than Richard would ever be except for the sperm donation and a one-night stand with Emily – which was almost inconceivable under any conditions.

"Yes, well ..." Richard didn't finish his sentence. He often did that. The pause, ellipses written on the air, that were a substitute for all the effort it would have taken to complete the thought. It had been too too lucky that the girls had met years ago, even under the difficult circumstances of Fred's death. Calls like this, however infrequent, satisfied his dim pretensions of parenthood. Emily, too, had it down to a science. She negotiated every bump in the road of her daughter's life with, "Oh, dear, you know your father." No ellipses. Just that one sentence. It dead-ended everything.

The phone call ended somewhat unceremoniously. Well, well, Evan mused. Richard was almost listening.

CHAPTER SEVEN

Parker was worried. She knew how to live with people who were indifferent, but that didn't include Maggie. As they walked back to the apartment, having gone to see "Casablanca" (for the 4th time, at least), Parker was carefully eyeing Maggie, trying to determine the size of the load of grief her friend was carrying.

"Definitely better on the big screen," Maggie said and Parker agreed.

"Nice print," Parker said.

Maggie allowed as how it was.

That pretty much ended the chitchat because Maggie said she needed her beauty sleep, so she went to bed and closed her door. Parker curled up with a book on the couch and read until her eyes were gluey. After awhile she turned in, too. She needed a better plan anyway, if she and Maggie were to weather this storm. Because she was still short on bright ideas, deliberately mimicking Scarlet O'Hara, told herself she would think about it tomorrow.

A few days later after work, Maggie met up with Denny at the Carnegie Deli. Denny: who was practically her brother, was occasionally her father-confessor as well and had long ago been nominated as Complaint Department Employee-of-the-Year. Also he was Denny of the exquisite Dutch-school still lifes. As Denny The Painter, his work was practically inhaled off the walls by the schooled and unschooled alike. As Denny The Friend, his calm good nature was a balm to her soul. She was closely examining the photographic proofs he was showing her when someone bumped her arm as they squeezed past and hurried out the door.

"*Excuse you*," she called, glaring ferociously at the back of the departing diner. Turning back she said, "Which reminds me, yesterday I actually thought I was being followed. There I was on 34th Street, looking in a store window at lunchtime, and someone bumped into me there, too. What is it with these people? Am I invisible? It's disgusting. Didn't even excuse himself. Just rammed me with his shoulder and kept going. Later, while I was at the bus stop, waiting for the cross-town, I could have sworn I saw the same creep. What's that about? Anyway, it couldn't have been the same guy, but I shook my fist at him, just in case. Whoever it was, he turned and went the other way."

"Want me to follow the one who just offended? If we hurry ... I can punch him in the nose for you. I wouldn't mind getting violent on your account," Denny offered cheerfully.

"Thanks, anyway. But the next lurker that messes with me ... I'm telling you. I'm going to pop him with my handbag." The righteous anger had exonerated her indulgence in self-pity for the moment. She returned her attention to the photographs. "Denny, these prints are beautiful. Boy, you are working with one great printer. The colors are perfect."

"Yes, he's a really good guy. I'm picking out the three best and these will be printed up. I'm sending one of these to anyone who ever expressed an interest in my work or hinted at a commission but didn't follow through."

"It's a great idea." (She suppressed the thought that while she languished in Slough of The Unknown Artist, he would probably be swamped with work within weeks.) She didn't begrudge him his success; she was just chittering inside herself like an agitated monkey because she wanted to have a real breakthrough of her own and felt she was unwilling to face the work it required to engineer such a turnaround. She handed back the photographs. It was fun being around Denny. They had been pals since sixth grade when they shared a cubicle in the workshop at a Saturday class for gifted children. They had both decided never to ruin their friendship by trying to turn it into something it wasn't. He was practically her brother, and that was fine with both of them. Actually it was better.

Maggie thought it was great that he had a following. Each show he did garnered him a list of commissions. However, as he explained, since he painted very slowly he wasn't rich, either. "Weird, huh?" Maggie agreed.

After gorging themselves on enormous hot pastrami on rye sandwiches, she kissed him goodbye and walked cross-town, letting her mind wander. It was amazing how one could navigate the crowded streets of Manhattan and still think one's own thoughts. At least summer was imminent. Maybe things would get better. If she wasn't going to draw – and the unmentioned moratorium on making art had lasted nearly four months so far – she'd better re- think her reading material. After completing the miraculous cheetah painting, she had done nothing.

Cowboys hang up their spurs, generals their side arms ... and artists? Their brushes.

She needed a new writer for her Tomb of the Unknown Artist for lounging on the couch. Maybe Dickens? Having demolished "David Copperfield" for the third time, new blood was needed.

That night, while standing in the living room, as Parker unpacked her backpack, Maggie asked her, "What book has that great line? "I am born"?

"Oh, gee, I don't remember."

"It's all right. It's not Italian ..." and Maggie grinned. "I know! It's Dickens. *Oliver Twist*. First chapter. First line. "I am born." Boy, doesn't that say it all? Now let's see. What's for dinner?" She opened the refrigerator door.

"How about I cut up some of that cold chicken meat and mix it with the romaine ..." which she picked up to check for freshness, "... and let's see. You shred the carrots and ... do we have any Parmesan ... do we? *Do wop, do wop*," she sang, faking it. "Ah, yes, here we are – got the salad dressing. Cool biz."

They sat down and ate a pleasant dinner. Parker wondered, what is this? A Maggie who is never going to do another drawing? Was it possible?

As for Maggie, she had tired of Dorothy Parker and her renegade, smart-ass Algonquin friends. Wodehouse was fun but ... a thought came. She hadn't been back to the library in ages.

"I'm going to look for something new to read on Saturday. Want to come with me?" Maggie asked.

"Mmm ... no ... not really. I've got a new practice tape ... Italian for business. It's got all kinds of words I don't know. When I learn this, it's going to double my vocabulary, at least."

"Are you angry with me?" Maggie asked.

"Of course not. Absolutely not. You know, someday I am going to get to Italy – if I have to swim there. I mean it."

Maggie assessed Parker's reply. She knew that steely, determined glint. "Yeah. I know. But flying would be easier."

Parker smiled. "Flying would."

"It's all right. Are we still going to the movies on Saturday?"

"You bet. *Boudu Saved From Drowning* is playing at MOMA. We cannot miss that."

"Oh, Lord, you said a mouthful."

With that they finished dinner on a pleasant note.

Late Saturday morning Maggie left on her book-buying junket. Through the partially closed door Parker's bedroom, she could hear 'Sara 'assegno o contanti?' ... 'Sara 'assegno o contanti?' (Will that be check or cash?"). Maggie closed the door to the apartment quietly and locked it.

When she got to the library, she was pleased to see their favorite reading room again. It still possessed some of the best ceiling art in America. Ms. Browning was not there that day, which was just as well, Maggie decided. For some reason thought gazing up at the ceiling made her flinch. She had to leave immediately. Hustling out of the building, she thought a nice walk to the Guggenheim would do the trick but once she got there, she changed her mind and only visited the gift shop. But that, too, made her feel antsy, and she didn't like the feeling so she hurried out the door. Getting back on the bus, she went downtown to a used bookstore she hadn't visited in ages. Once she arrived there, she felt her whole body relax. Free to wander, she puttered through the stacks and basically hung out, chatting up the clerk when he wasn't making sales.

In the end she came home with an old, well-thumbed copy of Alexander Dumas' *"The Three Musketeers* in French and a good bi-lingual dictionary. Here, possibly, was something worthy to counter the dark thoughts that came around to haunt her. Reading this would be work. It would require her full attention.

Parker knew Maggie was trying to pull out of her self-imposed slump but she talked with Evan and Barbara anyway. The agreed-upon strategy was simple: leave Maggie alone for a while longer and they would all keep an eye on her. If this funk continued until Chanukah, they would work out something else. Evan felt strongly that a gentle hands-off sometimes worked wonders for their moody daughter. Parker was willing. Maggie knew nothing about any of this in any case.

All three watched Maggie's progress surreptitiously as the summer passed, the fall and finally the holiday season. It came and went. There was some fun, some parties, the New Year's Eve dinner (deep dish pizza and rented movies and a late-night walk around the block), smiling at strangers, playing their tinny noisemakers. January came and went while Maggie kept reading. Translating the book was arduous but fun in a grim, weird way. The girls worked at their jobs, had a mid-week dinner in the kitchen with Randall and Cook, dinner again with Evan and Barbara on Friday nights, movies on Saturday night. The friends just kept plowing along, just as though nothing had happened – as though Maggie had never gone to art school, never had any flaming ambition to succeed. Parker didn't know if she could keep this up much longer. She called Evan and Barbara and told them so.

"Hang on a little longer, will you, Parker?" Evan asked. "I'm making some inquiries. "She agreed. He didn't explain and she didn't ask.

The winter passed, spring was beautiful and June arrived. The city was in bloom. On any given Saturday and Sunday afternoon Maggie could be found sitting in a window seat (having graduated off the couch when Parker was home). Her dedicated reading jag was turned full on. She loved D'Artagnan and Constance, hated the weak-kneed King. Enjoyed a full head of steam over Richelieu's machinations. There was swashing and buckling. There were hearts to win and broken hearts that couldn't be mended. It was the just the right remedy for what ailed her – total immersion in another world, other people. The laborious translating of each sentence only upped the ante. It was something to look forward to. Each weekend afternoon about 3-ish she would take a break, usually hanging out in the kitchen with a cup of herbal tea and a couple of slices of cinnamon toast. It was a safe activity, it was a routine. It suited.

This particular Sunday, it now being August, while enjoying a momentary idle in her reading labors, she found attention focused on their new toaster. It was a handsome red Art Deco thing with chrome appointments.

Emily had sent it as a seriously belated house-warming gift, which was laughable, however, the toaster itself was charming. It gleamed. The girls were very careful to keep it as pristine as possible.

"You really are a cute thing," she said to the object.

While doing the washing up, Maggie had a thought. An hour later, resting on her drawing board was a heavy-weighted, peach-toned pastel sheet of 11 x 17 paper on which could be seen a simply drawn outline. She paused. With care she filled in the main section with a blush of red chalk using her fingers to spread the colored dust, leaving small glints of untouched surface for the highlights to come. Giving the work a quick gassing with non-fixative spray, she looked over what she had done. She knew she liked what she had done. Pastel, she reminded herself, had to be worked in layers. It would never do to rush and thereby lose the light-toned background too soon.

Meticulously she washed and dried her hands. Up went the drawing, pinned to the living room wall for review. Of course there was still more to do. But she wasn't in a hurry. She could see it in her mind already. Down came the heavy sheet of paper again. With the same care as before, this time the empty background was worked delicately until a sheen of pale blue sky filled the background. She liked the negative space – liked the contrast of peach, red and blue. Kind of fauve, maybe she thought. For the shadows, these would be a rich purple. Oh yeah. The planned-for empty space remained empty. That was being reserved for a group of cottony cumulus clouds.

Hands were washed and dried again. Once more the drawing went onto the wall for review. She took some big breaths. Okay. I know what to do. She took it down and laid it on her drawing table. Now with all the skill at her command because clouds (the demon bastards!) were tricky, they too joined the scene. Fragile smears of white, pink and grey brought the mass of clouds to life. The merest hint of peach-toned paper remained, untouched and inviting.

A slow smile spread across Maggie's face. With the certainty born of years of drawing creatures, she executed a pair of exuberant pink flamingo wings fully extended, deftly joined to the sides of a perfectly executed copy of the bright red toaster! Up onto the wall went the drawing for its next review. A kind of pealing of church bells rang through her. *Ding dong. ding dong.*

Maggie washed and dried her hands a third time, cleaned up her workspace and climbed back onto the window seat to read. Nearby, on the wall, while she sweated her way through the long, complex sentences, she could feel the drawing. It was radiating.

6:30 p.m. Footsteps. That would be Parker. Maggie snuggled into the loveseat pillows and continued reading. A key sounded in the lock and the door opened. Maggie knew the whole sequence of sounds. *Thunk.* That was Parker dropping her backpack on the chair by the door. *Clink* went her house keys in the dish. *Chunka-chunk* – off with her clogs. *Sfft, sfft, sfft.* That was Parker padding down the hall to the living room in her socks. She walked over to the couch. Maggie said nothing. She just flicked her eyes in Parker's direction and went back to her book.

The clock in the kitchen one room away could be heard ticking. Parker scanned The Wall of Honor. Maggie said nothing.

Long pause. She, too, got out a book (Italian, of course) and spread out on the couch. Maggie got up and filled herself into the other end. "Shove over," she said to Parker and tucked her feet into Parker's side.

Parker looked over the top of the book she was holding. "The new drawing is genius. Now leave me alone, I'm studying." But they were both smiling – inside and out.

The next month found several more new drawings going up. Maggie attacked every piece of furniture they owned. With a creative vengeance, she drew the stove, the refrigerator, an old food mixer; even the hand-held can opener was drafted to pose. She particularly liked their hairdryer. All kinds of appliances, in fact, were the special grist for Maggie's new artistic mill. Some things got snouts or tails. Other objects received manes, paws, ears. The level of invention was wild and uncensored. One Sunday when Mrs. Pantopoulos, their neighbor, came over from next door with a plate of ginger-spice cookies to share with the girls, she found herself face to face with a wall full of ... well, she didn't know what to call them.

"So now you are some kind of mad scientist. Doctor Frankenstock, is it?"

Maggie came and stood next to her visitor. She sampled a cookie.

"Yum. I think you mean Dr. Frankenstein. Could I have the recipe?"

Mrs. P was looking intently at the third drawing from the left on the top row, pointing with her own half-eaten cookie. "Maggie, why does that lamp have a tail?"

"It's a very good question, Mrs. P," Maggie acknowledged.

She looked at Maggie for an instant and said, "When you know the answer, you will say it to me?"

"I will," she replied with a smile. "Boy, those are good cookies, Mrs. P. Can I have another?"

"Have the plate ... I going now. I am washing shirts for my nephew." A lamp with a tail. She didn't think she would tell her daughter-in-law about this. Her family might question her judgment, letting two young women into their apartment building. The building hadn't seen a tenant under the age of 60 in a long time. Better to let sleeping dogs sleep.

"I'll bring the plate back later, Mrs. P. These are really really yummy ..."

Maggie did bring the plate back, after it had inspired a new drawing. On the wall the drawing included a dinner plate with a striped tiger's tail, ears and paws. Moreover, this 'creature' was looking directly at the viewer as it padded across a living room floor, behind which was their own real couch. In the drawing, on the wall above the couch, were suggestions of other drawings, as a salute to an earlier generation of Impressionist artists who often included their own earlier works in the background.

By the end of September, the wall was getting full. On Saturday nights before going out to a movie, if anything good was playing, the girls would spend a few minutes silently reviewing Maggie's production for the week.

One Sunday afternoon Parker said, "There's still nothing wrong with wanting to be successful." She was looking at three drawings. Two rough sketches and one a finished piece. What Maggie had done to their vacuum cleaner was pretty damn great and funny.

"I know," Maggie said. "The thing is: I forgot that the work had to be worth the effort, all by itself."

Parker nodded.

Maggie was thinking about her art. Parker was thinking about Italy.

CHAPTER EIGHT

Maggie finally agreed to participate in a few different group shows through the fall but she didn't include any of her new work and she wouldn't explain why. Also she withdrew the cheetah painting and just showed the Baby Giraffe series.

"Think of the new work as my Helga series," she told Parker. "If Wyeth could keep a secret, so can I. Maybe it'll all see the light of day and maybe not. Please do not rat me out to anyone"

Parker gave her promise. Besides the two of them, no one else knew about the new work except Mrs. Pantopoulos, and as she explained: she had no one to tell. "I don't think anyone going to believe me, what you do. I cannot explain so good."

When Maggie patted Mrs. P's hand as she handed back a plate which had previously contained a dozen delicious oatmeal cinnamon cookies, she only said, "You spoil me, Mrs. P."

"You good girl, Maggie," and Mrs. P, smiling her puzzled smile, toodled back down the hall to her own apartment.

Maggie stood in the doorway and wondered if everything about America still puzzled Mrs. P even after all these years.

The schedule of shows had Maggie hustling to keep up. She still had her day job, of necessity, so on top of also ferrying artwork back and forth, helping to hang other artists' work, getting out promo and taking her turn at the phones, there was little time for introspection. She couldn't even explain to herself why she didn't want to share this new work with anyone. It was just something she felt. She merely took it on faith that this was the right thing to do. Meanwhile sales of her known work were still slow, but each one was a victory. That aspect of being an artist never changed or grew old. The people who bought her drawings and paintings were heroes to her and her eyes almost teared each time she made a sale. If the purchase happened when she was out of the gallery, she wrote the buyer a personal letter. Whether it made a difference to the buyer or not, she couldn't say. But she felt it deeply each time a piece went to its new owner.

The celebrations were modest because Denny had gone to visit his family for a month and decided to stay longer. He called Maggie. "My parents aren't old yet but ... you know how it is. They won't last forever."

"Don't stay there too long, we need you, too," she replied.

They both knew she meant 'I need you.'

"See you in awhile," Maggie added and that was that.

Martha was dating a man; it looked like it might be serious. "Can we meet him?" Maggie asked.

"God, no," Martha replied. "Maybe later, when I'm sure. He already has to contend with me."

Maggie felt Martha's dry smile come down through the phone wire. "When you're ready ... but tell him we don't bite."

"Ah, but you do ..." she cracked. They both laughed and hung up.

So, Maggie and Parker were on their own. That was when Parker decided she wanted one of the pastel drawings – before it was too late, she told herself. The day those works went up on some gallery wall, the fireworks were going to start. Maggie was going to be a sensation. Parker planned her approach. She would do it while they were sitting on the steps of The Met. She planned to ask on Sunday afternoon while they were enjoying toasted bagels and cream cheese. The steps were full as usual, even though the day was only partly sunny.

Parker leaned close and said to Maggie, "Will you let me buy the first one? *The Red Toaster*?"

"Certainly not .. I'll give it to you."

"No. Can't let you do that. I'll buy it. I have to buy it."

"I can't *sell* my work to you."

"Yes, you can. That drawing – it's kind of like your "Demoiselles d'Avignon" or whatever Picasso called it. When you get famous ... no, don't interrupt ... when you get famous, I'll never be able to afford you. So, this is my one chance. And I want that one. A hundred dollars ... okay? It's not enough but ..."

Maggie felt very odd taking money from Parker. But when she looked at Parker, the other's face was so full of determination, she relented. "Okay but I have to make another Toaster. Will that bother you?"

"Absolutely not. After all, I will own the first one. Hah!"

"You very funny girl ..." and they lapsed into quiet.

After finishing their snack they got up and went inside. They were going to look at the Egyptian artifacts that day.

Maggie kept on drawing. It didn't matter to her that no one else knew that she onto something entirely new. Even if it did mean delaying her entry into The Big Time. Maybe losing that print contract was for the best after all. She had wanted "it" so badly she actually used to ache physically. It had distracted her from looking for new challenges, new ideas. Maybe this was better. She was definitely on firmer ground. She realized she didn't ache anymore either.

Very late one night, in early October, when the weather was turning chilly, after Parker had paid Maggie for the drawing, she padded in to Maggie's room and sat on the edge of the bed in the dark and waited. Coming out of her sleep, Maggie felt a weight on the bed. She turned over and finally cracked open an eye.

"What ...? Can't you sleep?"

"No. It's something else. I have news."

"Well, gee ... that great but it's ... uh ... (squinting at the illuminated dial on the clock) "... oh, the hell with it. You know how to tell time. Okay, I'm up." She turned on the light.

Parker took a breath, settled herself and launched. "I don't know how it happened, but Richard's got a job. Can you believe it? He's being paid to review a new golf course in Jamaica. The review will be published in one of those in-flight magazines. It's a one-time assignment for now but ... my Daddy? Working? Huh. That's totally strange. Naturally he and Emily will be in Jamaica ... doing the research."

"Naturally," Maggie replied. Still squinting. She wanted to turn off the light.

"Well, okay. I just wanted to tell you. I know it's late and we have to work in the morning."

"You woke me for that?" Maggie asked.

Parker stayed where she was. "No. That could have waited. It's about Richard and Emily – as parents, that is." Looking at the clock, she thought: sometimes one has to communicate at very inconvenient moments. This was one of those moments. She plowed ahead. "I still can't help it. It gets on my mind and just grinds and grinds ... I mean, Maggs: he's my father. How can he not care? I just don't get it. And what about Emily? She hardly ever calls!"

"Tired of being angry about it?"

"Oh ... maybe."

"Richard and Emily are ..."

Parker finished the sentence for her. "... who they are. I know. I know."

"So, you know. Now what?"

"They are selfish beyond belief ..."

"and ..."

"You can't just have a kid and then ignore them, like they're ... oh, an ashtray ... and the people don't smoke anymore!"

"But they did. That *is* pretty much how it went. I'm sorry about that, kiddo." She gave Parker a wry smile.

Parker shook her head but said nothing.

"Hey," Maggie said, tapping Parker on the arm.

Parker looked at Maggie. "I was thinking about us, actually. I've been thinking about it a lot lately."

Maggie nodded. "Okay, come on." Wrapping herself in the bed cover, she handed the blanket over to Parker. "It's chilly." A few minutes later they were sitting on the couch in their usual places, nursing cups of hot tea. "Talk it out," Maggie said. "I'm listening."

So Parker did, starting with third grade, when the first year of her life with The Malones began. "They really couldn't leave it Randall and Cook."

Maggie was thinking: sure they could – and did. Standard practice for Richard and Emily, but she kept her peace.

Parker sighed. "Poor Fred. What a horrible way to go. In a motorcycle crash-up in the middle of Riverside Drive. I still miss him. Did you know that? Twenty years old. That's too young to die. The only Feldman who actually cared about me."

It was true, Maggie thought. Twenty is way too young to die.

"Richard and Emily came home from ... wherever ... just for the funeral and they were gone again. Like now. Here and gone again. Like I don't even count."

"Right," Maggie said. She always tried to keep her replies to the minimum when these discussions came up.

"Good old Mrs. Harriman. Randall and Cook spilled the beans to her and it was like setting fire to dry tinder. Think what would have happened, how it would have all played out if Richard hadn't fired Mr. Harriman in the first place. Sure pissed off Mrs. Harriman. That was a good one," and she chuckled.

"You could have been living in a closet under the staircase ..."

Parker looked puzzled.

"Like Harry Potter?" Maggie prompted.

"Oh. Yeah." She paused. "Boy, Mrs. Harriman didn't like Richard after he fired her mister. Well, Richard's loss was Uncle Barton's good luck. Harriman was a first-class chauffer. He's like a New York cabbie." Parker took a moment and began again. "Mrs. Harriman came to see me, to see how I was doing. Found me all alone. I heard her talking to Randall and Cook. It was only a matter of time, she said. Those two are bound to find a way to unload that child. That man ... really gets my goat.' That's how I first found out: Richard and Emily really didn't want me."

"That's hard," Maggie said quietly.

"Yeah, that's hard. When you're nine ... *nine*." She shook her head.

"Well, you can thank Gramma Nonie and Miriam Sedgewick," Maggie added.

"I know. Mrs. Harriman went straight to Miriam and from there it was right back to Nonie who called Miriam. The two of them came to the apartment. They had me pack a bag. A half hour later I was at The Malones."

Maggie nodded. "I remember. Nonie and Miriam were so cool. They acted as though Emily wasn't even there. Which she was. I saw her. Standing at the front door to our apartment, looking in. She had a weird expression on her face. She was just standing there – like on the sidelines – watching. I heard Miriam say to Evan, 'I give it ... oh, say, an hour – Richard and Emily won't even miss the child.' She didn't realize I was still in the hall.

"Miriam was right, of course. They were perfectly happy without me. Didn't miss a beat."

103

Maggie nodded again.

"After two weeks, when Nonie and Miriam realized that Emily and Richard were planning to abandon me completely, Miriam called Emily. I was in the den watching *Leave It To Beaver*. Miriam said, 'I'm calling your mother.' I didn't know what to think. She said, 'Meet us at The Malones.' She was talking to Emily. It didn't sound like a request. I don't think Emily dared to cross Miriam. Not if she wanted to keep her place in good society.

" 'A whole new set of parents will do that child some good,' " is what Miriam said right to Emily's face when she showed up. I had followed everyone to the front door. Hell, I thought I was packing up again. Your Nonie stood back a little listening. I guess she didn't mind letting Miriam handle Emily. 'Why you two ever bothered to have a child is a mystery to me.' Boy, was Miriam angry.' "

"That felt good, I'll bet."

Parker smiled. Maggie could see her friend's face, now that the pitch black of night was passing and morning was beginning to light the living room. "It did. Someone fighting for me. This was new. I mean, Randall and Cook were great, but we're talking a long time back. Now they aren't afraid. They're like: so fire us. We'll just go work somewhere else. Emily looked like someone had punched her or something. " 'You misunderstand us, Miriam,' " she said. ' I am terribly sorry about Fred. It's a blow to us all.' "

"When she said that, it really pissed Miriam off. 'Do you *not* understand? Parker can't be left *alone*. She's nine. Nine! He was only friend that child had – besides Cook and Randall – and he is now dead. She can't cope with that all by herself. ' " Parker turned to look out the window. The sun was now coming up. Maggie and Parker could see each other now. Turning to face Maggie again, she continued. "So, Emily got all indignant. 'I know you think you are doing the right thing – but really, you're interfering, you understand. Parker is our little girl.'

"Then *do* something to help her, or so help me ...' " I thought Miriam was going to punch her lights out. And Miriam is a lady." Parker nodded her head remembering that.

"I heard that. I came down the hall. Nonie was holding your teddy bear."

"Yeah. Somehow it got left at the apartment. Emily was looking at me and I was looking at that teddy bear. All I wanted was to get a hold of the teddy bear so bad." .

"That's when Emily said, 'We'll come see you.' I just looked at Nonie, then at Miriam. Barbara and Evan and you. What a mess."

"True," Maggie agreed.

"So Nonie says to me: 'You go play with Maggie. Emily and I want to talk with Evan and Barbara. Go along now. We'll see you in a little while.' So I did.

"We went back to my room."

"That's right. Right after that Emily got her walking papers. I found out the next day I was staying with you. Emily said she would call."

"But she didn't," Maggie said.

"No. She didn't call me. She called Miriam twice and Miriam said I was fine." Parker put her cup of tea down on the little side table. "She called me at the beginning of the summer.

Wanted to know how I was getting along. I was fine, sort of."

The early morning sun was slanting through their living room window. Maggie and Parker remained where they were – both still stretched out on the couch, facing each other. Maggie thought Parker was done for now but she went on with the remembering.

"The next Sunday night, while we were all sitting in den watching re-runs of The Ed Sullivan Show, I saw you hunkered down in the corner of the couch. Suddenly Evan reached over and pulled you gently onto his lap. You sat there for a moment or two, all stiff, and then you went all limp and you gave this enormous sigh enormously. Ten minutes later you were sound asleep.

"I remember that. After that, it was like I was a member of the family. Like Barbara had had twins. The only thing that didn't happen was that you didn't formally adopt me. Personally I don't think Richard would have objected if you had."

"We still can, if it'll make you happy."

"No," Parker said, smiling ruefully. "I don't need that."

"Isn't it amazing that I was never jealous? I never felt I had to compete with you for Mom and Dad's attention."

"It's because we were like twins."

"Right. How good is that? I mean, nothing's perfect. We know that Evan lets nothing come between him and one of Barbara's brisket dinners but ..." and they stopped to have a good laugh. Her father's obsession for an uninterrupted dinner so he could *kvell* over his wife's cooking was legendary. "Do you know that Barbara is still trying to get me to 'do something' with my hair. Yeah, like that's ever going to happen." It was, as Maggie described it, as though her head of dark red curls were some kind of Mount Everest that Barbara would never give up trying to climb. The girls laughed again.

"They're great parents. So, you want to know, what's my beef?" Parker asked. It was the $64,000 Question.

"Right."

"I want it to be different."

"I understand."

"I've turned it around in my mind a million ways and it always comes out the same."

"I understand," Maggie repeated. She understood the dilemma only too well.

"So you think that maybe he'll change?"

"Richard? Hell, no. I think he'll stay the same. And Emily. Those cats are probably never going to change their spots."

Parker peered at the clock. "Oh, shit."

"My sentiments exactly. But I'm glad we had this little talk. Now it's almost time to get dressed. Do you want to take a shower first or should I?"

"I'll go first." She set aside the blanket. "I kept you up half the night."

"It's true."

"It ... it just gets me crazy sometimes."

"Which is where we started. Go take your shower. We'll have breakfast out somewhere."

"I'd like that."

Parker walked slowly towards the bathroom.

"Parker?"

"Hmmm?"

"If it's any concession ... it could have been worse. You could have been left on the doorstep of an orphanage. I mean, I wouldn't have put it past them ..."

"No. Richard would have wanted a tax deduction. That's probably what pissed him off the most. That he didn't get one was only because his accountant wouldn't have let him get away with it. You have no idea ..."

"I'm afraid I believe you."

Parker remained in the doorway. "Sometimes I'm such a fool."

"Well, you're our fool and we love you."

CHAPTER NINE

By November life had finally normalized. Maggie was feeling good about her work. On the weekends Parker was taking an immersion course in Italian conversation while Maggie was apt to laze on her favorite big floor pillow, mulling over the color plates of some art book if she wasn't drawing or going for walks.

One Saturday afternoon, she decided to revisit a book of Whistler's society portraits. Maggie loved looking at them. She loved the size. He painted *big*. She liked big. She liked his directness and bold shapes; she liked the negative shapes, too. In fact, she felt nothing but admiration for the artist whose signature was a butterfly with scorpion tail. Looking up at the wall, a new drawing was featured. In the lower right corner she saw the neat, modest "M. Malone". Couldn't she do something better than that for a signature?

Grabbing a marker and a sketchpad, she started working with her name and signature.

She tried every version she could think of. Well, couldn't her name go somewhere else? Did everyone have to sign their paintings on the lower right, like a report? If not, where? In an upper corner, as Van Gogh sometimes did? Or maybe something strong and very black like Henri Rousseau. She had even seen artists practically hide their name, tucking it vertically up a blade or grass or in the eave of a house. No, she wasn't going to do that. How about a *chop*? She could go down to Chinatown for that. No. Too pretentious. Well, Albrecht Durer and Henri Toulouse-Lautrec had set their initials in a design. She searched through her library of books with color plates and simply looked at signature after signature. She noticed she liked what Delauney did – and Degas – theirs being soft and inviting, even a little witty. Yes. She liked that. She didn't have to sign in dark gray, heaven knows.

She penciled in a grid of boxes on a small canvas and opening up her box of paints, proceeded to paint small squares of different color. When that was done, she proceeded to paint her name in complimentary colors. "Shades of Joseph Albers," she muttered and was still at it when Parker arrived home. Standing above her, looking over her shoulder, Parker waited for Maggie to look up, which she finally did.

"Well? What do you think?"

Parker looked down at the page thoughtfully. "That it's definitely time to retire M. Malone, Accounts Receivable Clerk."

"Funny, funny. Ha. Ha. Which one do you like best?"

"The orange square with your name in red. Just 'Maggie'. I like it. Like 'Madonna' or 'Prince.' "

Maggie examined the square thoughtfully. "Well, they are both musicians ... but you get the idea. I'm going to show Mom and Dad when we go over there for Thanksgiving dinner."

"I think they are going to like the new signature, too," Parker agreed, thinking about news of her own, but decided it would keep. Evan and Barbara should see the new signature first. Also, with Maggie's permission, Parker wanted to bring along the now framed pastel of "The Red Toaster".

"It's time," Parker said. "They'll keep your secret."

Maggie agreed. The following Thursday, before they all sat down to partake of Barbara's delicious cornucopia of food, using the appropriate amount of ceremony, Maggie and Parker unveiled 'The Red Toaster' pastel and her new signature. Evan and Barbara were suitably flabbergasted at the wild new direction of Maggie's art, but they loved it and they told her so vociferously and with hugs. The dinner that followed was a happy affair.

Finally, Maggie thought, things are finally sane again.

Evan and Barbara both had the same thought. It had been touch-and-go but somehow they had all made it through. The table was cleared and Barbara brought in the coffee and a plate of Gramma Nonie's brownies. Nonie always went to Miriam's home for holiday dinners, "... because we're both old and the dogs (meaning Nonie's three retired greyhounds) are slowing down and I don't want to bring them somewhere new ... it really works out better for everyone." It had been that way for years.

Sitting around, enjoying a second cup of coffee, Parker decided it was time to unveil her own news. Opening an envelope, she passed it to Barbara, who read it and handed it on to Evan. It made the circuit of the table and arrived at Maggie, who had noted the pleased faces. What could it be? Evan was nodding his agreement. Barbara reached over and patted Parker's hand just as Maggie read the paper and lurched from her chair with an agonized screech.

"You *can't. You wouldn't ... you can't!*" Maggie moaned. "You can't leave!!"

Parker had known Maggie would not take the news quietly.

"I'm not emigrating. It's Italy – not ... not ... uh ... not the sub-Saharan Desert. And my visa is for a year. A year. One year. As in: three hundred and sixty-five days ..." but Maggie was not listening. Her eyes were wild. "Listen, I felt really bad when I didn't get that scholarship. It was sort of crushing, but I got over it. I made up my mind. One way or another ... I was going to make this happen. I told you. If I had to damn well swim. And in the meantime, we got our apartment and ..."

"We're having a good time, aren't we?" Maggie wailed.

"Well ..."

"Well, what? What!!"

"It's been almost four years since we graduated. I've been waiting about half a lifetime for this. I could be an old maid if I don't go now. You know how it goes. I know you've been through some very bad times and I would not leave you when you were so unhappy, but things are good for you again. Okay, for sure your career is not where you want it to be but you're on a new track now and I think it's great. Maybe even brilliant. You need to keep working. Maggie, I have to do this. It's my idea of paradise. You can't tell me not to go. Please, Maggs ..."

Tears were rolling down both girls' cheeks.

"Mom? Say something. Dad! Make her stay. I ..."

Barbara stood up and held out her hand. "Parker, dear ... come on into the living room while Maggie and Evan have a talk."

Maggie sat back down and moaned. She went so far as to petulantly kick her feet. Parker and Barbara retreated to the next room.

"Don't say anything, Dad. Just don't! Don't fix it. You can't."

Evan knew his daughter well. As long as she was still sitting in the chair, there was the possibility he could reason with her. Taking a moment to fill his cup from his wife's fresh pot of coffee, he thoughtfully stirred in a couple of sugars and added a dash of milk. He took a sip. Yes, the coffee was fine. He cleared his throat.

"You know this is something Parker needs to do, don't you?" The trial balloon had been floated. Maggie was crying. He tried again, speaking very softly but not placating. "If you think about it, this girl has never really been on her own. She has two sets of parents, for heaven's sake, one way or another. How much more looked after and cosseted could she be? Here she is, nearly twenty-five, and her life really hasn't started."

Maggie was still crying, but the first storm of tears had subsided to dribbles.

He kept going. "Why? Because she's been looking after you – and don't tell me otherwise."

At this point Maggie opened her mouth to protest but only a squeak came out. She closed her mouth and looked down – searching for help somewhere in the design of the rug, perhaps.

"We all know she's been holding your hand. Is that really fair? Is that her entire job in life? When is her life going to start, hmm?" He rested his case.

Looking in the mirror over the long mahogany chest against the wall, she saw her mother and Parker reflected, hanging back, but listening in. It was true! God, it was true. She had been sucking up the help and support a long time ...

Parker watched, a tentative smile hovering. Now Maggie was smiling back, albeit a little ruefully. Holding up her fingers slowly in a "V" for victory, she said, "Rome will be great. They'll all love you almost as much as I do." Parker hurried back in the room to hug Maggie as hard as she dared.

"Yeah, well ... you'd better write me – a lot. It may be the only English I get all year long," and they both laughed at that.

By January everything was in order. The girls had done all kinds of careful financial planning. It was time to fill a suitcase with Parker's favorite clothes and shortly thereafter she was ready to go. At work she turned her work over to her replacement. She walked the new girl through the procedure. "Maggs will help you. She knows the ropes." The new girl, an Antioch student, looked askance but Allen Rushman, their boss, promised her, "Everything will be okay."

Of course, people promised that all the time but somehow the interne wasn't entirely sure that she would indeed survive her brief internship in the real world. She really wanted to hurry to get back to the safe haven of college before real life came down on her like a load of bricks. Oh, well. She would hope for the best and pray she survived the next four months.

With only 10 days to go, Maggie and Parker were making the most of their remaining time together. Parker had been emailing resumes and was armed with a list of potential employers, " In case I don't feel like being on vacation for a full year with nothing to do but eat pizza and tour the country."

No one knew for sure how it happened, but extraordinarily enough, Richard came through with a job for her in Milan. No one wanted to speculate if Evan had threatened to 'sic' his *minyan* from Temple Sinai on the mostly absentee parent, but since every one of the men in Evan's prayer group had a network of contacts everywhere, who can say what pressures were threatened or brought to bear. Maggie herself wondered if someone had actually intimated that it was time for Richard to help his daughter.

In any case, Richard had made the right calls, did what had to be done; after that he simply sat back, watching from the sidelines as his wife's time and attention were occupied entirely by his daughter. He had already received his thanks, and considered them more than due. Staying otherwise silent, he put on a bland face. Inside he was angry. Enjoy it, Parker, my dear, he railed to himself. That's the last time anyone gets the better of me.

As for Emily: she did what she knew best. She took Parker shopping for clothes. Her daughter now had a new, second suit case filled with dreamy things – from underwear and stockings all the way to a new coat, hat, scarf, boots and shoes.

Anytime in those remaining days when Emily had a free minute, she looked to her forbearing husband and saw the signs – the jealously he thought he had managed to conceal – and much as it upset him, she knew it couldn't be helped. At least shopping with her daughter was activity Emily could understand.

When there were just a few days to go before Parker left, Emily and Richard had finished their evening sitting side by side in bed, they were talking a little and reading copies of the same book. She looked over and noticed that Richard was only pretending to read. He sighed loudly as she turned a page.

"What page are you on?" he inquired.

"200," she said.

"Oh," he replied. "You're ahead of me."

"I had a little time today while Parker was getting her hair done and a manicure."

"Mmm," he said.

Emily laughed dryly. "All right," she said softly, and marking her page, laid the book on

her night table. She could hear a soft rustle as her husband used the control wand and dimmed the lights until there was total darkness. She leaned over and whispered in his ear, "Come here, stinker," and the stinker smiled back, getting ready to kiss her.

"You are still first. You will always be first."

* * *

Maggie and Parker sat in the living room at their apartment that same night. It was still hard got Maggie, knowing that Parker would be leaving shortly.

"You know, it's unbelievable. You're going to Italy and Emily has just bought you a king's ransom's worth of new clothes."

"It's true," Parker replied. "What else was she going to do? Oh, Maggs: sometimes you simply gotta love a mother like that."

They both had a good laugh.

They talked once again about how Richard had managed to get Parker a job. A real job. It was quite a miracle. The company had been thoroughly vetted by Evan even after Richard had guaranteed their credibility. The fact that he had further extended himself by making sure there was money in a bank account to help his daughter handle the first few months' expenses (which were generally always more than anyone planned) was an even bigger surprise. The upshot of it was that Parker would be the new go-for girl at Fortelli's, a clothing accessories firm located in Milan. They needed an attractive, smart, American girl who could speak and write and read perfect Italian to deal with their many English language-centric customers and now they had one.

Immediately after Parker's plans were settled, Richard and Emily shared the news that they had committed themselves to a monster tour of Australia. It was scheduled to last a year or more, possibly. Nothing about the country, its spectacular reefs, the far western cities, Alice Springs, Ayers Rock, nothing would be missed. It was to be an in-depth tour. This was a special trip because it also included adult college courses on the country's history and culture. Even a stay in an Aborigine village was arranged. It was to be the definitive experience.

"Why am I not surprised?" Maggie said to her mother, while standing in the kitchen. They were talking about the Feldman's monumental trip to Australia.

"Are you asking me?"

"No, Mom. Not really."

"Leave it. Richard stepped in when it was really needed. We must give credit where credit is due, daughter."

Maggie looked askance at her mother. "Did I ever tell you how smart you're getting to be?"

"No. But I wouldn't mind hearing it."

"Mom: well you are. One smart cookie."

"Thank you, daughter. Now, please set the table, because your father and Parker will be arriving shortly."

The next day Evan and Maggie went to the airport with Parker. The girls had one last hour together and it would be an entire year before they would see each other again. Her flight was an economical red-eye she had booked online. Barbara had stayed behind and visited with Nonie, who also did not like airport goodbyes.

It was Richard's idea to have both departures happen the same night. Ironic and convenient. Richard would be Richard to the end, Evan noted as he and Maggie waved Parker off. At a different terminal, that same night, even as Parker's plane was lifting off, Richard and Emily were already nestled in the comfort of their first-class seats, heading in the opposite direction.

"Richard," asked a sleepy Emily, "Do we have the name of the *pensione* where Parker is staying?"

"We do," he promised, taking small appreciative sips of the lovely wine just served.

"Good." A pause. "Richard?"

"Yes, Emily?"

"Does Parker have our address in Adelaide?"

"She will ... I'll send it first chance I get."

"Oh, good ..." and with that Emily turned her head the other way and slipped into the beginning of a full night's sleep. She never ate on airplanes.

Richard observed his wife. He made sure she was well covered with a comfy blanket, and her silk eye blind was in place. He also checked to make sure her hair was smoothed. She never liked to look frumpy, no matter what. He took another sip of the wine. Of course, I will send her our address and our itinerary ... *when I'm good and ready.* Imagine others thinking he wasn't willing to help his daughter, now that she was being launched. It galled him. *They* could call it a businessman's lunch. He called it Blackmail Incorporated. Evan Malone would be Evan Malone, to the end.

He examined the wine in the dimmed light. Those two inches of pale wine had no idea what he had been through: surviving ten penal years of sleep-away private school followed by six years of higher education deliberately situated on the opposite coast from his parents' home – all this being his father's idea of how to raise a child. Grim but effective. What didn't kill a man toughened him. Now his own daughter was a very pretty girl, and smart. And tough. Parker would do well. She would be a credit to them all. He had done his part. No, he wasn't jealous in the least of Evan and Barbara's fostering. They needed Parker. He didn't. Emily found it difficult to cope. He knew he was a demanding husband. He needed all his wife's attention. And in that he had little to worry about.

Looking at his wife, he wondered, how had he managed to find her? The needle in the proverbial haystack, he called her. But not blind luck. Never that. He knew he was owed. Emily was his. And vice versa. The wine in the glass knew nothing of the sort. It just continued to taste delicious.

After a light dinner he turned off the overhead light, adjusted the airflow, checked his wife's blanket once more and then, assuring that his own silk eye-blind was well settled, thereafter emptied his mind in order to accommodate the long night's sleep.

That same evening a thirty-something fellow in a denim jacket and jeans sat bundled up, having a smoke while sitting on the steps of a brownstone near Maggie and Parker's place. No one was close enough to hear him mutter, "It's show time ..." as he flipped the unfinished cigarette towards the gutter the way he had seen it done in old black & white film noir. It was the only kind of movie he liked.

Down the street a hundred feet further along Oscar waited out of sight standing in the shadows of a tree; he could hardly be seen. "Pretty soon now, Maggie Malone." He stood awhile longer before walking away. He had already noted Nick's lurking. It would come to nothing.

* * *

At work Maggie's improved attitude had been duly noted and in consequence she was pulled into the office to help coordinate field activities for the northeast corridor, the Antioch interne proving able to handle Parker's job. Being indoors during the cold northeast winters was an unexpected bonus and she relished it. She was willing to feel not too guilty spending the winter indoors (for a change), happy to be able to sit warm and snug at her desk while looking after teams of dedicated people who tramped the streets of various American cities getting signatures for petitions demanding a stop to various kinds of military-industrial- environmental malfeasance.

At the little apartment, new drawings were added to the living room wall at regular intervals. No one was allowed to visit and no one guessed what she was up to. She and Parker had never been the kind of invite people over for dinner. Now Maggie continued to make sure all her socializing occurred elsewhere. If Denny suspected anything, he didn't ask. He approved of the verve in her step. Whatever it was, was fine with him. Maggie's other artist-compatriots were similarly disposed. She would tell them when she was ready.

For Maggie, it was a pleasantly monastic life and she was actually enjoying her anonymity when in February of the New Year, surprise of surprises, she got a call from Corinne, the assistant to the assistant manager at Obayashi's Fine Arts. They wanted to give Maggie a show.

"Really? Corinne, this is great news."

This time Maggie did not do somersaults. She was pleased, but determined to remain calm. Her life nor her happiness would hinge on one show. Her priorities had finally straightened out. Coincidentally a recently revived interest in animal art was cross-fertilizing with various clothing designers' interest in animal print clothing. The fashion magazines were saying every woman should have one animal print blouse, pants, scarf, shoes – something – and that's when Maggie's art twigged Hiru Obayashi's memory. They wanted to be sure Maggie still had the terrific cheetah painting. As it happened she did. Hiru also remembered Maggie had a portfolio of first-class colored pencil drawings of the other Big Cats as well. Everyone involved was supremely pleased. The show looked to be a genuine hit.

The meeting with the show's curator, Moki Hokai, went well. He was very pleased with the series. He wished there was another painting, but there wasn't. The big question was: where they would hang the cheetah painting, to cause the biggest impact? It was while the gallery was prepping for the show that Corinne noticed the change in Maggie's signature and pronounced it "Very chic." Maggie's small, loopy writing, now placed in the left corner inside a small eccentric orange rectangle and her name in red would be immediately recognizable.

There was going to be one show before Maggie's. Obayashi's roster of old warhorse-artists was finally being turned out to pasture. It would be a heroic retrospective, an enormous catalog *de raison* and a clean sweep. Most of these venerables weren't even painting anymore. They were simply living on the fumes of their past successes. Hiru felt it was time to buy a large quantity of drinkable champagne, throw a party, sell everything possible that was still gathering dust, hold a charity auction and bring down the curtain. Let new faces have a turn at stage center. Maggie's work would be the linchpin of the next show. It would be a good start on a new era of talent. She would make a suitable splash. The gallery owner was very pleased.

Maggie dug out the manila file still stuffed with names for her mailing list and created a postcard announcement. Later the gallery would do a better one, but she wanted to get a head start on promoting. She called Denny to get some advice because he had headlined many more art shows than she had. For the next month, she spent Saturdays working on whatever new drawing was on the board and on Sundays she would hand-address the cards while listening to the radio.

In the meantime, the warhorse art show was scheduled for early June. Her solo show would open right after Fourth of July. Right then, however, it was the Ides of March. The telephone rang. Maggie hummed as she walked over to the telephone. That should be Parker. It was her turn to call. They tried to talk once a month on Sundays.

It was Corinne ...

She had been bumped again. Maggie couldn't believe it! Because of her pal, Frieda Goetz. Hiru had asked Corinne to personally call and express his regrets for this sudden change of program. Even after the phone call ended, Maggie's mouth was still agape. She didn't know what to do, she was so frazzled. She was beyond getting upset.

"Et tu, Brutus," was all she could say aloud to the empty apartment. But she didn't even cry. Why bother? This kind of thing is nothing new to me. Damn them all.

She stoically gathered up the unmailed postcards and the list of names. Thank god she hadn't invested in the postage yet or mailed them. Just thinking about the phone calls she would have had to make to announce the cancellation was a nightmare. Everything went back in the desk drawer. She called Evan and Barbara. Giving them the bad news, she said she was fine and rang off. Treating herself to a pizza, she turned on the television. Football.

Good. Every violent scrimmage was cheered. The high-fidelity sound system reported every grunt and groan on the playing field and each was a temporary mitigation to the silent wound. On the Monday she went back to work as though nothing had happened (again). It was true. Nothing had happened. Again.

On the following Sunday, she did talk with Parker. First she shared the devastating but brief news of another show being pulled out from under her. That didn't last long. They pushed on to chat about everything else possible. A few days later Maggie couldn't resist mailing Parker one of the postcards she had prepared. Scribbled across the notice in red marker was an 'End of story, but don't worry about me'.

By Wednesday Maggie wanted to scream after all. When she got home, instead of sitting down, she changed into some old clothes, grabbed her purse and walked out of her apartment slamming the door as hard as she could – harder than she had ever slammed a door in her entire, mostly well-behaved life. It felt good. Damn them all. Anything loose shook or rattled. The drawings on the wall quivered en masse. Damn them. Damn them all. Mrs. Pantopoulos opened her door and came out into the hallway cautiously. She shook her head at Maggie, who was standing there in front of her apartment door, still shaking with emotion.

"What for you make the door to close so hard that way and frighten my cats? I surprise at you."

Maggie felt quite chastened. "I'm sorry, Mrs. P." It was all she could manage to say before she hurried down the stairs.

She was off for the little pocket park a few blocks away. That would be a safe place and relatively unvisited. She needed somewhere she could calm down (or cry – just in case she did blubber). At least she had remembered her hankie. She would sit in the inhospitable cold until her behind froze. She had tried so hard not feel affected ... was it fair? What the hell was going on!

In the weeks leading up to Frieda's opening, Maggie saw for herself that Frieda's work was hot. Iconic, quite religious. Lots of gold leaf. Dazzling. Very dramatic. She was so hot the Arts Calendar was doing an article on her.

Maggie knew her own work was good – if one considered only the animal drawings (not the new stuff which she would permit no one to see). But even she believed that great animal art couldn't compete with what Frieda was doing. So, Maggie was good versus Frieda, who was sizzling. Not a difficult choice. The opening of Frieda's show, like her arrival on the scene, was like foreign matter entering the atmosphere. She was blazing. Of course it was exciting.

It was hoped that Maggie would still have the next show, because after Frieda she understood that Hiru still wanted to show her Big Cat series – coordinated with a new textile designer – except that Olga Navratilova had also blown into town. Olga, a newly arrived Russian artist, was doing amazing gold and jewel-colored dip-tychs. Apparently gold leaf was having a bigger revival than animal art. So Olga had a smash opening at The Modern Review Gallery and Hiru was so impressed, he decided to extend Frieda's show to make the most of the sizzle. Olga and Frieda were the toast of the art scene. Maggie could only watch from the sidelines. There was paradise with all the trimmings – just out of her reach.

Maggie talked with Corinne. Maybe in the fall, after things had quieted down? "Let's look at that," Corrine replied.

As of right now, the only two galleries interested in Maggie Malone had put their interests elsewhere. She was back to Maggie Who? Maggie What? Maggie When?

At least she was still drawing and she still liked doing animal art. But now she divided her time between genres. Therefore, on any given Saturday afternoon, Maggie could be found on her old bench at the Zoo but Sundays were spent in the apartment making pastel drawings with more and more outrageous combinations.

Spring arrived slowly. It was April but the city was under the iron hand of another cold spell. Apparently Mother Nature hadn't looked at the calendar. Maggie had to work all muffled in a long coat, a long scarf wrapped around and around so her nose didn't freeze. On her head was the familiar red wool cap with a bobble on top. She kept her mittens near by – taking breaks to warm up her chilled fingers. Winter boots were still required foot covering.

Maggie looked around. She considered the few leaves obstinately stuck to the trees even after the winter's hammering. "You missed your chance," she groused to a lone leaf as the wind tore it loose. Having struggled mightily to hang on, it finally fluttered down. "You could have joined the Big Rake-Up in November, you know. Gone out in a blaze of glory – or at least ended up with all your buddies in one of those huge environmentally safe green bags ..."

She moaned softly. That same old door had shut on her again and she was locked out. How weird was that? Did someone hate her? Or is this how it happens? Is this how Renoir and Cezanne felt? Shut out by the State-approved Beaux Art? All dressed up for a show and no one to come see the work. Rats. Rats. And double rats. Where was the king who would offer a Salon des Refusés now? Oh, that was the Emperor Napoleon. The point was ... she heard William come crunching down the path through the remnants of the last snowfall. His undone boot buckles clinked. In his hand, a rolled green hose.

"Do ye want to come look at a baby duck? I've got one recuperating in our little hospital ... she's a rare 'un."

She shook her head. "No, thanks anyway. I just want to sit for a bit."

Maggie had, in her excitement, personally invited him and Maeve to her show so she had to call and cancel the invitation. She felt a fool.

He sat down next to her and put the hose to one side. "Christy Brown did it with only his left foot, you know." He rested his arm across her shoulder and down her arm. She could see his big mittened paw out the corner of her eye. He tapped the side of his nose with his free hand. "It'll all come right. You'll see."

"I guess so. I'm just being a sad sack today. Frieda is doing such great work. And Olga. I can't blame them. They're so ... popular. It's just that I've never had that. It must be wonderful."

He pulled out a clean hankie. "You'll have your turn. I'm sure of it. Here now. Mop up."

She did. Tears she hadn't noticed were ambling down her cheeks.

"Blow ..." he ordered. "Go on. It's just snot. It'll wash. Give a big blow."

So she did, emptying both nostrils. William wrapped the hankie and put it away in a pocket. "Maeve will wash it. I have another, anyhow. I always pack two. Well, that little duckie is waiting for me," he said picking up the hose and walked in the direction of his workshop.

I'm a cry baby, she thought, but feeling marginally better for the cry, she got up and took a few steps before she remembered her presentation portfolio. It was leaning against the bench. Having been out visiting galleries again and getting nowhere, she had come to her favorite bench to mourn — and maybe do a little work. It was a strange feeling, but for an instant she had the idea of leaving the portfolio — just abandoning it. But oh, no, she couldn't. Her drawings were like her children. She couldn't leave them. That would make her ... what ... like ... um ... and Maggie shuddered. Like Richard. Oh, god. Walking back the few steps, she grabbed hold saying, "Come on, we have to go home now," and munched out of the Park towards Fifth Avenue.

Now I'm talking to my portfolio, she noted. How pathetic is that?

On the other side of the path, in a tweed overcoat with the collar turned up and galoshes covering his feet, was a tall man. William, who was standing in the doorway of his work hut with the door open, looking down the path at

Maggie's back, knew he had seen this man a number of times before. William enjoyed making note of the regulars. This man was one of the "fans" that he had mentioned to Maggie. This was the man with the suede Russian hat and furry earflaps, who now remained seated, continuing to be thoughtful. William shut the door again.

Outside on the bench Oscar stayed seated. He didn't like seeing Maggie so unhappy, however necessary to their plans it might be. He got up and followed her out to the street, passed her by and kept walking. With the flaps down and his scarf turned several times around collar and mouth, there was very little of his face to be seen. He was just another pedestrian. As it was, he didn't think she would recognize him. Parker might have, but Parker was in Milan, sound asleep, hours ahead in a different time zone. Oscar turned and headed uptown.

Maggie had, in fact, recognized the man by his coat and hat. She thought for a moment he might approach her but it didn't happen. It's just as well, she thought. I'm in no condition to talk to anyone today.

Her next destination was the library. It was some kind of comfort to be planted in her old seat at the table where she and Parker had spent so much time writing papers. After pulling some books on Italy, she found she was in no mood to read. Her eyes kept getting misty. (Oh, stop it, she said to herself, getting testy.) The book on top of the pile she pulled was "Milano and the Roots of Industry". That's where, tomorrow morning, she imagined Parker would be up to her elbows in straw, unpacking and cataloging a new shipment of goods.

If Maggie had looked up, she would have seen a slightly familiar, winter pale, thin, thirty-something fellow in a plaid shirt and dark jeans standing near. But she didn't. Nick smiled inwardly. He walked over and stood by the end of the table. Pointing at her pile of books he asked, "Are you finished with those?"

Maggie realized he was talking to her, but she was in no mood to talk to anyone. "Sure. I'm done." She continued examining the carpet. She hadn't noticed it was Nick.

"You like Italy, huh?" He was still there.

She didn't reply.

Nick was enjoying giving Maggie a dig. His skin itched. He needed to get out, go upstate, into the woods all alone. It was time to shed.

Finally there was the sound of feet departing. Maggie looked up in time to catch a glimpse of a denim jacket as he walked away, the books in front of her being gone. She packed up, making sure she had her portfolio this time, walked out of the room and across to the landing at the top of the stairs. She was missing Parker something awful. No one to hold her hand this time. She would have to muddle through on her own. Maggie sighed. The library was closing. Time for her to go home.

Back in the Microfiche Room, Elizabeth was barking at Nick. "You need to watch what you do ... oh, ick." She wrinkled her nose. "Get out of here. Find someplace. You're about to shed right here. Ick. You really smell."

He almost smiled because what annoyed Liz, pleased him. "I know. It's driving me crazy, too."

"Well, handle it because I can smell it from here." She wrinkled her nose again, moving towards the door.

Nick took a self-examining sniff. It wasn't that bad. Not that anyone here would recognize the smell, which in fact, was a lot like musty books.

Out on the street, Maggie hefted the padded strap of the portfolio onto her shoulder and walked slowly. She hadn't intended to, but she ended up in front of Obayashi's anyway, thinking about earlier times.

Through the big picture window looking into the gallery, she saw a man sporting a silk cravat and cane, his shoulders covered with his coat – like an impresario – talking to Hiru. She wondered who the swell was. All I know is, they aren't talking about me, she sighed.

But as it happened, the two men were talking about Maggie. Arthur Cotillion had voyaged from his little paradise of Fleetwater to talk to Hiru. Hiru thought Maggie was something special and it was only a coincidence that Frieda and Olga were having breakout shows at the same time. He wanted Arthur to sponsor Maggie. Maggie wasn't the first artist that Hiru had directed to Arthur. Since Hiru had very good taste, Arthur was willing to make a rare trip into the city. If Maggie had kept looking in the direction of the two men a moment or two longer, she would have seen Arthur, but it didn't happen. She felt it was lame to be standing there and looked away.

But Frieda, who was in the gallery, spotted Maggie and waved at her to come in. Arthur and Hiru had already moved inside to Hiru's office to have a cup of tea. In the meantime, Maggie waggled her head, 'No,' to Frieda but

Frieda hustled outside before Maggie could do anything about getting away. The portfolio was too big for running. Besides, she and Frieda were buddies.

"I feel like a fool," Maggie said, getting a little misty again.

"Well, you aren't. Curators are fickle. That's all. It could as easily have been me. For them, it's just business. You are a marvelous artist. Your turn will come. I know it. Now listen, I already telephoned Denny and Martha. They are both available and we are all having dinner. I was just about to phone you anyway. Saves me the call. We always say the person who gets a big sale or a big show has to pony up for dinner. This time it's me."

"Make it a horse and I'll come," Maggie joked. It was their old joke – as in "I'm hungry enough to eat one".

In place of her heart was a medium-sized lump of cement, but at 8 p.m. that evening Maggie was at Tobey's Bistro with her shredded emotions temporarily stapled back together. She could not let them know she was upset. It simply wouldn't do. This dinner would be one for the road because the group was also breaking up, so to speak. Martha was leaving for London. The potentially special boyfriend had evidently bombed out and Martha was acting like nothing was amiss. Apparently no love lost. Maybe Maggie would ask what happened and maybe not. What a lucky break that Martha was going to stay with relatives rent free because, as she explained it with her typically dry delivery, "The house is so big even now there may be other people living there they don't know about in rooms not yet visited." Typical Martha. Maggie always liked being around her. She would be missed.

As it also turned out, Denny was going back to Denver again. His favorite part-time job was waiting for him – clerking in a music store in the downtown. He would keep painting, of course. There wasn't a classical gallery anywhere he couldn't get a toehold in, but he painted so slowly it was difficult to get full-time representation. Some unsuspecting curator would get all excited, hang the current crop of his paintings, watch people come in and scoop them up and then the commissions would start rolling in. That's when Denny The Slow (he called himself) showed his true stuff. Art buyers would find out how long they would have to wait, which was usually just marginally longer than was comfortable, so that it drove the gallery owners wild. That kind of waiting was just not their style. In the meantime, some of the commission orders would stick, so Denny could paint – slowly and carefully – which was the way he liked it. All the razzle-dazzle of openings didn't interest him. He just liked to paint.

"I'm not a factory, Maggs," he explained. "I don't paint assembly-line style. I'm a modern Henri Fantin-LaTour, with one major exception: I only have one speed when I paint: slow. Still they will try to rush me. It can't be done." He gave his familiar laugh. Frieda was nodding her agreement, even though she painted at lightning speed comparatively speaking, which was making Hiru one happy gallery owner.

Maggie laughed, too. She would miss Denny the most. Mourn this change later, she told herself. I have enough trouble as it is.

"Yes, our Frieda is a race horse of an artist," Martha was saying in between bites of romaine lettuce. "She paints fast and beautiful."

Denny patted Frieda's head. "Pretty horsie ..."

Martha leaned over and tapped Maggie on the hand and whispered in her ear. "Don't look now, guys, but someone is admiring our Maggie."

"Where?" Maggie whispered back. How could she look without turning her head?

"Over there. The older guy. He's having dinner with ... uh-oh. He's looking our way. Careful."

Maggie waited a minute. She had an idea. She reached into her pocket book and took out the little mirrored powder compact. That way she could check out the man without him seeing her use it. Huh.

"Too old," she said into Martha's ear. "Too much hair." Way too much "boulevardier' for her.

The man's dinner companion was wearing an antique silk cloche on her head, and it masked everything but the outer edge of a severe profile. Maggie would have bet even money a dame like that wouldn't take kindly to her date taking even a casual glance in other directions.

"Not my type, but thanks anyway." She and Martha had a quiet laugh.

"Frieda said he looked European."

"Is that supposed to make a difference?" Martha asked.

"With some women it does," Frieda replied. "They think it is a bit exotic, I suppose."

"An Eskimo is exotic ... an Australian Aborigine is exotic ... a Ubangi is exotic ... we've all been to Europe – except our innocent Maggs here – but if you've seen one

European, you've seen them all – present company excepted, Frieda dear," said Martha.

"Thank you."

"So, Maggs," Martha continued. "When I get to London, I will call you. Here is my new phone number."

"It's a date ..."

There was more chitchat and exchanging of information and dinner naturally ended on an upbeat note because one of their own had Arrived. Frieda: fast and talented. It was the perfect combination, they all had to admit. For Maggie it seemed like everyone she cared about was headed for greener pastures. After dinner, the four stood out on the sidewalk for a breath of fresh air.

Frieda was saying to Maggie, "... and they have some really nice galleries there. I love your giraffes. Give it a try?"

"I haven't done giraffes in over a year, Frieda ... besides, I'm ..." Maggie suddenly shut her trap.

Thank god Frieda wasn't quite listening, Maggie thought, because I almost spilled the beans and that would have been a huge mistake. Frieda was still carrying on:

"I think you are giving Stubbs a real run for his money."

Denny rolled his eyes even as Maggie settled a friendly look on her face. She was going to let it pass, but not Martha.

"Frieda. That was two hundred years ago and George Stubbs specialized in horses."

"Of course. All I meant was ..."

"We know. We know. You mean well. That's the point," and Martha gave her a little pat on the arm. Was Frieda really that dim? Sometimes Martha had to wonder.

Frieda handed Maggie a thin stack of business cards. "You must go check out these places ... I think these are the best but go see for yourself. Promise me? Be in touch."

Maggie stuck the pile in her coat pocket. "Thanks, Frieda ... here's a taxi." *Kiss, kiss..* Frieda was due back at the gallery and the taxi hurried off. Denny and Martha joined Maggie in a group wave. While Denny was fixing his coat buttons, Martha gave Maggie a hug and whispered something funny and unrepeatable in her ear.

Maggie smiled. "You're a good friend. I'll miss you, too."

"Good. You can come see me. London's not that far away. There's certainly enough room ..." she quipped. They did another group hug after which Martha was put into a cab and she was gone.

Denny and Maggie stood together sampling the night air.

"And then there was one." Maggie quipped.

"Agatha Christie," Denny noted. "Is there a body in the den or something?"

"No. But I think the butler did it ... anyway. It's just that you guys are going here and there. And I keep getting shut out of shows. Totally weird, don't you think? Is it too much of a coincidence, you think, Denny?"

"I don't know. Maybe. Kind of weird, if it was true.

"But, I mean, why do it? We're basically your typical unknown artists, really."

Denny nodded. "Yeah, could be a little weird." He turned to Maggie and untied her scarf and re-tied it. "There. That's better."

"Do well in Denver."

"I will. You'll be okay. You've got good family ... like me. We're lucky."

"I suppose."

"No. No supposing. Frieda and Olga are hot, but they don't have family here to back them up. You think Obayashi and MRG are any kind of substitute for what we have?"

Denny could see Maggie's face clearly. There was a street light as well as the illumination from the sign outside the restaurant and the line of small spots over the canopy. He put his hands on her scarf ends and tightened the knot a fraction. It nudged her windpipe. "You listening?"

She could feel the pressure on her throat. "Yes. I am. You're right."

"That's my girl. You have my address. You know the phone number. No maundering. Get busy. Your turn is coming. You better believe it."

"There's a taxi ... hey! Taxi! ..."

The cab pulled over. "Where you going? This is my last trip," said the fellow through the open window.

"Other side of the Park?"

"Get in."

Another quick hug and Denny was gone, too. What a night. What a year ... what a life ... it was as though someone had turned down the volume on her life. She was alone. Frieda still being in New York didn't count. They would never find time to get together. It just wouldn't be the same without Denny and Martha. Rats. And double rats. She needed to walk off some of the stored up unhappiness so she decided she might as well stretch her legs a bit; she'd find a cab if she was too tired to walk the rest of the way.

Walking down the avenue behind her, very quietly, in an almost stealthy manner, was a man in a dark coat who had been standing outside the restaurant when Frieda's cab drove away. With the collar turned up and fedora pulled down low, it would have been difficult to identify the watcher. Accompanying him was a woman with severe profile wearing the silk cloche. They were talking softly, and from time to time, one or both looked particularly in Maggie's direction.

Considering the funk she was in, she wouldn't have noticed. But if she had, by that time she was too far down the street. Still this covert stalking was not being entirely overlooked. Close by the entrance to the restaurant, also standing in the dark, was Oscar, watching it all from the tree he was standing under. No one guessed his presence. Having shed a few weeks earlier, he now smelled fresh. More human, he conceded. Less like old books.

He knew he was beginning to like what they were doing less and less. But he didn't want to transport home. And it was also true that the credits for his service were accruing nicely on Mindar, and even if he didn't like Mindar, he didn't have a better plan yet. For Oscar, life on Mindar had felt like a slow strangulation. Most of the inhabitants had conformed to 'the change' without difficulty. There were still a small population 'in transition' and a very tiny faction who had never changed. But the way life worked on Mindar, still, the fact that there was no art – no culture to speak of – bothered only a few. This was the reason for all of .... this. Arthur was certainly right about one thing. Earth is a gold mine where art is concerned.

It was obvious to Oscar that here on Earth most artists' life were – what was the word? It was a British word. Oh, yes: dodgy. Artists here are very likely to have a very dodgy time of it. Oh, certainly, some were doing well, but most were living on a par with the servant class. Yes, there were people who supported 'the arts' but for those missed the mark of making work that was popular and highly desired, a career making a living wage wasn't going to happen. Of course, there were the artists who went the wrong way altogether – ending up as drug addicts, alcoholics and so forth. Or they just gave up making art altogether. How ironic to think that they would have been celebrated and feted on Mindar as though they were all Michelangelos. Even if they weren't, no one would have cared. That's how starved for art were those who still knew the difference.

Sometimes it happened that what one didn't have anymore, they didn't miss. Oscar thought about that. We used to have a culture. There's little evidence of it now. How do you lose a whole culture? Ah, well. That was easy. Just evolve. The metamorphosis from humanoid to herpetoid ... a few million turns of the planet, a few million changes of night into day and voila. There we are. Most of us. Sunning ourselves on a rock was our idea of a good day – the new standard of comfort and everything we aspire to.

Except for a relative few, of course. These are the ones who have the maddest appetite for art. So, for those who can afford to come here and indulge ... well, tie on your napkin. Dinner is being served. Aesthetics the appetizer, the main course and the dessert. Because, as our observers had noticed, Earth was absolutely awash with art of every kind.

He couldn't help it that he didn't like Mindar anymore. Life on Earth had changed him. It suited him here. Not Elizabeth or Nick or Arthur. Not them. They didn't care about the art or the artists. They were in it for the money. Literally. It was no skin off their cold-blooded noses that the way they were handling things, artists were going to get used up like tissues.

The problem was this: you can't just *give* an artist everything they want. Take away every vestige of a challenge and simply concentrate on making art to the utter exclusion of everything else ... it wasn't a balanced life. Such people would break. The results were a disaster. Whether the artist was great or not, an unbroken diet of fame and limelight just wore them out. The Mindarians didn't care what the art looked like. They would buy anything. They had no sense of taste at all. As for the artists, they didn't understand this. Their dream was a career like a conveyor belt of riches from the hands of the buyers, right into their maws.

Arthur had done the research: the artists of Earth were his goldmine. He had put together a plan and got the commission to establish a colony. If it worked in Fleetwater, there would be more outposts. Right now Arthur was here to supply those on Mindar who still missed the good old millennia of the humanoid culture before the metamorphosis was complete. For those who were rich enough to pay for all such a trip entailed – a small fortune.

The way Arthur described it, Earth was like an orchard. It was engorged with ripe fruit ready to be picked. Mazes, that was just the way Arthur talked. Of course, the supply was practically endless. If everything went right, they'd all be rich – all those who were part of this Mission, that is.

When it began, Oscar had wanted to be rich, too, but now he was changing and he didn't feel the goal was money. In their future, they would be lapping up the luxuries, soaking up the heat and the violet rays at the far end of the light spectrum at the Noave Coalition or some such place. That's where they would be, if everything played out the right way. So far, Arthur was getting it right. But when this assignment was finished, what would he, Oscar, do? Where would he go next?

He hadn't counted on coming to feel more affinity for these humans.

But what about the human artists who were going to suffer? It was starting. Annette was already unwell. There had been others, too. So far it was only a few, but the body count was sure to be noticed at some point. Then what? What about his part in this? Oscar now had serious misgivings. He had to think. How could he make this all come out right? It was the logical thing to ask ... but for Oscar it was the first time he had ever ever *ever* actually considered that there might be a way to help Maggie. Which meant ... not helping Arthur. Which meant ...

Oscar heard a police siren's insistent cry off in the distance – the pulsing *makewaymake waymakewaymakeway* ... it was just as well. He couldn't finish the thought. He was due back at the gallery in the morning. He would think about this later. Not a lot later ... but later. If he started walking now, he'd have enough time to get a good stretch and be back at his apartment for a good night's sleep before taking the train down to Fleetwater.

PART TWO:
Fleetwater

CHAPTER ONE

Maggie made do with letters and occasional phone calls from Parker, but in April she decided she needed a vacation. "It's a good thing for me to get out of town," she wrote in a short note to Parker. "I'll tell you what I find out."

All that saying goodbye had just about worn out her emotional reserves. She went to Penn Station and bought an all-day pass for the Long Island Railroad's southern route. These passes were very handy. One could get off and on wherever one wanted all day long. If Frieda had not gone to the trouble to call her and insist she check out this "little haven," she might have dropped the whole thing but as long as she had the time, what would be the harm? It was only a day trip. It was Long Island.

As the train zipped along, she looked at the business cards Frieda had given her. Most of the galleries were in one town ... the motion of the train was making her sleepy. *IcandoitIcandoitIcandoit* ... she yawned away some of the distraught emotion. A little nap won't hurt. It's okay now – *itsokaynowitsokaynow* ... the motion of the train was hypnotic ... the city was blending into trees and land ... her eyes were getting heavier ... she was standing behind a huge wooden palisade, peering through a very small peephole. Beyond was a wide, dusty plain. No horizon. Just an enormous flat plain without trees or hills. Something was coming. She couldn't turn away. The dust plume was mesmerizing. Slowly something unreadable was heading her way. Her heart muscle banged with excitement and terror.

On came the swirling dust, looming larger and larger as it approached. The dust settled. She peered through the peephole. Up up up, looking to see what it was because it was huge ... it was at least 100 feet high. Da Vinci's great war stallion! It was wonderful. Not alive and yet its mane was fluttering. And the eyes ... they looked real. How did it move? Oh yes. Underneath its four legs was a platform, on four huge wheels. But where was the driver? or the legion of men and the ropes needed to pull it? Trails of smoke were curling from its nostrils and its mouth was opening. Now a fore leg lifted. Maggie stiffened. Down came the fore leg, its hoof thundering enormously on its platform.

There's no such thing as a horse that big ... she thought she heard Parker's voice. It was Parker! Outside the gate with that creature! "Let me in!"

I can't do that, thought Maggie. Remember? You can't trust a gift horse.

"Let me in," called Parker ... something bumped Maggie's leg. She let out a cry and her eyes flew open in shock.

"I'm terribly sorry." An older gentleman, white hair, white bristle mustache and snapping blue eyes was looking at her closely. He was dressed in a tweed coat and his hat was a trilby. "I'm terribly sorry to wake you up. I was trying to get into that seat," and he pointed to the one facing hers by the window.

"Uh, oh, sorry ... I must have fallen asleep ..." She pulled her legs in and sat up.

"I ride this train all the time," he remarked. "I always tell myself I'm going to see the scenery but, you know, I almost always fall asleep, too, if only for a few winks. Must be something about trains ..."

Maggie was looking back at him a bit vacantly.

"Never mind," he said. "I was chattering. You just sit back and make yourself comfortable," and with that he sat down and settled himself.

"It's all right. I shouldn't be sleeping anyway," she explained, trying to smooth her rumpled hair. "I've got this brochure," and held it up. "Think I'll do a bit of reading."

The man nodded. "We'll both read," he said agreeably, opening up his newspaper to its widest.

Maggie unfolded her "Visit The Sound!" brochure but she didn't feel like reading and put it aside. She would look out the window instead. The city had long since filtered away. It was pleasant to see surprising swathes of open pasture where the snow had melted. Dotted here and there were placid black and white cows grazing on grass or grinding circular on strands of hay pulled from convenient bales. Maggie relaxed, allowing herself to enjoy the scenery unfolding.

Today there was no eagle-eyed Martha sitting next to Maggie to notice she was again under scrutiny, this time by a rather nondescript-looking thirty-something. He was wearing a denim jacket and frowning at her from time to time over the top edge of an old issue of 'Cahier du Cinema'.

Actually Nick was glaring at the older man. James! I thought he was dead! That old fool. What does he think he's doing? The man's nothing better than a traitor.

Enough time had passed since he had last seen the man that he had supposed James Fuyard had done everyone a favor and died and instead, here he was, well-dressed and looking fit (unfortunately).

Nick knew his cinema and his actors possibly better than he knew his real job ... and decided Fuyard looked a lot like a now-deceased American character actor, Charlie Ruggles. That old coot! Since Nick thought mostly in identities, who looked like who, who reminded him of who, his life was, as often as he could arrange it, like scenes from his memory storage of film, which he felt life resembled. Whenever possible, Nick liked to insert himself into these scenes and give them cinematic life.

Well, I know a little something about expedition policy, he growled mentally, taking out a little notepad. He wrote a few words. Of course this would be reported. We have to do something about Fuyard. Maybe it will be me. The idea of causing trouble always cheered him up.

Nick wondered if he had been equally noticed, but the older man gave no such sign. They were just both passengers on the train. Well, never mind. He would keep his eye on them both – Maggie and Fuyard. He went back to reading his magazine.

The next day when Nick went in to work, he stopped by the Reference Desk to tell Elizabeth the news and almost did report the sighting. Reaching into his shirt pocket to take out the little notepad, he was just about to speak when he noticed she was frowning at him. It served to interrupt his none-too-reliable train of thought.

"Don't you wash?" she asked sharply.

"What do you mean? Of course I wash." He noticed a vague, greenish, scaly patch by his wrist. "Oh, that," he said licking a thumb and giving it a rub. "I've scrubbed and scrubbed ... that won't come off until next time. If anyone asks, I just say it's ... scoliosis."

"Psoriasis, you dunderhead. Don't you know the difference between your spine and your skin by now?"

Elizabeth knew Nick's place in the team was an error. It was just too late to replace him. Which reminded her of the original team ... which had included James. Not that she had liked James very much, it just that he was ten times more valuable. But he had up and left. That had been a bad time for the group. Anyway, that was a long time ago. She didn't want to think about it and she didn't have to.

"I was trying to tell you something." Nick said as he waved the small notebook at her.

"There's no time now. You have work to do." With that he was dismissed and he knew it.

Well, my little slitherer ... you had your chance, he growled to himself as he put the notebook back in his pocket. He had tried to do the right thing, hadn't he? If he wrote a regulation report now, it would have to go to Arthur and the only result of that would be trouble for little Nickie. It wasn't his fault Elizabeth wouldn't listen to him. Somehow he would end up with the blame. There would be an argument, naturally. Of course he, having tried to do the right thing, would be penalized ... it would go on ad nauseum like that. For what? For that old man? So James is alive. So what!. So he didn't transport home after all. Who cares? So where's the problem? ...

Hours later, after work, taking a walk and having a smoke, Nick reviewed the matter. It was a rare moment of clarity for him. Mindarians weren't supposed to be walking around unsupervised on other planets, especially when an expedition was on-project. Maybe I'd just better send a dispatch to the home office. It'll have to be later, though, when I get back to Fleetwater. On the weekend, he decided, filing the thought.

But 'later' didn't come. He left the notebook in his shirt pocket, which ended up in the laundry. The Fluff 'n Fold attendant picked the dry and mangled thing out of the dryer and tossed it in the trash and that was that. Seeing how Nick's moments of such clarity were very rare, there is how matter ended. Out of sight, out of mind. It was too bad. He almost got it right – just this once.

Perhaps Maggie might have recognized the thirty-something from the library and wondered that they had ended up on the same train, but it was such a small point of no importance, and on this particular day she was busy willing herself to notice the classic red barns instead, all of which made her feel nostalgic (for times and places she had never lived). Mini-palatial estates were filling the view, which irked her unreasonably. In the distance, the ocean – only an unremarkable narrow gray band – had become an interesting counterpoint in her painterly mind. She hadn't done landscapes in years ...

A blue uniform walked through the car, stopping at each occupied seat to punch the ticket sticking up. "Copper Springs," he called as he exited to the next car. "Cawww-per Sper-rrringggsss ..." is what she heard through the closing of the hermetic door.

"Well, nice to have met you, young lady. Good luck."

She had forgotten all about the man sitting opposite. "Yes, you, too," Maggie replied as the man packed up. She settled back. Turning her head to the window, she felt the train come to a stop, shifting as it did so. A few people were leaving the station including the man in the trilby, who was looking at her as he passed her window. He tipped his hat to her as he walked by. How quaint, she thought. Even nice, come to think of it.

Soon the train was on its way again, and after passing a series of open fields, the outskirts of a new town came into view. Unexpected rays of sun shot through the cloud cover, spearing the roof of a pottery factory sharing space with a tinsmith. A wooden sign announced the village of Fleetwater.

Taking a quick look at the business cards again, she noted that most of the galleries Frieda had visited were, in fact, in Fleetwater. If Frieda thought it was worth a look, Maggie would give it a shot. Decision made, it felt good to stand up and walk.

Stepping down the metal stairs, Maggie was happy to have firm ground beneath her again. Spotting the exit, soon enough she was outside train depot, looking around. It was more sophisticated than she expected. Definitely country – but upscale. Not at all hick. More Banana Republic and The Gap – a little less L.L. Bean. She didn't notice the magazine reader from her train ride had also left the station; apparently he was going in her direction (whichever way that might be). Even if she had noticed, in her current state of mind it probably wouldn't have mattered.

Crossing the street, Maggie joined a lively crowd of well-dressed people sauntering about as though it was already late May, not the tag-end of a still-chilly April. Hmm. They don't look like bargain hunters. According to Fleetwater This Week, the art scene broadsheet she had picked up off a bench at the exit to the station, there was a whole district of art galleries. Let's just see what the day-trippers are buying, she remarked to herself.

Maggie's stomach growled. Looking around, she needed a food break. Spotting Gus' Donut Shoppe, she was happy to fine out it also served very good sandwiches. A couple of the house specialty – sugar-glazed chocolate crullers – would be her dessert. Munching on a cruller, she began her gallery trek. Reviewing the town map, she picked two streets to visit. Maggie kept notes at every place she visited as she went along, even if it was only a quick look through the window.

Interesting place, she thought. No two galleries were the same. Some offered coffee. Some even had a snack tray. Some places were stark and spare, one or two were closed for the day. A few were positively and incongruously Victorian with fat love seats sporting antimacassars and small mahogany side tables. One gallery had a grouping of Adirondack chairs facing away from the window. Each seat was filled by a person; the whole group was intently looking at a line of small canvases being attended to by a person in tidy pantsuit covered with a natty green apron. This reminded her that her feet were also getting tired so she took a quick turn into Las Pampas, the next gallery with an open door and found herself a fan-backed grass chair. It was good to sit down. She allowed that a series of large paintings concerned with potted palms on antique rugs – a style that somehow combined Henri Matisse and Wayne Thibaud – was a good way to occupy her attention. On the way out, the receptionist looked up at her and smiled. Apparently no one minded all the in and out of browsers mingling with people who obviously were spending money.

Refreshed, she was back on her jaunt again.

At one point, traffic on the road was stopped while a large van was filled by several industrious young men loading large bubble-wrapped works of art which corners, she noted appreciatively, were all correctly protected with cardboard sleeves. I think artists get treated well here.

The hours went by faster than she would have wished. Soon it was time to go home. She strolled back to the station and waited. Digging into the waxed bag from Gus's, she ate the last of the indecently delicious crullers. Another decision had been made. She would come back tomorrow. It looked very much like the artists here were flourishing. Buyers were abundant. It wasn't that she didn't like her day job. In fact, she did. Quite a lot. The people she worked with respected her; they were nice to her. She'd gotten a raise and a better appointment ... but what about her life as an artist? She wasn't getting anywhere. She had never planned for that eventuality while she was growing up, making all her grand plans. It had not really crossed her mind that she wasn't one of the lucky, one whose work would of course draw sharp breaths of amazement, followed by the breaking out checkbook, credit card or cash. She hadn't planned for the hard slogging in the Slough of the Unknown.

The heartbreak of Obayashi's understandable treason, which was still agonizingly fresh, came back in a flood. Maggie knew she had to do something to assuage her misery. Before she boarded the train, Maggie stopped by the Donut Shoppe again to pick up one of Gus' free, promotional postcards showing the man himself in his baker's toque and double-breasted white jacket, standing in front his store proudly holding a tray of crullers. It was printed in sepia (a nice touch). The counter girl let Maggie know she could buy a stamp here, which was handy and necessary since the Fleetwater Post Office had already closed for the day.

There was just enough time to jot a quick line to Parker.

April 18: Found a whole town full of galleries on the Island. Am checking out the competition. How's Milano these days? Love, Maggs.

She hurried aboard the train.

CHAPTER TWO

For the next few days, Maggie commuted to Fleetwater until she had finally visited all the galleries, or at least all the galleries she was remotely interested in.

The art being exhibited ran the gamut from the really good to the really awful (in her judgment) but that was to be expected. In fact, as far as she could tell, art gallery curators and patrons were very tolerant of all kinds of artwork.

Ten Thousand BC was showing a series of lively, abstract, pencil doodles. They weren't even framed – just push-pinned to the wall, which presentation seemed perfect. In another gallery, The Potemkin, an artist she remembered from a night class several years earlier, was showing collages assembled from old black & white photographs. Just next door at Farquahar-Holtz, they were showing a teenager who did extremely elaborate robots in ballpoint pen. Further down the street, 7/8th's-sized legal forgeries of Arthur Dove were being highlighted; while in another gallery was the work of an artist following in the footstep of Jamie Wyeth (but not himself a Wyeth, of course). There really was something for everyone. Abstracts, little seascapes. (Say, was the A. Rousseau the same gal she went to school with? It looked like it could be. Maggie would have to give her a call and visit.)

She strolled past a long narrow gallery showing flower paintings a la Henri Fantin-LaTour. Gotta tell Denny about that. Next in line was a slight, eccentrically-shaped showroom filled with messy expressionist pieces in broken color and, at the end of the street, a guy who did black paintings with spooky little white boxes that sort of lurked at the viewer. She hurried past that window. The thing she most noticed: the variety was tremendous. Everyone was selling.

By week's end Maggie knew she had made a decision. On the Monday she went back to work. Sitting down with her unit manager, he got the shortest version possible of Maggie's request. Seeing as how he was helping to save the planet from environmental destruction, she had to explain convincingly why she needed some time off. Could they find someone to temporarily replace her? Could she come back later on? Any time, he replied. She was one of his best people. Would two months be enough? "End of the summer – tops," she promised.

It was a done deal. She had a month to groove in a replacement; after that she had three months to fix what was wrong with her life. Three months. Maggie had enough money to cover her expenses and three months sounded like enough time. But she felt like she was on the limb of a tree, slowly crawling the wrong way. I've got to make enough changes before it's too late, before someone saws off the limb while I'm out here at the end – still clueless.

What would be the best way to finesse the rent on two places? Maggie's best resource (besides Parker) was her

Gramma Nonie. She called Nonie and asked if she could come over. Nonie said she could.

Entering the apartment, she looked around at the lace doilies and antimacassars covering the arms and backs of several sofas and half a dozen chairs. Tucked up amongst this well-padded comfort were three greyhounds. The dogs looked at her with eyes only, from wherever they were nesting, but otherwise failed to move a muscle.

She gave Nonie a hug, took a seat and laid out her plan. "So, what do you think, Nonie?"

"Don't you think the dogs are adorable? Just look at those darlings ..."

"Come on, Nonie. You know I love your dogs. I know you love your dogs ... could we pul-eeeze get down to business?

"Is that how you make sales? I don't think so. You can't take five minutes to kibitz?" Nonie's eyes were sparkling with mischief.

"You never kibitzed a day in your life. That's why you won't move to a retirement place. Don't give me 'kibitz'."

"Nice try, eh, doggies?"

Two of them looked up from their padded pillows and yawning widely went back to their indolence. The third got up and very carefully picked her way across the room as though she was walking a tightrope. It was a little sad, but Maggie knew that rescued greyhounds often had skewed spatial responses, considering the restricted lives they lived. The brown and white female with one pirate patch over her eye laid a narrow muzzle on Nonie's lap.

"How are you, Moe?" Maggie asked as she reached over to pat the silky back. The dog accepted the caress.

157

All right, Maggie thought. She wouldn't mind a little reminiscing after all. "It was William's da who sponsored you and Grandpa Terry, right? I've got to keep the family history straight in my mind. There's quite a bit of it, you know."

Nonie recognized the strategic move otherwise known as 'keep the old lady happy', but she liked talking about her Terry and the brothers. It would do Maggie some good to talk about the family and give her ambitions a rest for half an hour.

It didn't make Nonie sad anymore to talk about the men. Nothing would bring them back. Apropos of nothing she said, "I try not to worry about the ones I can't save. At least there's a society now for their cause. But these are mine. They're just big lap dogs, they are. Big babies, really. So quiet and sweet."

To prove it, the two quiet, sweet boy dogs, like gentle ghosts – Eeny (a smoky grey) and Meeny (a pale cream with white paws) continued resting on the couch throughout this short narrative on their account, showing only by the prick of their ears that they were listening.

Once Eeny sighed. It was as if to ask, 'How could I ever be the cause of trouble?" Meeny yawned, making his jaw squeak. And just to prove even that exertion was too much, they went both went back to sleep.

But Moe, the female, was different. On any given day she gravitated to Nonie wherever she might be in the apartment. This afternoon, while Nonie sat in a big wing chair, drank tea and ate butter cookies from a round tin, she burrowed her sleek head into the old woman's lap, gave contented grunts from time to time and simply stood still for petting. As much as Nonie would give, Moe would remain to receive.

"I can't have more than three of the dears at any one time. Someone would find out there's a crazy lady with an apartment full of dogs ... then there would be trouble," Nonie explained as she continued smoothing her hand from Moe's forehead back over her long, silky ears and down her backbone. Moe, to prove she was listening to her history, slapped her muscled whip-like tail a few times and settled down again, resting her head in Nonie's lap. Only the mantel clock could be heard ticking loudly.

"I miss him." It was true. Even after all this time, she still missed Terry.

Maggie got out of her chair and went to rest on the arm of Nonie's chair. "I know you do. We all miss Grandpa Terry."

Nonie would always say she had a good life and nothing to complain about, that she had friends and her dogs ... until, in the end, after any narrative of any kind, she would finally admit she missed her Terry and there was no getting around it. Having said so, whatever was due to come next in the conversation could begin.

"So, now. About this thing you're wanting to do ... do you want me to tell you that you are doing the right thing?"

"Well, I wouldn't mind that, I'll admit ... but ... the thing of it is: it's a bit more than that, Gran. Is there any one of your pals has a nephew or niece that could maybe take my apartment on a sublet? I've still got money saved but I don't want to use it all. In case I'm a washout in Fleetwater."

"You think someone in one of these galleries will find favor in your work and give you a show?

"Golly, Gran. I hope so. I wouldn't be taking three months leave of my job just to hang out on Long Island. I mean, it's a nice place to visit but ..."

"I see," she said. "Well, let me think about it and see what I can come up with."

"You want me to take the dogs for a walk, while you think ... would you like that?"

"You're really in a hurry."

"I'm going to be 26 years old this year, Gran. I don't have any more time to waste. Either I can make this happen or I can't. I see that I can't do it here in town. I don't know why doors which open right enough keep closing again but they are. Out on the Island, these small art colonies seem to be doing a thriving business. I think it's my best shot. Something inside me is saying: do this, do it now ... I don't know why. I hope I'm right."

"Well, it's only for a few months and you have your job waiting ..."

"That's the size of it."

"Okay. Come on, all of you. Maggie is going to take you for a walk. The dog-poop baggies are by the front door in that basket."

Eeny and Meeny unwound themselves, stretched, yawned, and slowly made their way to the front door and waited patiently to be attached to leashes.

"Come on, Moe," Maggie coaxed. Refusing to move, she kept her body glued close to Nonie's side, apparently studying the floor from a few inches away. Maybe it was only a tasty crumb wedged into the parquet which had captured her attention. Nonie looked at Maggie.

"She's still a shy thing. Their whole lives are spent in a kennel and on a track. She's newest, so she's still getting her bearings. Big rooms are a challenge. Okay, Moe, my love. Go with Maggie." Nonie bent over. Her hands smoothed and smoothed the narrow face, flattening down the ears. Finally the dog shook itself. "There you go. She's ready, aren't you?"

Moe answered with a sneeze.

"I'll be back in an hour," said Maggie kissing her grandmother's soft, powdered cheek left the apartment, three leads firmly in her hand, the sound of many doggie toenails tapping on the marble hallway as they followed behind.

Nonie closed the door and stood a moment. "I think it's time to call Miriam."

Miriam Sedgewick was her good friend. Her best. They went way back. How far back changed, depending on the occasion and who they wanted to impress, but it was decades nevertheless, and it was true that the old ladies had been friends nearly since Nonie arrived in New York, however they fiddled that date.

After due consultation, Dudley Cross, Miriam's nephew, was tapped for the job. Besides being a member of Evan's tax consulting team, he was a young man who ought to be ready for a bit of adventure. He had been content to live with his grandparents, Henley (Miriam's sister) and Barton, since the tragedy of losing his parents in a crack-up on the Interstate during a winter storm ten years ago. Life had quieted the quiet young man further.

161

His parents had been colorful people. Dudley had always felt ill equipped to compete. So he went to work for Evan. This was easier than being a young man 'making the scene.'

However, ten years was enough mourning, Nonie decided. Whatever Dudley might call it, 'growing up,' 'being responsible,' the truth was, he was a nice-looking drudge. It was a shame and a waste. His life was in danger of becoming one long yawn – a dire condition which Nonie planned to remedy. It was her express opinion that it was time to let the poor boy (26 years and counting) to do something on his own before he was permanently soldered into the bachelor life of a well-kept child. (God help us all and The Saints preserve us.)

When Maggie returned with the dogs, who had evidently enjoyed their stroll. Meanwhile, Nonie was happy to report she was already in negotiations so Maggie spent another half-hour while the dogs stood around Maggie waiting for more petting.

"Come back in a few days," Nonie said, ".... you can take the dogs for another walk while I complete the deal." She smiled mischievously.

Maggie returned for the follow-up visit. First there was the usual tea and cookies and reminiscing. Last up was a walk with the dogs. Maggie was allowed to have the news, which Nonie gave her granddaughter with great satisfaction. She delivered the blow-by-blow description of Dudley's being sprung from the Sedgwick/Cross family mid-town, well-appointed, brownstone jail. Maggie had to admit it: it was definitely entertaining to hear Nonie tell the story.

"You're a terror, Gran and that's the truth. You and Miriam – what a pair"

Nonie smiled. It was true. Every bit of it.

After that, it took a further bit of nagging to get the manager of Maggie's apartment building to agree to the sublet. Eddie Buchanan had been manager of the building for five years. This job was his retirement fund. He saved the rent and invested it in the highest yield funds he dared. Compounded monthly and annually, combined with his Social Security benefit and his Navy retirement, he would have enough to get the hell out of New York and go somewhere for the last twenty years of his life. Probably buy himself a little boat and sail around the islands – Bahamas, for instance. Nothing would be allowed to interfere. Nothing. .

"Dudley's a true gentleman," Maggie explained.

The manager raised his eyebrows in alarm at this information.

"He's the nicest boy," she promised.

More alarm. "What's the matter with this guy?"

"Nothing. Absolutely nothing." But at this point, Maggie wondered if Eddie would he be happier if she told him Dudley had spent some time in jail for federal crimes. "I'm trying to show you he'll be great. Listen, you have my phone number on Long Island. All you have to do is call; I'll hop of the train and come back. Please, Eddie ... please??"

"All right, Ms. Malone. All right. Keep your shirt on. You bet I know where to find you – and your Dad, if it comes to that. Bring this young heathen around for me to meet and if he passes inspection, it will still be on your head, but you can do your sublet. Now, are you happy?"

"Yes, I am.. I'll bring Dudley over tomorrow. You won't be sorry."

"I know I won't. I'll sue you, you know. I'm not afraid of Evans & Cross. All that name means to me is that they have deep pockets."

"They do. But you and I both know I am not going to jeopardize my tenancy. Right?"

Eddie Buchanan nodded. He liked getting huffy. It made people pay attention. Couldn't have them thinking he would let himself be walked on, like a welcome mat. He'd done twenty-five years in the Navy. That was nothing to sniff about. No one messed with Eddie Buchanan.

"So, let me get this straight: if he never calls me to get a hairball out of the plumbing or ask for help changing a light bulb or lets the bathtub overrun and drip through the ceiling to Ms. Bingham's apartment underneath, I'll be happy. If he should just be silent as a mouse, he will be a great tenant."

"That's the deal."

"Okay, you two come around tomorrow and I'll fix up the sublet lease." With that he closed the door.

Re-runs of "McHale's Navy" went on at 4 p.m., two episodes back-to-back, and he didn't like to miss his program. It might be silly, but he liked it anyway. Civilians had no idea what it was like being in the Navy. After that was re-runs of "Magnum, P.I." – another ex-Navy man. And that took care of a whole different era. That meant it was 6 o'clock and he could open a beer, unbutton his shirt, loosen his belt, take off his shoes and relax and fix himself some dinner. That meant god help the tenant who let something go wrong between 4:00 p.m. and 8:00 a.m. the next morning, Monday through Friday.

He told everyone who lived in the building: "I'm a manager, not a slave. Even God rested on Sundays. But that was when the world was young, so I'm off on both Saturday and Sunday. Got it?" They all did.

Maggie was getting excited. She was closing in having all her logistics in place. Just as soon as Mrs. P had met Dudley and had given her approval, because Mr. Buchanan and Mrs. P were thick as thieves and it really required the approval of both. That done, the deal would totally be sealed and Dudley Cross would be her sublet.

Naturally Maggie owed Nonie another dog walk. Standing in the foyer, the dogs quietly waiting by the door, Maggie asked the old lady, "Did you actually threaten Dudley with ending up a Grandma's Boy? That's language even I wouldn't use. It's positively frightening, Gran." Nonie shrugged. "There was a job to do. Barton Silverman is not an easy man to deal with. Miriam and I know how to talk turkey when we have to. Henley is seriously spoiled. Barton can't spoil me. I'm independent. But Henley is lazy. Barton keeps her that way so she won't rebel. It's true she can run a house. Barton likes that. 'Course he thinks it's still around 1890. The man is positively Victorian. Haven't you noticed?"

Maggie had noticed but there was no prudent way to mention it and no purpose, so she kept quiet. Evan and Barbara thanked her for keeping silent. They were also close to the Silvermans and the Crosses, so there was no use trying to change something that wasn't going to change.

"Think about it, Granddaughter. There are two ways to trap a soul. Give them nothing (that's what the British did to us) or give them everything – that was America until the politicians screwed it up and now it's turning into some kind of Socialism. Oh, don't argue with me," and Maggie closed her mouth. She was beginning to understand that she did not know her grandmother very well and it was time she did.

Noni smiled at her granddaughter. "Henley has everything. She can share Dudley a little bit," and Nonie made a sign with her thumb and first finger about one-half inch apart.

Maggie had heard this argument somewhere before. Deprivation being the usual form of coercion, this notion of treating the prisoner very well was very attention-getting. Rarely used though, she decided. Jailers are cheap. So: you can also keep a person under your thumb by giving them exactly what they want. What a concept.

"I think they broke the mold when they made you," Maggie said admiringly, putting her arms around Nonie's skinny shoulders.

"They did. Sure but the Irish saints didn't want to have others like me to deal with."

By mid-June Dudley was firmed situated in Maggie and Parker's apartment, and Maggie, loaded with a suitcase and a duffle full of art supplies, was off to Fleetwater to 'find herself' or finish sawing off the limb of the tree she was on the wrong end of.

CHAPTER THREE

The train ride was uneventful. She had a nice nap, letting the conductor's voice calling, "Fleeeet-wa-taaah" wake her up. The room she needed, she had already rented. It was a one-room studio up a hill and around the corner from Gus' Donut Shoppe. Knocking at the manager's door, Maggie stood waiting with her suitcase and duffle bag. Now she wasn't just a daytripper. Now she was playing for blood. Turning around, she looked up and down the road. Yeah, it's gonna be one hell of a summer. Hearing the door open behind her, Mrs. Aubrey was standing there patiently, hands clasping a kitchen towel.

"I was drying the lunch dishes when I heard you ring." She tossed the towel onto a nearby chair. "Follow me, dearie."

Maggie hefted her bags, following the matronly shape of her new landlady up the stairs. Located on the second floor, on the ocean side of the house with a large rectangle of lawn that met a fence dividing it from the property next door, was a room with pale blue walls, a wood floor covered with a Persian rug and a comfortable sofa in a softly-faded cabbage roses cotton print dividing the living space from the bed and night table. There was an armoire and a closet. She liked it that the sink was separated from the toilet, which was in a little cabinet of its own. She noted the desk and chair. Just as long as there was room for an easel and a taboret and some wall space to hang her paintings to dry.

"You sure you aren't going to mind the shower being down the hall? I gotta a room coming up with its own tub."

"No, Mrs. Aubrey, it's fine. As long as I have my own toilet, this'll work fine for me. It's nice to have a refrigerator in the hall. That'll come in handy."

"It does. Just mark your food clearly. People staying here are really pretty good about minding their manners. Shouldn't be anyone eating your sandwich or drinking your milk."

"Actually, I think I'm going to like it. It's a nice change. More like camp."

Mrs. Aubrey nodded. "We do what we can. Got artists going in and out of here like a revolving door and then there's your type ..."

Maggie looked puzzled.

"Oh, that's the ones that stay the summer or the fall because they intend to make something of themselves. They aren't just playing at being artists."

"That's an interesting way of looking at it," Maggie replied looking around her room. "So, here I am."

"That's right. Here's your key. You should lock up, of course. Not that we have much crime but better safe than sorry. Can't promise no one has light fingers, you know." She paused. "Anything else I can do for you?"

"No, I'm good. I'm here and I like my room and I think it's going to be fine."

"You can put nails in the wall. It's expected. Every couple of years I just have them spackled over and repainted. I didn't get to mention it before but I will make a nice tea with little sandwiches and cakes if you have visitors, or if you just want to treat yourself. Sometimes, if I know people are going to be around, I do a late afternoon tea anyway. That's how it was where I come from."

"England?" Maggie asked.

"Yes. I lost my English accent some time back, but I'm London born and bred. There's a few of my people still alive back there but I'm not much for traveling. Got my place here and that suits me. Well, I've just about talked your ear off, I expect."

"Not at all. I like the idea of having tea. You can count on me. All my family are all in

the city and we haven't made any plans for visiting. I've got too much work to do. I'm on leave from my day job, so I need to make every day here really count."

"I'll get out of your hair. Come down when you are ready and I'll show you around once more – laundry room, the basement lockers where you can store things. Just ask me."

"Thank you, Mrs. Aubrey. I really appreciate it."

Shortly thereafter, Mrs. Aubrey was gone and Maggie was standing in the middle of her new temporary home.

"Oh, my god. I'm really here. Well, I'd better unpack."

While putting her clothes in the various dresser drawers, she thought about when she originally signed the lease and had explained that she was an oil painter. It was a bit of a shock to find out that instead of receiving a healthy list of do's and don'ts, she was the recipient of a discount for being a 'visiting artist.' Now there would be afternoon tea. Of course, Gus' Donut Shoppe was practically next door. Parker might be eating gelato but

Maggie was thinking about those sinfully delicious chocolate crullers. Oh, yeah. Things were looking up.

During the unpack, Maggie found a small framed sign near the fuse box by the door. "Do not pour turp' down the sink, do not smoke in the room, no radio playing after 10 p.m." and more of the same. There you go, she nodded. A healthy list of warnings. Now she felt better. People had been so polite to her here in Fleetwater, she was beginning to wonder if it was natural. It was the same sensation she got while watching a re-run of "The Twilight Zone". Something was going to happen. The director would put the camera on something – like a flag. Then there would be that camera shot of motion of the wind announcing the storm to come. It was a bit like that. Or like waiting for the axe to fall. Or maybe it's just me ... there is no axe. Or storm.

People are being nice and welcoming. What's wrong with that? Well, Parker would be totally suspicious by now. But I think it's fine, so there you go. It's easy to become jaded. TV makes you think that people have hidden motives where none exist. Otherwise there wouldn't be any drama – nothing to keep people occupied while they sell us laundry soap and cars. Now this, she thought, looking out her window, this is real life. She finished unpacking.

There were three entrances to the house. A side entrance she passed on a landing that took her out to the fenced yard, the front door and a back door leading out to trees and a sandy pathway.

Maggie exited through the front door but following around to the back, it turned out that by taking the path, she ended up on the next street over, and there was Gus' Donut Shoppe, looking as inviting as ever. Entering the shop, a young woman in a formerly white apron was moving fresh trays of donuts and crullers into the showcase.

"Chocolate crullers?" she asked Maggie.

"No. Better not. They are way too addictive. Just two plain cake donuts for me." With that, she took another free postcard, bought a stamp and wrote a quick message.

"Gee, I don't know where the mailboxes are," she said to the counter girl.

The girl flipped her long mane of hair out of the way revealing the name badge. "I'm Veronica. I need a new hair net. Hate those things ... anyway. You can give it to me because I have to make a run to the Post Office at 4:30."

"Really?"

"Oh sure. I do it for a few of the houses around here. There's no house delivery. I guess Mrs. Aubrey forgot to tell you that. We all have to go to the Post Office for our mail."

"Well, I need to rent a mail box."

"Oh, no. Mrs. Aubrey has a box for the house. Every house has a box. Your mail will come to the box for the house. She goes over in the morning some time, usually, and gets the mail from the day before. Come on. I'll take that."

Maggie wasn't sure. This was all so different than the city. Well, in for a penny, in for a pound, so she handed over the post card that was now embellished with two pale chocolate finger prints – a thumb on Gus' apron in the photo on the address-side and a left index finger on the under side. The message read:

June 19 ... Dear Parkie, I think you'll like Fleetwater. The start of Gallery Alley is only 15 minutes from my room. It may not be the Italian countryside but it's pretty cool nonetheless. Love, Maggs

In the next few weeks she got herself settled in and the town fairly well scouted. She went to Gallery Ten Thousand BC and picked out an art card reproduction of one of the pencil doodles. $6.00, but worth it. She liked the kid's work. Parkie had already sent one page of onionskin in reply with lots of news. Therefore, this time she wrote:

July 10th: Dear Parkie, The people who run these galleries are very pleasant. This is a nice change. Here are lots of new faces whose work is plenty of getting wall time. With any luck, me, too. Did I tell you I'm expanding the new series? And I'm using oils again. Will send you a photo. Love, Maggs

In fact Maggie had already picked out a gallery she thought would do her justice but she wasn't in a hurry to reveal her interest. The scuttlebutt was that this gallery had a very energetic approach and a serious promotional budget. Postcards, mailings, big openings, the works. The first month was already partly gone but, just for the moment, working on the painting in progress was more important.

Taking walks to Gus' for lunch, and splurging twice that week on a decent dinner was restorative. Otherwise, she was keeping the tightest rein possible on her expenses and making do. In fact she was too occupied to register the presence of the same thirty-something in a denim jacket who traveled the same schedule on her irregular day trips by train into the city to visit her family, Gramma Nonie and check in on Dudley. It turned out Dudley was winning hearts all over the place. Already he was carrying Mrs. P's groceries up the stairs for her and putting out water for her cats. He had been caught picking up trash around the back of the building. The building manager nearly *plotzed*. Would wonders never cease?

By the end of July it was evident to Maggie that things were going well but she wasn't going to be able to do everything she planned in just three months. She went back to see her supervisor at The Green Coalition and asked for an extension. It turned out that the temp filling her place had done a great job and when she finished her internship, he had a replacement for her. "You're sure you can spare me?" she asked with not a little amusement.

"You always have a place here ... well, maybe not *that* place," her boss replied looking at the current busily efficient temp deftly handling the traffic on her desk.

"I can always go back to getting signatures."

"We'll see ... when you get back. In the meantime, go! Did I tell you that you look good? So, I know it's working for you. If you get nice and famous, tell the interviewers about us. We always need good PR."

"Of course. Thanks for everything. You're great. All of you. You guys are the best," and Maggie hustled back to the train station.

This time she didn't stop to see William or say hi to Randall and Cook at the Feldman's apartment, or even visit Nonie. No stops, no dilly-dallying. Breathing a sigh of relief when she got off the train in Fleetwater, she hustled straight to her room and changed into work gear. After that she was off to the little garage-cum-studio she had decided to rent. The painting she had planned was far too big to work on in her room. This day her hands were itching to get to work. It felt so good. Like when she had made the first "Red Toaster" pastel painting. She knew she was on the right road. The demand to work was surging through her. She had goals, she had a purpose.

July 27... Dear Maggs, From all reports it looks like you've done your homework. No surprises this time. The gallery manager at La Nouvelle Vague, Oscar Valenzuela, sounds suitably eccentric. When are you going to show him your portfolio? I'm crossing all fingers and toes for you. I am on your side ALWAYS. When I come home, I still think we should sign up at the Computer Tech Institute. I know a lot about import-export now. I'll be an expert. We can go into business together and you can still paint. Tony is <u>still</u> delicious and I'm falling in love with him more and more, but this year is going to end and I will be coming home. I have no idea how I'll juggle a long-distance love affair – if we are still together – but I'll figure something out. Super News Flash: My dad sent me a check! I nearly fainted. The money is great but can you *believe it? Maybe Evan's friends enjoyed beating up on Richard so much the first time they went back for second helpings? We just know Richard didn't volunteer – or did he? He could have taken a break and just flown himself first-class to Milan for the same money. Emily could spare him, don't you think? It would have been good. Father and daughter discovering Italy. Oh, listen to me. Kind of pathetic at this late date to be thinking such thoughts, eh? Anyway, I called Evan and Barbara. It was so good to hear their voices. Have you had another date with the new guy? Miss you but then again, Italy is fantastic. Love, Parker*

Maggie finished reading Parker's letter. Another date with the new guy? Yes, there had been another. The better question was: how had such a pleasant, unassuming man as Boyd managed to find his way to her door? Actually, Gus was to be thanked for the introduction. She was sitting at a table outside his shop taking in the sun, taking a break and munching of one his ultra-delicious chocolate crullers when she happened to mention to Gus that she needed a carpenter to build a large canvas with a gallery wrap.

"Boyd MacArthur is the guy," Gus told her, enjoying his smoke. "Lives up that street there," pointing the way. "Little yellow house with the blue shutters. Tell him Gus sent you. He'll do a good job."

The carpenter was as good as Gus' word. Followed her directions to the letter. She was very impressed. Even though she had stayed to sidewalk-supervise most of the construction, he handled her intrusion with diplomacy.

This new painting she was planning was going to be huge. Maggie had never attempted anything this size before. Even as he was hammering the supporting cross bars, she wondered at her own audacity.

After she paid him, instead of leaving immediately, he stayed to chat. So she told him about the painting she was planning and he told her a little about himself. It all went so smoothly. He was easy to talk to. Maggie really didn't have anyone like that now that Parker was far away and her artist pals were scattered. After telling him about Parker, she asked him, "Do you have a best friend?"

"I probably count Gus as a friend."

"Not your best friend, though."

"Not like you and Parker." He got quiet and asked, "Want to get some of this good night air?"

It was an offer she didn't want to refuse. She nodded yes so he graciously pulled back the heavy sliding door and led the way out to the road. It was about one-quarter mile down the road to the marina. They took their time. When they got their, they settled on a spot by the long railing looking out over the water.

The night treated them to a symphony of seaside sounds and smells. Water sploshing, rigging sighing, chains clinking, the sound of a head on the closest little sloop getting flushed, some laughter signaling they weren't alone. There was the tang of oil and a lacing of pine. Not much farther out on the water, several louder parties were very definitely in progress and the night was young. A splash sounded. Another and more to follow after that.

"Hope they aren't skinny-dipping. The town fathers frown on it ..."

"Town fathers? It sounds so ... puritanical. Is there a law against it?"

"Yes. A blue law, no less. But of course, the police have to catch you at it."

"Do you ...?"

"Me? No." He shook his head. He grinned. "No drinking, smoking ... or skinny-dipping." A pause. "You?"

She grinned in return. "Oh, god, no. I suppose there is a certain freedom to a full and unfettered salt water swim ... but ..." (someone yelped a dozen yards away) ...

"There you go," remarked Boyd. "Jellyfish. Unh-uh. Not me. But you like the ocean?"

"Oh, yes. I like living near water – the East River, that is ... still, the Atlantic is right there", and she pointed. "Yes, I like the ocean."

"So, tell me. How did you happen to meet Parker?"

"Oh, that was in 3rd grade. Her cousin, Fred – he was looking after her for the summer – her parents were away (as usual) ... she adored Fred – he died in a motorcycle accident. It was a bad loss for her. Richard and Emily – (here Maggie shook her head) ... you have no idea how clueless they were. Still are. They came back for the funeral and they left – the next day. Unbelievable. There was Parker, all alone. Just Randall, their butler, and Cook, his wife. They are very nice people – don't get me wrong. Now we've known them for years but still, Parker was just nine. My Grandma Nonie and her best friend, Miriam, they sort of kidnapped Parker and brought her to our apartment. And she stayed. There I was with a sister. It was like being given a twin."

177

Boyd nodded. "So, you really didn't mind having a sister?"

"Absolutely not. She changed schools and came to mine. I think it was in gym class that we really bonded. I hated climbing 'The Rope'. So I went on strike. Actually I couldn't climb. No muscles to speak of." She bent her arm to show him.

He gave her bicep the smallest tweak and nodded. "I see."

Maggie continued. "Ah, yes. I can see it now. Me standing in front of the teacher saying, "You can't make us. I know my rights. As for Parker, she just jumped right in: 'We've been studying the Constitution,' she says. Poor teacher – getting quoted to like that. It was pretty hilarious. Well, of course my parents were called. They had to come to school – for the both of us. The Phys Ed teacher gave me some other exercises to do – because you aren't allowed to fail gym. Parker had already passed The Rope, so it was a non-issue for her ... well, there's more, but that's how it started." Maggie didn't feel like talking about Fred. It wasn't the kind of night for that. She was feeling happy. "So, what about you?"

"I passed my grammar school years in a one-room country school house in Maine. I didn't like being an orphan, but you know, one doesn't have anything to say about such things. I wasn't abandoned. My parents were killed in a small plane crash. We don't know exactly how it happened. The first part of the landing was fine, a wheel crumpled, the plane skidded, flipped, the fuel tank exploded ... I was only a couple of months old. A lady was babysitting me while they had gone on this trip. My parents had no relatives. I don't know how a person can manage to have no relatives but there you go. So, I was an orphan. Half the kids in our little school were wards of the state. My main interest was learning enough so I could get out of there. It isn't that the people were bad or anything. They took pretty good care of us, I'd say. Some of the matrons were mothers with children of their own. So, we made out okay. I just decided I should concentrate on improving myself. It's not quite as lofty as it sounds. I think I still hold onto that. Curious but a little cautious. Anyway, I know I can take care of myself. We were eating granola for our morning chow long before it was fashionable."

He said it with a such slow smile, so it took a few seconds for Maggie to laugh.

Leaning towards Maggie, she suddenly got the idea, if this was just the right moment … it was going to happen … and it did. It happened: the kiss. Soft lips meeting, just the right amount of pressure. It lasted just the right amount of time, as well.

"Well … okay," she said taking a breath, her face a few inches from his.

"Yeah …" he agreed. After a bit he said, "Listen, I know it's our first date (if you can call taking a walk a date), but I already decided I'm going to ask you out … if that's okay with you."

Maggie nodded. She meant to say something but she couldn't decide what, so she just smiled at him and nodded.

He took her hand and put it firmly through the crook in his arm. "Now I'm going to escort you home."

Their footsteps sounded on the boardwalk. Continuing on, they reached the sidewalk proper, each street light illuminating them in its bright pool of light, a few seconds later disappearing until the next pool. Maggie's place was halfway up an almost-hill. They climbed the steps onto the porch and stood holding hands.

"Maggie ..."

"No. My turn."

"Okay. Your turn."

"I like you, too. I think we are both late bloomers in the romance department. No one is hustling anyone for a one-night stand, right?"

"Right. That's what I wanted to say."

That's when he surprised her, when he stepped in close and put his arms around her. This time it was full body contact. The whole package. She let herself be held for an instant and then she put her arms around his waist. Time passed.

Boyd finally pulled back. "Goodnight," he whispered, his voice a bit husky. She nodded in reply. "I'll call you soon or come by," he said taking the key from her hand and fitting it into the lock, pushed the door open.

Oh, yes, Maggie thought, as she read Parkie's latest missive. There had been a second date. It was every bit as good as the first one. Of course things change. Sometimes the best starts get frittered away. People know so very little about each other in the beginning. Everyone's on their best behavior and before the little things happen which can ruin or weary the best beginnings. Things begin to interfere and spoil the best of starts. What had he said quietly into her ear at the last moment before he took the key out of her hand that first night? "You can count on me." He had kissed her once more, hard and fast and walked away quickly ... it made her heart beat very fast.

"How's the painting coming along?"

Maggie put Parker's letter away and squinted as she looked up from the lounge chair she was sunning herself in. It was Gus. At least he was blocking the sun, to be polite. It was very bright outside today.

"Really good. Thanks for asking."

That seemed to satisfy his interest because Gus took off his apron, hung it on the hook by the door and walked down the road to have a smoke. He usually didn't like to smoke near his shop. Didn't want the smell of Virginia's finest to mingle with his donuts.

Closing her eyes, Maggie mused: what exactly was she going to say about Boyd to Parker when she wrote back? With her eyes closed tight against the hot sun, she resumed her daydreaming. When Boyd had reached the end of the path leading to her door, he had turned around and waved. A little gesture, done so naturally; it charmed her.

Boyd did come back two days later – this now being his third visit – he knocked at her door about 8 o'clock at night.

Maggie was in the downstairs living room when she heard the knock and came to the door to answer.

"No male visitors," Maggie said mischievously seeing Boyd standing there.

"Mrs. Aubrey knows me. Otherwise, of course she doesn't let the boys go catting around her female tenants. I think it's a good policy," he said with a grin.

They walked over to her studio-shed. From the beginning she had decided Boyd would be the only one permitted to see the painting she was working on. She felt he had proven himself. Sitting quietly in an old leather club chair that had been there when she took over the shed, he made himself at home, reading a book, paying no attention while Maggie worked.

That was the start. She would tell Parker everything, she decided, as she realized more and more that Boyd was 'a keeper'.

Any time he was there while she worked, he would mostly sit and read, but usually, after awhile, he would get up and come to stand beside her, silently looking. He'd go back to his reading while Maggie got on with it. Having occurred to her early on that he approved of her art, she knew he liked to watch it come to life and she felt safe and calm in his presence. Even better, he had no comments to make, no helpful hints, wasn't interested in discussing the whys or wherefores, didn't object if she painted out what had just been painted in or anything else. He would just be there. His steadfast, silent, interest provided more sustenance that she could have ever hoped for. All unasked. That was the point. He was there because he wanted to.

The train whistle sounded. Maggie's afternoon rest was over. Afternoon punters would be pouring through the streets any minute now in time to get the last run back to Penn Station. The sun was still high.

What she was thinking was: maybe that awful axe she had become so familiar with wasn't going to fall on her this time. Maybe she wasn't going to saw off the wrong end of the limb and come crashing down.

The on-shore wind was giving a good shake to the stand of trees next to Gus's shop. Time to get home and put on a sweater. Even in August, at the end of day it would turn cool even though during the middle of the day the heat could be mesmerizing. In those moments, sometimes she got the image of a snake warming itself on a rock. It was a funny image, Maggie thought. She roused herself, walked home and changed into warmer clothes.

Standing by the window sash facing the road, she noticed someone walking away, across the small lawn. They hopped over the fence, crossed the road and disappeared into the woods. The details of the man were bled out by the afternoon light, but the direction of his movement said he had been at or near her window. Looking in? At me? Naw. I'm on the second floor. There's nothing to see.

Off in the woods, Nick snickered to himself. "Well, that ought to bother our precious Maggie Malone just a little. Can't have her feeling too comfy. Your time is coming, Miz Malone. 'Course it's too bad she can't slither ... but never mind. There are other fish for little Nickie to fry here in Fleetwater, and he licked his lips in appreciation of the girls he found attractive who would ... slither, that is.

But Maggie was unnerved. It was the first time since she arrived that she didn't feel entirely comfortable. She decided she would mention it to Gus. He had lived here a long time. He knew the locals. He was, all things considered, one of the long-term locals himself. Plus she needed more of his freebie postcards which she was sending regularly to keep in touch with friends and family.

Putting on a windbreaker, she jammed a beret down. That would hold her hair in place. The salt air had wreaked havoc on her best hairdressing ministrations. When her curls had become an unmanageable mop she had cut them shorter, which helped a little. This time she went out the front door and walked down the hill instead of cutting through the back. After dark, she didn't take shortcuts. Turning the corner, she finished up at Gus's in under five minutes.

Inside the shop, she waited her turn. It was the early dinner crowd. That meant people who had cars and were staying the night or planned to drive later. She stepped to the counter and ordered a sandwich and coffee. She would bring it with her to the studio.

"Gus ... got a question."

He tensed for an instant, then leaned over the counter by the register. "Shoot."

"Are there ... um ... well ... any new people in town?"

"All the time. What do you mean, Maggie?" he asked while slicing bread from a fresh loaf.

"Well, like a guy. Maybe 5'10 or 6'. Dark hair. Thin. Wearing a leather jacket and jeans. That kind of a new guy."

Gus stopped cutting and looked up.

"That's a pretty particular description ... did you see someone like that?"

"Yes, I did. I think so. Outside my place ... it looked like he was walking away from the house, like he might have been looking up at my window ... he left off, cutting across the yard, over the fence and into the woods. It's kind of ... well, now it sounds like of silly ... anyway, I just wondered. Do you know anyone like that?"

Gus looked thoughtful a moment. "No, I don't, but I'll keep an eye out. Do you want to go over to the police station and make a report?"

Maggie shook her head. "No. There's nothing to report. Maybe it was just someone cutting through from the backyard to the street. I've done it myself. I'm getting very good at short cuts. There isn't a yard I haven't cut through, now that I know my way around."

"Well, Maggie, I think you're safe. We run a tight ship here in Fleetwater."

Maggie paid for her sandwich and coffee and left. Walking to her work shed, she thought about what Gus had said. What did that mean? 'We run a tight ship here in Fleetwater.' Who's *we*? Probably Gus was on the town council. That must be what he meant. At least he had been in Fleetwater a long time. People like that had input. Their longevity counted for something. Especially store owners. This wasn't like Maine and Vermont. Places where if you weren't born there, you were a foreigner – forever. Still, Fleetwater residents were a pretty tight-knit group themselves. Maggie was sure they tended to stick together to make sure things are going smoothly ... that must be what he meant.

Having sorted that out, she walked to her shed and let herself in. Standing in front of the large easel, she considered the loose washes of color recently blocked in. The door rattled. "Boy, the wind is really up tonight." She put down her sandwich and went to the door. It took two hands to slide it open. Looking around, no one was there ...

of course. She knew that. Boyd didn't rattle the door. He knocked and said his name. But Boyd wasn't there. Everything looked as it should. Okay, she said to herself, that was the wind, and to prove it, the wind which was pushing the trees determinedly to the west, gusted again. Closing the door, she locked it from the inside and went back to her painting. She would be finished with the first layer of washes very soon. Time to plan the next layer of paint. Fat over thin – otherwise it would take ages to dry. Or you get those crackles. Don't want those. Do we?

Maggie had calmed down. Of course she was safe. How many short cuts had she taken in the past weeks since she arrived? Why can't a guy cut across the lawn without being suspect? Anyway, if Gus knew something, he would have said so. She poured fresh turp' into a clean can and dipped her brush in it and swished. Okay. Another two hours of work and I can pack it in.

That night before she went to sleep she wrote a short letter to Parker.

"Dear Parkie, My appointment at the gallery is for mid-August. I know Oscar is a bit prissy, but from everything I hear, he's also a real go-getter. The owner of this gallery is Arthur Cotillion. Met him once briefly at a party at the marina. Kind of goatish, I suppose, but that's the art world for you. He's loaded, so this place is well backed. If these guys don't want me, there are several other galleries here who do, but this is the gallery I like best. They've got buckets of money and aren't afraid to spend it. I like the street and the galleries on either side. By the end of the summer I am going to have

representation, one way or the other. Do not worry. Everything is going fine. Love, Maggs"

Down at the docks, his shop closed for the night, Gus was sitting on a bollard having a smoke. A shadow shot across his own. "That was stupid," Gus said, without looking up.

"Arthur said to keep an eye on her, so I'm keeping an eye on her."

Gus took a puff. "Yes, but not looking in her window. Not lurking. How stupid is that? Maybe Oscar is right. Maybe this job isn't for you."

Nick moved in front of Gus. "Oh, you and Oscar, huh?" His fists were clenched.

"Listen, *dicht-la (friend),* maybe you should work on controlling your hostility. You knew this job would be dealing with another species. If you aren't up to it ..." He sniffed. "You need to shed," he remarked dropping the cigarette, grinding it out with the heel of his work shoe. Picking up the stub, he stored it in a small metal box and put it back in his pocket.

"I know I need to shed but Arthur never lets me alone long enough to do it! I'm going. Right now. You tell him." He scratched at his arm through the leather sleeve of his jacket.

"If you're taking one of the cars, don't forget to fill the tank," Gus called with a chuckle, but Nick just kept walking. He watched the other turn the corner. If we don't watch out, he's going to ruin everything. He could. What does friend Boyd say ...? That old carpenter's adage:

'measure twice, cut once'. I think we didn't measure twice when we brought Nick here.

CHAPTER FOUR

Almost two weeks later to the day, at one o'clock and on time, Maggie entered La Nouvelle Vague Gallerie. When the receptionist told her that Oscar had unexpectedly stepped out, Maggie had to stifle her disappointment. Everything would be okay. This time it would not go wrong. Finding a suite of chairs, a table with magazines and a bouquet of fresh flowers, she sat down and forced herself to get interested in the latest issue of *Art in America*. At 2:30 she went back to the Receptionist. Again she was assured Oscar would return soon. Another hour went by. Maggie walked over to the reception desk for a third time, putting on her best poker face.

"I'm really sorry," the girl said in advance of the question. "I don't know what's keeping him. I apologize. Really. He's due back ... he's definitely expecting you."

Just then Oscar walked in the door. Being tall, he was hard to miss – all six-foot two-inches and naturally slender. He looked a bit like the image of Valentin Desosse from one of Lautrec's poster – with no La Goulue. She realized his hair was actually brilliantined. Oh my, this fellow does have style. He was dressed immaculately in a white dress shirt with pin tucks, pleated dove-gray pants, white linen jacket, two-toned wingtips (dark cream and white), pale pink suspenders and a floral bowtie. Maggie could hardly take her eyes away. He was terribly sorry to keep her waiting. Having popped out of her seat, he invited her to sit down again.

(In fact, Arthur had kept him away on purpose. Oscar thought it was unnecessary but Arthur was in charge.)

"It's okay ..." she said still standing up. She didn't know his true character yet, but there was something in his tone that quelled the greater portion of her fear and she relaxed a bit.

They shook hands. In silence she handed over her portfolio and press book. Oscar took his time as he reviewed it. Arthur had instructed him not to hurry. ("This has to look authentic." "Well, of course. It is authentic," Oscar had replied. He really wondered about Arthur sometimes. What goes on with that creature when he says such things?) He placed the portfolio carefully aside and picked up the 16"x 20" canvas painting Maggie had brought with her (still unframed) and scrutinized it very closely. He liked it immediately. He especially liked the finished surface. Even after years of reviewing artists' work, he could still be surprised. A smile lit up his eyes. He had expected something different. Based on what Arthur had told him, he apparently didn't know what Maggie was actually doing these days, Oscar mused. Well, he would, soon enough.

First he looked into her eyes, then at the painting. Her own visual take was quite unique. Distinctly creature parts and objects worked into a seamlessly executed new life form ... Pegasus had wings, he recalled, but at least he was still an animal. Maggie had taken the matter a few steps further. It was also quite humorous. Oscar felt his chest gills fluttering with appreciation. He pulled his attention back to the business at hand. Indicating the photographed work in the binder, he said, "I see that your work is going in a very new direction. Quite interesting."

It was a good thing, too, because Annette Rousseau, their last sensation, was nearly worn out – in just under a year. Happily she was in recovery, but in the meantime, Arthur needed someone new and special right now. It took a lot to feed the aesthetic appetite of the Fleetwater population. He was certain Maggie would do very well. Her work was very strong. With her knowledge of animal anatomy, her ability to draw and keen sense of color, if she stayed on this course, she might last a good three years, maybe more. Practically a record. It would take the pressure off them to keep finding really good new talent. Oh, yes. Fleetwater would be a happy place.

"I think we should see Mr. Cotillion."

Maggie was thrilled. Naturally she knew she had to show a calm exterior but inside she was dancing. The Endless Winter of Being Unknown Maggie Malone was finally over. Oscar would not, she was sure, recommend her to the owner, only to have his recommendation overturned. As she explained to Parker in her next postcard, Arthur Cotillion did look, he liked what he saw and told her so.

What he actually said was, "Well, well. Quite new. Very ... very ... off-the-beaten-path. Very avant-garde in a ... Henri Rousseau/Rene Magritte sort of way." Arthur reflected that if she could graft flamingo wings to a toaster with artistic skill and aplomb, Mazes knew what else was coming.

The three of them, Oscar, Maggie and Arthur all sat down in his office to discuss how to proceed. She would definitely have a presence in the fall group show. But there was more. While working on the first of the large-scale pieces, which she was telling no one about, she said she had also planned out a dozen smaller-format paintings on this new series called, "The New World". Half of them were already done. "Toaster (Two)" had been done twice. The original #2 was a pastel, and now, done again, in oils. She assured the men she could be ready. No impasto to deal with, everything would be dry and ready to frame by late November. Arthur approved heartily because he wanted to showcase Maggie in the Christmas Show. He decided that one of her paintings would be used for all the promo. ("That will do the trick," he told Oscar. "That's an offer she can't refuse. Then she's ours.")

Oscar wondered again if Arthur understood: Maggie already is ours. We're in overkill. He knew how badly Maggie wanted to be in their gallery. Arthur was so busy trying to hook her and she was doing everything she could to be hooked. As if we haven't already interfered with her enough? She couldn't be more ours if we had kidnapped her at gunpoint. He had long since questioned to himself the necessity of their shady tactics.

Giving his attention back to the conversation at hand, Oscar heard Arthur say that both the earlier Giraffe series and Big Cat series drawings ought to be kept in a portfolio, all unframed and displayed so art patrons could look and turn the sheets of heavy paper (with gloves, of course). He felt these would sell easily. One wall would be devoted to her new work. They would finalize the PR program at their next meeting. Everything else was agreed, the gallery split, the fine print in the contract, etc.

"I'll have to take the contract to my lawyer," she said. "But it won't take long. A day or two at most. I'm sure you understand."

"Of course we do." He smiled and showed an even row of teeth. He would have preferred to strangle her. Imagine having the gall to check the contract. With snakes, it's all up front. Just rattle or hiss or coil. But humans ... and their myriad of emotions ... ah, such convoluted ways.

Maggie had already packed up to go. Heading towards the door, Arthur walked along. "So, my dear. I hope you are as pleased as we are."

"I'm very pleased, Mr. Cotillion."

"Oh, call me Arthur. Everyone does. We don't stand on ceremony here ... by the way. Did I hear you say that little painting is "Toaster (Two)"?"

"That's right."

"If I may ... I hope it's not prying ... is there a "Toaster (One)"?"

"Actually there is. It's mine, though. You know, some artists only paint to sell ... I was never painting for myself ... but ... I decided I would keep that one. I think of it as ... um ... sort of like a ... baby picture. "Two" is much better anyway. I had to get my footing, you know. Such a change."

Arthur looked at Maggie and smiled in reply. "Of course. Of course. Completely understood. We shall see you shortly ... you can make all the day-to-day arrangements with Oscar. He'll take very good care of

193

you." They shook hands. His was cool and smooth. Hers warm and slightly moist.

Maggie left. He watched her walk down the path to the street. Well, well. Not quite the silly I thought she was. She just lied to me. Possibly told me something close to the truth about that painting of hers, but not exactly. Hmm. We shall have to continue to keep our eye on her.

On the other hand, Maggie could hardly contain herself. When Arthur asked her about "Toaster (One)" she knew immediately what to say. The only person who knew about Parker was Boyd, and she knew she could trust him. The only two who knew about her big paintings were also Boyd and Parker. Just exactly why she didn't want to say that Parker owned the painting wasn't clear, but Maggie knew it was right. Otherwise *it was all so fabulous, so divine.* Things were just opening up just perfectly – like a rose going into full bloom. It was ... over the top wonderful. Of course there would be many long days of production ahead but she could do it. She wrote Parker a long letter detailing everything.

When Parker wrote back that she wouldn't be coming back at Christmas after all, Maggie didn't know whether to laugh or cry at first. But the emotional storm was brief. What the hell! How could she be upset with Parker? Life in Milan was good for her, the way life in Fleetwater was good for Maggie. Nothing really touched the friendship. Wasn't that the important thing? She read Parker's letter again.

25 August: Dear Maggs, I hate not being there for your group show. I know it will be great. I was so sure I was coming home in December. But I've cashed in my return ticket, otherwise I'll lose the money. Mr. Fortelli was determined to get my visa extended. He says he really needs me. The showroom is doing really well. We have a lot of new accounts. He's giving me a raise. How can I say no? So now I'm crossing my fingers for you. Let's talk at Thanksgiving. I'll be at your show in spirit if not in body. Send me photos. I should be able to take a month off in the spring. Remember I love you.

Kisses, Parkie

Nov. 18th: Dear Parkie, The "New Faces" show was intended to prime the public for the upcoming Christmas extravaganza and it did exactly that. I sold three pieces. The thing here is, if you have lunch with a gallery owner at The Yacht Club, that means things are happening. So, I had The Lunch! Everyone here knows I had The Lunch. Arthur is par for the course. He's what I call "Standard Issue Gallery Owner": late middle age, a bit stocky around the mid-section, a good head of hair just going grey at the temples. You know the kind. Wears it a bit long to show he's hip, cravat at the neck and carries a cane no less (no limp). Oi vey.

No time to get home to see the folks lately so phone calls have to make do. Can't wait to see you – you prodigal child. What a year this is turning out to be. I wish you could be here in December ... but, hey! You're hot, too. Did I tell you that one of my new pieces will be the image for all the promo? I'll mail you one as soon as they come from the printer. Boyd says hello.

Love, Maggs

Dec 6th: ... Dear Maggs, Wish I could be there but oh, I love Italy. Tony and I had a squabble but it's okay now. The motorcycle thing was hard for me to get past – reminded me of Fred – but I did. Glad you and Boyd are still hitting it off. Right now I definitely feel too far away from you. Don't forget to call home – that means Nonie, too, right? And Dudley. I think you ought to invite everyone from The Green Coalition to the show, even if they can't come. Make them happy to have supported an artist now getting good notices. Have you heard from Denny or Martha? We certainly know how Frieda is doing. Her news is reaching our shores as well. But you will be bigger. Ha! Ciao, Parkie"

Dec 28 ... Dear Parkie, This year is almost over. I'm doing a pretty good job of keeping in touch – even if it's quick phone calls and postcards. Denny sent me some of his press clippings. He's up to his ears in commissions. He's getting more money for his paintings at the gallery so he might actually get ahead financially one of these days. He likes his parents, so living with them is no problem for him. He told me he does his own cooking and laundry. Such a boy. Now he needs a girlfriend. Martha is fine, too. She's invited me to come visit but of course I can't go ... (yet). Too much to keep me here. She got permission to work at The Tate and copy the masters. Well, that's a new direction for her. I guess we are all going in new directions.

You don't have to worry about me. Just think good thoughts. That's all I need. The Christmas Show was *totally exciting. It was fun being the poster girl. Do you know you can now buy postcards of my work!? I sold the cheetah painting for big bucks: $10,000. That's 10 big ones. My share is $5,000. Isn't that great? Arthur was very smart. The guy who bought it had to sign a special contract about not making prints without my permission, and there was a clause arranging for paying me if he gets my permission to create a print; also he can't use the image for a corporate logo (apparently why he really bought the painting) without my okay ... I could go on. The thing is: Arthur and Oscar caught it before the guy basically did a bad thing. I learned a lesson. I need to keep my eyes peeled. I am really grateful for the protection that Arthur and Oscar gave me. Still the painting sold. The buyer was kind of a jerk, you know. Gave me a wink and said,, "It doesn't hurt to try" as he handed over the check. Oh, Parker! By the way, you should know, Oscar is a very good guy. He works really hard. Does whatever Arthur asks. Oscar hardly takes a day off, in fact. As for Arthur? He comes around once in a while. Him and his snazzy girlfriend. She's way too chilly for us mortals.*

I miss Nonie.

Yes, I am still seeing Boyd. He would be hard to do an extended background check on (of course I know what you are up to, silly girl). He's an orphan! Been living in Fleetwater for about 8 years now. Very polite, very down-to-earth. I would bring him home to meet the folks but there's no time. We manage to get together for lunch when he comes over to my studio. Very rarely we steal time to have dinner together. He likes to come and watch me work. I'm so glad he was there for the Christmas Show – as if there was anywhere else to be on December 15th! If you couldn't be there, then at least Boyd did a fine job as substitute.

Love, Maggs"

In Parker's next letter she announced that she and Tony were officially in love. There was a lot to do before they were officially engaged but as least all handholding and stealing of kisses was now sanctioned. There were numerous family dinners to attend because, of course, Parker had to be introduced to everyone on both sides of Tony's family tree. Evan was right. Parker needed to make a life of her own and by going to Italy she had done so.

Maggie called Evan and Barbara on New Year's Day. They were very proud of 'both their girls'. Evan reminded her that Parker had a good head on her shoulders and if she said the family she was joining through Tony was worthy, it was so.

"You mean, having Richard for a father has not entirely screwed her head on upside down and ruined her judgment."

Evan remarked that at least Emily was known to be civil. He would credit the woman with that. The way Evan looked at it, Parker now had three mothers watching her back because Tony's mother, Lucia, was her latest acquisition.

Things were going so well that Maggie took a few days off the first week of the New Year. She and Boyd had a great date on the 31st that included dinner and dancing. It was very romantic. They were going to say up almost the whole night but changed their minds, thinking that meeting for a January 1st breakfast would be sensational. The final kiss was, of necessity, fairly long. Neither wanted to let go. But then they did.

At 11 o'clock next morning, they were seated at Gus' sharing the morning paper (like an old married couple, Boyd teased), having eggs, bacon, fresh donuts, coffee. The shop was full. Gus opened every January 1 – albeit four hours later than usual because he was determined to sleep in one morning in the year). The line of people was waiting for him was expectedly long – and good-natured. He would close the shop all day on January 2. The sign always said the same thing: "Gone Fishing", although everyone knew Gus didn't fish. It gave people a good laugh. There were a few other places open so everyone found somewhere else to eat.

Meanwhile, that first morning of the New Year, the restaurant was full to the seams with regulars so there was no question of hurrying the waiters or the kitchen. This gave Maggie and Boyd extra time to dissect the Christmas Show, and how opening night had been a great success. Everyone had made sales. Arthur was to be congratulated for his selection of artists. She said she wished Arthur was a little less smooth, less unctuous, but as he was doing a good job of promoting her, she was willing to reserve the rest of the perhaps mild dislike that was forming about him. Maybe there were other, more appealing facets to the man's character. She remarked again how Arthur was lucky to have Oscar. She noted Arthur's treatment of Oscar was not quite nice enough, but again, maybe she was spoiled.

Boyd agreed.

"Hey, I'm not spoiled!"

Boyd laughed.

"Okay. Maybe just a little."

Maggie allowed she'd not had a great deal of work experience except for working with the Green Coalition – they were an especially nice group of people. Yes, she had spent several summers doing secretarial work in her father's office where, surprising to her, some of the women rather resented Maggie's presence. They were glad when the summer was over. So was she. Still, that wasn't enough to judge by. But Boyd had fewer qualms about his reservations concerning Arthur's behavior.

"You're having a great ride, Maggs. Enjoy it, but let's be smart. Arthur is doing what's good for Arthur and right now what Arthur is doing is also good for you. He's a businessman. Right now, you are sensationally good business."

Maggie had to agree. It was true. Such a lot of excitement! Oh, the money! Even with the gallery split, she now had a very nice boodle of money in her bank account. She also loved her holiday gifts. Back in her little room she had spread the goodies out on her bed to admire each one. Nonie had sent her a finely-framed photograph of herself and the dogs. That went up on the narrow mantel over the fireplace. Her mother had sent her a brand new sweater, "nice and long so it'll keep your backside warm while you work in your studio." The silver bracelet from her father went on her wrist immediately. "I'm only taking it off to wash," she said to herself. Parker had sent her a beautiful, oversized Italian (what else?) silk scarf. The print was old pre-World War I bi-planes. Maggie loved it. She loved it all. They knew her well and had picked perfect gifts.

In return everyone wanted Maggie's artwork and that's what they got. Maggie originals. Each person got a tiny (6-inch square) painting – something specific to each.

When she gave Boyd his painting – a pair of pliers with duck feet, he laughed out loud at the unwrapping ... and kept laughing. He told her how much he loved the painting. "It's going right on my mantel." It was the best Christmas Maggie could remember.

Boyd wanted more – because he was ready to use the "L" word. He wanted to tell Maggie how much he loved her, but somehow the timing wasn't right. He wasn't sure why, but he trusted his instincts. He would wait. In the meantime, they were getting along 'like a house on fire'. If this was not the time to rock the boat, the right time would come and he'd know it.

By February of the new year Maggie understood that not only had she definitely developed a following, she was actually a bit of a celebrity. People came into the gallery and specifically asked for her work. They waved at her on the street, and sometimes a new artist in town approached her for some words of wisdom. Of course, art postcards of her work were now available at the gallery. She noted with pride how quickly the stack dwindled and had to be refilled. Maggie just couldn't believe her good luck. Everything was really really working out. It was just the way she imagined it. People continued to request a look in her portfolio – her animal drawings and pastels were continuing to sell. Visits more often than not concluded with a drawing being carefully rolled in tissue and taken away in the distinctive La Nouvelle Vague paper tote. Her small format paintings were still leaving the gallery at regular intervals.

The upcoming big solo show was scheduled for the following October. What she needed most was to concentrate on getting all the work done! If she had shown discipline before, now she had her eye on the prize. Denny, William, Martha – they had all predicted her turn would come. Now it was here. She knew her plan for the oversized paintings was an enormous challenge. She would have to hustle to be ready but it would be worth the effort. She was sure.

Having said nothing to Arthur about the large paintings, he assumed he knew exactly what she was doing – both the work completed and those still planned. Why she was keeping the big paintings a secret was not entirely clear to herself, but it was so. Therefore, she had to keep up with making smaller format paintings and somehow still have seven large paintings ready as well. The scope of the work was herculean. The idea was to unleash them all at one time. It would make a huge splash – shock the hell out of everyone, basically. No one could guess what Maggie was really up to. Sometimes she had to gulp herself. It was such a lot to do in such a relatively short amount of time. (The stories of how long it took Picasso to complete Gertrude Stein's portrait haunted her.) Her only advice to herself was: keep going. Don't look back. Hadn't she damned the torpedoes? Wasn't she moving full-steam ahead?

"Feast or famine ... feast or famine ... I swear, I swear, Denny ..." she mumbled as she cleaned the last of her brushes after a particularly good day's work. Turning her head this way and that, seeing how the light reflected on the brush strokes, she noticed a passage that needed to be more smoothed out. Tomorrow would be too late. The thin layer of color would be dry. "Rats, rats ..." Maggie checked her watch. "Okay. Ten minutes max. I can do it. .this night is over." She opened up the can of turp' and poured a few fresh inches in the glass.

Suddenly she laughed out loud. It really was quite funny. This was life being bad?? She laughed again. Hope no one decides to walk by right about now. They'll think some crazy person is talking to themselves. This was the best her life had ever been. She was an artist. A working artist. It was wonderful. In fact, it was paradise. It was everything she ever imagined. Arthur was giving her everything she ever wanted. How could this not be good? She ended up staying an extra hour as it turned out – not ten minutes. It's got to be right. That's what I know.

So it went. Some days were better than others, but in the end, if only because she was doing the work she had dreamed of all her life, all her days and nights were good (... except on the nights when it was one or two a.m. and she hadn't accomplished her target for that night. "No sleeping yet. Argh. I need a new batch of fresh turp'. No rest for the wicked.")

Some days she knew what was coming and some days meant new territory. It was tricky going because the work was intended to be both iconic and mildly humorous. What made it all work, if it did, would be the exactitude of her drawing and quality of the brushwork. And the finish.

Smooth and silky, as though it had come from the hand of Van Eyck.

Not being afraid of color, each piece was truly dynamic. It was fun to let her imagination loose. Those moments were wild and heady.

Throughout the last months of the winter she managed to finish Painting #4. The next three were going to be even more ambitious – more complex. She knew, of course, that any painting she made must get her full measure – whether big or small. She joked once to Boyd that if she opened a production line on the Toaster and Eggbeater paintings alone, she would probably be in Fat City for years to come, but the thought also gave her the willies. When a print series was mentioned in passing by Beth to Arthur, she being his companion and business partner, Maggie firmly squashed it. She'd had enough of that, thank you very much, and the subject was dropped.

Although the turnout for the Christmas show was outstanding, Maggie did wonder in passing why no one from Modern Review Gallery or Obayashi's had showed up. Beth, she was told, ran a very tight ship. If she was in charge of getting the invitations out, there was little chance of error. Maggie kept reminding herself to call the galleries herself, but in the end she didn't. She didn't want to find out that Beth had left these people off the list deliberately, which would mean having to confront her on the matter, or that Hiru and the MRG people had let the invite pass and Maggie really didn't feel like dealing with that ... either way, she wanted to be got too busy to think about it anymore. She had already decided she wouldn't ask Arthur. He was always very dismissive of anyone except Fleetwater's social register of patrons anyway. There was absolutely no way she could even intimate that Beth might have failed with the invitations. Arthur apparently worshipped the ground she walked on. Maggie didn't think Beth was all that big a deal and didn't bother to associate with her unnecessarily. Beth was usually locked away in an office somewhere so there wasn't much opportunity for getting acquainted or even close observation. No, Maggie had no time to fiddle around with such details.

It fell to Boyd to drag Maggie away from her studio for occasional necessary breaks. "Come on. You were inside so much last summer, you are totally pale. At least come get some fresh air. If you don't make the occasional appearance, people will wonder if you are being chained to your work ..."

As Maggie explained to Boyd (and Parker, when Maggie had time to write), Monet had his water lily paintings – his "nympheads." She had her "Big Appliance" series. Sometimes she quite laughed out loud. It was such a hoot. Think Warhol. Think Rosenquist. Think Hockney. There were others. She laughed again.

"They'll be writing you up in text books on modern art. You'll see." When Boyd said things like this, Maggie would look to see if he was perhaps just pulling her leg – out of its socket – just a little – but in fact he was in earnest.

"Maybe they will," she agreed cautiously.

She knew she was being more than a little superstitious. Remembering the parents in "The Good Earth" as they entered the emperor's great city, hadn't they suddenly decided that bragging wasn't a good idea? What the gods give, they can take away. Maggie thought that maybe she, too, should be a little more circumspect. But the gods couldn't possibly be interested in Maggie Malone. Right?

CHAPTER FIVE

Finally the snow was mostly gone. With only the slushy remains edging the streets and roads, it was pleasant to take a walk with Boyd. Anywhere would do. Across the town green and around the square, or all the way to end of the main road to where the sidewalks ended or down to the marina. They would buy a bag of Gus's plain crullers because, as Maggie noted, "I can't give the birds sugar-coated chocolate fried bread. God would strike me dead." So they would break up the crullers in the 'throw-a-bite-eat-a-bite' method until the bag was empty.

She was no longer a Starving Artist, she informed Boyd, as if he needed to be told.

"How could you ever starve?" Boyd asked. "You've got parents. You can always go home."

"Ugh," she shivered. "Can you see me? Some fifty-year-old living off my parents? I don't think so."

He buttoned his lip. For him the solution was a moot point. It was one of the rare points where Maggie didn't seem to understand him. Well, we can't agree on everything, he reminded himself. Otherwise, he did understand her very well. Moreover, the success of the December show was now buying her the time she needed – if she painted like a fury – she should to be ready to blow the socks off everyone come next October and that was where all her attention was focused.

Sometimes they discussed Arthur Cotillion.

"I think he's an old pirate, if you want to know the truth. Scratch his surface and it's still all surface. Rusty sheet iron just beneath. Don't worry about hurting his feelings, Maggs. Just remember, he doesn't own you. He's a gallery owner. A businessman. He's not God. When the relationship between you two winds down, and you might as well realize that it can, because very few of these gallery people are *that* loyal, it's not like they are putting money aside for your rainy day ..."

"I know. I know."

"Come on. Let's walk over to the gallery. You need to tell him you're going into the city for a little visit anyway. It'll be fun to watch him squirm. He hates to have you out of his sight – I think that's funny."

"Are you sure that growing up in all that cold and snow didn't do something to your mind?" Maggie quipped.

"Maybe. But we thaw out in the spring ..." he replied with that slow smile she now knew so well. He took her hand and they walked over to the gallery.

Entering the open door to his office, Maggie walked up to Arthur's oversized desk while Boyd remained behind, leaning on the doorjamb. Arthur covered his annoyance at Boyd's presence and rose to meet her.

"How lovely to see you, Maggie. Everything going well, hmmm?"

He would have been more disturbed if he realized that the musicality of his voice increased as the falseness of his intentions increased and that others knew it, too. Today he was positively lyrical. Too bad the insincere rarely can afford such insight into their own character, Boyd noted to himself.

"Just came by to say goodbye for a few days. I'm off to see my folks ... Boyd's agreed to do guard duty on my studio." Arthur's eyebrows did a little dance. "Well, we don't want anyone peeking, do we?" As if Maggie didn't know that Arthur very badly wanted a peek.

Arthur noted that Our Maggie is getting to be very sure of herself. Dear old Boyd is evidently here to provide the muscle, if necessary. "Why, Maggie, dear girl. Of course you must go to the city, by all means. Enjoy yourself. Enjoy the family. It's beautiful weather. We consider ourselves very lucky that Boyd is a part of our little group now," and he nodded to Boyd with a smile with all the warmth of a cobra.

Arthur had already decided that Boyd was a liability. But what to do? That was the question. At first it had seemed wonderfully convenient that Maggie had a beau to squire her around. A local man – no one with family or outside ties. However, now this local fellow was no longer handy. He was encouraging her to rebel. Arthur was sure of that and if there was one thing Arthur was not going to permit, a rebellion was it. I'll take care of you, my fellow. You can be sure of that. When it suits me.

Boyd carried her suitcase to the train and gave it to the porter. There was no time for him to bring it aboard himself. They had a quick kiss.

"I'm sorry you can't come, too, but I understand. You've got your own work to do."

"Maybe I really should come with you?" However, he did have several clients waiting. On one hand, he was one of the best carpenters around. On the other, there were several others in the area ... ready to step in if he wasn't available. So, he couldn't make up his mind. Stay or go with her on this trip.

Maggie made that decision for him. "Oh, no. You are staying here. Just please, check on my studio. Make sure everything is locked up ... those black velvet curtains are perfect. No one can see in. You have all my phone numbers in New York. You call me, if you have to. Listen: here's an extra key. Also, I'm probably being silly, but every time I see someone crossing the lawn I get nervous, which is ridiculous. I thought I saw someone hopping over the fence last week – and someone probably was – and I know it means nothing but maybe you can go air out my room on Wednesday, but don't forget to lock the window. Pull the curtains and tie them tight. Check on the studio ..."

"Come here." He pulled her close. "Not to worry. I'll guard the fort while you're away."

"I know. It takes such a huge load off my mind. I mean, if anything happened to my work ..."

"You can count on me," he said, looking at her directly. It was not said quickly.

That, Maggie noted, was the second time Boyd said exactly that in his particular, quiet, matter-of-fact way. It tugged on her heart in way that words could not describe.

"I know I can. It's one of the reasons I feel so good about us ..."

They hardly had time for one final kiss when the conductor called out the final "all aboarrrrd" so she hurried to take a seat.

Boyd had known he was smitten with Maggie from the very start. He was pretty sure she loved him, too. Knowing as much about her life as he now did, agreeing to look after her studio and room while she was away was an important responsibility. This time, when she came back, if everything was still the same between them, there would be a lot to talk about. Time to go into the city, meet the family, the whole thing. Present his case as to why they should allow him to marry Maggie. He had no doubts about who would be taking care of who. Boyd was satisfied. If Maggie agreed to marry him, it would be a done deal until the day would come when they were old and worn out – when their spirits left these mortal forms behind; they would still be together. He wanted her. Warts and all – and so far, there were very few warts. She was everything he wanted in a partner, in a friend ... in all the ways they could be together. If she wanted him like that ... well, then. The matter would be settled. That's what he wanted. He knew his own character. A little plain, a little stern ... but able and loyal and kind. He could take care of her. He could do that. He could be the one.

The train glided out of the station. He waited until it was out of sight. Boyd had already decided he would take a turn around her studio before heading out for the day because Murphy Elias wanted new shingles on the roof and outside walls of his sunroom. This job was going to pay well. With this invoice paid, Boyd would buy an engagement ring for Maggie. His Maggie Malone. Girl Artist. More than enough happiness for one man. With that thought in mind, he headed for her studio for a final check.

As for Maggie, the trip home for her was a treat. She was well used to the ride and enjoyed doing nothing for a change. Then she rested when she got in. Dudley was out so she made herself a light supper and fell asleep in Parker's room. The next morning Dudley was up and out before Maggie could have a quick word with him. Her second day in the city she dressed up in a light-weight dark blue suit, white blouse, low black patent leather heels (since the sidewalks were clear) and a small envelope bag on a gold chain. Hopping a cab, she went cross-town to see Barton Silverman, Dudley's great-uncle. She wanted Barton's agreement to let Dudley continue keeping the sublet on her apartment for another year. Henley had already agreed but Barton's approval was important.

It was so strange. Parker could hardly get her parents to care and here were Henley and Barton, and they would suffocate Dudley if someone didn't step in. How contrary life could be!

Barton was a hard nut to crack in the best of times, but he certainly handled Evan's business interests well enough. She beamed her best smile at him and took a seat. Barton harrumphed but clearly her effort at dress-for-success was noted. She knew he preferred Dudley at home in the family apartment. "He has his own separate entrance," Henley had bragged to Miriam, which remark was duly reported back to Nonie. "So do prisoners at Sing Sing. It's called a cell door." It had definitely been a coup, managing to spring Dudley from the family grip.

So, here was Maggie again, making a second visit. More like a supplicant, but never mind. Barton remained cool but in the end, seeing that Dudley was noticeably happier, he agreed to let the young man extend his stay in the sublet. Maggie sailed out of the office a happy camper and hopped another cab back to her old apartment. She knocked on Mrs. P's door. Opening the door, she gave Maggie a big smile and soon they were having tea and cookies.

"If you hear him bring home a girl at 2 a.m., break down the door, Mrs. P," Maggie told her. "I beg you. His family is really really conservative. If we are going to bust Dudley out, we have to do this by very careful, very small increments."

"What for you think I am listening at the key hole? You do not think good things of me!"

"I think we are all lucky to have you here and that you know just about everything that goes on in our little building. Between you and Mr. Buchanan ... you can't fool me, Mrs. P. The FBI and CIA should have your skills."

"Now, Maggie: what for that young man so tall with the nice glasses on his face can not do at the one o'clock in the afternoon that you think I should kill his door at two in the morning?"

"It's the principle of the thing. We have to guard him or his family will drag him home and we don't want that, do we?"

No. Mrs. P did not. In fact, anyone daring to move out of the building almost always felt compelled to have a negotiation with Mrs. P first. Eddie Buchanan, the building manager, might be under the impression that he was the one to be talked to, but in fact it was hurting the finer feelings of Mrs. P that was almost unforgivable, such that tenants were known to start months earlier broaching the subject with her, discussing their plans – marriage, change of location, etc. "I looking after our boy just fine. You go back to the beach and have a good time."

Maggie could not convince Mrs. P that she wasn't just living the high life at the beach but the look on Mrs. P's face told Maggie that it was useless to try. However, having completed her main task, she was now free to spend the rest of the visit with her parents and Nonie. It was great to see her family but the itch to get back to Fleetwater was also very strong. She was ready to begin work on Number 5, the next big painting. Completing the first four large pieces had given her lots of confidence. Still, every day at the easel was a challenge. How had Rembrandt and others of his kind done it? A studio of unpaid apprentices most likely! Every day it was one step at a time. Thank god there hadn't been any major mishaps yet.

Maggie boarded the train at Penn Station and made herself comfortable. She had picked up a book on 19th century Russian art in the sale pile at the MOMA bookstore and meant to entertain herself and expand her art history horizons on this trip. Normally she just looked out the window until a nap overtook her.

A few minutes had passed and she was just a few pages in when she heard a voice say, "How do you do, Maggie."

Looking up, she was surprised to see her oft-time companion of these trips, the nice man with the white bristle mustache. It always seemed to Maggie as though he lived in a time warp. He sounded almost English, but really it only was the syntax, the calm graciousness, rather than the accent. Always unhurried. Yes, that would be a good word. Unhurried.

"Why, hello, Mr. Fuyard, how nice to see you. I didn't know you get all the way into the city. Somehow I thought you lived further on ... I'm usually sleeping when you get on anyway."

"So I noticed. Yes, I do get off a few stops earlier than you. At Copper Springs. But my solicitor is here in the city. At my age ..."

Surely he wasn't fishing for a comment, she thought to herself. That wouldn't be like him. She didn't know a person who seemed more self-aware and less needy, except maybe Boyd. But she had missed a few words.

"I have a niece. Well, I call her that. Actually, she's the daughter of a friend, and I have no family, so Anne has become my niece. I really couldn't treat her as a surrogate daughter but niece and uncle suit our relationship admirably. We may live forever, as some of the more spiritual amongst us believe, but these bodies certainly don't last indefinitely. I wanted to check on a provision of my will. She will have my money. Anne deserves it. She's very kind to me."

All of the foregoing was news to Maggie. She had sometimes wondered if Mr. Fuyard would ever share more of his personal information with her. Maggie, of course, blabbed quite a lot on these trips when they happened to meet up. She sometimes despaired of her own uninhibited, unrestrained willingness to talk to just about anyone ... but he seemed so interested.

"You promised to call me James, hmm?" He was smiling. Almost a portrait of the perfect Jane Austin-type uncle.

"All right, James. I'm very glad you have a niece ... Anne, that is."

"Really? Why?"

"Well, I think you're a nice man. Nice people shouldn't be all alone."

"That's very kind of you. One doesn't always know the impression one is making. One forgets. We're making impressions all the time, influencing others even in small ways. Even these small influences might be of value, even if no one realizes it."

"Are you being philosophical?" she quizzed.

"Well, I believe I am. Going to see my solicitor has made me a bit introspective. Let's look out the window and see what's new, eh?"

Facing opposite as they always did, they turned their glances outward. Nevertheless, their conversation was resumed almost at once.

"But tell me. Really, I'm quite interested ... how is life coming along for you in Fleetwater? Every one of these towns is different than the next. People lump them altogether, but it isn't true. Each has its own identity."

"I like Fleetwater. It's pleasant. Very ... how shall I put it? Apolitical. Uh, well, since you ask ... oh, uh, James, can you keep a secret?" Maggie asked quite seriously. She was dying to tell someone about her big paintings. "I mean, do you know a lot of people in Fleetwater? ... because I really don't want this to get out." It all came in a rush.

"The truth? I used to live in Fleetwater ..." He held up a hand.

Maggie's face lit up with surprise.

"But that was quite some time ago. It is an interesting town. Quite a wealthy crowd, of course. All very art-minded. The truth is, I think I'm just a bit more pedestrian. I like art well enough ... and of course I know you're an artist. But that's different. There's only one of you. Copper Springs is more retired dentists and engineers. They just aren't interested in plunder. I hope I'm not being too critical."

"Oh, no," Maggie calmed down. She knew she mustn't pelt him with her questions. "I understand you perfectly. The Fleetwater crowd ... well, they take their art ... how shall I put it ... 'seriously' isn't quite the word. There's a kind of emotional heat. Yes, that characterizes it. Not everyone, but there is a whole group ... you know what I mean. Anyway, I think you're right. And astute. The thing is, I'm painting the best ever ... which brings me to my secret." She was watching his face intently.

"I give you my solemn vow, your secret shall be kept by me inviolate, unto my grave," he replied.

"Good, because I really would like to tell someone. I really want to share this with someone ..."

"Happily I can be the right someone," he said finishing her sentence and the thought.

So Maggie did, describing the first red toaster painting and the carrying on through to the latest on her easel.

"You are happy with this new direction?"

"I think it's my best." With that she sat back in her seat. She didn't realize how tensed up she was until she started describing her journey to this new direction her art had taken.

Fuyard nodded. "As I told you before, I'm really not an art connoisseur. I tried. It's why I went to Fleetwater. The town is quite rich in such resources. It just wasn't my milieu. I'm very happy where I am. But I'm also very happy for you."

"Is there a 'but'? A reservation?"

"Have I implied one? I wouldn't want to influence you like that. It's not my place. An artist should want to succeed. What's wrong with that?"

Whatever she originally meant, Maggie jumped at the point he was making. "That's exactly the argument Parker and I have had for years! You've hit the nail on the head. An artist should want to succeed. It's normal. It's natural."

"If I could be so bold for a minute."

"Go ahead. Be honest." Maggie was bracing – again – for The Lecture. Did everyone she knew have "The Lecture" stored inside them? Like it was a gene she was missing, that she was somehow defective and they were required to supply it? Boyd was the only one who didn't lecture her. Well, actually that wasn't true. Nonie didn't lecture. Certainly her mother didn't ... anyway, James was speaking.

"I think your friend Parker worries about you. She is tremendously fond of you. So, her way is to caution you. Because life has cautioned her."

He had it exactly. Maggie nodded. "You're right. There's nothing wrong with wanting it all." She remembered Fred. Poor Fred. That would be a reason enough to caution anyone.

James interrupted her thoughts. "I believe your friend Parker means well. Maybe a little caution isn't unreasonable, hmm? Let's just say that all your friends want everything to turn out right for you. How about that?" His voice was very kind.

"That's what William says. He's a friend of the family. He's a sort of an uncle to me, I suppose. He and Maeve don't have children. He says the same thing. It's not that I don't love Parker, because I do. She's my best friend in all the world .... in ... all the universe! ..."

"But she worries about you."

Maggie nodded.

"People do have their own natures, their own ways ... and if we love them, we make allowances."

"I have my dream. She has her cautions. Gee. I never looked at it like that before. Explaining it this way, it seems very simple. Thank you, James. Thank you so much."

It was time to calm down, sit back and just relax. Turning away, she looked out the window. Cows. Probably the same cows as last time. Which reminded her. She would get a book from the local library about cows. It was time to do a cow painting. She had a theory, as yet unshared. Every artist should do a painting of a plain brown paper bag, a black square painting and a cow painting. Of course the chances of sharing this oddity were nil but she enjoyed the thought of it nevertheless.

The door to the passenger car opened with a pneumatic *'thip'*. The conductor was past them calling out the familiar, "Cawwwwper Sperrrrinnngsss ... Cawwwwper Sperrringgssszzz," and moving to the next car.

"My goodness. That's my stop."

"Did I bend your ear?"

"You did not," as he touched the top of her hand lightly, the one resting on her knee. "It's an honor and a treat for me to know you. I mean it sincerely. The things you say interest me and I appreciate our time together. Your secret is safe."

"Thank you, James. We only know each other on this train, but I feel we are friends." His hand was warm. Now where had she seen that gesture before? Oh, yes. That was the way Gramma Nonie put a hand on Moe's head. So soothing. It was very dear, the way she did it. Maggie wanted to remember it, learn from it. Maybe it was in her, too ...'dear-ness' ... although she wasn't sure about that ... but James was saying goodbye. She shouldn't miss that.

"Good luck with the painting. Next time we meet up, you'll tell me all about your progress, eh?" and with that he neatly tucked his newspaper under an arm and left the train. When it pulled out of the station a minute later, he was still standing on the platform. He tipped his trilby to her as usual and she waved in return.

Maggie felt good. Really really good. Sitting back in her seat, while Fleetwater was still a few minutes away, there was just time enough to gather her thoughts and relax. Maybe it was a bit sappy to have a heart-to-heart with an 'uncle' but that's what it felt like, and all in all, for whatever reason, she felt cleansed of some worry, released from a concern, like the smallest stone hidden in a shoe finally found out and thrown away. Now she could move ahead without that nagging worry.

What was it he said? Oh, yes. Parker has her cautions. I have my dreams. Yet, somehow, it's a friendship forged in heaven. She was glad to be home again. The trip home to New York was done. All targets accomplished. Maggie was ready to pick up the rhythm of her life again. Right away, she went by Boyd's cottage and left a note tacked to his door. "I need another. MM" Suitably cryptic, in case anyone was nosey.

That evening she went to Gus's Donut Shoppe and Boyd was there, which he normally would be, if he was in town or available. More than a few treated the shop like an unofficial office. Boyd and Maggie greeted with kisses and sat down. Maggie was just about to tell Boyd about James when she changed her mind. I think I'll just keep this to myself for now.

She told him she had left a note on his door.

"Same size?" he asked.

She nodded.

Boyd looked her over and decided Maggie needed to lighten up. She puts in more hours than an Egyptian slave working on one of the pyramids at Giza, he calculated. He would make her smile. Leaning over a few inches, he reached her neck and nuzzled it.

"Come to me, my little thing," he whispered.

She giggled.

"Your neck, it is so lovely ... I must take a bite ." and Maggie laughed.

He was taking the smallest nip with just his lips when his cell phone rang. "I have to take that. Hello? Kids did what? I'll be there."

Maggie gave him a disapproving look.

"One o'clock. See you," and he closed the phone. "Some hooligans pulled off a whole wall of the shingles I just hung for Murphy. Have to see what I can salvage and do the wall again." He gave her neck one last kiss, one to the cheek, and one on the lips.

"Kisses good. Hooligans bad," she said.

"Yes. It's not the kind of work I prefer to do twice, although it pays well." He checked his watch. "We still have time ... let me see. Where was I? Oh, yes. Biting your neck ..."

Boyd pulled her over again and pretended to nip. They were both feeling silly and good.

Maggie sat up. "Wait ..." but she was laughing too much to talk. "Wait ... I've got one ..." and she launched into her Simon Legree. She hadn't done it in ages. They were both laughing as she clasped her hands piteously.

Boyd pulled a red scarf from his pocket and wrapped it around his neck. It was the end of the day and the air was a bit chilly from an onshore breeze.

Maggie stopped what she was doing. She was staring. Something from the past, something from ...?

"It's you!"

"What do you mean?"

"Oh, this is too good! I'm sure of it. Ohmygod. Wait 'til I tell Parkie!"

"What is it??"

"Listen! Did you ever visit New York ... like, maybe four or five years ago?"

"Yes, I did. Picked the worst time, too. The weather was brutal. I took the train up to the city because I needed a break. Turned out it was just as cold there – or worse. I can handle the cold, but ... anyway, as long as I was there, I decided to walk around. It was ridiculous. The wind chill factor was ungodly. I got so cold, I couldn't stand it. Gave up and ducked into the Main Library. I mean, I was desperate. Still, it's a great building."

Maggie was smiling. It was! It was him. The Tourist!

"Anyway, I remember there were two very silly girls in front of me ..."

The memory resolved in his mind quite clearly. He turned and looked at Maggie. " ... You!"

She was nodding hugely. "Yes!! It's me. It was me. And Parker. We were the two silly girls!"

"Well, I'll be darned ..."

"*This is so cool.* Wait till I write Parkie."

You," Maggie said with a big smile. "Imagine that."

He didn't mind Parker hearing the good news at all. He more more determined than ever to propose when Maggie returned. He had already ordered a ring. He didn't want anyone in town slipping up, so it was all arranged through a dealer in Copper Springs, a man who could keep a secret.

Meanwhile, here she was – so bright and beaming. Of course they had to hug and again.

"Ahemmm ..."

The lovers looked up. It was Gus.

"It's all very cute and lovey-dovey but this is not the place. Would you mind continuing this outside? I've got customers waiting for a booth," he said with a wry face.

"Sure, Gus," said Boyd, coloring nicely and Maggie, also blushing and holding his hand, nodded her okay.

They scooted out the door and went around the corner by the side of the shop to resume their conversation.

"You," he said.

"Yup," said Maggie.

"Well."

"Yeah."

There was a short silence.

"I have to go," Boyd reminded her. He didn't want her to leave.

"I know." She didn't want to leave, either.

They could both feel the bond between them. It was growing tighter and stronger with every passing day.

"I'm coming back as soon as I can. Well, I might have to spend the night there. It might be faster. Gee, Maggs ..."

"I know. Okay, one more big hug and then we gotta get going."

"Okay...err ... Maggs?"

"Yes, Boyd."

"So, you know I'm crazy about you. Right?"

"Yes, right, I know."

"And ..." he prompted. It might have been the longest ten seconds in his life ever.

She looked him straight in the eyes. "I feel the same."

"That's all I needed to know," and he kissed her hard and hurried off.

CHAPTER SIX

Maggie wrote Parker a long letter a few days later full of the amazing news. Parker wrote back saying she did remember a guy in red scarf who had laughed at their silliness. She said it was 'a sign'. She wrote how glad she was that Boyd was turning out to be such a good guy, for Maggie's sake ... and when was Maggie going to send her some of Gus's fabulous chocolate crullers? Parker mailed her letter and got on with the unglamorous task of unpacking a gross of small, eminently breakable gewgaws.

Maggie kept painting. It was long hours each day spent at her easel. Layer by layer, she went at it, filling the canvas, 'cycling through'. The time flew by. Number Five was finished. It had taken much longer than expected. It was much more ambitious than the first four.

Exulting at first, then she sagged with relief. Still no one was allowed to see any of it but Boyd. No one guessed. Even with all of the work on the big paintings going on, Maggie was still making smaller format pieces, which Arthur and Oscar were allowed to see. As far as she could tell, no one had a clue.

All Maggie would tell Arthur was that she would be ready for the October solo show and to trust her. He agreed, reluctantly. He had never been shut out before. He always had a hand in what his artists did. But Maggie was adamant. In the meantime, Boyd built the canvas for Number Six and she was out of the gate in a flash, but this time the work was taking longer and longer because this painting was an even bigger challenge. It was complex. It had to be done right. Even if Maggie felt like an unstoppable force, the fact was she had to paint from early until late each day, six days a week just to get anywhere. Boyd insisted Sundays were their day and he also made sure she ate regularly. He called at her studio and if she was still there, he would come to walk her home to make sure that she would get at least eight hours of sleep.

"Did you ever see a movie called *The Red Shoes*?" she asked one night, sitting down for a break right after she changed out the dirty turp' in the can for fresh.

"No. What's it about?"

"Well, it's two stories, really. One about a ballerina and the jealous dance master who mentors her and how she falls in love with another man, a musician. Naturally there's a lot of goings on in the story but basically the bad guy/mentor tells her nothing is more important than dancing. She's not all that strong but she won't give up the man she loves and manages to keep dancing. There's an inner story, a ballet folk tale about a pair of magical – really cursed – red dance shoes. In the end the real ballerina is so tormented by the manipulations of the dance master, she ends up killing herself, just like the girl in the folk tale, who can't take the red shoes off ... it's like they've become one and the same. Kind of like that."

"Not very cheery, is it?"

"No. But the dancing is great. It's the way the two stories intertwine. When someone is obsessed, you know, everything gets twisted around it. Sometimes I think I'm like that."

"Is that what you're worried about? Painting until you drop dead?"

She hadn't realized she was feeling that way until she started explaining things to Boyd. Of course doing all that painting was so exciting, but on the other hand, there was a suppressed sense of hysteria, too, which she was just beginning to recognize. Maggie nodded again.

"I'm ridiculous. I mean, I know it's crazy to even think like that. I mean, art is seriously important to me but I'm not ... you know, over the hill. Even this series isn't anything like what Michelangelo was up to with the Sistine Chapel. I'm not gonna be lying on my back for years doing a ceiling, fighting with a Pope for control of my life. I realize Arthur is hardly a substitute for the Pope. But you know what I'm saying? I have other things, other people ... I have my family ... I love doing what I'm doing but I know it's not going to cure cancer, or help get us to Mars or make us elect a better president. See? I know that. They're ... just ... paintings. The shows are just shows. It's not going to last ... we both know it. It can't. Artists are like flavor-of-the-season. Even if it lasts years, it's still not forever. Listen: only a few of us get into the history books or create an art movement. I know my work isn't going to do that, no matter how good it is. So, things are going to change. It has to. I have no idea what's going to come next. Arthur certainly has other people in the pipeline. Not that he's telling me but I have to be realistic about this."

She had more to say but she just ran out of steam. Boyd was standing now. He could see that she was quivering with emotion.

"Well, I like you whether you paint or not – now, I think you should paint, because I see how happy it makes you, but it's not like you have to. Not like that."

"So you think it should change. That we won't always be here in Fleetwater."

"Oh, I see. Well, you never said you were going to live here forever. Your family is in New York. Parker is in Italy ... and isn't your friend, Martha, in London? Don't you want to visit her? That would be great. It's a great invitation. Don't you want to see a bit more of the world – the one out there – not just the one in your imagination?"

"Well, sure, that is ... I mean, I think ... I don't know. I didn't plan that far ahead. Um ... well, you and I ... we never ... I mean ... are you ... that is, what will ... you ... uh, do if I ...."

Boyd nodded. So, that was it. Part of it, anyway. Actually, in a way, it was great, because it meant that Maggie was looking at the future, too – a future they could share. The very small velvet box in Boyd's jacket containing a modest diamond ring almost nudged him, literally.

"Well ... couldn't we go together?" There. She had said it. She would collapse with relief. She smiled an enormous smile as Boyd put his arms around her and she let herself be held.

It was a huge relief to him, too. "Of course we can ... and we're going to talk all about it, just as soon as your show is over. I promise you ... but listen, I need to say something here. I know it's wonderful work you are doing and there's nothing wrong with a great big challenge – like climbing Mount Everest or something ... Arthur is very possessive. Which is all right, in its way but you do have a right to leave. We both do. I can work other places. You don't have to stay here and paint until you die. Really. You don't."

Boyd watched as he told her these things. He could see it in her eyes. It was what she needed to hear. Even while Canvases #6 and #7 haunted her sleep ... until she could make them real ... she still needed to hear exactly what Boyd was saying. Of course she wasn't going to end up with syphilis in Tahiti or cut off her ear. There wasn't going to be any mad-sad-bad endings. She knew she possessed the ability to reason and judge. Still, there had to rest points, points of moderation in her life. It was just that she had been struggling for so long, she didn't realize that she had nearly overrun her goal. Finding Boyd ... that had never been planned for – she hadn't given anyone a serious look since art took over her life, which went all the way back to grammar school. How did that happen? But here indeed was a wonderful man and now they were talking about their future.

He took her hand. He could feel the roughness from all the washing. He adored that hand. He raised it to his lips and brushed it lightly. "Is that better?" He was still watching her closely. She smiled, so he smiled back. There was a light in his eyes which made Maggie's heart sing. She nodded.

"Good." Then he kissed her. "Now I'm going to sit down and do some more reading ... "Lake Woebegone Days" is very good reading ... you: paint. Your fans await."

So it went. The summer completed itself. October began to loom. Sometimes strange, random thoughts went

229

through Maggie's mind at night before she could will herself to sleep. Each thread had to be followed – in case it might be important. They rarely were. Still she chased them ... and in the end, the brightness of the morning sun would wake her up. Whatever Maggie knew about painting or didn't yet, she decided that this series was going to be great. We'll see ... that's what she promised herself. We'll see.

Working on Number 6 meant that 7 was not far behind. There was no time for dates now or strolling. There were only stolen minutes to share a kiss, a rare quarter-hour to call her family and write to Parker, who was now in the throes of planning her wedding with Tony. Of course she had to stay in Italy. There was no fussing. This Maggie was a different person. She was on a mission. She was on fire ... now all she had to do was keep her head down, dodge any stray bullets and she was home free. October was fast approaching.

She paced herself, planning her days, working to the schedule she set for herself, making every brush stroke count. In early September she suddenly decided to take two days off. Again Arthur didn't make a peep. He didn't dare. Months ago he had realized that stepping back was the way he stayed in control. She promised him the work would be spectacular and he believed her. Now all his attention was focused on lining up the best opening money and influence in Fleetwater could buy because every gallery was wired for big openings. The town was flooded with people but come October 18th he wanted every big gun with deep pockets in *his* gallery.

Boyd naturally agreed to watch after the shed and her room. Maggie didn't even have to ask. He said, "Everything will be fine. See you in two days." They kissed one more time. She climbed aboard. Maggie was on her way to the city again.

Some hours later she was sitting in her mother's living room, just taking a breather, when the doorbell rang. Barbara said, "Don't get up," so Maggie leaned back in the big chair. She was so glad just to sit here and vegetate.

When Parker walked into the living room Maggie nearly had heart failure. She gave a huge shout and leaped up. She hugged Parker so hard she nearly broke a pair of her ribs. Barbara just stood back and let the girls hug and cry and squeal.

"Why didn't you tell me! Oh my god. You are really here. Let me look at you! Oh god, you look so ... Italian!! How could you not tell me you were coming!"

"Because Evan and Barbara thought surprising you would be more fun ... because I wanted to see you here in the city and take the train to Fleetwater with you *so we could share that*. There's just enough time to say hello to William and Nonie ..."

"Oh, god, it sounds so good ..."

"Please note, Miz Malone, the full dance card ...". Parker held up a small plastic rectangle.

"What's that?"

"It's from Tony's father. He says I worked myself to a fragment (he meant 'to the bone') and this is my reward – *our* reward."

Maggie's eyes were glittering. "How much is on that thing, Parker?"

"His papa loaded it," she announced. "I've been a very good girl. His son is going to get married to a girl who will do the laundry! I can cook. Randall sent me his best recipes and I've been taking some cooking classes ... Vincent is one very happy almost-papa-in-law," and the friends laughed and laughed.

She flapped the plastic square in front of Maggie.

"A thousand?" Maggie asked.

"More ..."

"Uh ... twenty-five hundred?" Maggie whispered.

"Double that."

Both girls laughed out loud and squealed.

"You've got to be kidding."

"I should be, but I'm not. We don't have to spend it all in one place, you know. That would be kind of piggy. Of course, just one visit to Emily's favorite dress shop and I'd be walking home with one small underwear box ..."

"Another words ... we're going to do some serious shopping."

"Amen, sister."

"Did you know about this?" Maggie asked, turning to her mother.

"We did. Parker told us. We're not sure we entirely approve ... but it's not our money, not our son-in-law exactly ... far be it from us ..."

"It might be lira, for all we know," Maggie joked.

"It isn't," Parker answered. "So, listen, we're waiting for Evan. Barbara, tonight, let this dinner be my treat."

"Not tonight. You girls need to get together ... tomorrow night will be soon enough," Barbara replied as Evan walked through the front door.

232

"Daddy, look! ..." Maggie called out, still in an uproar.

"Yes, I know. Welcome home, daughter ... wonderful to have you here. " He gave her a hug and a kiss.

"Come along, Evan ... I have dinner for us," said Barbara as she towed Evan out the living room. "We'll be in the den if you need us, but I can't think why. Goodnight, girls."

"You haven't seen everything," Parker grabbed Maggie's face. "Look." She held up her hand. On it was a spectacular square-cut emerald practically shooting sparks.

"Oh, my god," Maggie squealed. "It's gorgeous!" Parker screamed. They both jumped up and down. Finally they calmed themselves and sat huddled together on the living room couch ogling the jewel, examining the sparkle.

"My word, that's divine. You could put your eye out with it, if you're not careful."

"Awful, isn't it?" Parker gave it a polish on her shirt and held it up. "I told Tony it was too big. Let's not be nuts about this, I said. I can live with a nice little diamond. His father said – and I quote – "Tony. Shesa nicah girl. You don need sucha bigga dimon. She love you. You marry. Betta you gif her a nicah little rock," (stone, he meant). "You tella the worl this issa girl for you ..."

Maggie laughed. "Tony's papa sounds like a really nice man."

"Vincent is a lovely man. But Tony gave me this "rock" for an engagement ring anyway. This is such a wonderful family. I'm going to be a part of it. They are the loveliest people. The kindest people you'd ever want to meet. The papa, he takes me for a walk around the courtyard (which is huge) and he says, "I know Richard forra longga time now ... since we do some busy-ness together an' I know Fortelli a longga time. Heesa a good man, too. I say to Richard, what for you don come to Milano to see you lovely daughter." Gawd, Maggie, I almost went through the ground. No one ever talks to Richard like that."

"But Vincent did."

"Uh-huh. That's when I realized it didn't matter anymore. Richard got me to Italy. He did that one thing ... uh, conception duties aside ... he gave me money to get started ... well, you know. Richard is Richard. Why they ever had a baby is beyond me. They shouldn't have. Maybe he and Emily were harassed in some way. You know, pressured by his family. In his younger days I'll bet rich young men were always been pushed to have a child, especially a boy, to keep the family name going – that kind of thing. Then they had me. A girl. Oh my."

"Your father is not a happy man," Maggie said simply.

"No. He's not. He and Emily are more like distant relatives. It would be very bad if I was all alone but I'm not. I wasn't! Even Randall and Cook – always there for me. I just didn't see it that way. If you want to know, Evan is my real dad. I told him so this morning when he picked me up at the airport. I know you don't mind sharing. In fact, you never did.

"Even though I used to talk like I thought Evan was my Dad, I felt like he was ... on loan, you know? Even with all the stuff. Dentist, doctor, eye exams, school plays, bandaging my knees ... but I also went to see Richard and Emily ... it was confusing and I felt disloyal. I just couldn't roll with it. So, there we were, Vincent and me – suddenly I did see it. In the garden, taking that walk. It all came together. You are my family. It isn't some pretend thing. It's not a name thing. It's not a loan. It doesn't matter that it's not the same bloodline.

"And in Italy, boy, I can tell you. When a family takes you in, you *belong*. Over there, the family is in your hair all the time. I love it. So, there we are and we're strolling and I realized how it all works."

"I am truly glad for you, Parkie." Maggie looked at Parker, relief in her face – it accompanied a burden Maggie had been carrying for her friend for so long and now she could unload it. God bless Vincent.

"Thanks. It's been a long haul. I mean even Nonie's *dogs* think I belong. I was the only one who didn't get it. It was in front of me the whole time. I had it all – the family I needed and wanted the whole time. Why didn't I know?"

Maggie kept silent because she knew Parker wasn't finished.

"Anyway, so Vincent says to me, "You fahther, heesa man who iss hard to know. But he has some good. Heesa smarta fella, he love you mama, you know this.""

"I told him that I did know that."

At which point Maggie gave Parker a big hug, which said it all.

"So we're going to Fleetwater for your 'really big shew'. Next stop: Italy with me, because I need to marry Tony. Okay? You wouldn't make me go through this alone?"

Maggie shook her head no. Of course not. Wild horses couldn't keep her away. It was wonderful. Somehow she would figure out how to get Boyd to Italy with them ... and even if some Doubting Thomas (make that Arthur) said: that'll happen when pigs can fly ... in her case, at least in paint on canvas, all kinds of things that couldn't, did fly anyway. So, somehow it would all work out. Boyd would be included. If Parker could be part of their family, why not Boyd? There was room for one more.

The girls jumped around some more, and when they were exhausted, they crashed out in their old bedroom. For the next two days they swanked through two extravagant shopping trips, a great dinner with Evan and Barbara and a visit to see Nonie and the dogs.

Maggie could see she needed another day or two in the city so she called and told Arthur the news. Then she called Boyd, but he was out, so she left a message for him.

On the way back to the apartment at the end of third afternoon, they stopped off to see Randall and Cook. From there, because Maggie couldn't visit with Randall and his wife and not see William, they went to the Park where they were proudly allowed to see the latest baby ducks receiving his special care. It was a fabulous afternoon.

"I'm famished," Parker announced. "I had no idea a victory stroll could make a person so hungry." Off they went to the Carnegie Deli for lunch and battle planned.

"Got to meet this cutie of yours," Parker said with a twinkle.

"Boyd isn't quite the 'cutie' type. He's a very nice, sensible person." She stopped. It wasn't that she didn't think Boyd was handsome, because he was good-looking. It was just that she didn't think of him as a cutie. He was more than that. So much more.

"Uh-huh," Parker coached. "But he is cute ..."

Maggie thought about the last time she had seen him. It was at the train station. He was holding her hand. Maggie had hated to let go.

"Well, yes, he's good looking but for me the main thing is that he's trustworthy. And very sweet. And kind. You know, people can go one of two ways: needy or self-sufficient. He's definitely not the needy type." She turned to Parker. "I really like him."

"I know you do. You're allowed. So, let's go meet this fellow of yours. You're going to meet Tony soon enough. Isn't there something about 'marry a girl and you marry their friends'?"

"Yuh. Something like that," Maggie agreed.

Parker grinned. She really was itching to meet this man of Maggie's. Protectiveness only goes so far when one is thousands of miles away in Europe. Now that she was home again, she felt like some of the old Parker mistrust niggling – with a new target. Once she met this Boyd fellow, she'd know for sure. Either she could relax or he could just damn well watch out because Parker Feldman was the new sheriff in town and she would go gunning for anyone who messed with her best friend. Now it was time to head to Fleetwater. The afternoon was waning.

They finished eating and went to pick up their suitcases. Barbara had left them a nice note. Evan was, of course, long gone to work. Hurrying into the kitchen, Maggie did a baby giraffe sketch in several quick strokes with a stub of white chalk on the little blackboard next to the shopping list. Parker left x's and o's.

"So that takes care of that," Maggie said washing the chalk off her fingers. "There's one more train to Fleetwater today. We've got time to make that one if we hustle."

Outside the doorman whistled them a cab. In no time they were at Penn Station. Actually when they reached the platform, it turned out that they were just in time which meant running all the way down the platform and hollering, "Wait! Wait!" to the conductor looking both ways, about to signal the engineer.

The conductor recognized Maggie quite well. She was a regular. "We don't hold the train for just anyone," he said with a wink as Parker hurried up the metal stairs just behind Maggie.

"Thank you," she replied breathlessly. Inside the car the friends found two seats, stored their backpacks on the overhead rack and landed heavily on the cushioned seats. Maggie turned to Parker saying, "They were not holding the train for me."

"Actually they were, but it was sweet. You've come a long way, Maggs."

But Maggie still out of breath from their sprint so she just smiled and took more deep breaths.

They had hardly just settled in when, to her happy surprise, a man with the white bristle mustache approached. "Is this seat free?" He was asking about the seat opposite.

"James, how nice to see you. Of course, sit down. Parker, this is James Fuyard. This is the gentleman I told you about. We've shared this trip a lot of times, haven't we?"

"Indeed. How do you do?" He extended his hand to her.

Parker returned the favor. His skin was soft and smooth and a little cool to the touch. It was a reassuring hand, in fact. She was inclined to like the man already.

"Your friend and I sometimes have the luck of riding the same train ... but, if I remember rightly, this visit has been a long time coming. so you girls probably have lots to talk about. Don't let me interrupt," he said.

"Nice to meet you, too," Parker replied pleasantly. She watched him as he settled behind his paper. He was gracious. His voice sounded kind. Parker decided she definitely liked this avuncular fellow who had befriended her Maggie.

All three settled in for the ride. Parker took note of all the points Maggie had written about; it was time to see the real thing. There were indeed swaths of grassland, a glinting ocean, trees, housing estates – and Maggie's favorite: cows. Big, placid, cud-chewing cows.

Just before Mr. Fuyard got off at Copper Springs, as usual, he pulled out a silver card case. "Maggie, I've been meaning to give you my card. I nearly forgot again." He handed her one of the snowy white rectangles. She read his name in the center. Elegant black script. There was a Copper Springs post office box address in one corner and a telephone number in the other. "One never knows. I feel we are well enough acquainted. I should like you to feel free to contact me if the occasion arose."

"Thanks, James. Um, I have a card, too ..." but after searching in her backpack all she found was a postcard left over from the Christmas show.

"Of course. From your show. Well, this is even better, if you don't mind my saying so. I know the Nouvelle Vague Gallery well. That is, I did. It's been so long. Is Oscar Valenzuela still the manager?"

"You know Oscar? This is so great ..." Maggie would have said a lot more but the train was leaving and there was no time. James was out the door and on the platform and seen tipping his hat to her through window, as he always did.

"I'll tell him I saw you," she called out but she wasn't sure he heard her through the glass.

"Oh, isn't that the best?" Maggie said cheerfully turning in her seat. She put the card into her pocket. "I don't know what James and I talk about sometimes ... anyway, it isn't about the people in Fleetwater or Copper Springs. Oh, yuh. This is so cool," she said, sitting back. "I have to remember to tell Oscar."

Now the train was well on its way again. Fleetwater was not far ahead.

When they arrived, Maggie pointed out everything of possible interest. Living in a place like Fleetwater, she felt it was all about the details. She knew them by heart and wanted Parker to savor each one, too. Dropping off their bags in Maggie's room, she escorted Parker to Gus' Donut Shoppe. He was at the counter exchanging out two empty trays for two just filled. A fragrant chocolateyness wafted. The goodies were obviously just out of the oven.

"God, those smell good. Hey, Gus. Look who this is. Can you guess?"

He took a moment. "How do you do, Parker," he said pleasantly. "Welcome to Fleetwater. How about half-a-dozen?"

"No! Four's plenty ..." Maggie yelped.

"Nice to meet you, too, Gus ... yum," Parker said, as the tongs delicately moved one cruller after another into a crisp white waxed bag. The smell was divine. She reached for her purse.

"Oh, no. Put your nasty money away. It's no good in this town," Maggie said swatting her hand. "She's rich," she said, with a nod towards Parker. "But this is my treat."

"That's nice," Gus said with a rare smile. "We have a lot of rich people here. You'll be quite comfortable," he remarked, enjoying the banter.

Parker reached for the bag. Her emerald ring was impossible to miss.

"That's quite a rock," Gus remarked appreciatively.

The girls would have said more but both were already well into their first crullers, mouths filled. Maggie pointed at her mouth and shook her head. Parker did the same. They waved in happy silence, signing big 'okays' and 'v' for victory'. Gus waved back. "Come back later," he called. The girls danced out the door.

The air was brisk. The sun was almost down but it was a pretty day so they decided to sit outside for a bit, with their jackets zipped, scarves, hats and gloves in place. They munched and talked. Parker told Maggie how a minivan had nearly crashed into her airport shuttle the other morning when she arrived at Kennedy International. "It was crazy," she said. "The driver actually fled the scene! Can you believe it? But I'm alive so phooey on him."

Parker was so matter-of-fact about the accident that Maggie had nothing to say. Then it was Maggie's turn. She described the much-vaunted competition for the local library commission at Bettie and Freddie Austin-Miller's palatial home, named Valhalla, which every artist within shooting distance wanted to win. "It's an amazing house," she bragged, not realizing how her viewpoint on such buildings had changed in two years. Now they were potential showplaces for her work – not the source of some inexplicable annoyance.

"They're making the short list for commission now ..." She stopped. Suddenly she didn't want to discuss her career anymore. "I'm *so* glad you are here. Did I tell you Boyd had to go out of town at the last minute? I rang his phone and there was message on it for me. You'll meet him. Don't look at me that way. He had to buy some special materials for a job. He's due back tomorrow."

Parker rolled her eyes but Maggie's cell phone rang, interrupting. Parker wasn't listening. She was deciding to hold off discussing the results of the background check on Arthur. Parker was happy that Maggie's boyfriend had come out clean as a whistle but Arthur? Oh, the man had money all right. The investments seemed solid enough. No complaints there. But where did he really come from? The trail seemed to pick up in Fleetwater back in the 1970's. It was like he came out of the ground – figuratively speaking. Anyway, there would be time enough for such exchanges of intelligence later.

"Hello, Mom ..." Maggie was saying. "My hair? ... my hair looks fine. I know the sea air 'adds volume'." She turned to Parker. "I've got big hair," she mouthed with a grin. "New York big, not Dallas big. That would be too big ..." (she grinned at Parker again). "I am listening to you. Just because I don't do everything you say doesn't mean I don't love you ... no, I don't need a hair cut." She looked to Parker. "Tell her I don't need a haircut," but Parker laughed and refused to take the cell phone. "Can you not trust me? Pu-leeezze ..." she said in a mock wail.

Maggie tried to hand over the cell phone to Parker but she was not going to take it. "Oh, no. Mothers and daughters. Frightening stuff. Just frightening ..." she remarked, keeping her hands to herself. Instead, she took another cruller.

Now Maggie was holding the phone up so Parker could hear Barbara saying, "Do you talk this way to Arthur and Oscar? I don't think so."

"Arthur and Oscar are not family. Don't be ridiculous! I love you for calling. Everything's great. We had a great trip. Tell Nonie I love her and the dogs ..." She rolled her eyes. "Yes, yes ... here. Talk to Barbara ... you have to." This time she thrust the phone into Parker's hand.

Parker could see she had no choice. "Hi, Barbara. Yes. The train ride was fun. It's not so very long. Listen, Maggs and I are off to get our nails done. I'm going to keep her pruned and polished, I promise. She looks great, which proves that I'm looking after her." Parker eyed Maggie. "She's under my protection now so you can leave everything to me. I love you, too. "She handed back the phone. "It's Evan."

Maggie harrumphed and took the cell phone back. "Hello, Daddy."

"How's my little girl?"

"Oh, gawd, please don't talk like that or I'm going to barf."

"Barbara, take your hands off the phone. It's my turn. I'm speaking to our

daughter ..."

Maggie heard her parents fighting for control of the receiver as line went dead. "Oops. I bet Evan hit the "off" button by mistake." She laughed. "Parents. You gotta love them. They'll call back." Putting the cell phone away, they finished their second round of crullers. "Delicious. We'll save the rest for later."

"Coffee," they said in unison and bounced back into the shop. Gus was not there. Veronica, the counter girl took care of them. "They don't call all that often," Maggie was explaining as they left the shop carrying double-paper cups of hot coffee. "They don't want to pester me," she explained. Off they went, strolling down the road, resuming their chin wag.

Inside Gus' Donut Shoppe, well out of sight in the office in the rear, Beth Barrett was feeling placid. She had recently molted and was feeling good. Moreover, she and Arthur had shared a very satisfactory late night coil and squeeze. All things considered, Beth was in a good mood. Standing by the side window which overlooked the marina, she saw the various yachts' running lights twinkling in the dark. Perhaps she could even appreciate them as well. Slipping just the tip of her tongue between her teeth, she smelled all the interesting smells. She dialed a number on her cell phone. Her call was answered. Listening for a moment, she nodded her head. "Don't worry," she replied. "I've got this," and she closed the phone. Outside the running lights were still twinkling in the near black. Maybe that's all that's missing in the Noave. Running lights.

CHAPTER SEVEN

The second morning after Parker arrived, she set up an email account at the E-Café, located on Main Street. She still had a wedding to plan. The next few weeks would pass quickly. Summer had officially ended and evidence of the beautiful, cool fall weather the Island was noted for was everywhere.

Maggie painted with the shed door wide open, knowing no one would bother her. There was an unspoken policy that artists-in-residence, of which there were a number, were to be left strictly alone. It was a very rare occurrence to turn around and find someone lingering in the alleyway, but strollers were quickly shooed away in any case and weren't seen again.

Parker's routine was to wait while Maggie picked up a take-out breakfast at Hadley's, walk with her to the shed each morning, then stroll over to Main Street to visit the galleries and shops. At lunchtime she would pick out a restaurant to have her own meal at a more leisurely pace. After that, she would window shop again down the streets until she reached the E-Café. By now she was now a regular customer. Happily she knew what she liked and didn't dawdle about her decisions. By cell phone she talked with Tony every day and Lucia, her mother-in-law to be, every few days.

Maggie had arranged for Mrs. Aubrey to fix up a camp bed for Parker in Maggie's room. It made the space more than a little crowded, but neither of the girls minded. Maggie also arranged for Parker to receive mail at the Post Office so that boxes of samples and catalogs from Italy arrived, which Parker inspected, made her selections and replied to Lucia quickly. Between the faxing and her Internet connection, Parker carried on with the detailed planning almost as if she'd never left Milan. It was true that Signor Fortelli also sent her email reminders that the office was practically hanging in abeyance until her return. (Not entirely true, but it made her life in Italy continue to be real, so that she was looking forward to going back.) She always sent an appreciative reply because she really did intend to go back and work for him again, albeit on a slightly reduced work schedule. There had to be plenty of room for her and Tony.

In the third week of September there was a short fuss about the silverware pattern but in the end, even though Parker felt that Lucia's choice was too elaborate, she wisely decided to give her mother-in-law the final word on this. After all, all the styles were heavy silver no matter what. So that was that. The smoke cleared quickly. Between Parker and Lucia, all the details were well in hand. Now Parker had some time left to walk around and get to know Fleetwater better. What better way than to stroll along the streets of Gallery Alley. It had obviously been just one street in the beginning. Now it was tight formation of half a dozen short streets.

The routine worked well for Maggie, too. She was working full out, driving herself to complete Number Six, so it fell to Parker to make sure Maggie ate at least two nourishing meals a day, seeing as how Boyd was still away working. "You know what they did to the Suffragettes," Parker would threaten, and if Maggie did any foot-dragging, Parker would politely take the brush Maggie was holding, place in the turp' can or swish it clean and lay it on the towel.

"I hope Tony knows this dark side to your personality," Maggie would growl but she had to relent. Arm-in-arm they would walk to one of several favorite eateries or picnic from a hamper.

The one really odd thing that Parker could not fathom was Boyd. He was still away. She didn't want to be suspicious, but it bothered her. Every time she was finally about to meet him something came up. He had been notably absent since just before she arrived. Parker couldn't decide if it was just coincidence or if other forces were at work. "Have you heard from you-know-who?" she asked as they took a dinner hour at Olaf's Swedish Table as the friends *kvelled* over the delicious meatballs.

Maggie held up a finger for the one-minute time-out and chewed. Clearing her mouth with a sip of coffee, she finally replied, "Boyd called me this morning after you left. I hear from him nearly every day. He was packing to leave when the client shows up and says "One moment, son," and shows him a design. 'It's a tree house. Maggie,' he says to me. 'I've never done one. It's a great place. The tree is perfect. Huge old oak.' 'How long will this take?' I asked. 'Three weeks max.' So I told him he had three weeks. 'I promise,' he said, 'and then I'm coming home. God, I miss you, but you will be happy to know I've made a pile of money. This client is one rich guy. Actually all my current clients are loaded. Everything I do has to be top of the line.

That's the way I like it. Anyway, I told him, if I do this, this has got to be the last thing because my girlfriend is having the biggest art opening of her life and I have to be there.'

Parker's eyes opened wide with interest but kept silent as Maggie continued.

" 'So, then he says 'I hope you are my girlfriend because if you aren't, I won't have any excuse to leave.' Parker, I was smiling so hard I couldn't talk. So then he says to me, 'Well, you are, aren't you?' and I said, 'Uh-huh.' Then it was quiet on both ends, if you know what I mean."

Parker was familiar with the game of love now and she nodded.

"So then he says 'I miss you' – again."

"He said that twice ..."

"That's right. Twice. I am definitely counting."

"And you said ..."

"I said, 'I miss you, too.' So then he said, 'You're okay with this?' "

"And I said, 'I'm okay with it. Come October 18th, you will be here. Right? Even though I've got Parker ... who, by the way, is beginning to believe you are a figment of my imagination, but we'll leave that alone for the moment ... I need you here, too. Please.' " I said, 'Please.' I wasn't planning to. It just happened. God, I hate sounding needy. And he said, 'I'll be there,' and I said, 'All right ... uh, Boyd?' – because he wasn't talking ... and he says, 'I'm still here,' so then I said, 'Measure twice, cut once, fellah,' and he laughed ... and that was the call." Maggie took a deep sigh and settled her chin onto her hands folded on elbows in front. "It was divine."

In the face of such a report Parker could not say anything untoward. She was not going to be the one to tarnish the bloom of this romance – it was Maggie's first serious boyfriend. Was it just too convenient that Boyd was suddenly not available for her scrutiny? What was going on? No answer came so Parker kept her peace.

Now Maggie was working flat out. Parker's only job now was to make sure everything ran smoothly for her. The last three weeks before the opening flew by. Maggie stopped painting the week before the show.

"Everything has to dry. Number Seven will have to wait. I did my best."

"Arthur won't know the difference anyway, since he knows nothing about the big canvases anyway," Parker offered. What she was thinking was: mess with my friend and you will be sorry.

"It's lucky I don't do impasto," Maggie was saying as they stood inside Giovanni's Frame Emporium. It was agreed that while the small format pieces should have some congruity, they needn't be framed all the same. Giovanni would sort through the variations while she and Parker voted 'yeah' or 'nay'. It took a few hours but they did what they came for and that was a load off Maggie's mind. After that some conferencing with the printer was necessary to make sure the colors on the art card reproductions were perfect. Just having Parker there, after all this time of having to make all her decisions alone, was pretty great.

"Just be glad I'm not Georgia O'Keefe. You do realize she created her own personal white paint and required every gallery to re-paint their walls for her shows. Do not talk to me about what it took to get her okay to reproduce a piece of her art in a book. Oh, my god."

The man behind the counter just nodded. Actually he wasn't going to ask, but he didn't think that was the point anyway. Maggie was not the first highly exacting artist he had worked for and was indeed silently glad she wasn't another Ms. O'Keefe. Parker nodded her approval where needed. After that they were off to the gallery to check in with Oscar where they had daily briefings.

It was Oscar's new, bright idea, he explained, to hire a couple of very presentable young twenty-somethings to go door-to-door to the surrounding homes as well as visit the affluent businesses in downtown Fleetwater. Each person on the list received a small gift bag which included a handsome invitation to the first day opening and an by-invitation-only to the opening soiree. The following day the doors would be open thereafter day and night to everyone for the run of the show. By the time several hundred invitations were handed out, there was plenty of local chatter about who had been lucky enough to find a pretty girl or good-looking young man standing at their door or store in order to hand them one of the coveted goodie bags. The list of respondents was equally enormous. Maggie's opening was going to be the event of the season. It was turning into a circus, of course, but no one was complaining.

This particular afternoon Oscar was in full battle mode. Besides his own work, he had a whole day planned for Maggie, beginning with the photo-op he had arranged to be done at the Marina where Arthur and Maggie were to be snapped having a business lunch.

Parker was not invited to this so she went back to the E-Café, which was fine with her. She had no desire to share a meal with Arthur – the least said about that the better. They had already met and disliked each other immediately although neither said a word. No one wanted to rock the boat as planning the show was taking every attention unit available. Next up that afternoon Maggie was to be interviewed while designing a poster so the reporter and his photographer were there to grab shots of Maggie Malone, Girl Artist, in action.

Later on that afternoon, while Maggie was in full-promotional mode, Arthur was in his office, sizzling with irk over the failure of his campaign to cajole her into staying in Fleetwater. This trip to Italy was unconscionable! She didn't realize how actually furious he was. Fit to be tied, in fact, because not one of his artists had ever gone on vacation! But she didn't know Arthur that well, so she didn't know the signs. Oscar and Beth did. They knew Arthur's emotional storms. Something not very pretty was bound to happen, that was for sure. It gave Oscar and Beth cause for concern.

Arthur never realized how it might look to others, or how he affected others. He simply lived inside these whirlwinds. A rant would invade his mind and he would be compelled to stop, wherever he was, and listen while it broadcast to him alone. Local people already considered Arthur eccentric, therefore one more slight tweak out of shape seemed about right.

What Maggie didn't know was that this particular inner rant was insisting that Maggie would not leave. It simply wasn't acceptable, not with time running out and so much to do. She could not leave right after a show like this! It was impossible. It was outrageous. I won't have it! On and on. Around and around it went in Arthur's mind – at least several times a day. He was wearing himself to a frazzle.

By the time there were only three days to go until the opening, Oscar thought Arthur might actually burst a blood vessel. Happening into their leader's office while Parker and Maggie were standing nearby the front door to the gallery chattering about air tickets and so forth, Oscar found he was literally holding his breath. He could only pray that Arthur did not come charging out of his office and attack Parker or Maggie or both. After the girls left, Oscar sighed with relief. Arthur was still ensconced in his office. He, Oscar, busied himself at the filing cabinet while Beth kept patting Arthur's shoulder whispering, 'Now, now' as tenderly as possible. But Arthur refused to be calmed. "Get off me – the two of you! ... out – everyone," he hissed.

Oscar melted away and Beth backed off. A minute later he was seen walking out of his office. He slammed the door behind him, leaving the gallery in a red haze. Maggie was at her studio by this time so she knew nothing about this, and Parker was well on her way down the street to the E-Café, but Beth and Oscar knew. She looked at Oscar and shook her head. Their leader was finally having a meltdown.

Every chance thereafter he would croon to Maggie in his most alluring manner, "Now that you are a hit, your patrons and fans will be coming into the gallery just to meet you. Of course there will be more media interviews.

Parties, excursions, all kinds of thises and thatses ... and I need you. Your public needs you. Think of all fabulous opportunities to consolidate and expand ..."

Maggie listened to as much of this as she could and when she had had enough, she expressed her exasperation. "Arthur, listen. You need to cool down. It's not like you'll never see me again. Haven't I explained? I'm not *just* taking off. I've been painting like a ... like a *slave* ... for almost two years. I need to take a break. I need to breathe. Refresh myself. You just set up a commission list. I can probably do at least a few small pieces while I'm in Italy. I'm not going to be gone that long. You are welcome to raise the prices, if you want ... you do whatever you have to keep the patrons happy for a few months – but just stop it. The show will be huge, we're going to make a pile of money. We've put huge prices on these paintings. Not everyone has that kind of ready money ... I'm going to Italy to see my best friend get married. So stop this nonsense. Now ... I want you to come see the paintings."

All right. Arthur shut his trap. It was obvious, this girl didn't have a clue how to run a business. He would stop, just for now. Certainly he wanted to see the paintings which Maggie had been alluding to for over a year. No one had ever kept their work a secret before. It just wasn't done, but Maggie had managed to do the impossible anyway.

She took him by the arm and waltzed him to the back of the gallery off of which extended a large open room with racks full of stored paintings and long plain white walls on which eye-level shelves had been built to hold smaller works. The bigger canvases could be leaned on a floor-level shelf to be viewed (or admired – or both). Oscar had ordered the covered paintings to remain covered while they were conveyed to the gallery from Maggie's shed during lunchtime.

They had been set up in sequentially around three sides of the room. That's the effect Maggie wanted. Oscar had agreed. They were best seen shoulder to shoulder, which is how Oscar had lined up them up.

Beth was there, in her usual spot, standing close by Arthur. She really didn't care about art very much, to tell the truth, but Arthur did, in his own selfish way, so she had to be there, too.

Maggie prayed that seeing the six huge paintings, all arrayed in a continuous line wrapping around the room would be quite the spectacle she had been planning and dreaming and working so hard at for so long. She had often muttered that if Monet could do it, so could she.

"Okay, Arthur. So, you know Claude Monet had a whole room in the Museum of Modern Art in Paris just for his water lily paintings. They're set in a big oval. You walk in and you are inside this magical world ... right? Well, here's my version of that. Oscar? If you will do the honors ..."

With that Oscar folded up the heavy covering and unveiled the first; then he unveiled the next, and the next, working his way down the line until all six were revealed. He went and stood at Maggie's side. He hoped it would be a triumph for him, too.

Oscar thought they were marvelous. Inventive. Colorful. So beautifully drawn. Beth murmured her version of being appreciative. But Arthur was agog. "Oh, my," he said. In fact, it was all he could say. He beamed at Maggie. Walking forward, he stood again, about six feet from the paintings, looking again at the first ... moved on to the second ... like he was doing a military review. He approved. Oh, my, yes. He approved.

From further away, Parker kept her peace. She had already seen all the work and loved it (naturally). Mainly she was there to provide emotional support. Maggie looked at her from time to time – waggling her eyebrows and grinning. Parker nodded and gave her a small 'v' for victory sign.

But, as Maggie was soon to find out, all this glorious artistic expression would not serve to halt Arthur's fussing about her trip to Italy. Having seen what she could do when she was totally unfettered, his resolve to keep her in Fleetwater was going to be renewed with even greater vigor; nevertheless he decided he would say nothing more about it for a few days. Not until after the opening. In the meantime, he decided he needed to rethink his strategy. In any case, Maggie Malone was not going to Italy. Not a chance.

That very night, during the dinner hour, he grabbed Oscar and pulled him inside his office, closed the door and locked it behind. "You will find me a replacement for Maggie Malone immediately. Do you hear?" he demanded. The man's hot breath was sour and repellent. Oscar leaned slightly away, while hoping Arthur wouldn't notice.

Arthur was ranting: here she was, finally – a fully primed and loaded artist, about to explode onto the public scene with greatness – energy and art like hers would feed the hungry aesthetic maw of Fleetwater's citizens for ...

two, maybe even three years, or longer ... possibly five ... lesser artists burned out so quickly. He was top dog and nothing was going to get in his way ... now that he had Maggie.

Oscar had heard enough. He decided Arthur had finally really and truly lost his grip. For now the man was still his employer – well, really, leader of their Mission – and he was still talking, (if you could call it that), and Oscar needed to listen, but Oscar realized his days here were numbered. What he would do, he couldn't hardly say. The whole Mission was unraveling even if it didn't look that way on the outside. But inwardly, Oscar knew it was true.

Arthur was ranting how about he wasn't about to let some rich, whiny brat (Parker) ruin his plans. He considered most of the other local art to be pish-tosh – not that it mattered – but he thought Maggie's work was truly something special. She was doing work his connoisseurs could sink their teeth into ...

Oscar tried to step back, but Arthur had gripped him by his coat lapel and his eyes were lit with fever as he looked into his glorious future. Suddenly he let go of Oscar, raised his hands in the air and kept talking – he was nearly incoherent. He wouldn't give up. He wouldn't! In three days' time the art-buying public, like a well-primed canon, was due to come roaring through the doors of the gallery and he, Arthur, had a target that even the sightless couldn't miss hitting. This show was like the side of a barn. "Just aim and fire!"

Arthur's metaphors were a mess but the message was clear. Nothing must interfere! Oscar knew there was big trouble brewing. Where was this all going to end? With no immediate answer, he continued to follow his punch list, because, whatever else happened, the opening was due to in three days' time and they had indeed spent a fortune to make it the biggest opening ever.

CHAPTER EIGHT

Showtime.

The weather was perfect. Fresh and brisk and almost, but not quite, cold. The harvest moon, now in its second phase, seemed to know it, too, was being counted on to do its part, so it was following a perfectly placed trajectory above the roof of the gallery and through the treetops. Luckily the towns along the beach and rail line understood the concept of light pollution and maintained a very low electric light profile at night. That meant the sky was sparkling with so many stars, it looked as though it was blanked with diamond confetti. The breathtaking effect was on full display.

Every one of the gallery staff was looking their best. Arthur was handsome in a perfectly tailored dark blue pin-stripe suit and a sumptuous cravat at his throat (his couture signature). Beth was quite his match in a red suit with a pencil skirt. The notched-collar jacket had a tiny, decorous peplum. Deliberately towering over everyone but Oscar, she clip-clopped neatly about in black patent-leather spikes while she ran the event like a general directing troop movement.

The assistants, known as Arthur's Girls, were also out in force: long narrow-sleeved leopard-print tops and silver-threaded chocolate brown broomstick skirts over paper-thin knee-high chocolate brown suede boots. Beth had insisted their hair be worn smoothed back into small ballerina knots. ("It's chic and trouble-free.") Earrings could be studs of pearl or some small stone or nothing. "Nothing that sparkles," she warned. Arthur's Girls needed to look great, uniform and efficient. Each one was carrying a small Lucite clipboard containing notes on all the artwork in the show, a price sheet, sales forms and business cards. They had been drilled mercilessly. They knew when to talk, when to be quiet or nod pleasantly or do nothing at all. "Keep a pen in your hands at all times, look interested, don't annoy the guests and know where you're needed before we have to ask." This was Beth's mantra and all six girls knew it by heart.

Veronica, Gus' counter girl, who had ached to be hired as one of Arthur's Girls but was turned down, was selected to act as Communications Relay. She was to be on extra-special high alert. She was wondering aloud what her appointment really meant when Beth looked at her sternly and said, "Just be ready." She stalked off. Veronica shrugged and left the gallery. It was only a short walk back to the Shoppe. She was hungry. There was still time to get a sandwich if she dressed now.

Inside the office-cum-changing room set up at the gallery, Veronica found her outfit for the evening on a set of hangers. It consisted of a pair of skinny ink-black jeans and a hip-length, green-ish/gray long-sleeved t-shirt with the image of Mercury on the front. "If you say so," she said aloud to the empty room as she changed her clothes. She smoothed back her long black hair and wrapped it into a tight Psyche's Knot. Into her ear lobes she pinned small pearl studs. Taking a final check of herself in the mirror, she nodded approval and let herself out the back door of the Gallery, walking down the pathway beside the building. It was two short blocks to the street and another two to reach Gus' Donut Shoppe. The door was open, which meant Gus was there. "Hey," she called. He was sitting in a booth having a cup of coffee.

"Hey," he replied and continued to sip the hot liquid. "You look very nice."

"Thanks. I don't see what the big deal is. It's jeans and a jersey."

"It's neutral-chic and your friend there," (indicating with a nod of his head at the image on her jersey), "is Mercury. Messenger of the Gods."

"Oh." She paused. "Was I supposed to know that?"

"Probably," he shrugged. "But I don't know if the good citizens of our fair town do or if they would care, even if they did know. They think they are gods," saying which he smiled to himself.

"Uh, would you care to explain that?" Veronica asked as she poured herself a glass of milk and went to work on building a medium-sized roast beef sandwich

Gus watched Veronica over the rim of his coffee cup. "No."

"Fine," she said, slipping into the booth, sat opposite to Gus and began to eat. "Mmmm. Good sandwich," she commented and continued eating. She knew Gus was watching her and that was what she intended. He already was aware of her – in the way that a man should be. Naturally he thought he was way too old for her, but she would handle that, when the time came. She had already made up her mind. Now she just needed to be patient, while Gus decided to agree with her. After eating, she covered herself with an apron, washed her dishes, finished wiping down the serving counter and cashed out her drawer.

"Aren't we taking this all just a tad too seriously, Gus?" she asked as she handed him the bag of money.

He got up to straighten the paper menus in the 'Take One" box by the front door. "Which part of tonight's festivities are you referring to?" he replied, almost smiling. He didn't mind a little game of 'high school cat & mouse'. Veronica was a cutie and she knew it.

"All of it, I guess. With six Arthur's Girls, I really don't see why they need me. I mean,

it would have been fun to dress up nice and hobnob, but "Communications Relay"? I don't

know what that means. When I asked Beth, she wouldn't answer. Sort of stupid, if you ask me."

"I see. You've lived here most of your life but you just don't know these people very well. I do. They take their art very very seriously."

"Now, listen, Gus. Everyone – and I do mean *everyone* – knows Maggie is going to be a hit. She's already in the big time and this show will just make her bigger. I mean, it's in the bag.

People are gonna pay Arthur the fortune he's asking for her paintings. Every big shot around here wants to own something Maggie painted. They all gotta have at least one on the living room wall or they'll be considered failures and has-beens. So," (here she put her hands on her hips), "what is the big deal?"

Gus was smiling. He didn't do it all that often. Veronica amused him. He liked her no-nonsense feistiness.

She was pretty. She was human. The genuine article – contrary to the genus of many of Fleetwater's fair citizenry, as he was wont to describe the town's inhabitants. Mating was a difficult proposition. Certainly there was no mixing between races. Well, no one had tried it so far. The concern for what would be the result unnerved everyone. Therefore, all the children were the humanoid offspring of human visitors who decided to settle down here. So far, no one had yet twigged to that, although it was likely that eventually someone would. Another thing to worry about.

He wished the problem didn't exist, because Gus liked Veronica more than any other female he knew – or had ever known, for that matter. He had never been one to coil and squeeze – snake balls weren't his thing. He just hadn't thought much about mating and nesting and all of that. What surprised him was that he had just figured it out. He liked Veronica. That's what he knew. However, he was 15 years her senior. Such an age difference on Mindar was nothing notable. Here on Earth it did matter. It caused comment and controversy. Also there was Arthur to deal with. He would throw a fit, of course.

Suddenly, just at that moment, Gus was also thinking, much to his surprise, maybe he didn't care if Arthur would disapprove because the chances of Gus shipping back to Mindar were becoming less and less likely. He had known it for awhile. He just hadn't admitted it to himself so openly. He also realized that if he actually expressed his feelings for this human girl, and she reciprocated, it meant eventually telling her everything. That was not permissible per their Mission orders naturally. Getting involved with an alien life form was really really asking for trouble.

Leaving the group was one thing – like James – but staying here and domesticating with a human ... was he serious?

"What are you thinking?" Veronica asked as she sat back down in the booth.

"Oh, nothing much."

"Hmm. I don't think I believe you. That look on your face is not a 'nothing much' kind of look. I thought we were just having some useless conversation here – even though it was pretty one-sided. I guess you may be tired of being the duly elected the Complaint Department ..."

"I was thinking," he said, interrupting her.

"Yeah, well. I guessed that. I mean, one minute we're talking – sort of – and the next, you're kind of ... uh ... um ..."

He looked at her and he was still smiling. Apparently he had decided. Let The Mazes protect him from what he was about to do.

"I like you."

"I like you, too, Gus. A donut shop is a good place to work, if you like donuts."

"I don't think you heard me. What I'm saying is I *like* you."

This made Veronica go utterly silent. Her eyes opened a bit wider. "Oh."

Those eyes were way too much 19-year-old for him. "Never mind," Gus said. "I'll cash out the other drawer. You go get dressed. It'll be fine."

But she was still sitting.

"Go on. You're done for the night. Scoot."

"You said you like me."

He hesitated. He thought that dangerous moment had passed. Apparently not.

"Yes. I did say that."

Well, this was a river he could cross only once. And in that moment he knew he wasn't going back to Mindar when the Mission was complete. James had not confided in anyone when he jumped ship, so to speak. One day he was there, a member of the team, and the next he was gone, leaving only a note to explain himself, which Arthur would have ripped to shreds considering the rage he was in, if Beth hadn't salvaged it. None of the team ever got the idea that James had met an Earth woman and wanted to domesticate. It wasn't like the King of England abdicating his throne for an American divorcee. It was worse. James had left the group all by himself, to be by himself, to absorb the human body he was wedded to until he was totally human. He had already expressed his extreme disagreement with the campaign targeting young Maggie Malone. Since Arthur would not give up this ill-conceived plan, James wrote, that left him no alternative. He was leaving the group. He would live and die a human being. It had never happened before. It had never even been considered possible.

Gus continued in silent review of their group history. None of the others really knew James very well. He thought James would survive here. And he would survive well. He had a quick mind. It was his ability to take well thought-out action that had appealed to Control in the first place. They always wanted to send out steady types. In which case, Arthur was a mistake, and once James was gone, Nick – his replacement, who should have been a hard working little slitherer – had turned out instead to be a bit of a psycho with pretensions.

It was assumed that everyone eventually would be going back to Mindar except James, and a new group would take their place. Except that now ... well, he would have to take the next step, if he was staying. Really staying. Was he up to this? Feelings, commitment, being a member of a group of two, life shared, life as a human? Did he want to do this?

"You are some deep fellow. I just thought you were the quiet type."

"I am the quiet type."

"I'm listening."

"So I see." He smiled.

Veronica smiled back. Gus really didn't smile that often, she thought again. He had a pretty good smile. She'd been working for Gus for nearly three years now. That had given her a chance to see a lot of him. So far, she liked what she saw. The rare smile was a bonus.

Looking out the window, Gus knew there was no foot traffic. The whole town had migrated to Gallery Alley. The restaurants over there were handling all the business of feeding the populace and the huge influx of visitors. No one in a suit or a cocktail dress would be buying donuts. He could close up if he wanted to.

"I may have started something here that isn't such a good idea," he said and picked up the cash bag and walked it to the small safe in the office.

Veronica stayed put.

Gus came back out of the office, walked over the other register and cashed it out. He made a second trip into the office and locked that bag in the safe as well. When he came back out, he noticed that she still wasn't doing anything about leaving. In fact, she had started to drink his cup of coffee. That little minx.

"You want a cup of your own?" he asked.

"No."

Gus nodded.

"You want a donut? I can make you a box."

"Okay. I like ..."

"I know the kind you like," he said and proceeded to fill a box with plain crullers, a few raised, a couple of powdered and some chocolate glazed. He closed it, tied it with string and walked over to the booth. He set it down.

"Thank you."

"You're welcome."

She pulled the box over and untied the string. Lifting up the lid, she surveyed the contents. She took out one of the plain crullers. Gus watched. Breaking it in half, she offered him one.

What is a snake like me doing with a girl like this? he asked himself.

"You must be doing some mighty deep thinking, Gus."

"I am."

"Want half?" she asked.

He took the piece of cruller and set it down on his side of the table. Then he took her hand. He was alert to see if she wanted to pull away. Even a molecule of uncertainty in her presence would have registered. He was on high alert.

"No," he said looking at her with great interest. "I want it all."

Chapter Nine

Penelope and Stacy (the nieces of Mrs. Austin-Miller) were on hand as extra help, to do

as they were told, whatever that included – having been warned to stay sharp! Beth had them dressed in freshly-washed medium-blue jeans and white, long-sleeve t-shirts with the gallery logo on it.

Parker had whispered to Maggie during a run-through the day before the actual opening, "You'd think it was the job of the century – those girls. Like the Rockettes or singing with Ray Charles."

"It practically is," Maggie whispered back. "Working for Arthur does seem to be a stepping stone up."

"Well, stairs go both ways ..." Parker mumbled.

"Never mind, sister mine. All will be well. I'm hungry. Let's get dinner. I want a steak and a big baked potato. I'm sooo hungry ..." and they loped off to Hudson's Surf & Turf.

Everyone involved with the planning understood that the windows would be covered with lined, black velvet curtains which would permit no light to come through. Each panel was stitched to the next. There would be no peeking. For the two days prior to the show the Gallery was closed in preparation. Elegant signage out front announced the opening. The buzz was huge.

Finally it was the end of the afternoon of the big day. Parker had a little free time so she moseyed over to the Gallery. She was happy for Maggie to be having all this fuss made over her work. For one thing, it was totally deserved ... for another ... but a conversation between Arthur's Girls and Beth caught her attention and she arranged herself to listen in. "General Beth" was giving her troops their orders. That woman. My god. Who talks to people like that?

Parker noticed The Girls were paying full attention and didn't seem to mind. Parker had heard enough. As far as she was concerned, it was just more like bullying – and if not exactly like Richard's style, it was too close to it for comfort. Parker needed to get some fresh air immediately. She'd make one quick stop at the E-Café, then it would be time to go help Maggie dress.

At 7 p.m. The Girl of The Hour sat in a club chair and watched while Parker dressed first. She thought her friend had chosen wonderfully. Taffeta silk. It was a unique, red Stewart plaid, one-piece jumpsuit. Wide pant legs, sailor collar and a dramatically long black silk middy tie. Her shoes were Chanel black leather flats with black patent leather toes. (Well, more French-Scottish than Italian tonight but she still looked great.) Over her long straight blond hair Parker had fitted a black velvet beret with its jaunty comma of material at the top center. The beret looked smashing settled straight across her brow.

Now it was Maggie's turn, seeing that her makeup was finished. Parker had even spritzed her face with some stuff to keep her make-up from needing a touch-up. Zipped into a new black wool and silk-blend sheath dress, the lines perfectly fit her curvaceous figure. They had picked out the dress together in New York with the largess of Tony's credit card. "I could have paid for this myself. It's my opening, you know."

"But why not allow us the pleasure of contributing ... at least let's hope none of the dress shop people in

271

Fleetwater figure out it isn't one of theirs ..." and they laughed.

Taking command of the hairbrush, Parker gave a final stab at Maggie's abundant dark red curls which were shiny and fresh and newly pruned. One side was almost tamed by an antique diamond barrette which pulled the left side up high, behind her ear.

"Very fetching, " she said, admiring. "Now, show me ... I have to make sure you didn't chip the polish."

"I wore surgical gloves most of the afternoon. It felt stupid ... but now I'm glad. It was a good idea," and she gave Parker a peck on the cheek. "You really are watching my back."

"Show me," Parker ordered. "You can't fool me or distract me with superfluous compliments. This girl," (pointing to herself) "is now officially a 'maven'. What small detail gets by me, I ask you? ... I'll tell you. Nada. Zip. Nyet."

"That's why Fortelli is desperate to keep you."

"Which is exactly why Signor Fortelli wants to keep me. But we'll discuss that later. Hands," she ordered a third time and Maggie presented her hands. Inspection was passed.

Maggie was glad that Parker had wrestled her to the nail salon. Her hands were now in that condition Maggie termed "do-nothing soft" and absolutely free of any miniscule bits of paint. Her nails had been soaked, cuticles trimmed and dressed with a warm peach lacquer. The ends French-tipped.

"Ta-dah! Maggie Malone. Girl Artist. Great hands. Okay, now: shoes ..." Parker ordered and Maggie slipped on a pair of black medium-heel patent sling-backs. "Walk for me." Maggie did a circuit around the room. "I am English-y stylish. You are Continental chic. Clothes do speak volumes."

"Did you know," Parker said, "that movie directors sometimes had a set built three-quarters-sized just to make the lead actor look bigger? They did that for John Wayne in "Rio Bravo". And he was already six-four. But it worked. He looked huge. All those little details – they all add up. So, tonight you are an inch taller than me, because I am wearing flats."

"You are a very devious young woman," said Maggie, shaking her head in mock dismay. "We may have made a mistake taking you in when I was younger ..."

"... and it's way too late now to back out," Parker laughed, finishing Maggie's sentence.

They both laughed. Parker continued, "I know it's a small detail but tonight is your night. It can't hurt." (*And where is Friend Boyd?* The rat. She wouldn't ask. Maggie hadn't mentioned it so she wouldn't either.)

At this very instant Maggie was checking herself in the mirror, noting that she looked as she felt. Very dressed up, a bit flushed with excitement but totally ready.

"I'm ready for my close-up, Mr. DeMille," she mimicked in a low throaty purr, glancing at her friend from the corner of her eye.

Parker laughed. Parker almost always laughed at her jokes. It one of the ways Maggie was sure that her friend was happy, that their friendship was secure.

They heard a knock on the door. "Maggie?"

They both recognized the voice. "Coming, Beth. Just putting on the finishing touches."

"Well, we need you. Now."

Parker opened the door to let Beth see the finished product.

"You do good work, Parker. I'll give you that. You do good work. Maggie, you look ... perfect. Come along ..." Turning around, Beth headed back down the hall to the main room of the gallery, expecting that Maggie and Parker would follow. Which they did. No sense staging a rebellion over this Maggie and Parker had agreed when they compared notes earlier in the day.

The opening was bigger, better, more exciting, more electric than anything Maggie had imagined. It was beyond huge. She really was The Girl of The Hour. She beamed like the lighthouse at Land's End.

It all began at exactly 8:00 p.m. sharp when Arthur's Girls dramatically unlocked the wide double doors, placing unalike but same-sized dolphin sculptures like chocks to hold them back, then melted away while Arthur and Beth bracketed the doors to greet the milling crowd now swarming in. They drew back the long velvet curtains so passersby could now look inside again and see the artwork displayed on the long, freshly painted, matt walls. When it got too cool, or the crowd no long generated enough body heat, the doors would be closed. For now, people were streaming in with great enthusiasm and there was enough motion and body heat aplenty to make the two rooms comfortable.

Guests were directed to the bar on the left to pick up filled champagne flutes. Next stop was the buffet. Clever black Chinese take-out boxes with handles were laid in rows. Each had already been filled with a delicious sampling of dim sum, wontons and spring rolls. That way the people could saunter about with the small box, assuage their appetites, munch and sip, while admiring the art filling the walls.

At 10:30 p.m. the gallery was still full. Looking around at the happy throng, Maggie escaped into the Powder Room. She knew Boyd was missing in action, but he had called. She would forgive him because Parker was here: Thank you, God. Thank you, God. "Come as soon as you can," she said and he promised he would. She turned the cell phone off and tucked it back inside her evening bag.

She examined her image in the mirror and saw that it was time to repair her lipstick, "Red Excitement". That dramatic name had given the friends a good laugh when they bought it. Giving her hair one last check, she knew it was time to get back out there and "win one for the Gipper". The fact was the evening was going brilliantly, each phase smoothly segueing to the next. Oscar had really and truly orchestrated this evening. Maggie also had to admit that Beth was doing a fine job. As for Arthur, he was reveling. She peeked out the door of the Ladies' Room. Across the floor she could see Oscar chatting with a small group of very well-dressed attendees in front of one of the big paintings.

Next she spotted Beth, standing nearby Oscar, listening attentively. Maggie didn't begrudge the woman her ability, but there was something that niggled at the corner of her mind about Beth. Not every time. Just sometimes. A memory perhaps? Something Maggie saw ... that reminded ... but no.

Presciently Beth turned and looked in Maggie's direction just at that moment and caught her peeking out from the door to The Ladies. (Hiding in the Powder Room, are we? Come out of your egg, little one. It's perfectly safe.)

Seeing that look on Beth's face, Maggie decided, even while not knowing the significance, Beth Barrett was a strange person and yet she was running the logistics perfectly. Even being nice to me, in her own weird way. Okay, Beth. Truce. For tonight. Because, for the next two months, I won't have to see you or think about you or wonder what's really going on. I'm pretty certain, it can't be entirely kosher, Maggie concluded.

Scanning the crowd further, Maggie found Parker standing in front of one of the small- format paintings having a nice chat with a total stranger. It would be so good to have Parker all to herself again – okay, not exactly all to herself. There was Tony and his family and Mr. Fortelli ... anyway, this time next week Maggie would be in Italy with Boyd helping Parker and Tony get married. (She had decided Boyd was definitely coming with them. Now she just had to tell him – when she saw him.) Life had never been this good. Maybe it never would be again but right now, it was so good it almost hurt.

Beth was smiling. But she had another reason. Everyone who was anyone of consequence had molted. What a bother that had been. It had amused her that certain individuals (who would remain nameless) had gone nearly hysterical trying to find a safe place to shed.

But everyone had managed. And now, here they were. All smart and smelling fresh. It was quite a turnout.

The transport had taken a few of the older members of the community back to Mindar. It was time for some of those almost-gone-native to retire. All their human friends thought they were relocating to Miami. So they were. Almost. It was similar, she supposed. For her, Miami couldn't hold a candle to the Noave.

When Arthur found a free moment, he threw back a second glass of champagne, hoping that would calm him down, which it didn't, and subsequently dragged Oscar into his office, holding him by the lapels again. He was practically hysterical. "You will find a replacement for Maggie Malone or I just may find a replacement for you. I will not be thwarted! Do you hear me? Handle it or you could find yourself on the next transport ship out of here!" and he marched out of the office alone. Oscar stayed behind. It was the crisis he had hoped would never happen. Arthur's plans only included success and dazzle. Some remedy would have to be found. Maggie's departure was causing chaos. Oscar was no fool. He knew why he had been included in this Mission. This was where he, Oscar, excelled – accomplishing targets out of practically thin air where others would fail to achieve. But he also knew, if it wasn't for Maggie, he might have gone home a long time ago. Since Mission Control had approved Oscar's petition to be a part of this adventure, Arthur had no choice but to accept Oscar. So what if Oscar had insisted on being South American. It was the identity he wanted and it was the identity he would have. What Arthur had insisted was that Oscar work for the gallery – and not retire as a citizen of

Fleetwater. As long as he was here, he had to work. Oscar had agreed.

All Arthur's demands, blustering and denial couldn't erase the fact that Maggie was going to Italy just at the very moment when a mob of newly-arrived, very rich, aesthetic-starved Mindarians were settling in for their big feed. We've promised them, and oh, by the rings of Saturn, we are going to deliver someone, something, somehow. But there wasn't enough of Maggie's work to satisfy everyone. It was a dilemma. It was a terrible dilemma.

Oscar could just imagine the absolute ream of complaints about to be filed. It would be an electronic report storm hitting Control. The Expedition Council on Mindar would do what Councils like that always do: shift the demand back down – and it was all going to settle on Arthur's head and shoulders in very short order. And what landed on Arthur, landed on Oscar. Life was going to be hell. The Noave would be chilly by comparison. Moreover, all these rampant emotions were playing havoc with his body mechanics.

Walking out of the office, Oscar nearly bumped into Arthur, who, it turned out, hadn't progressed very far after all. He was standing in the short hallway with closed his eyes. Hearing the other close behind, he waved Oscar away with a limp hand. So Oscar excused himself silently and continued on towards the exhibition space itself.

A backward glance at Arthur's face was like reading newspaper headlines in blazing 48-point type. It would be up to Oscar to find someone of Maggie's caliber to replace her.

Arthur heard Oscar pass him in the hallway but his attention was on the trouble to come. All Arthur knew was that Maggie's intention to go to Italy was unspeakable. She couldn't do it. It was ... treason!

Oscar was certain that, in the long run, the Mindar locals living here wouldn't care a whit which artist it was. Being the toast of the town was just a big bonus. Anything with color and a frame stuck around it, a big opening, all the dressing up, the glitz – that's what made these people happy. If you could now call them 'people'.

It struck him with force that this problem had been brought about because Arthur now thought there was a difference! He never used to before. Of course his taste was mercurial ... even with his high hopes for Maggie's success, one couldn't be certain which way Arthur would blow for the next artist he championed. Oscar did realize, however, in a relative blink of an eye, something about Maggie's art had upset Arthur's equilibrium. What Mindarian had ever considered the quality of the art? Frankly: never. When did a Hostess Cupcake and Gateau Chocolate de Grand Marnier stop being the same? And yet, it had happened. Maybe this change in Arthur's taste was a fluke? That remained to be seen. For now, he was raving about having great art and great artists and nothing less would be acceptable. The local Mindarians were echoing his chant. Actually, Oscar realized ages ago that all artists were not equal. It's just that understanding wasn't part of the plan. It was wisdom gained through experience. The only promise to visiting Mindarians was: art. Aesthetics. Color. Paintings. Drawings. Later on it would be music and dance, and all the rest of it. Everything we don't have anymore on Mindar.

Oscar sighed. Maybe what I need is a rest. A good long rest. Shed this body and just find myself a big warm rock and have myself a long snooze. It had been over a decade since he'd entertained the thought. He tried imagining a nest, eggs, a quiet sandy place and waves of radiation blanketing his form. On the opposite side of the equation: a bed with pillows and linens, a baby that cried and needed diapering, a home with a roof and windows and doors ... I shouldn't have to even think about this. It shouldn't be happening. Mindar and Earth are more than just worlds apart. Our living forms are totally divergent. Maybe we should have all stayed home on Mindar and minded our own business in the first place?

And yet ... perhaps it was inevitable. Having lost all ability to make art, we were going to have to do something about the problem. Life with no aesthetics? Oh, no. Well, this was a hell of a solution.

To compound the problem, Oscar felt that some familiar part of himself was slipping away. He rarely spoke Minda anymore. He was even forgetting the prayers. With every passing day, he was changing. Some changes were more imperceptible than others, but he could feel it. How he cared about nuance, how he recognized quality. That was all different.

Everything on Mindar had evolved into a form of utilitarianism. Everything was designed for ... what we really are. Earth was a ridiculous planet for anyone of our kind to attempt to live on. It wasn't suited for anything but humans. All the unnecessary décor, additions, trimmings, bits and pieces ... all a Mindarian ever needs is a large flat sunny rock and he's happy. Of course you put fifty of us together and we're going to have a great big happy writhe ... but otherwise, to be frank, when you're built like us, what else is there?

And so Oscar concluded: we've been here too long. Mining the aesthetics here on Earth was a great idea. In fact it was The Great Idea. But it's changed Arthur. He's in the middle of it and doesn't see the forest for the trees. He was never that steady and now he's an emotional mess. Nick is totally wrapped up in French movies. He thinks he *is* a French movie. James is gone. No one saw that coming. As for the Mindarians here? We should just load everyone onto transports and take them through the reversal process. The trip is a long one. Plenty of time to reacclimate. One good group slither and they'll forget all about houses, chairs, feet and eating quiche ... and in that instant Oscar remembered clearly the argument between Arthur and James which had had such enormous repercussions.

"Let's get out of here, before it's too late," James had insisted.

"We have a Mission."

"But it's going wrong. Can't you see it? It was an experiment. Okay. The experiment was tried and found wanting. We'll find another way to restore culture to Mindar."

Arthur snorted. "And what exactly will you paint with? Your snout? On what? We don't have canvas on Mindar! We have just enough hybrids to do what those of us who have totally acclimated can't do anymore. Don't be ridiculous. Everything is going just fine. Here they have thousands of artists. Or millions, even. Why shouldn't we have it? It's just laying around – like stones on the beach. It's here to be harvested. So, let's harvest." He had walked to the middle of the gallery with arms open wide. "Can't you just smell it?" He flicked his tongue to catch the fragrance. It's delicious." He gave a small shiver of pleasure.

Oscar remembered how Arthur turned around and said, "I like having this human body. It's quite useful. I shall perhaps miss it for awhile when I get home but that time will pass and life will go on."

"But what if you can't get used to not having a humanoid body? What if ..." James stopped.

"What if ... what?" Arthur asked.

James just shook his head.

"Just as I thought. Oh, no. We're not leaving. Our plan is working. You just need to stop being a ninny and get to work."

So Arthur wouldn't leave and James wouldn't stay. No one knows where he's gone to. The Mazes only knew if James was still alive. Maybe it would be better if he wasn't. The idea of him being caught trying to shed ... no. That would have been in the newspapers. Okay ... so anything could have happened and none of it good. Anyway, his replacement was the totally unsatisfactory Nick. Terrible. Just terrible.

Oscar found that his thoughts were getting all mixed up. I don't know who I am anymore. This was perhaps the one problem he felt inadequate to handle. It even made one want to cry (if tears were possible). Oscar had never tried to use his tear ducts. Just the theory was enough for him.

"All right," he whispered to the spot which Arthur had just vacated. "I'll find someone to replace her somehow."

CHAPTER TEN

Back in the front room everything was going swimmingly. Three Hollywood arc lights stationed outside in the street continued scanning the darkness in silvery figure eights. Why not? After all, this was IT. This was her night. Oscar made a quick trip outside to inform the lighting engineer he could shut down at 2 a.m. but not before.

Meanwhile, Maggie was back in The Ladies. She closed the inch of open door again and went back inside. She needed another minute. Taking care to smooth the back of her dress so it wouldn't wrinkle, she sat down in one of the nice chairs. Movie actresses used to rest on tilted boards, she reminded herself – like Marilyn Monroe on the set of "The Prince and The Showgirl". Maggie had read about that. Well, she didn't need a board to lean on.

What she had done was stuck it out through all those bad times and disappointments – terrible enough to crush a lesser person ... but she had held on. So, now, just outside the door was her dream – her idea of paradise. Not the quiet, sensible I-just-do-my-work sort of artist. No. Maggie had wanted to cause a sensation and now here it was. The only thing inside the gift horse was a happy mob of hungry art patrons. They had been waiting for her signal to come piling out ... and now here they are. She would remember this October night as long as she lived. Arthur had spared no expense. Oscar had pulled out the stops, hadn't he? He had even hired a sommelier!

Ever since the gallery had begun representing her, there had been sales. Even the smallest of her paintings had gained interest. Maggie now always had commissions waiting to be filled – even while she executed in secret the six big ones. It was with those that she had taken her biggest risk. Arthur, she was pleased to note, had immediately appreciated the scope of the big paintings and decided that owning one of these would have to cost the lucky art patron a small fortune. Keep them rare – don't make too many, he said. After which he said a great many other things. Most of which made equal sense.

One way or the other Maggie Malone, Girl Artist, had arrived. And when she came back from Italy, the canvas for Number Seven would be ready and waiting to be created.

She took another peek out the door of the restroom – her third such visit because her bladder didn't know how to calm down and cooperate. Just for an instant Maggie had a flash. She remembered a dream: looking through a peephole in a fence of some kind looking at ... what? Was it a horse? Oh, dreams. They take life and mix it all up. It's all nonsense. Here comes Parker. She'll make me come out. I wish Boyd was here. That stupid client of his, telling him the stepladder for the tree house was wrong. Poor Boyd ... letting the door open another few inches, she made Parker squeeze inside.

"Well, Arthur's Girls certainly are doing a fine job ..." Maggie noted.

But Parker wasn't listening. Something had her attention. Something about "The Girls" ... something about ... what? their quietude ... no. What was it? ... She interrupted Maggie.

"There's something about The Girls – it reminds me of ... Oh, I don't know. It's right on the tip of my tongue ... it's important. Oh, god. Let me think. Where was I when I had the thought ... okay. I was at the reception desk ... wait. I can remember. I have to." She put her hand on Maggie's arm. "I'm standing at the desk and ... and Beth is talking to ... Veronica. That's right. She, Veronica, that is, has her back to me. And I'm seeing ... what am I seeing? Her clothes, the door ... no, it's Veronica. It's ... it's ... ooh ..."

The door opened and Beth walked in. Her almost-black wavy hair and blue eyes contrasted dramatically with her pale, unsuntanned skin. "We need you ... oh, am I interrupting?"

Was everything Beth said always spoken in that low voice reminiscent of Lauren Bacall, but in this case, a slyly supercilious tone? Parker questioned herself silently with supreme annoyance.

"We'll be right out. Our Girl Artist needed a break. Me, too. Five minutes, okay?" Parker answered calmly.

"Of course." Beth backed out.

"Where was I? Come on. Help me with this," Parker insisted.

"You said you were looking at Veronica ..."

"That's right ..." Parker closed her eyes again. "Okay, so I'm looking at Veronica's back ..." Parker sighed. "It's her hair. That little knot. It's that little ballerina knot."

"Very chic," Maggie interjected. "Of course not everyone looks good in one of those. You have to have really fine bones and ...

"Don't interrupt."

"Sorry."

Parker opened her eyes. "No, no, it's all right. Who do we know that used to wear their hair that way?"

"And this is important because ..."

"I wish I knew. It seems important." She saw that Maggie was being extraordinarily patient. "Okay. Forget about it. Let's go back in. I'm going to figure it out later. Let's go,

Artist Girl. Your fans await," and she pushed open the door to let Maggie through just as Stacy walked in.

"Please. You need to come out. The natives are restless ..." was all the girl would say and darted quickly through the swinging door, back to her assigned station.

Maggie and Parker exited the Powder Room, stopping to see who was where and what might be needed.

Up on the walls was art of a style and subject matter that three years ago would have been unheard of from the hand of Maggie Malone. *Did I really do all that?* It had started with the toaster. She knew that. But look what had followed. Somehow she had taken a really good idea and from that created a whole new visual language for herself and these people loved what she was doing. That was for sure.

Take a big breath, Maggie, she said to herself, silencing all other editorial thought, and with a pat on Parker's arm, she stepped into the flow of the room again. In the instant she could feel Arthur Cotillion almost boring a hole through the wineglass sipping, crab-salad-on toast-points snacking throng until his eyes reached her. Maggie waved her fingers and pointed towards a group of patrons standing around one of the big canvases. See you there, she mouthed.

Coming to stand by Arthur, Beth was whispering in his ear. "Maybe Little Miss Maggie isn't going off to Italy after all, hmmm?" He desperately wanted to ask what she meant but there was no time.

Just like any humanoid woman, Beth slithered away before he could hook her by the arm and demand to know more. She had work to do, including take count of the unopened bottles of wine. Moving towards the bar, she considered her own theory concerning Maggie's departure. Namely: she's not going anywhere.

Beth came back across the floor and grabbed Arthur's handsomely suited arm. He was looking out the large front show window, enjoying the night sky, taking a moment of respite himself. She pulled him in close, shoved her delectable tongue into his ear and diddled it. His eyeballs nearly popped. Electric currents ran madly up and down his spinal column. The skin around his neck flushed bright blue, which was luckily quelled by the voluminous cravat that swaddled it.

"Now, you be good and we'll have more of that ..." and she flounced off again. Beth was not going to wait for Oscar to step into this breach.

Arthur was speechless. Sparks of light were going off in front of his eyes. Oh, Mazes, he would be good, he promised himself. Whatever it took, tonight he would be perfect. In spite of this rebellion by Maggie, it was hard not to be nearly saturated with pleasure already, as he looked around the room, knowing there was still more to come because Beth had promised.

Oh, meteorites – the evening was still young. He noted with great satisfaction that everyone who mattered here in Fleetwater had come (despite being tantalized by other invitations). Considering that Fleetwater was a cornucopia of art, it was more a matter of what to buy first (and how to do it without attracting undo attention from outsiders)! Arthur could name a few who had shamelessly spent a fortune on interstellar travel to get here in time, despite the strain of making such a journey. And what about the trouble of getting fitted for human bodies and systems. Learning to walk upright. Learning human speech. What to do with arms, legs, the whole lot. It was quite amusing in a way, in a challenging, interesting, horrid, perverse sort of way. Mindarians so liked their leisure, but the pull to be here was enormous for those who still remembered, still had any aesthetic sensibility.

So Beth was taking care of the new arrivals – these very important people – the cream of Mindar's crop of high society. They had been promised. Now they were here to see for themselves. Luckily for everyone, The Earth Girl's new paintings were *truly* the feast Arthur had promised them. Hadn't Beth said to Arthur just that morning: think anaconda eyeing the biggest, tastiest rabbit ever? Oh, yes. Oh my, our Mindarians will pay handsomely for even one of these rabbits. And just think: we alone have more rabbits than you could ever hope for.

After all, where Arthur, Beth and 'everyone who was anyone' came from, *there were no more rabbits*. There hadn't been any rabbits in centuries. Who could say why? Actually, who cared! But Earth? Ah, Earth was Rabbit Heaven – if you had enough money, enough credits, enough pull. This place was Rabbit Heaven, indeed. Oh, my word, yes.

Beth's promise of a crazed night had interrupted his focus. Arthur knew he needed to regain his composure. He stayed by the show window and continued to look out. Actually, it was just a place to stand and let be for a few minutes. All the hubbub was behind him. He wasn't looking at all. His attention was all on the flaps over his ear valleys that continued buzzing with joy. One of these days he wouldn't have to wear those damn fake coverings. Transport home to Mindar was just a few measly decades away. Come on, Earthlings. Let's go! Everything will be easy pickings: a quick bit of 'take me to your leader and Bob's your uncle.' Wasn't that the ultimate plan? At that point no one will care what we really look like.

All the prep work had been done: Area 51, The Grays, Crop Circles ... random abductions to prime the fuse. Oh yes. That and another fifty years of 'science fiction' would do the trick nicely. It was easy. Meet the poor struggling writer in a downtown café, get him drunk, drug him, plant the story, he writes it, it gets published and voila! Earth people eat this stuff up. Mindar might be a pimple on the ass of the universe right now, but in fifty years we'll have a treaty with the United Nations.

The leaders of Mindar were even now thinking big: stadiums full of pulsating patrons eyeing voraciously the art displayed in tiers from floor to rafter like the official salons and galleries of old Paris. People will have to wear binoculars to see the goodies at the top, and wriggle down in order not to miss a single piece of art lining the bottom row on the wall. They won't want to miss a frame. And they will buy. Oh, my. The walls will be empty when the buying frenzy is over. Department store basement sales won't be able to hold a candle to our consumption. *We know how to buy!* Everyone happy, saturated, filled to overflowing, excited beyond measure ... until the next time.

Wasn't it just the most delicious plan? Planet Earth was simply lousy with art. Aren't most of the artists and their art going to waste here? Expeditions from Mindar had toured some of the other solar systems but frankly, each fell short of the obscene amount of art being made here on Earth by comparison. Well, we won't have to withhold our full interest much longer. Not to worry, my hungry darlings. Those of you still biding your time on Mindar won't have to wait much longer, Arthur gloated. Not much longer at all.

It was a small matter that filling every need an artist desired actually sometimes killed the artist – or at least, wore them out badly. After all, what was a short, dramatic, successful life compared to the draining obscurity most of them languished in anyway? I mean, he thought, let's be reasonable. There are positively countries full of these poor wretches!! What a waste.

There will be shows, tours, art marathons, year-long parties, raves, competitions, garlands awarded, money, gratification of every kind, lights, glamour – oh, comet, isn't it our destiny to fulfill and even exceed every need, every dream of these poor, underappreciated artists? After all, we can. Give us an economy and we can trade. Our finance is unlimited. Mindar is nothing if not lousy with mineral wealth. We are filthy rich. We can afford it all.

Back on Mindar Arthur had thought long and hard before taking on this assignment. He had studied up and decided the expedition really did suit him perfectly. Of course some of the dears will expire. It couldn't be helped. Paint for a year and fall over dead. Sculpt, sculpt, sculpt and oops. Two years later, worn to a frazzle or ... perhaps dead as a door nail. Arthur giggled to himself. The image was very impelling. Some artist – white with marble dust – poised with chisel in hand and – whoopsie daisy – over he goes. Too bad. Another giggle. It was all rather humorous. It wasn't as though something bad *had* to happen ... it just seemed to work out that way.

So far the plan had only tapped into the visual arts. But think!! What about the poets. Hah! Even more of them than painters. More poets than grains of sand on the beach ... er, or was it poems written? Well, anyway. Millions more of them.

And musicians. Ah, the scrape and squeal. Lovely. Triangles, bongos, pianos. Divine, all of it. Every tootle and arpeggio.

His mind went sailing while behind him the grand opening partied on. Mentally he tallied up the players in the project: the players and the played, actually. Mindar wasn't the only place suffering along. He could export! There are scads of planets where the populace is still squatting by fires scratching their naked behinds. They're not even up to charcoal drawings on cave walls ... or places like ... still can't pronounce the word ... places like *that*. There were worlds he knew of where there was so much metal and shine, but it was the art that had been lost. Sacrificed, in some cases. Like on Mindar. Nary a painting or a mural. So, they need us. Come to think of it, isn't funereal art also big business? ... now Arthur smiled (because to laugh out loud would have drawn attention and he wanted this respite to remain private) ... but he did remember it well. That time when he had laughed so hard he nearly fell off the rock he was sunning himself on ... oh, but it was pleasant business remembering that ... but now something *wonderful* was wafting his way. Arthur sniffed. The tip of his tongue, as canny and accurate as the most modern detection equipment, still infused with reptilian cells, made note of breadth and direction. It was everywhere. Delicious.

He set a subdued look on his face. That way he could inhale and still maintain his decorum. Oh, my. It was almost overpowering. He thought he might expire with pleasure. He knew this smell. Mindarians exuded it with their breath and sweat. Such a perfume. The air was ripe with it. Like enormous masses of blooming flowers unleashing their delectable come-hither scents. The throng of art-lovers was right now so busy loving Maggie Malone's paintings, they were oozing hormones of every lovely sort. He could almost eat it with a spoon. And what about the adrenaline? It was almost as luscious as their own happy musk. He loved the smell of that, too.

So, it had turned out that being of ersatz human construction wasn't an entire waste.

Arthur recalled many art exhibitions presented over the years. Many moments of someone standing before a painting in his gallery simply exuding, many times when the good citizens of Fleetwater went quietly, happily mad with all the art ... how does one explain it to someone who doesn't feel it? He remembered Annette Rousseau's opening was quite the thing ... the aroma in the air that night was wild ... but was it *this good*? He had thought so until now. Why did this evening seem so much better? The scent surrounding was so much more potent, it nearly drove him wild.

Maybe he had finally proved to them all that he knew what he was doing. It wasn't a matter of luck. That was part of the pleasure – getting it right time after time. It also meant they loved Arthur Cotillion. Yes, indeed. Oh, the emotion of it was exquisite. Admiration. Wasn't it just divine? It certainly was the elixir he lived for. Kept one young, too. Nothing quite filled Arthur's need so exactly. Not even Beth. He needed to drink deeply of this. And he did. It filled his nostrils and face cavities and he exulted. It washed over him and he smiled. It sloshed through every pore and orifice!

The least he could do was smile. No one would question a smile. Mastering the muscles required to smile was nearly a competitive sport for some Mindarians, but Arthur had done it. Oh, he could smile. He had a catalog of smiles and he used them the way a musician plays an instrument or an artist uses different brush strokes. This was his satisfied smile. The one that only follows when lust has been satiated. That's when Arthur knew he needed to cool down before turning to the throng filling the gallery.

He was indeed feeling triumphant. Without sufficient funds, life on Mindar was for drones. He had no intention of being called back before his account was bulging. He would be so rich, he would never have to go back to ... ugh ... what it was he did before. Luckily his talents were in the multiples. That meant, he wouldn't be leaving Fleetwater as long as he could deliver. Maggie would change her mind. She must. Anything Maggie Malone's heart desired he could provide. Want for nothing. Desire nothing. Just ask me. I can make it all happen. Just paint, Maggie Malone. Above all, paint. And when she was worn out, as was inevitable, there would be another (just like her) agonizing for IT. The Big Time.

His first one hundred years on this outpost had been among the most successful. Others on the same Mission elsewhere had failed miserably or their ability to produce results were so limited, it was hardly worth the effort, but Arthur knew how the game was played.

With so many artists, came so many opportunities. Oh, yes. Earth was prime territory. It was really almost laughable. One just had to know how to handle his fellow Mindarians. The time it took to travel to this outpost could be agonizingly inconvenient and, as he remembered, it was no easy business learning to mimic a Terran ... and all that surgery business. Dreadful. So the trip was a long one, but it was needful. There was so much to accomplish. Of course, once that task of transformation and indoctrination was accomplished ... ahhh, the rewards. All hail the rewards!

From across the room Arthur heard the well-known booming voice of Stewart Rangel (former leader of the dissenting party on Mindar). All that woolgathering and scent invading his cavities was heavenly but now there was work to do. Arthur knew when enough was enough. He turned around to face a room full of activity.

Stewart, that reptile, had already paid $10,000 for a small, early Maggie Malone painting entitled "Eggbeater". He was swooning with delight as his treasured painting received a red dot. Arthur knew the creature had millions of credits on account. (Maggie, of course had no idea who her new patron was.)

Next up was Reed Stamos. That was him over there, drinking champagne, laughing affably. Paid a fortune to look that handsome. Also filthy rich and him hardly out of his shell. Standing beside him was Pinky, his live-in society girlfriend. Half of her clan, The DeLillos, were still damp, but there you go. That's the nouveau riche for you. Their idea of an inaugural swim was a hop in a heated pool in a gated community. Looking at her, however, Arthur had to admit she was quite a cunning little package. And now Reed and Pinky owned "Home on the Range". Having paid $35,000 for the mid-sized canvas, they were nearly floating on air. Spending all that money was wonderful. They would have paid the same for a velvet Elvis, if the truth be told. It just didn't matter! Being society people on Mindar, they had paid a fortune to boot a former Premier and his consort off the transport and take their seats. They were the kind who thought just walking upright was a hoot.

Arthur looked around. He caught sight of Philip Neyman chatting with Maggie. A large potted palm couldn't hide the man's bulk. He still reminded Arthur of a monitor lizard. His family tree was a scandal. Checking his watch, Arthur noted the dial showed nearly 11:30 p.m. He stepped closer, peeked through the fronds to see better.

Phillip had just purchased "Winged Victory" for an impressive $150,000. (Maggie was staggering with all the success this night was bringing.)

Poor Philip. He was so happy, so entranced he had almost inhaled Maggie herself. Right after he purchased his piece, he had to be dragged away by Arthur before something truly dreadful happened – *the way he kept sniffing her.* "My mother loves horses," Philip enthused to Arthur as he was strong-armed over to the buffet.

"Eat a spring roll (and get hold of yourself)," Arthur had hissed into the other's ear.

Just as Arthur left for other points in the room, he looked back and saw Philip reach for the whole plate. Well, happy people are hungry people. Buying art gave some the munchies. Arthur shrugged and kept going. He was needed elsewhere.

When the Fosters bought "Portrait of the Artist As A Young Hellion" an hour later Maggie almost fainted. Quarter of a million dollars – *ca-ching, ca-ching.* Happily Arthur was standing there when the deal was closed, so he was able to get a hold of her elbow as she started to slowly sink to the floor, but it turned out that she had no time to faint or even savor the moment further because the Heilbroner's were also discussing a commission.

Wasn't even the scuttlebutt of it all just so much fun? The Fosters were originally reformed clean water smugglers. They had emigrated to Mindar and tried to corner the market on fizzy water. Of course the Governing Council shut them down as soon as they found out. fizzy water ruins the molting cycle even as it adds a certain drug-like 'frisson' to the experience. It wouldn't do to interfere with a natural cycle in that way. Warmed and cozy is one thing. Too glassy-eyed to shed? ... oh, no. The combined stench alone would kill their population. Either that or drive the inhabitants to a mass migration ... and The Fosters would be on hand, of course, with their fleet of transports, it so happened ... that was all put a stop to before it got out of hand. Mindar's citizens had learned the hard way early on that they had to clean up after themselves. There wasn't any such thing as 'trash collecting' on Mindar. One simply had to keep one's own nest tidy and in good order. It was the law. That's why the Heilbroners were on hand. They being the prosecuting attorneys. The Fosters, they had learned, were adept at fomenting trouble quickly, so the Governing Council sent a prosecutorial staff wherever they traveled. Where the Fosters went, Jim and Lola Heilbroner were always close at hand, in case the Fosters suffered a relapse – albeit a limited possibility here in Fleetwater, but the Fosters were so enterprising – and always enthusiastic about it in the wrong way – they had to be watched. Let them spend, but let us keep watch.)

When "Portrait of the Artist ..." (Number One in the series of the big paintings) sold for two hundred and fifty thousand dollars at midnight, Maggie decided she was having a hard time breathing.

Beth merely watched it all unfold, moving silently here and there, ensuring a smooth operation. It charmed her that Maggie had no notion of the truth, how she had been selected, scrutinized, followed. How her life had been manipulated. Now that was delicious. Sowing the seeds of a destruction was something that actually pleased Beth.

Had Arthur yet mentioned to Maggie that he was bringing Annette back for an Act II? He knew the art patrons now ogling Maggie's work would suddenly stampede to see Annette's charming little paintings without missing a beat. Would Maggie know how to take that? People suddenly no longer interested because they were looking at small-format landscapes with the same elation? Of course Annette's work would sell like candy. Beth wondered: is Maggie the jealous type? Oh, if she was, that would be amusing.

Seen from her position by the buffet, Beth could tracked Arthur as he walked in Maggie's direction, taking his time as he threaded through the still-crowded room. He certainly did love the attention, the adulation. They would be lucky if the doors could be closed before sunup. Photographers had already stopped him several times, and hovering nearby was someone from the Fleetwater Sentinel-Observer anxiously waiting their turn to interview him. (Try not to pontificate, my slitherer, she thought at him.)

What Maggie most noticed was how pale Arthur was. That man should get a little sun once in a while. She would mention it to Beth, in case the woman cared about Arthur after al ...

oh, here comes Arthur.

"That's two so far ... two of the *big ones* ..." he crowed *sotto voce*.

It was great news but Maggie couldn't help noticing his neck. Even though it was covered by a cravat – with that a wild, profuse floral print – so lavishly snuggled under his chin ... was his skin tinged with blue? Was there an aneurism cutting off the blood flow to his brain? Well, no. The mottling was fading now, and it was hard to see anyway under the long hair, so like a maestro.

"Well, my dear. Are you pleased?" He didn't mind if people heard him say that.

Sometimes Maggie felt there was something truly odd about the man. That tongue of his – darting in and out. The only thing missing was the bifurcation at the tip. She concentrated on her reply.

"This evening ... it's utterly fabulous. I don't think you can know. It's the big night I always wanted. I promised myself, if tonight is all there is and someone else is the IT girl tomorrow, at least this was wonderful. I hope you know that."

"Well, well, my dear. I can appreciate your sentiment but listen. You are a success. A genuine success. Your run isn't going to be over for a good long while." (Well, one had to lie about certain things. Of course it wasn't a complete lie. Her run was going to continue – and finally it would be over. For sure.) "I have big plans for you." Indeed he did. Maggie was strong. She loved the limelight. She had many more paintings in her, he was sure of that. She was a regular artistic dynamo. Lucky for us because the frenzy had just begun. Let her art fill the empty aesthetic gullets of the many here in Fleetwater ... even now coming this way is the next ship from Mindar ... and the next and the next ... Maggie must be here, making art, to satisfy that hungry maw.

As Maggie looked at Arthur, a random thought interfered. He may be a bit silly, but he really was dedicated. What was the matter with Parker? Arthur

Cotillion was no Trojan Horse. Here he was, 'inside her gates,' and there were no attacking hordes suddenly revealed.

"I believe a buyer for Number Three is in the pipeline as well. You'll see," he was saying. (In fact, Arthur had been beating off salivating patrons nearly since the doors open. They were indecorously scrabbling like women grabbing willy-nilly at a yard sale. He demanded that they show some restraint. 'Handle yourselves properly or go home'. And the overheated art lovers had tamped down the lids on their evident ardor because no one wanted to go home. They all knew that Arthur didn't mean their townhouses or estates in Fleetwater. He meant *all the way home*.)

Oscar captured Maggie by the elbow. "Excuse me, Arthur ... but I need Our Darling Girl right now."

Maggie looked around for Parker. She was standing by a small table talking to some people. She turned to smile in Maggie's direction. In reply, Maggie mouthed: See? (Meaning, if it wasn't for Arthur, none of this would have happened. Right?)

Parker nodded. It was true. Arthur had delivered — beyond their wildest dreams.

    * * *

One couldn't say the night ever ended. People just finally ran out of steam, they were tipsy with wine and the feeling of (temporary) satiation. Most of her small works had been purchased, and very few of her drawings still remained unsold as well. Purchases were carried home on the spot, if possible. Several stayed to be re-framed. Three of the six big pieces had been purchased, so even with the standard 50/50 gallery split, that meant Maggie was now financially a rather rich young lady. Arthur had hinted there was great interest in the other three large-scale works. Wasn't is marvelous, he told Maggie? Hadn't Arthur assured her that she had nothing to worry about?

Actually the only reason there was anything left on the walls was because Arthur had finally snapped at Morgan Milstern, a very high ranking, ultra-rich Mindarian who could hardly control himself in his ardor to own two of Maggie's remaining three large paintings. Arthur promised to considered his offer, mostly because, money aside, it was understood that Morgan needed some art of magnitude with which to control his personal entourage. Left to themselves they would have behaved more like a pack of hyenas at a kill.

In fact, Morgan had experienced an epiphany that night, standing in front of a wall of Maggie's outrageous paintings. Some notion had gotten hold of him and he had begun to entertain the thought that not all 'rabbits' were the same. It was an idea not to be denied. No, suddenly *not all art was the same*. He thought Maggie was something special. And he liked her, too. Of course this was tantamount to heresy, but there it was. Naturally he didn't dare risk telling Arthur that he believed this girl should live. Morgan would have to think about that later.

"Rein them in," Arthur was saying, "and two of the big ones are yours. It's as simple as that."

Morgan, the financial tycoon, went back to standing at his place before the wall. Up until now getting big paintings had been more like big game hunting. Heads on the wall, bagging the most exotic ... in the next few days,

Morgan would be back with a select few friends. One of them would be permitted to purchase the last of the big paintings, the rest would be left to pant with want. It was one way to use power.

As Arthur watched Morgan leave the gallery, he considered it interesting how he and Morgan often thought differently but the end result was the same. A useful ally. Yes, theirs was a relationship that was developing nicely.

Morgan, on the other hand, was developing something else – a dispatch – preparatory to actual filing. The over-excited mottling hidden by Arthur's voluminous cravat had been spotted by Morgan after all. That was a no-no. Maybe Arthur's time running this project was coming to a close. Maybe it was time to consider handing over the reins to someone younger – like Morgan.

The air in the gallery was getting chilly as the number of remaining visitors thinned out. Arthur instructed two of his Girls to close the doors. "With finesse," he cautioned. "Everything must be done with finesse." She really doesn't have a clue, our little Maggie, Arthur thought with a pleasurable sigh.

At three a.m., being the last two to leave, Parker and Maggie staggered home. They were both sure human feet had never been so tired. Arthur and Beth locked the doors and stayed behind because there was still work to be done.

Oscar said his goodnight – or rather 'good morning' – about 4:30 and headed home. It was just easing past the darkest dark of night. In another hour or so, the sun would be cracking the horizon. It had been grand ... but of course there had been other such nights. He remembered them well. Whatever was wrong with Mindar, no one could say they weren't eager – about certain things, that is.

He was really quite exhausted but he dawdled so long he was still moseying down the street to his cottage when the sun flared over the water, sending long radiant shafts of light across the landscape. He stopped to admire it. Beautiful ... and distracting. It didn't pay to get distracted. He knew the Mission had a problem. We may have to start selling prints even though they all knew Maggie was dead set against it. (And whose fault was that?) They had no permission to make prints. How would they convince her?

The small stock of her paintings being held in reserve wouldn't last very long. Then what? Right now the people wanted Maggie. It had to be Maggie. So much effort had gone into her build-up and into the big solo show, she simply outshone the competition. How others might view her work was of no consequence now. Here in Fleetwater, under these newly changing conditions, their gallery couldn't take just anyone who came along anymore.

He moaned a little. The game had changed. Now they had a reputation to maintain. Not that the other galleries weren't also beginning to feel the pinch, too. Somehow, the issue of quality had snuck in. Oh dear. Really, we're heathens. What do we actually know about art!?

Oscar stood at the entry to the marina and looked down the walkway. A swim had never looked more inviting. He'd ruin his clothes. Stripping down to his skivvies would never be forgiven if anyone spotted him. Instead, he pulled the end of his bowtie and it came loose. Well, that's better than nothing.

If Arthur thinks he can win by playing both sides of this game, he's wrong. This fact of discernment was throwing a major spanner in the works. Oh dear, it was worrisome.

Oscar felt a bit furious. Things had been going fine, just fine ... and then ... what. What had happened? Hmm. It's all to do with Maggie ... James leaving, Nick nearly murdering Parker. Morgan Milstern was positively strutting when he left. What was that about? Now Milstern is one ambitious snake-in-the-grass. So, what's happening? When did we actually start drifting off course?

His arms sagged on the railing. The sky was lightening. It really was a ... (yawn) pretty ... place. He really was tired. The sounds of the new day were beginning. Early birds living aboard their boats were flushing heads, actual birds in the woods beside the road leading into the village were tweeting. The *slap slap* of the tide was hypnotic. Well, the tide was always coming in or out, of course. It has to. I know why, he laughed to himself: because it's a permanent installation. Oscar chuckled at his own joke. Looking at the ocean is a show which never closes. I am getting silly.

Just at that moment, coming down the lane behind him, heading out to the main road, was the dull sound of a large truck shifting through its gear changes. Just a different kind of music, he mused, listening. He went back to his thoughts.

Our great leader, Arthur Cotillion, just *had* to specialize, he mumbled critically. Damn him. He remembered those first decades James was still a member of the expedition and much appreciated by Oscar. Now he sometimes he'd forget about James for months on end. He didn't like that. James had been Oscar's only real friend. *Vig hanish dal. (Never forget.)* Sorry, James. I mustn't let that happen.

At some point James and Beth had gone into the city and one day they stumbled onto a little slip of a girl who was doing marvelous drawings of the zoo animals in Central Park. Maggie Malone. Before that the Fleetwater galleries just took what came along. Artists wandered in, 'convinced' Arthur he should take them up, be their mentor and voila. Everyone had a good time. James had wondered aloud if the little Earth girl might not be something special but it was Beth who had picked up the idea and developed it. James said, no, let's leave it alone. We're doing fine, but Beth was adamant. It must be presented to Arthur. He was expedition leader. Yes. That was what did it. Turned their world upside down. James had seen Maggie first, but it was Beth, that conniver, who had taken the idea to Arthur. James was so sorry. It was really all his fault. Oscar had forgotten that this didn't all start with Arthur, so it wasn't entirely fair to blame him. James always said he should have stayed on Mindar. He was the really loose cannon. Beth did not understand him. And for that, Oscar knew, we lost the best man of us all. Now we have Nick. And he's a loose cannon, too, only he's considerably more dangerous. Fancies himself a thug. Oh, Mazes, why did it have to get so complicated? Did things always have to twist and turn? Why couldn't we leave well enough alone?

Something bright struck Oscar in the eye – oh, it was the sun coming up and spreading out. Kind of like an announcement. Good morning. New day here. Now what have we got planned? Looking out over the water, he realized how truly entrenched in human life they had all become. That was the plan, but so *very* deeply? It was a two-edged sword. One must mirror these humans deeply enough to be believable, but not so deeply we can't go home. Surely not.

In those early days, Fleetwater's citizens didn't set down roots. Mindarians came and went at more regular intervals. Now look: yachts. Could we be any more human?

Fleetwater is, to all intents and purposes, an honest-to-God human village. God?? God?? *We don't have a God!*

He remembered how, back in those pioneering early days, there was a lot less surgery, more prosthetics. But, as the technology to morph really got going, it wasn't enough to look human, the visiting Mindarians wanted to feel human, think human, be human. And now, complicating the matter was this new appetite for really fine art. Now everything was getting mixed up. See, that's how humans make it so difficult. This is good, that's awful, this is better, that isn't as good – blah blah ... that's how it got so complicated. We used to say: stick a frame on it, slap a price tag on it, throw a party ... and there you go. Why mess around?

When he thought about how many credits Pinky and Reed had spent to look like they did, to walk around utterly human ... they weren't the only ones. These 'people' almost believe the lie. Some of them have been here for decades now. They aren't going home. They are home. One only wonders how the human part of these bodies doesn't simply take over? Biologically it's been known to happen.

After all, Mindar had 'absorbed' several visiting life forms. Did those others miss being who they really were or was it okay, finally, to be a blend? After so many generations had passed, Mindar was all they knew. The rest was history and folklore and used-to-be. So, did it work the other way? Could a surgically enhanced Mindarian turn human?

If it walks like a duck, quacks like a duck, and swims like a duck ...

He revisited his memories again of how the trouble had started. It was Beth who had mentioned to Arthur how she and James had come across Maggie. They both saw her sitting on her bench, drawing away. Thinking about it now, Oscar speculated for the first time that maybe it wasn't so much the art James had responded to as that Maggie was a very fetching child. What if ... if ... a flash desire to hatch a nestling had cross-flowed with seeing a child artist at work and ... well, it was water under the bridge now. What's done was done. Beth had blabbed to Arthur. Idle speculation turned into a 'could we? And a 'what if?' After that first instant, James was all for leaving the girl alone ... but Beth and Arthur had already decided to make Maggie a test project. As if we didn't have enough to do. James: you should have kept your trap shut, Oscar thought fiercely. Wasn't the nesting instinct sometimes just mad-crazy? He didn't know a species yet that was exempt.

James and Arthur had squabbled. "We ought not to interfere this way," James said. "There are so many artists, we don't need to be silly. She's just one artist. Who cares?"

But no. Arthur and his pretensions. Arthur, you fool!

Beth knew Arthur's mania for getting things right and big and splashy – he was the one who had said the drawings were especially good. That was when the issue of quality had reared its ugly head for the first time.

James tried to deflect the oncoming 'train'. "Fleetwater won't care. They'll take anything. When you've got nothing, anything will do ..." but it was too late. Arthur had taken the bait. Is that what Beth intended? To bring this trouble down on us? Oscar wondered. She seems to be there every time there's a problem. It was an unhappy time as the arguments between James and Arthur escalated in frequency and volume.

When Arthur wouldn't come to his senses, James disliked like the idea so intensely he wrote a dissenting report. James never was one to hang back when it came to an argument. He'd been a known scrapper in his day. It was one of the reasons he was picked for this expedition. James was fearless.

"You're changing the game plan, Arthur. It's not a good idea. We don't want to draw a lot of attention to ourselves. We have plenty to do as it is," James reminded. But no. Arthur loved the idea of making the game bigger. He wanted to see if he could make Maggie come to Fleetwater without anyone ever discovering the manipulation. Thus began all that covert surveillance. Maggie was the new toy. Beth and Arthur were just having the best time ... and in the middle of this all, one day they realized James was gone. Unbelievable. He wouldn't be a party to the plans being made for the Earth girl. He couldn't protect her so he took the only other action he could. Maybe they wouldn't be able to pull off this scheme without him. Arthur was outraged. Leave the colony? It was unheard of! Not on Arthur's watch! James had done it, nevertheless. It had disappointed Oscar mightily.

In the end, James sent word through a circuitous route. His message included the sentiments that he wasn't coming back. Ever. He liked it here on Earth and he didn't like the way the Mission Plan had been altered and he had no reason to ship back to Mindar. In fact, he admitted he had been "feeling more and more Terran for some time. Take what I earned. Split it amongst you. Goodbye."

All of that because of the day a bad decision was made by two creatures who really couldn't leave well enough alone. Which decision James refused to go along with. That's when Nick joined the crew. He was the new 'tool'. Another mistake. Selecting him was also Beth's doing. Which was queer. For a capable person, her few errors loomed large.

Once or twice in the years that followed, Nick had spotted James walking in the city. He told Oscar about it. "Tell Arthur. He's in charge," Oscar said. "He should know," but Nick wouldn't. It was no good reporting things to Arthur. It would only upset Arthur to hear about it. Nothing would be accomplished. James wouldn't come back. Better by far for Nick merely to note his presence and leave the man alone. How the creature lived was his business. Just as long as he died quietly and avoided an autopsy. Well, James would make sure of that. So, Oscar had shrugged. It wasn't his report to make. He hadn't seen James. He couldn't confirm it.

And now, here we are. It's the morning after Maggie's big show. We've done it. Congratulations, Arthur. She's a certified hit. The risk of dying young isn't the worst thing, you'll say. But now you're playing right into the hands of the arbiters of taste who started all the trouble in the first place.

Oscar could go no further in this line of thinking. He had to sleep. Somewhere mixed up in all of this was a need to forgive James. After all, he didn't do it on purpose, even if he did trigger the deluge. Whatever happened, right now, today, Oscar needed a really long, restful sleep.

As he passed Arthur and Beth's cottage, a rustling could be heard through the open window. He knew the sound of slithering when he heard it. He marveled. Those two. How did they have the strength? He kept walking.

The next day, while Arthur and Beth were curled up together, sated in every way, Oscar was still next door, still sprawled in his clothes because he had never managed to get undressed but had worried himself to sleep just as breakfast was being served all through Fleetwater.

Maggie and Parker, having gotten a good seven hours, were both feeling in reasonably fine fettle, at that moment had been delivered via limousine to Valhalla, the Austin-Miller's mansion. The to-die-for invitation to lunch had been made and the girls lost no time accepting.

What a layout, huh? Parker asked by way of a nudge in Maggie's ribs. Richard was rich but this? Parker had to laugh. This was ridiculous. This was serious wealth. Between last night and today, she had never seen so much wealth on casual display. Valhalla was stunning. Sitting in the solarium, drinking coffee, the girls quarterbacked the results of opening night, waiting for the lady of the house to appear.

Half a dozen of Maggie's small works had been scooped up for between $5,000 to $10,000 each. "For that alone, I could *plotz*," Maggie whispered,

"Do you know Stewart Rangel?" Parker asked, changing the subject.

"Just the name. He's the one who paid $10,000 for a small "Eggbeater". I almost got him mixed up with Reed Stamos but his girlfriend, Pinky DeLillo, came over and I realized who was who. They bought "Home on the Range" – for $35,000. They've commissioned a new one of my mid-sized "Toaster" series. They want it to be yellow, so it will match their kitchen! God bless the idle rich."

"What did Philip Neyman get?" Parker asked.

"He and Oscar had a huge discussion. That's when he purchased "Winged Victory". That's the Deux Chevaux with Pegasus wings."

"Right. That was Number Three?"

"No, that was Number Two, for which, ohmygod, he paid $150,000. I could scream." Maggie took a breath. "The Fosters bought "Portrait of the Artist As A Young Hellion." That was the first one. I know it was self-indulgent to paint it at all but I was really feeling my oats ... two hundred and fifty thousand smackers. Yikes. Number Three was "If Pigs Could Fly". That also sold for $250.000. The Heilbroners got that one. I rather like them. That Morgan Milstern guy is real player – you should have seen him, Parkie. Walked around like he was the Mayor of New York ... I hear he's going to buy something. I think he doesn't care as long as it costs a lot of money. How weird is that? My poor paintings – hanging on the walls of a home owned by a certified heathen ..."

"But you are now rich, Maggs. Officially," Parker concluded.

"I'm freaked, is what I am."

"And rich."

"Well, yeah, that, too."

"Even with the gallery split, you are one rich baby girl."

"Yes, I am ... Parker, I wish Boyd would call. I really want to tell him all the news."

"Well, his client just had to have another step ladder."

Maggie had missed the hint of sarcasm in Parker's voice. Which was just as well because it was out of character for herself so she shut it down. Boyd will show up. Just be cool, she told herself. He is not going to let Maggie down. I'm sure. But it he does, I will kill him, torture him first ... and then I will kill him

"Yes. The client claimed the ladder wasn't safe and he couldn't take a chance and he had already paid Boyd mucho buckos. I can understand it ... I mean ..."

"From what you've told me, I really find it hard to believe Boyd would make a mistake ..."

"Um. That's true."

"Well, no one's perfect. Not even Boyd, although I think it's close."

Maggie's cell phone rang. It was Oscar. John and Aggie Fitzhugh had walked into the gallery this morning, and paid $300,000 for Maggie's enormous 12'x 20' "School For Angels". Which left just one of the big paintings still unsold, if Morgan Milstern came back with a certified check. She just listened, uh-huhed and hung up.

"You better pinch me, Parkie".

"Why?"

"I can't stand it. That was Oscar. Number Four just got a red dot." She turned to Parker. "I'm exhausted. Do you know that? All this ... this excitement, adulation, the money ... I'm just totally pooped. Is this normal?"

"Certainly. You've been working flat out for a long time ... but, it's fun, right?" and Parker poked Maggie. "Watch it. Here comes Beth. I see her in the hall. Oh, it's okay. She's going the other way." But she lowered her voice anyway. "Look at this," and Parker showed Maggie a clipping from the Fleetwater Sentinel-Observer.

Maggie read the article. She looked up at Parker. "Some anonymous Japanese businessman paid $70 million at least ten years ago for that Van Gogh. I can't believe he's going to sell it. He was quoted as saying he would never sell it. I didn't know the Eagletons were that rich."

"Even if they are, how do you suppose they got hold of the identity of Mr. Anonymous? His real name has been kept more secret than ... the combination to the safe at Fort Knox," Parker noted, stabbing her finger at the newspaper cutting.

Beth's shadow fell on the space where they were sitting. Her hearing was especially sharp. While some got lazy living in this paradise, she had not. Had she not just been on the telephone with Arthur trying to get him to squelch that horrible story about the Eagletons?

"Call your friend at the paper. Have him pull that story," she demanded. "If a national wire service picks up on this, we'll have all kinds of trouble raining down."

Arthur demurred that Beth was getting all worked up over nothing.

Beth didn't agree. Arthur's response had been way too human, way too 'now, now, the little woman is overwrought' for Beth. Arthur has been here (on Earth) too long. He's lost his perspective.

It was a gross mistake to allow – nay, encourage that story to get into print, even locally. If the Eagletons want to have a copy made of the damned painting, let them and be done with it. But this? Saying they plan to own the original – and if it can't be done, get a copy made by that, oh, what's her name? ... the one who does legal forgeries. The whole thing was stupid and Arthur was letting the story run. Stupid man. Stupid, stupid man. He could have arranged the whole transaction silently, but no ... Arthur liked the limelight – way too much.

Standing at the door to the solarium, Beth realized there was no damage control regarding that newspaper article that she could effect right now that would in any way improve their situation with Maggie. That show must go on.

"Excuse me, Parker, but Bettie was wondering if you could spare Maggie ... she's in the library. It's down that hall on your left."

"Great," Maggie said, jumping in. "Think I'll take my orange juice with me. You just sit back and soak up the rays, little sister ... I'll be back. Thanks, Beth," and she hurried out of the room.

Beth sat down in Maggie's recently vacated chair. "Are you having a good time?"

"We are having a lovely time, thank you. This is all so exciting for Maggie. You can't imagine how long she's been working for this."

"I suppose I can try."

Parker picked up her coffee cup and gave it great attention. That was a pretty lukewarm reply. Anyhow. The less conversation she had with Beth Barrett the better. Really, she wanted to be able to scrutinize the woman and that was easier done in silence.

"So, how long are you visiting us?" asked Beth.

Parker especially did not like the "us". Too royal by half. "About a week. My fiancé has a private jet. Maggs and I will fly to Milan on Friday."

"I see. Private jet. Very elegant. We'll miss Maggie, but of course you're getting married and you want to have your best friend there. Of course."

Beth Barrett was looking at Parker with a piercing gaze. She agreed with Nick. The girl didn't scare, so it was time to get rid of her. Nick would have to arrange an accident which he would just barely manage to survive (lucky him – and if he screws up, well, that's no loss either). Nosey Parker will be an unfortunate, tragic statistic. Maggie will be devastated, of course. She will have to start painting immediately – to help cope with the tragedy, of course. Beth gave herself a tiny, internal hug and allowed the smile it engendered to appear on her face. The cranky muscles would just have to lump it this once. "Well, I must be going. I have things to do. Enjoy yourself."

That woman is as phony as a three-dollar bill, Parker noted. I've got to find out what's going on. Parker registered the image of her departure. Beth Barrett was medium height and nicely trim. Her hair was shiny black and waved prettily around her face. Somehow, though, it didn't match her personality which was precise and measured. And fake. She could swear it. That woman is fake through and through. I just can't prove it. Always wearing spike heels and very feminine dresses. Somehow the mock-up is ... wrong. She really looks like the button-down type.

Maggie returned to the solarium. "We talked. No deal yet, but she is definitely interested. It's not like I'm the only artist who can do the job. I have to admit that. It's just that I want it so much more than anyone else!"

Parker wasn't listening.

"What's up?"

Parker whispered. "That Barrett woman."

"Listen, Parkie. I think it's a good thing you are getting married. All that delicious wedding business is making you cuckoo. Time for you to have some really good, unbridled sex ... oh yeah, I'm going to let Tony handle you."

She glared at Maggie. "Keep your voice down, please?"

Maggie wasn't tracking. "Bettie is serving lunch. Whatever it is, it'll be yummy. You should eat ..."

Parker pinched her arm to shut her up.)

"... what! Ow. That hurt. "What is it?" Maggie asked.

Parker looked around and shook her head. She put a finger to her lips. Maggie didn't know what the trouble was, but the message had finally gotten through. They had been friends long enough. Certain actions were a signal. If Parker wanted her to play act, she would.

"She picked up her voice. So two more days and we are out of here. Let me get going. People are expecting to see me at the Gallery. We know there are more sales in the works."

"I don't like leaving you here," Parker whispered.

"I'll be fine. It's lunch. I'll make an apology for you. Bettie will understand. I'll take the train up on Thursday night and meet you. Please stop worrying."

"Yes, do go back to New York and stop worrying ..." Beth Barrett was saying as she stood at the French doors between the foyer and the sunroom again. Sashaying in a few steps, she said, "We'll make sure you get to the train on time ..."

Parker was trapped. That woman had been listening in, like a damn spy. Just as they'd been doing for years, Parker put her arm through Maggie's. It was their signal to say nothing and stay cool. When was the last time had Parker invoked the signal?

An image came to her, vaguely in the first instant ... it was ... no ... yes. Maybe at the Public Library? Oh, that was at least six years ago ... they were standing by the elevator. Oh, right. From across the room, they could see Ms. Browning, the librarian, was talking to some overdressed impresario-type ... ohmygod ...

Suddenly Parker knew. Certain pieces of the puzzle that had been driving her crazy were falling into place, and the way they were falling was beyond alarming. What should she do? Play act. Like she had never play acted before.

Turning to Beth she said, "Hearing you say that makes me feel so-o-o much better. I just love this girl, don't you?" she trilled, putting her other arm around Maggie and gave her a hug. Quickly she whispered something in the tiniest voice to Maggie and then in a normal voice said, "Now I'll just throw my things together. Beth, if you wouldn't mind, could you arrange for the limousine to take me to the station ...?"

"Of course. I'll have Nick drive you in."

Shortly thereafter Parker was in the back seat of the limo, the motor idling when she called Maggie on her cell phone where she was still sitting in the solarium, nursing a last cup of coffee.

"Oh, Daddy, that's awful!" Maggie said loudly enough so anyone within earshot would hear. "I'll be there in a couple of hours. You just tell Nonie to hold on. I am coming to see her. Tell her I love her ..." and she hurried through the huge day room to hallway leading to the foyer. Out the open front door she saw the limousine moving very slowly down the driveway. Parker was supposed to be waiting for her! What could she do? Without thinking she picked up several of the smooth charcoal black pebbles that filled the driveway and pelted them at the rear window. Several pinged but the car didn't stop so she grabbed another, larger handful and threw them, too. Thwack! Crack! Maggie ran. As fast as she could. The car slowed down.

She came along side and smacked on the window. "Stop, please stop!"

The car stopped and the smoked glass window came down. The driver's scowling face met hers. "What's going on!? Oh, Ms. Malone ... sorry about that but ..."

"I'm so sorry about scratching the car window ... oh, Parker. It's my Nonie. I just got a call from Evan and

Barbara. They're at the hospital. I have to go home right now. Please, I need to go to the station, too."

Looking at the limo driver straight in the face, Maggie knew that Parker was right. This fellow was the library guy! And Beth – good god. Beth Barrett was Elizabeth Browning, the librarian! What was hell was going on? What were they trying to hide?

Parker picked up where Maggie left off. "Thank God you caught up with us. Another minute and it would have been too late."

That was Parker, Maggie rejoiced. Good old Parker. We should be in the movies with acting skills like these.

"No problem, Miss Malone. Climb on in."

Maggie quickly climbed into the roomy back seat next to Parker and grabbed the intercom phone and said, "I'm sorry, driver. I left my purse in the sunroom. Damn it. I'm sorry. It'll only take a minute. We can still make the next train back to New York if we hurry."

The limousine backed up to the walkway by the solarium and Maggie sprinted in, hurried past the foyer, throwing the news at Beth who was standing by the hall table scrutinizing the morning mail. She dashed back out the front door again. By the time she got into limousine again, she was totally out of breath.

"I'm okay ... (huff, puff) ... I'm okay. I'll just have to get into better shape if we're going to have these emergencies. But never mind me. I'm blathering. Let's go. *Brr.* It's chilly. Oh, nuts. I didn't bring my coat. Driver ... we need to stop at my room. I have to get a few things. I won't be more than a minute."

All the way to downtown Fleetwater Maggie was stealing hard looks at the back of the Nick's head. Each time his eyes shifted in her direction, she would give him a dazzling smile. Her "I'm-Maggie-Malone-I'm-worth-a-fortune-and-I'm-Number-One-Artist-at-La-Nouvelle Vague-Gallery Smile." No one ever messed with Maggie when she was wearing That Smile. No one.

Almost two hours later while Parker and Maggie's train was almost about to enter the city, Beth was inside the Gallery storming. She was beyond angry. She had a hard, mean grip on Nick's arm.

"You are hurting me, you witch!" he grimaced.

Her ear canals were swimming with chilly fluid. Her tongue flicked in and out picking up the myriad of smells. "I gave you an order to kill that bitch," she snarled. The gills underneath her hair were turning a pale violet. "If you can't do as you're told, there's room for you in the cargo hold of the next transport out of here."

Nick's skin was gaining an angry yellowish tinge. It was the color of attack. That was a bad sign. Beth took a step back just as he pulled away bristling.

He was sick of being threatened: Beth, Oscar, Arthur. "What was I supposed to do? You heard what happened. Maggie threw stones at the back window. I slowed down to see what was going on and she climbed in ... something about having to get back to New York right away because her old granny is in the hospital. Now, I don't think you didn't want me to kill Maggie, too, did you? Not the goose that's laying the golden egg, hmmm?" The sneer in his voice was naked. He held up a hand. "You know what? I've got some news for you. It's about James. *I saw him*. He's

322

alive and well ... and he was talking with Maggie and her friend on the train. How about that!? Wonder what they were so chummy about, huh? Well, there you go. Now it's your problem. Because you're in charge. I need to shed, so today's the day. Right now. I'm out of here."

"That's fine with me. Fine with all of us, in fact. Go home. All the way. I'll put that into the paperwork. Mindar: that's where you belong." She reached out, took hold of his arm once more and dug her nails in – right through the cloth to his skin. The news about James was shocking and upsetting, to say the least, but she had other, more pressing worries. That Parker dame was still alive and Beth was sure Parker had finally recognized her. And that story in the paper. Oh, Mazes. What a mess.

Meanwhile Nick didn't blink an eye. "Don't waste your venom on me. I've been inoculated." Yanking her hand off, stepped back and crossed his arms over his chest. His stance said she might be his senior in the field for right now but this interview was definitely over.

"Just shut up," Beth ordered. "Get out there and make sure the car is all clean and ready to go. You know Arthur likes everything to be perfect. You need to get out of here. Don't you dare shed even a skin cell in the limo. In fact, I never want to see you slither again," and opening the door she shoved Nick out into the vestibule and slammed the door harshly. "That nitwit! I'll wring his miserable neck myself."

When Arthur walked into his office a few minutes later, he saw at once that Beth was beyond upset. The skin around her neck was still mottled a violent orange. For him, it was erotic. He loved high emotion. He really thrilled to the scent of it.

"Here, here ... come to me. What's the matter?" he hissed invitingly.

"That witch is going to ruin everything." She slithered into his arms and tucked her head on his shoulder. The news about James was ... oh, did she dare? Arthur hated even the mention of James Fuyard, which occurrence was rare, but it happened because his name was on various documents and there were instances when they needed to be reviewed. At such times Arthur just glowered and time suddenly seemed to drag to a stop for an instant or two and then the bad moment would pass.

But Arthur was smiling. He was back to feeling in charge. Their early morning romp had done wonders for his temperament. Now he would fix hers. He knew how to handle Beth.

"And which 'witch' is it this time? Hmm? Tell Arthur, do," he purred. One could practically hear his tail rattling.

She made the decision in an instant. Say nothing about James for now. She'd deal with that later. At the moment Arthur was holding her in a way that she really couldn't resist. She needed some comforting. She deserved it. Didn't she? Wasn't she *that* upset?

"That Parker Feldman creature. She knows who I am. I'm sure of it. I was going to have Nick drive the limo off the road. Make it look like an accident. He could have managed to get away and she'd be dead. Either that or he could always just ring her silly neck. It was a beautiful plan. We were simply going to get rid of her ... but Maggie needed a ride to town at the last minute and my plan was all spoiled. It's not fair," she whimpered, stamping her foot petulantly. Arthur so loved to comfort her ...

"Well, of course it isn't fair. Oh, you poor thing. It was such a good plan. Come here to me. Let's have a squeeze." Actually Beth was now so closely entwined in his arms she could have hardly come closer.

"Oh, Arthur! We don't have time ..." but there he was – flicking his tongue on the gills behind her ear, bringing a sheen of pleasure flowing into her innards. "Oh, my ... do you think we should?" Being coy was good for a quick tickle ... but oh my... oh my... in fact, her vocal chords were vibrating deliciously in response already. He could hear the vibration. It was all too too yummy.

She really needed this. She deserved it. Look at the sacrifices she made ... and here was Arthur, giving her his most convincing look, one that said he was primed, full of promise and ready to deliver (again – despite their early morning romp).

"Well, maybe ... half a squeeze ..." she conceded as the gills behind her elbows fluttered erotically. She purpled through and through. The color was sensational and so stirring. Arthur was not one to waste such an opportunity, even in trying times.

He walked to his desk and took the 'Do Not Disturb - Conference Call In Progress' sign and hung it on the outside doorknob by the chain and locked the door.

"Oh, you," she said playfully giving him a slap when he came back into her arms. "You are such a snake."

"Aren't I though," he gurgled with pleasure as the two cold-blooded bodies sank to the rug, corkscrewing together. He peeled off her ears. It felt wonderful to be free of them. He peeled off his own with a sigh of relief and set all four on the desk. The hormones of two unique and separate species went speed racing through their bodies – heading for their respective organs. Her dark eyes were saturated red with passion and through the translucent coverings she was gleaming at him with desire. His were nearly black and well-filmed over.

"Come here, you ..." he commanded, covering her frame with his own. Their clothing fell away easily as their forms thinned out. His pale skin had already turned bright turquoise. Beth was now a brilliant emerald mating green. The liquid inside his ear holes fizzled and popped. She could smell his tantalizing aroma. Her body was taut with need. Wrapping his arms around her, he pulled her closer still. Soon the last bits of human angularity gave in, turning their bodies fluid, boneless. Their mating knot streamed gloriously through all its curls and turnings. Except for their coloring, at consummation it would have been impossible for an outsider to guess where one of them began and the other one ended.

Outside, Viola Higgins, the office maid, passing with a feather duster in hand, saw the sign on the door and shrugged. Putting an ear to the door she heard something rustling. She gave herself a knowing nod and walked on.

CHAPTER ELEVEN

During the train ride back to New York, Parker kept looking around, suspicious of everyone. So Beth had been using another name. Pretending the whole time. Damn them. As far as Parker was concerned, it was safe to assume Arthur and Oscar were also in on this scheme! It was monstrous. Frieda had sent Maggie to Fleetwater ... did she know? Was she a willing part of this ... conspiracy? Why else did Maggie end up in Fleetwater? It was so hard to believe. I mean, Frieda was a bit silly but ... so Maggie wasn't wrong. Maggie's failures here in New York weren't just the normal, difficult course of events after all. Look how her shows kept getting cancelled. And that lost print contract! Oh, god. It now all made a twisted sense and yet she could hardly believe it.

Parker looked at Maggie who was deliberately looking out the window or napping. I don't blame her. The few times they chatted, they were unwilling to talk about anything except the weather and the sports until they could get somewhere they were sure they wouldn't be overheard. Even at the Penn Station, standing by the phone booth Parker kept vigil.

"You really think someone is going to come running by, push you out of the way, lock me in the booth, rip the phone booth out of the floor and make off with me in it?"

"Just dial, smarty pants ... I will stand watch."

Maggie rang Arthur to tell him that she had to stay in New York a few extra days because Nonie was in the hospital. Arthur had seemed unusually mellow, according to Maggie, when she reported the particulars of Arthur's end of the conversation to Parker as they left the station.

"Well, with all that money flowing into his coffers, what is there to object to? He has all of your work there at the gallery."

"But he was kind of *obstructive* before. Why the sudden change?"

"Oh, for god sake, Maggs ... there's nothing really right about those people. Why shouldn't he be changeable? They're a bunch of two-faced ... weirdoes!" Parker realized she was starting to raise her voice so she jammed it back down to a whisper: "Double identities ... and ... god knows what else is going on. They could be spies ... Nazi agents ... I don't know. Don't ask me. Come on, we have to get somewhere safe and talk," and she yanked Maggie through the throng of travelers.

"Okay. Okay. Right. You're right. There's a lot wrong with Beth and Nick ... and yes, Arthur. And Oscar, too – which is really sad and upsetting ... it can't be like he doesn't know."

"Oh, he knows. Remember the man that came to visit *Ms. Browning* on that afternoon at the library? Yeah?? Well, that was Arthur. I'm sure of it. I'm sorry about Oscar, but he certainly is part of ... this ... charade. I actually sort of liked him. Damn it ... TAXI!!!!" Parker yelled and they hopped into the cab which had screeched to a halt.

They went to Evan and Barbara's apartment, dropped their suitcases and hurried off. Securing a table in the café by the window at Rockefeller Center, they hoped they were safe. Who would try to interfere with them in such a public place? Finally they thought they might be able to relax a little. Out on the ice were numerous capable skaters in snazzy outfits shaking out the kinks.

"You're right." Maggie agreed. The evidence was incontrovertible. Once she recognized the limo driver as Nick, the library clerk, she realized that Beth Barrett was indeed the Reference Librarian, Elizabeth Browning. "But why?" She tried to think it out. "Even if you decided to dye your hair, which people do that all the time. And change professions ... she could have said, "Why, Maggie Malone. How marvelous. So, you've met Oscar. Terrific. Lovely to have you aboard. This is my new job – assistant to Arthur ... but she didn't. What have they been up to??"

"God knows, that's what! It's no coincidence, that's for sure," Parker replied with verve. "Of course she didn't say anything. Because she's a rotten-hearted, two-faced, no good, miserably schemer!" Parker was fit to be tied. Having gotten a good look at the chauffeur, there was no doubt he was Nick, the library clerk. Beth Barrett was Ms. Browning and ... Oscar – what was his part in all this? She wished she knew.

What they couldn't figure out was why. "*Why any of this?*" Maggie asked? "I mean, if they like my work, what's the big deal? My work is selling. We're all getting rich as blazes, why all ... *this?*"

Meanwhile Parker had calmed herself a bit. "Because there's more to it that we don't know about. That's what. Listen: does it strike you odd that all the art collectors at last night's show are strictly Fleetwater residents? I didn't figure that out right away but … don't look at me like that. I'm only saying … listen, Maggie. Where are all the city people? I know the invitations were sent. Surely some of them would have come, if only to check out the competition and go back to New York happy thinking that their artists are better than you."

Maggie glared.

"What I don't understand is what's the purpose for all this." Parker looked out the window. A little girl in a fuzzy pink sweater and pink felt wool skirt in the center of the rink was doing doubles.

Maggie sighed deeply. At least the night before had been quite beyond wonderful. Today she was … in the middle of … what? A spy caper or something.

Maggie felt all the joy had drained out of her. She pulled a newspaper clipping out of her pocket. "Okay. So, we don't get it. Yet. And look at this. The Eagletons are not going to buy Van Gogh's "The Irises" from that Japanese man. It's not going to happen. I don't care how much money they have. That man said he was keeping that Van Gogh forever, locked up, and that's that. End of story."

"So?"

"Well … what's the purpose of this news story? To let everyone know how rich you are? Why bother put it in the paper? There are a relatively few artists doing creditable, legal forgeries but who advertises using them? It's just silly. If they want a copy, they order a copy. Even if the copies are great looking. It costs a fortune, they have the money, so good for them."

She ran a mental list of all the artists she knew personally who were skilled legal forgers. Maybe Gerald

Darling? Ron Christ, the Aussie. Or Bettina Ferguson? She made a living doing that sort of work. "I suppose I could start calling around. Find out if anyone got offered the job. But why all the fuss anyway?"

"I think the story was a mistake," Parker said slowly. "I'll bet you anything it gets pulled. They won't do that again. (Whoever *they* are.) They'll have to find some other way to impress ... er ... whoever." She looked up to find a waitress hovering. She ordered hot chocolates, not wanting to say anything unless until the young server had left.

"Someone put it in the newspaper. But why?"

Leaning over the table, Parker whispered, "Because, well, the story was some kind of ... well ... mistake. Just a big fat mistake. Or maybe it was an attempt to get the owner to come out of hiding so they can negotiate? No ... that wouldn't work. It's like it's ... um, all inside out and backwards ... mixed up ... like ... like ... the ... person whose doing this ... doesn't understand PR ... because the guy won't sell (of course), so they order a big, expensive legal forgery. Is this all designed to introduce some new great, legal forger? Oh, my head hurts just thinking about this. It's stupid. That's what I know. It's all so very very stupid."

"You mean, the people say they're buying the Van Gogh, but the deal falls through so they order a fabulous forgery and everyone gets a ton of publicity? Who would do a thing like that. It's so ... lame."

"Yeah, well, it's not my logic. I don't think this way. But someone does. Someone in Fleetwater – seeing as how the Sentinel-Observer printed it. You know, some very odd people, very rich people live there. There's no telling what the idle rich get up to when they're bored." She changed her tone. "But not you. *You do not live in Fleetwater any longer, right? As of today.*"

Maggie had been looking out the window at the rink. The little girl in pink was now partnering with a little boy in a silver outfit. They were really quite good. Maggie's gift horse, it turned out, was full of strange people on an inexplicable mission that had somehow involved her ... she might be safe now but her paintings ... well, what was left of them – most of the small ones had been sold but two of the big ones were still at the gallery ... that is, if any of them were safe ... which nearly broke her heart. What a mess. What an insane, horrible mess.

When she thought about it, almost everything that mattered to her was there in Fleetwater. All her art work, all that money, her notebooks, her art supplies, her Christmas presents – which was silly except that somehow they mattered to. Except Evan's silver bracelet, which she was wearing ... and Boyd. Was he suspect, too? It was too horrible. A nightmare. Oh, her poor head ached. "I don't suppose you own a gun?" she asked, turning back to Parker.

"Don't be a nut. Besides, we're not going back," Parker said with finality, at which point the conversation lapsed.

It had been dark for an hour and still they sat. The lights around the rink had been turned on. Now the skaters were accompanied by fantastic shadows as they glided and turned. Currently there were a number of couples circling the ring, doing the classic forward glide in tandem, a young Elvis Stoyko-type was executing pyrotechnical/martial art moves in the far corner and three little girls all wearing identical black and white tuxedo outfits were giggling as they walk-skated along holding hands, occasionally all falling down on top of each other harmlessly and having a good time.

The friends ordered sandwiches and ate in silence. After the plates were cleared, Maggie went to the bathroom. When she came back, she sat down and cleared her throat.

"Um, so, Parker ... I need to tell you something. I know I should have told you before but ... well, I know you are not going to like this, but you have to know because now I think ... well, uh, that is ... I think ... that ... er ... oh, you are going to kill me ... "

Her friend showed two empty hands. "No weapons. Tell me," Parker prompted.

Maggie lost her nerve. She was suddenly giving all her attention to a young skater executing perfect triples to a pleased crowd of spectators.

"Ummm – before the Age of Aquarius ends, please."

She turned back to face Parker. "All right. Okay ... here goes ..." She took a breath. "William used to tell me that people were watching me at the Zoo when I was drawing. He called them my fans. But now I don't think so."

Parker glared but then she relented. She had her own secret. The one where she nearly died when she was pushed into traffic. Now was probably not the best time to mention it. But she would. Soon. Maybe.

Maggie pulled out a red bandana and wiped at her eyes, which were tearing up. "So, it's all a fake. I'm a fake and I'm back where I started. It's not fair. It's just ... not ... fair." Gulping for air she blurted out the rest: "You have

Tony. He's the real thing. I have ... God knows what I have ... because it's not real ... I know it's weak of me ... pathetic ... I'm sorry for complaining, but I was ... so ... happy ..." and the tears began in earnest.

Parker reached over and patted her hand. Maggie finished her crying jag and looked up.

"What?" she asked.

"I was just thinking. The only real argument I've had so far with Tony was about motorcycles. It was like: 'I'm Italian, I ride a huge, fast motorcycle. You must understand this. This is not going to change.' I had to explain about Fred. I was really worried, Maggs. Suppose he didn't get it? Everything was great but this one thing ... and it was important that he understand. But he did." Parker's eyes were shining with a few tears. "Once Tony understood, he said: "Listen, *cara mia*. I am not the Fred. I will not die of the motorcycle. You and I are going to have a wonderful life and make babies and finally we will be very old together. Yes? You will do this for me? For us?"

Maggie watched Parker remembering.

"So I said 'yes.' " she explained. Changing the subject, she said, "Now, listen, I'm serious when I say you are not going back to Fleetwater. *We* are not going back."

The outside rink had cleared except for one great looking couple in matching black velvet outfits swanning around like there was no one else there. In fact, the longer they skated, the more people gathered to watch them until the rink was in fact empty except for them. When they left the ice, they earned a big round of applause from the crowd.

Maggie knew she was aching to ask Parker about Boyd. Now she found she couldn't hold back any longer. "Parker ... what about Boyd? Maybe he's a part of all this? I mean, he could be completely innocent. He's never done anything to make me not trust him. I can't say goodbye to him on the telephone. I have to see him."

"But what if he's part of this ... I don't know what to call it – a conspiracy? Boyd could be one of them, you know."

"No, he couldn't." Her voice reduced to a whisper. "He wouldn't."

"And why not?"

"Because, well, for one thing, he isn't from Fleetwater. All the rest ..."

"We don't know for sure. Do we?"

No. It was true. Not for sure. Maggie had to find out. "Oh, God. Parker, we are really in trouble, aren't we?"

"What do you mean 'we', white man?"

That was funny so they had to laugh. Sometimes there was nothing else to do. They finished their war council with a plan.

On the Monday, still much to Parker's chagrin, they took the morning train back to Fleetwater after all. Mr. Fuyard, the nice man with the bristle mustache, was also on board but Maggie was suspicious of everyone now. Suppose he was part of this, too. Everyone was now suspect.

"I read in the paper that you had a very successful opening," he said with interest.

It was hard not to answer him. "Yes, thank you, James." How could she think he was an enemy? "It was a wonderful opening. The gallery did everything to help make it a success." There. Let's see what he does with that, Maggie thought, looking over at Parker.

"Didn't you mention you are going to Italy to get married?" he asked Parker. Without waiting, "Are you going, too?" he said looking at Maggie.

But Parker answered for her. "Yes, that's right. I don't know how long we'll be away.

I think it would be fun for Maggie to spend some time in Italy. There's such great art there, the museums, the antiquities ..."

"I think you're right, my dear. An excellent opportunity."

Maggie and Parker were flicking eye signals at each other. Maggie had an idea. "Do you remember how I told you I changed the signature on my paintings?"

He said he did.

"Don't you think it's interesting, about signatures, and names – how they can fit a person or ... maybe contrast. Take me, I'm half-Irish, half-Jewish. With this red hair and the freckles people wouldn't guess about my Jewish half unless I tell them. Of course, they say that many Jews had red hair – in the old days – like Solomon ... anyway. It's like that. Sometimes people don't know unless you tell them." Parker was now eyeing Maggie with signals of her misgivings.

Oh, God, Maggie. Don't.

"So, you know what else is cool? Names mean things. In Japanese, and Indian – American, I mean, and the English. Well, I was just wondering, isn't "Fuyard" French?"

For this Parker would have kicked Maggie.

"Yes, it is. Lots of English have French names. The Norman Invasion, you know."

"Oh, right. Anyway, so I was wondering, do you know if "Fuyard" means anything special? I mean," and now looking at Parker for an instant, "it's kind of fun to know this stuff" With every passing word or two, she was sounding more and more like a chatty ten-year-old and less like a post-college graduate. Parker really wanted to clamp a hand over her best friend's mouth and drag her away, now, before it went any further, but James was answering.

"Well, I do find the origin of names rather interesting."

He was taking the bait? "So, do you know?" Maggie persisted, making herself sound as 'tweeny' as possible.

"Why, yes. It's amusing, I suppose. Fuyard means 'runaway'. One wonders how that happened, eh? French revolution, the Foreign Legion ... hard to say." He gave just a little chuckle, let it run its course and fizzle away.

Maggie swallowed. Parker said nothing.

James picked up the dropped thread of conversation. "Well, you know how it is with names. Some are quite colorful, some record places and others are for families with long histories. I suppose mine's a bit colorful, to be generous about it."

"Yes, it is," Maggie said. She, too, had nothing more to say.

"Well, I must read my paper now, have to catch up ... if you'll excuse me. And if I don't see you again very soon, have a wonderful journey." Up came the paper as usual, spread wide.

He got off at Copper Springs and when he was outside the train, he waved, just as usual, and tipped his hat, just as usual.

"He knows, Parker. I'd swear it. I don't know who he is, but I think he's a good guy."

"I hope you're right." That was all she was willing to commit to. Mostly she prayed that they wouldn't turn a corner somewhere in years to come and face to face with Nick or Arthur or Beth.

To think that Maggie had been secretly stalked! Plotted about and against, manipulated, tricked. It was one thing to read about this stuff in a book or on TV but for real? It made her shudder. Gift horses, indeed.

Nearing the outskirts of Fleetwater, Maggie pointed out the window towards a large, unused pasture. Nailed to a post was the historical sign she knew by heart. It was there in the near distance, describing the day when a meteorite fell to earth, barely missing New York City. She recalled to Parker having been shown the story on her laptop by Mz. Browning-Barrett.

The conductor interrupted with a "Fleeeet-wa-tah", which meant they needed to gather their things. They had no more time to discuss astronomical phenomena or its significance.

On the train ride Maggie had made a decision. She would have to be strong and focused. No more damn crying. They left the station and went straight to Homer's Car Rental on Main Street. Step One of The Plan was that Maggie needed to see Annette Rousseau, the most recent "golden girl" in Arthur's stable of artists. Maggie had indeed known her through the years on and off, since

Saturday studio art classes many years ago. It was the same class where she met Denny. Annette and Maggie had been artistic rivals until each staked out their particular territory regarding style and subject – Annette would do abstracts, Maggie would copy Mary Cassatt. This solution obviated the need to continue feuding. Everything thereafter went fine. They occasionally shared brushes and visited the other's work cubicle. When Maggie phoned Annette, she was totally thrilled to see Maggie and immediately invited her to visit.

"Maybe she knows something. Anyway, let's scope it out," Maggie said to Parker as they whizzed down the two-lane highway in a rental car. What happened after that would all depend on what they could outright ask or glean. Finally a turn onto Spice Road, which became a bumpy track dead-ending at a medium-grey, painted saltbox house with salmon pink shutters and trim. The door was a sunny yellow. A few yards away was a marine blue studio-barn with grass-green colored door. The paint job looked fresh. It also looked like an homage to Matisse or Derain in that short-lived Fauve period. Maggie parked the rental and beeped the horn once.

"Hello, stranger," called a familiar voice. Maggie saw Annette standing in her painting smock by the door to the barn. "Who's the company? Is she competition?"

"Hi, Annette. No, this is my best friend, Parker Feldman. Her talents lie elsewhere. Like shopping and all things Italian – stuff like that."

Parker smiled and shrugged. "I'm not quite that shallow. I work. Anyway, how to you do," and they shook hands.

Maggie explained, "I know it took me way too long to make the drive. It's good to see you. The paint job is great," she noted with a nod.

"Thanks." She turned around and led them toward the painting studio.

Maggie noticed it immediately: Annette was walking like an old lady. How could that be? Was she ill? She was still very pretty but definitely looking haggard. It's like she isn't getting enough sleep. Maggie looked quickly at Parker who raised her eyes in question. She had also noticed the dark circles under Annette's eyes. Maggie shook her head as a signal. This was a 'let's just see wait and see.' Up closer they both noticed strands of grey were beginning to streak the temples of Annette's long black hair.

"Come on in. I'll make you some coffee," and Annette continued walking over to an old-fashioned stove sitting on a slab of cement. Circling the little eating area were several nicely cushioned shabby-chic chairs where they could relax and enjoy the warmth. Annette had already set out a dozen paintings for their review along a run of hay bales. It was a series small-format, horizontal landscape paintings. Silence ensued while they looked at her display.

The way Maggie remembered it, Annette's previous plein-air landscapes had been little miracles. Any time Annette did a show, she got top reviews. The fact was everything she painted, she painted well. While a grammar school dispute might have been settled with Maggie trying to copy Cassatt, it was Annette who had thoroughly inhaled the style and lessons of Eugene Boudin – albeit with a modern update – and exhaled a quality of art that meant there was every right reason why she was successful enough to buy property outside of town out here on the Island. This current work was therefore disturbing. They were ... just ... Maggie hated to think it – flat. Almost lifeless. The brushwork wasn't quite right. The groupings of people were missing something. And there some off-notes about the color, too, which was Annette's forte.

How could the quality of her work degrade? Had someone criticized her? Believing either the sycophants or the attacks of reviewers was likewise a fatal mistake. Maybe she had been coached to change her style? Not Annette. She had never been a pushover about anything.

"I don't know what to say, Annette ..."

"It's all right. I understand."

"You do?" Maggie was relieved.

"Of course. Arthur and I are making big plans. Nothing that would put a damper on your show, of course ... I'm going to be the opening for La Prochaine Vague Gallerie? He's gutting the second floor. They were using it for storage before, but now they are going to do it all very modern. I'll be Number One Girl upstairs and you'll be Number One Girl downstairs. There's room for everyone. It'll be fun. Later on he's going to add onto the first floor – because the old city council fogies will stop him from erecting a third floor. There's going to be a new, smaller gallery off the back. I saw the plan. It doesn't have a name yet. That way he can bring in more artists. Arthur has always been a great one for giving new people a leg up."

Maggie felt herself paling. She hoped it wasn't showing. There was a knot in her larynx. She spoke over it. "Yes, that's Arthur. Friend of the artist ... he ... uh, has he? ... that ... is ... so great." She had to think quickly. "I just knew

341

I had to come out here and see what you were working on. Arthur was so enthusiastic. Actually, when Parker goes back to Milan – she's marrying her boyfriend and ... you know. It's going to be great. I'm going to. My first trip to Europe. It will be very exciting. I'm going to go see Martha, too. She's still in London ... so, I'll see all the new changes at the gallery ... when I get back."

Annette was on her feet, heading for the coffee maker. She didn't see Maggie's face.

"Oh, no, please don't trouble yourself," Maggie said. "Parker and I have to go. Sorry to cut the visit short. I have to get back to the gallery. Arthur and Beth are waiting for me and Parker has to get to the station. We're leaving Friday. There's a lot to do. I wish we could stay longer. I'm so happy for you. Come on, Parkie." Maggie gave Annette a gentle hug, and with that hasty excuse, Maggie dragged Parker by the arm out of the studio. "No caffeine jolt for you," she could be heard saying with false brio. She almost heaved Parker into the passenger seat of the rented Volvo.

The wheels spun on the dirt and gravel as Maggie backed out; she did a k-turn and drove as fast as she dared down the track back to the main road. Once they reached it, she pulled to a stop on the shoulder.

"Did you see those paintings? What's happened to her!? Those are nothing like the work she was doing!" She took a breath. Turning to Parker she said, "You never saw the really wonderful paintings Annette was making. Those were little jewels. This stuff is so ... second-rate." She felt so disparaged.

"Well ... your work has changed ..." Parker had to take this kind of analysis on faith. She thought the little paintings were rather nice.

"You don't understand! Annette was doing brilliant work. Any amateur can do what you just saw. Her work was miraculous. She had plenty of offers but she wanted to live down here so she could set up an easel outside her cottage and go to work. Oh, crikey, this is bad."

Maggie could feel the grief starting to well up, but this time she just shut it down hard. One quick wipe and she was back in business.

"Listen to me, Parkie. That girl is not well. Did you see the dark circles under her eyes? It's like she's ... in the early stages of ... some disease. Annette was healthy as a horse."

"Well, people do get sick ..." but the look on Maggie's face told Parker to change tactic. "Okay. So you are saying Annette's paintings aren't good anymore? Right?"

"I'm saying not only is the work a real disappointment compared to what she's capable of, but she hasn't a clue *and* she's not well! *That* is what I'm saying. How could she not know this? Annette is one of the sharpest people I know. She's had successful one-woman shows in three countries! She's no new girl on the block and not a one-show wonder. Galleries can't get enough of her. When she told me she had moved down to the beach, I thought it was a great idea. Get a lot of work done, go back out and knock 'em dead again. She had a year of shows at The Vague and now she looks ... dreadful ... and she's ... making those pedestrian little *rectangle*s. Parker: she should see a doctor. She should be in a hospital – not be planning a new gallery with Arthur. Her hair is turning grey!"

Maggie lay back in the driver's seat. "I thought about telling her, but I don't think she would believe me. Not even if I put her in front of mirror and pointed it out. There was a look in her eyes. I ought to know. I've been there. They own her. Arthur and his lot – whoever they are." Her eyes were still closed.

"So, what's this about Arthur launching her again – in her own exhibition space?"

Maggie opened her eyes and looked at Parker. "Oh, that part's fine, I suppose. It's actually a good idea. Oscar mentioned it. The town council is a bit on the conservative side ... although they are right. No three-story buildings in the main part of town ..." but she was getting off the track. "Okay. Forget the town planning. Listen, Sherlock. The purpose of our coming out here was to find out if Annette knew anything about what Arthur and Beth might be up to ... because we are highly suspicious. Right? So, where does this little visit leave us? And do we know anything new?"

But she didn't wait for Parker to reply. "Number one, it's worse than we think because Annette is not well. That's for sure. Number two: her work is going downhill and she's clueless. Number three leads me to a new question: what's happened to the other artists that Arthur has championed? We need to find out. Four: where the hell is Boyd? We have to get back to Fleetwater. And I have to think who I can call to come get Annette out of here. She needs a doctor."

CHAPTER TWELVE

Arthur Cotillion sat at the back of the small concert hall and listened with enormous enjoyment to the Fleetwater Chamber Orchestra practicing the "Winter" section of Vivaldi's "The Four Seasons".

Allowing the music to fill up the space, his mind began to drift. Fleetwater society will love this Christmas season's offerings. He had such marvelous plans. He was only a dues-paying member of the planning committee, and of course it was a group decision, but these people hardly know good music selections from the prosaic. His input was vital if they were to have a really good – nourishing, he might add – program. Consider his upcoming retrospective on Tiny Tim. Such a cute little ukulele. And that voice. He had arranged to show clips from Tiny's visits to the Johnny Carson Show and his marriage to Miss Vicky ... it's going to be so delicious. Arthur swayed a little to the lyricism of the music filling the hall and closed his eyes to better appreciate it.

Behind him in the door, Boyd MacArthur was standing quietly, also taking in the practice session. He had just arrived back in town, finally. Peter Gelman, the infamous take-no-prisoners client who had tried at the very last minute to get him to stay for 'just one more thing' had finally been out-maneuvered. Boyd had told him 'no'. Definitively no. Absolutely no. 'The ladder is fixed. I'm out of here. I've got a commitment in Fleetwater. I appreciate your business, Mr. Gelman, but it will have to wait. I'll call you,' and with that he had loaded his supplies and tools into the back seat of his car and driven off. It was really incredible. What did Gelman think was going on? ... Boyd heard someone in the violin section hit a clinker. He winced. It was also obvious that one of the violins was out of sync with the rest of the section ... he winced again.

He realized Arthur Cotillion was looking at him.

"Good afternoon, Boyd. Nice to see you. Did you have a good trip? Too bad you missed our opening. We pulled out all the stops. It was quite stupendous, if I do say so myself." Arthur spoke with ingenuous good cheer as he turned back in his seat to face the stage.

Boyd was about to reply when Arthur called back over his shoulder, his eyes dramatically closed again, better to hear the blissful sounds, "We are very lucky to have musicians of this caliber." Unfortunately the erring musician hit another clinker but continued on, bowing furiously along with the others.

Was the conductor not going to say something? Boyd waited. Come on, he said to himself. You have to call the guy out for that. But Boyd could see that the conductor was definitely not going to call the guy out. Boyd knew himself to be a very calm and collected type of guy, but this was based on getting things right. When things weren't right, he hopped to it in one quick hurry and got them back on track. Otherwise ... otherwise? he queried himself. Otherwise I am not a happy camper. I wonder if Maggie knows this is my Achilles' Heel. I'll have to tell her.

He looked across the room of empty seats to Arthur. Did Arthur not hear those sour violin notes? The man was a nut for perfection. Why wasn't he saying anything? What was the matter with the conductor? Arthur must be pulling Boyd's leg. He occasionally did display a sense of humor. It was well known the man was a fan of Tiny Tim. And Abbott & Costello. And "Gilligan's Island". Low humor, of course, but perhaps it balanced out the man's insatiable demand for really great art in his gallery. Like doctors who play golf to blow off steam or Einstein riding a bicycle around the Yale campus ... er, no. I'm going overboard on this. Anyway, enough was enough. He, Boyd, was not going to say about it. Better to spend his time re-shingling the Garrisons' cottage – his next project – if you could get over calling that oversized outhouse a 'cottage'. Better that than to be engaged in conversation with Arthur Cotillion, as Boyd had learned over the years.

"Lovely," said Arthur. He turned around but Boyd was gone. "Too bad. He's missing the best part," he said to no one as he settled in again.

PART THREE:

Leaving Fleetwater

CHAPTER ONE

Boyd went directly to his apartment and unpacked, putting everything away neatly. Having changed into fresh clothes, he grabbed a heavier jacket and gloves. He thought about changing footgear but decided to leave it as is. The air was brisk.

At Hadley's he stopped to grab a sandwich. Once he had eaten, he felt better and hurried over to the train ticket office. "Hi, Gordon. Did you happen to see Maggie Malone and her friend, the one with the long blonde hair, Parker? Did they buy tickets for Penn Station today yet?"

"Yep, they came in, bought round-trip tickets. When they came back, they went straight down to Homer's and rented a car. I overheard them talking. Boy, that was some shebang. Best party I been to in a long time. I got one of them special invites. That girl sure does funny pictures. Boyd, they are supposed to be funny, aren't they? Oh, and the girls were heading for the ocean road but that's all I know."

"Thanks a lot. And yes, it is okay to laugh ... see you later."

Boyd checked for cars, jaywalked across the street and headed down to Homer's. The plastic clock sign hung on the window in front of the pulled shade indicated Homer would be "back in 10 minutes" so he buttoned up his coat and sat down to wait on the bench outside the rental office.

He decided to make use of the free minutes to consider Arthur and his mob based on his own eight years in the town. If Arthur considered himself a bit self-important that was forgivable. He did run a successful gallery. He was a well-to-do businessman, he sat on a number of social committees, had contacts in many places and now he was about to build a second floor gallery. That would be expensive and Arthur was a real big spender. That's one thing Boyd could say about Arthur. He didn't do 'cheap'. Boyd had done work for the man on numerous occasions. He paid on time, he accepted change orders with a modicum of civility, so that was all well and good. One point for Arthur's side.

The sun was warm. It balanced the chill. Thank god there was no snow. Boyd hunkered into his coat, closed his eyes and continued his ruminations. What else did he really know about Arthur? Eats at the Yacht Club, his main squeeze is Beth Barrett.

Speaking of Beth Barrett. Okay, now. She's one ruthless snake in the grass, as far as Boyd was concerned. Pretty-enough looking in her own way, he supposed, but much too obviously calculating. That she and Arthur actually got along pretty well was of no matter. As long as he, Boyd, stayed strictly clear of her, everything was fine. She seemed to feel the same way. So that zeroed out that point.

He knew that Arthur liked money. Happily he had plenty of it. Liked to get it, liked to spend it; was well known to "reward" his new discoveries with meals at The Marina and anyone in any profession. Well, no one could complain that he wasn't democratic. In fact, anyone was grist for Arthur's odd mill. Having taken a shine to Boyd for a job well done repairing the back stairs of his gallery at least five years ago, he followed that with an order for new railings in front and an overhang for bad weather. Delivering at the level of quality he insisted on had apparently merited taking Boyd to lunch. Which led to ordering a new mudroom.

Oh, yes. He remembered that meal all too well. Great food and possibly one of the worst social experiences of his life. Boyd had decided never to have another meal with Arthur alone, if possible. Megalomaniac was the only word Boyd could think of to describe Arthur. To know the man was to be distinctly uncomfortable. After that little lunch experience, Boyd managed to keep a professional distance. Several times after that, there were two absolutely necessary business lunches. For one of these, Arthur told him Beth had been invited to join them. She wasn't his choice in women at all. But what totally cooked it was when she dropped her napkin and ran her hand up Boyd's leg – twice. The first time might have been a mistake but by the third stroke, Boyd kicked her ankle – hard. She covered her yelp really well and that shut her down. Thereafter, whenever Beth did come around, Boyd made himself scarce.

If he hadn't experienced it himself, he would never have believed it. Imagine prim and proper Beth getting skanky with him. It wasn't as though Boyd liked Arthur. But he did respect him in very certain ways. He needed that or he couldn't work for the man, no matter how big a spender he was – and Arthur sure liked to spread the wealth. In fact, the man was, in a weird way, some kind of innocent. Naïve, even. Boyd couldn't explain it to himself any better. Well, people are any kind of mixture of different characteristics. Why couldn't Arthur have a streak of naiveté? And while Beth, was his 'true and loyal companion', she was not to be trusted. She simply wouldn't be allowed an opportunity to exercise her willingness to stray using Boyd.

Boyd thought: I am a long way from Maine. How did I end on Long Island? Wasn't the original plan to go out to sunny California? He wished he remembered who told him about Fleetwater. Since his memory was excellent, it bothered him not to remember this detail. Well, he would remember. It's there. That little thought – it's just hiding. He'd pretend it didn't matter, so that little thought would come on out.

Now, what about Nick? Boyd noticed the fellow got no respect from Arthur and Beth. He didn't think he, Boyd, could work in a place where people were openly disdainful. On the other hand, Nick wasn't the pleasantest guy. He wasn't incapable, he just seemed to object to almost everyone and everything on general grounds. Generally sour, another words, unless it was French New Wave cinema. So, that was Nick. Boyd just cut him all the necessary slack and that handled that.

As far as Oscar went, Boyd had always assumed him to be a homosexual until he overheard an argument at the gallery between Nick and Oscar. He had been sitting outside in back enjoying the weather; he was sketching designs for a bird feeder when he heard the men going at it verbally.

"You will stay away from her. Do you hear me?" That was Oscar.

"What's the matter? Is she too much for you, Oscar? She is what they call a 'fox'." And that was Nick. Boyd had no idea who the object of desire was but if Oscar was warning Nick off, that was reason enough for Boyd to think better of him after that. It seemed like Oscar was a decent fellow ... and that was a point for Oscar. Which begged the question, why was he involved with Arthur and his gang? Couldn't he find other employment? ... oh, here come Maggie and Parker, pulling into Homer's parking lot. He waved to them from his seat on the bench in the front.

So this is Boyd, said Parker's look to Maggie.

Yup. That's my guy, she smiled in return and waved back. "Be right out," she called. Boyd nodded.

Maggie parked the loaner and went inside to handle her bill. Meanwhile Parker sauntered over and introduced herself. He knew he was being vetted. She looked just the way Maggie had described her. They shook hands, just chatted a bit and waited. Informal and easy enough.

As long as he really really wasn't born and bred in Fleetwater, was what Parker was thinking mainly.

When Maggie returned, they shared a quick peck, did the formal introductions and with urgency said, "We need to talk," while taking his arm.

"You bet we do," he replied emphatically, "because something is rotten in the state of Demark. And, to use your terminology," Boyd said, "we need a war council. But first, sustenance." Walking to Gus', they three ordered large coffees regular and a box of chocolate crullers to share.

"I'm taking some home for Daddy," Maggie said as she took possession of the box.

Parker laughed. "No chocolate cruller from Gus' will ever reach the city."

"That's what you know ..." so all three laughed.

Boyd could see right away the girls did indeed have the kind of easy friendship he admired. He didn't have that with many people, except Maggie, really. It wasn't that many people didn't know he was an orphan – and he was okay about that – he had always just felt easier keeping a little distance. It was all right that he had come here the way many other people did, except for the very rich, who were already in residence. Most of the newcomers arrived on a whim, by train, and liking what they saw well enough and stayed. It had happened that way with him, too. If he could just remember how exactly he had heard about Fleetwater in the first place.

They sat down at the one table Gus had left outside for the most hardy and least intimidated by cold weather. Boyd got right down to business, ingesting the hot coffee and digging into the box of crullers. "What's the matter with Arthur Cotillion?" he asked.

"Well, you don't waste time. Is this Twenty Questions or rhetorical?" asked Parker.

"It's not rhetorical. But let me go on. I need to tell you what happened today, just before you came back (from wherever it is you went)," and Boyd described the music rehearsal.

"Maybe he just doesn't know a clinker when hears one?" Maggie asked. "Some people are tone deaf."

"Maybe," replied Boyd. "But what I got was that he thought the music sounded fine."

Maggie told Boyd what had happened at their visit with Annette.

Boyd nodded. "I've seen her around, of course, but only once recently. She was in town here to visit with Arthur the other day about the new second floor gallery. I didn't get a good look at her, but I trust your judgment."

Parker pulled out the newspaper clipping and showed it Boyd. "Look at this. There is no way the Eagletons are buying that Van Gogh!"

Maggie nodded her agreement.

"The question it begs: why bother to report it in the first place?" Parker demanded. "Maggie's been telling me the Eagletons are seriously rich, but $70 million? I'm sure that businessman wouldn't sell it for exactly what he paid for it. Try $100 million, maybe. Actually, no. I don't think anyone can afford it now." She took a breath and kept going. "But we also know the Japanese businessman who now owns that Van Gogh said he would never give it up. He was quoted as saying he was taking it off the market forever. So, if he did that, a person like that isn't going to permit the art world to know the painting has been sold. He wouldn't allow the publicity. The guy is a fanatic about his privacy. So, I just don't get it."

"And there's Annette's paintings," said Maggie jumping in. "They are utterly pedestrian. Annette is clueless about what's happened to her art. How can she not know? ... and I know I already said it once but she looks ill. I'm really worried about her."

Maggie and Parker told Boyd they were pretty sure Maggie had been stalked – for a very long time. After that news, there was a long silence. The sense of menace was strong.

"We have trouble in River City," Boyd said at last. He looked from Maggie to Parker and back to Maggie again. Suddenly she smiled. River City. Oh.

"Cute," she said.

"Thank you," he replied.

Parker waggled her head. " ... oh ..." She smiled. "Nice."

"That may have been the last bit of humor we can indulge in ... this is not a good scene."

"I'm glad you think so," said Parker. As far as Parker could ascertain, adding up all she knew about rats – Richard being the rat by which all other rats were measured – Boyd was a good guy, just as Maggie had promised. He could be trusted.

"All right. Two questions: are these people dangerous? And where does it leave us?" Boyd had put his two questions 'on the table,' – then he sat back to drink his coffee.

Maggie looked around and ensured that the area was otherwise deserted. The door to Gus' shop was closed. She lowered her voice to a whisper. "Besides the fact that there's no way to report this to the police nor do I want to be on the front page of The Enquirer mouthing off about weird, unprovable shenanigans, you mean?"

Boyd nodded. "Everything seems to be connected with Fleetwater itself."

"What about the doodles?" Maggie asked.

"What doodles?" Parker and Boyd both replied simultaneously.

"Jimmy Ferguson, 23-years old, Mohawk hair-do (nothing wrong with the Mohawk, I'm just saying it's a Mohawk) ... anyway, he's been at Ten Thousand BC Gallery for three years now. That gallery gets six hundred bucks a piece for each of his doodles and splits it 50/50 with him. He looks okay to me. What's wrong with him? I can tell you: nothing." Maggie crossed her arms over her chest and sat back. "He's 23 and he looks fine. But Annette is also my age and she looks about 65. AND you'd think someone would have tempted her to come back to New York by now – and the question to that is: why not?"

"Because," answered Parker, "the gallery people here do everything but blow their nose and wipe the behind of the artist they rep. You can look at me like that all you want, Maggs, but I'm telling you how I see it. Could the gallery split, the advertising and promotion here be that good?"

"Not the split. Mine's the standard 50/50. Nothing special or strange about that and I'm still been making out like a bandit," Maggie answered. "Of course, the advertising budget is outrageous. Arthur does it like he's Cecil B. DeMille ...."

"... or Ringling Brothers ..." Parker said, interrupting.

Which reminded Boyd. "This Jimmy Ferguson, Esquire, does not have a contract with his gallery."

"How do you know that?" Parker asked.

"Because he hired me to re-do the bathroom in his cottage and we got to talking. Didn't seem important at the time. But that was almost two years ago; of course maybe by now he does have a contract because his work is popular."

"No. Actually his show is finally closing," Maggie said. "He told me he's moving back to New York. He's homesick. I saw him at my opening. We managed a couple of minutes ... I told him I'd miss him. And I will ... well, I would have ... (Parker was glaring at Maggie) ...but of course we're leaving ... uh, I'll see him in the city ..." and her voice wound down to silence.

"So, that's takes care of Jimmy. A question for the table: what do you think is the matter with Annette?" Parker asked.

"I really have no idea. But it's worrisome," Maggie replied.

"Maggie, how do you feel? I mean it. Do you *feel* all right?" Boyd asked.

It wasn't a good moment for introspection but the question was more than fair. "Well, I've been working a lot ... and the opening was pretty exciting ... and exhausting, too. And, to tell the truth, the few days Parkie and I had in New York weren't exactly restful, although we did have a very good time ... we just didn't get a lot of sleep. I'd say I could use about two weeks of sleep, but other than that I'm pretty sure I'm fine. That is, I think I'm fine ..." she looked at Boyd, momentarily unsure.

"She's tired," Parker answered for her. "She needs a break and that Arthur is a slave driver, if you ask me."

Boyd looked at Maggie critically. "Anyone who has worked for over two years without a break like you have should need a rest." He leaned over, kissed her and they shared a quick smile. "The thing is, you think Annette was okay until she started to show exclusively with Arthur. That isn't conclusive evidence. You've been in two group shows here and had one blow-out solo show."

They all went momentarily silent. Where did all this leave them?

"Pack up," Boyd ordered.

"What?" the other two replied together.

"Pack up. Crullers back in the box, bring your coffees. We are going for a walk. Let's see what goes on in Fleetwater, when one is looking for anomalies."

Parker shuddered. She wasn't a wimp but she was glad there were three of them now, like The Three Musketeers. Boyd being a man definitely made her feel more courageous.

As for Maggie, the truth was, with Parker and Boyd here to back her up, she could look at the matter straight on: things are not right here in Fleetwater. Seeing Annette had clinched that.

The way Arthur and his lot had stalked her was definitely hinky. It was just so bizarre. She had been right. Of course, now it didn't matter. But the question was: why? Why go to all that trouble? Why not just invite her here. Galleries were always bringing in artists who would do well. Wasn't that the point? She reminded herself not to let Parker get started on the issue of Trojan horses, said a voice in her head.

"Okay," Maggie agreed. "We research."

It was cold. Luckily they all had coats and gloves and hats. Boyd was wearing his lucky red scarf. He knew it was silly to think the scarf lucky, but there it was. It had brought him Maggie, had it not? It was just a small superstition. He could afford it.

As they strolled, the bright blue afternoon morphed into a pitch-black winter night sky full of stars. It seemed incredible that bad things could be going on in such a pretty place. Maggie was still coming to grips with the knowledge that she had been stalked since childhood.

They walked purposely through town visiting every gallery that was open and pushed their noses to the windows of those that were already closed. Ending up back on Main Street, the three walked forward, Maggie in the lead, until the street became a dirt road, turned into a track, which became a grassy rut and finally they were all standing at the fence of a field in which nothing would grow. It had long since been given a clean bill of health and still nothing would grow. Not even a weed.

No one spoke. Maggie cut in through the fence rails and walked about a hundred feet to the center. Boyd followed. Parker was reluctant about this so she went last.

Maggie asked Boyd for his flashlight. It had lighted the road numerous times when they took walks after dark. Now she was using it to search the ground. Parker thought about breaking the silence but changed her mind. Maggie kicked through the loose dirt and the inert ground. There were depressions here and there. They looked like round burns. Fresh ones. But what did it signify?

"Let's go." Snapping off the flashlight, she gave it back to Boyd. They walked back to the fence and cut through the rails again. Maggie told them what she knew, what she thought. When she had finished, neither refuted her theory.

"I think you are right," said Boyd.

"You do?" Maggie had wondered if Boyd might tell her he thought she was mistaken. He was a very sensible man. Her theory was pretty outrageous.

Parker added, "Take a look at Beth's name. She broke it into two parts: Beth Barrett and Elizabeth Browning – the poetess ... she must think we're awfully stupid humans ..." She didn't finish the sentence.

"Cotillion," Boyd said. "Funny, because it sort of suits him. It's a dance."

"And Nick?" Maggie added. "Klausowitz ... Klaus ... some Santa Claus he'd make. He's not a nice person."

Parker finished it: "So, the names are just made up."

"I'd say so," Boyd concluded.

Maggie was glum. "My beautiful paradise has turned rotten. It's the shits ..."

She told Boyd how William said that people sometimes watched her. "I just thought they were admirers. So did William. How was I to guess?"

Boyd tried to comfort her. "You weren't supposed to find out. That's what underhanded people do. They work in secret. But listen: it isn't necessarily true that everyone was a lurker ... probably just these few."

Maggie rolled her eyes at this. Great. Just a few. But what a treacherous lot those few had turned out to be. And wasn't this exactly what Parker had been saying all along? Maggie had always treated it like a subject of debate, not a real issue. Well, the joke was on her. She obviously didn't know who to trust.

"Maybe this isn't a very big operation. Which means Arthur and Beth and Nick have been doing double-duty."

The girls nodded. They hoped he was right.

"What about Oscar?" Maggie asked. "I really like Oscar. Not that we were close friends but ..."

"You trust him," Boyd said. "Well, trusted – past tense."

Maggie nodded. She looked at Parker. Her eyes were pleading.

"By the way, how do you feel?" Maggie asked Boyd.

"Fine. Why?"

"Because you've done a lot of work for Arthur. You've been the recipient of his largess. We think that maybe Annette got sick after being around ... I sound ridiculous ... it's like being around these people isn't good for your health! Literally."

"I feel fine. The thing is, I do lots of work for different people."

"All Fleetwater 'originals'?" Parker asked.

"No. I get out of the town on plenty of occasions. I've done work all over this area. Also, I'm pretty much on my own."

"Copper Springs?" Maggie asked. Parker's head swiveled quickly in her direction.

"Sure. Been there on jobs ... why?"

Maggie and Parked exchanged glances.

"Do you happen ... that is, did you ever do any work for ..." Maggie didn't go on. "I can't. I can't stand it. Parker, you ask."

"Do you know or did you do any work for an older man, by chance? James Fuyard, some kind of English accent, white mustache ..."

"James? Sure."

Both girls groaned.

"Why?" Boyd looked from Maggie to Parker. With all the millions of stars blanketing overhead, he could see their features clearly.

Maggie shook her head. She wouldn't answer.

"Uh, because, we think he's one of ... *them*," Parker explained.

"James? Oh, no. He's lived there for years. He couldn't be. He's nothing like Arthur or Beth."

"Neither is Oscar, really. The thing is, we know James, too. Well, I know him, that is," Maggie said finally. "We're ... uh ... sort of ... friends. We seem to ride the same train a lot ... oh, Parkie. Not him, too."

Parker reached over and patted Maggie on the shoulder. "I don't think he's part of this." She decided to tell Boyd everything they had pieced together.

"But I think he was ... at one point ... now I'm just working it through, you understand ... it's like that whole conversation on the train was *coded*. Can you see that? Think about it. He wants you to go to Italy with me. He said to say hello to his old friend, Oscar ..."

"That's right. He didn't mention Arthur or Beth but he has to know them because everyone knows everyone else around here. His card! Remember, he gave me his card. I have to give it to Oscar. We have to go. Now."

Boyd and Parker didn't argue.

Starting back, walking briskly, Parker said, "I think we should go back Homer's and rent the Volvo again ... do you agree?"

"We don't have to," said Boyd. "I have a car. Let's see if we can find Oscar – but only if it's easy ... otherwise, what

365

I think, first and foremost is this: I think we need to leave. Right now. While we are safe ... even if we don't have the whole story. Even if everyone around here decides we were on drugs and out of our minds ... and Maggie, I think you have to leave everything that comes from Fleetwater in Fleetwater. That's going to be a sacrifice but it's just a feeling I have. Nothing from Fleetwater can come with you. I think that's important."

She agreed. Reluctantly. One way or another, all the paintings she had done were here in Fleetwater. Much of her work had been sold, although two of the big paintings were still at the gallery as well as the rest of the smaller format paintings ... but she had some notebooks in her room that were now pretty full of interesting sketches ... they would have to stay behind. It felt like a knife in her heart.

"Where's your car?" Parker asked while Maggie kept her silence, knowing what was occupying her best friend's mind.

"Back at this end of town. I pay for the space. The car is mine. I brought it with me. So, it's mine. It doesn't belong to Fleetwater. We're agreed?"

"Absolutely," Parker answered up immediately.

"Maggie?"

"So ... it's ..." She was having trouble finishing her sentence. "Let's just go."

Boyd put his arm around her shoulder. Parker put her arm around Maggie from the other side. They stood like that. Overhead an unseen shooting star was fleeing in a long arc through the darkness.

After a half hour of steady walking the road picked up again. Within a few minutes they were back at Maggie's room. She packed anything that was really hers and put it into her suitcase. Her hands quivered when she passed over the sketchbooks. She had done a lot of good drawings here in Fleetwater.

"I'm sorry, Maggs ..." Boyd said. She knew he was right. "You can do them again. No one can take that away from you."

"I know. I get it. I'm almost done." Leaving like this, sneaking out like thieves in the night, was difficult.

Parker had agreed with him. Nothing from Fleetwater could come with them. She went through her suitcase and took out a brand new jersey purchased at a local boutique to commemorate her Fleetwater visit, some art cards gathered from various galleries. Even a golf pencil picked up at Homer's. "It all stays," she said grimly and put it all into a now empty drawer in the dresser.

"Whatever is here in Fleetwater needs to stay in Fleetwater," Boyd said again with finality. "And that includes the crullers," which remark should have been funny, but wasn't. "That means all my tools. I bought all my tools here at the hardware store. They cost me a fortune ... it's the only way. It has to be a total disconnection." Maggie and Parker looked at him with sympathy. Up until now it didn't seem as though this tragedy touched him. But this leaving of tools brought it home. He was leaving, too. Leaving it all behind. It was truly upsetting.

Boyd's main concern was: would what they are doing be enough? He didn't want them being followed to New

York. Nothing like have enemies tracking you in a big anonymous city – people with greater resources than they had. He wouldn't say anything about it to the girls unless he had to.

"All right. Let's go." But Maggie and Parker were staring at him. "What?" And Maggie touched his shirt gingerly. She reached into her bag and pulled out an old sweater. Luckily it had stretched out with long use. He changed tops. The girls looked at his pants.

"Oh, no. Those stay. I have to wear something. I can't fit into yours jeans so forget it." It was true. Boyd was nearly six feet tall and Maggie only 5'4". "I'll buy some new ones as soon as we get to the city and burn this stuff." The girls agreed. It would have to do. He was leaving everything, too. Literally.

Boyd loaded Parker and Maggie's suitcases into the back seat and drove the car out to the edge of town. They were parked in the lay-by consulting a map when he realized someone else was there, standing by the side of the road. He stowed the map and very slowly let the car dribble forward a few yards. Was it Arthur? How would he know what Boyd and the girls had or had not figured out? He should be at the Gallery. Moreover, Boyd did not want a confrontation. He didn't know what these ... people ... were capable of. Or what kind of weapons they might be carrying.

"It's Oscar," said Maggie recognizing him first. She sagged with relief.

"What's he doing here?!" Parker whispered.

"Be ready in case I have to gun the motor," Boyd warned.

Maggie rolled down the window. "Hi, Oscar. What are you doing up so late?" She had to work hard to keep her voice neutral.

"You're leaving," he said.

"What do you mean?"

"You don't have to leave. The Austin-Millers want to give you the commission, Maggie. They told me so tonight. I went to your room at Mrs. Aubrey's but she said she hadn't seen you all day. I tried your studio, but it was locked. I walked all around town. People said they had seen the three of you just looking in the gallery windows ... I know you come out to the pasture sometimes. I come out here, too. To get away. So much hubbub ..."

The starry light was gentle on his face. His jacket was open and she could see his pink suspenders. The ones he always wore.

"Where's your coat, Oscar? A suit jacket isn't enough. It's cold." Maggie said kindly.

"Oh, back at the gallery."

She nodded.

"We want you, Maggie. We ... uh, we need you. You are one of our best. A real success story. Two years ... it's been two years ..." Oscar's voice was sad. "You're a real success story." He knew he was repeating himself. He was sounding like Arthur, which made this all the worse.

"Oscar, here ... take this," Maggie said in a whisper and taking James' card out of her pocket, shoved it out the window and into his hand which was resting on the rolled down window. "Don't lose this, whatever you do ..."

Oscar had just taken the card and slipped it into his coat pocket when a voice in the dark said, "Don't beg, Oscar." It was a harsh voice. "We never beg."

Maggie recognized it immediately. The chill might be a new tone but there was no doubt. Boyd and Parker recognized it, too.

"You're a fool." The voice was cutting.

Maggie knew he was addressing her. She didn't want to answer. It was hard not to. She was very used to being responsive to his wishes.

"I could make you stay, you know."

It was alarming. Frightening. The three of them, wondering if that was true, went stiff. Was being in a car any kind of protection?

"But I won't. Because you'll be back. You are a success here, Maggie. You are famous here. Here you are rich. And since you visited Annette – of course I know – you've seen that artists who aren't in my gallery tend to grow older a bit faster.

"But success will keep you young. Success such as my artists achieve," he was crooning. Of course, this was only partly true. The other part was that success sometimes burned his artists like dry paper set on fire. His smile faded. "Wait until you've been home for a few weeks. Don't be surprised at what you find in the mirror."

Arthur's words were ugly. It made Maggie's blood run cold. Parker was gripping Maggie's hand much too hard. It didn't matter. Maggie didn't want Parker to let go. In the driver's seat, Boyd's knuckles were showing white as he held the steering wheel. Who knew exactly what this person – these people – were capable of, if thwarted.

"You, too." This scorn was aimed at Boyd. "We've been very nice to you. We gave you a family." His hatred was palpable.

Maggie and Parker were almost mesmerized by the invective, but Boyd was not. He had met similar people when he was young. Being an orphan had taught him certain lessons, even those he would rather not have learned. It wasn't pleasant, the way a stranger would look him over, like an object, something to be selected or rejected. As though orphans were a group apart. Those experiences had tested him. Standing in line, being looked over like a cat or dog at the pound. Take me before I'm put down! All he knew was that he had been passed over again in favor of a different boy. Somehow he had survived the process. Now it was paying off. Arthur's eyes were blazing. Boyd's were cool and unreadable. And inaccessible.

"Stupid humans," Arthur sneered.

Beth called out, "Come, Arthur, we don't need her."

CHAPTER TWO

So, they were all there. Almost. Where was Nick? It reminded Maggie like nothing as much as Moses telling the Pharaoh that the Israelites were leaving Egypt. Someone else would have to do the slaving hereafter. But the Pharaoh didn't want to let them go. Where was God now, where were the seven plagues? What did Arthur have to lose? There were no 'first sons". How would the waters be parted?

"I want to talk to Maggie," he replied, closing in.

"Maggs ... don't listen to him," Parker whispered.

"Please, Ms. Feldman. Don't be so crass. We don't do that sort of thing. You've been watching too much television," Arthur replied, waving a hand dismissively. "Step out a moment, won't you, Maggie, hmmm? We should talk." He sounded more reasonable. Persuasive.

She opened the door and sat very still. Slipping her legs around, stood up. Could he do something to her? Violent or otherwise?

Arthur turned around and stepped to the rear of the car and waited. It was very convincing. After a hesitation, Maggie followed. They spoke very softly so no one could hear. Maggie kept shaking her head, Arthur gesturing with his hand. He made a cutting sign. Maggie edged back and got into the front seat again.

Looking out the window at Oscar, who was standing next to Arthur and Beth, she said, "Good-bye, Oscar. I shall miss you." To Boyd, "We're going now."

Maggie heard Arthur tell Oscar to return to the gallery. Saying it like he was the one Israelite who wouldn't be allowed to leave. It gave her the shivers. Oscar probably was a slave, when all was said and done. Unfortunately. There was no story in the Old Testament that covered this scenario. But Oscar had done her no harm. This she was sure of.

"Oscar ... come with us," she called out. He was a only few yards away. He could do it. He could be saved. Interrupting the pastoral quiet, they could hear a sniggering. It was Nick, looming directly in front of the car. His hand was up, holding something.

"Come here, Earth Boy. I want to have a discussion with you," and he motioned with his hand. In it was a gun. Nick laughed.

"Nick, stop this," Arthur ordered.

"Shut up, Arthur. Come on. Out of the car."

"Oh, god," Maggie wailed quietly.

Boyd turned to Parker and said in a low voice, "You take the wheel. If anything happens, anything – you both get out of here. That's an order. Maybe he just wants to fight or just threaten me because he can ... we'll see. Just don't panic. Remember, no looking back, no slowing down, nothing." Boyd knew about bullies.

"All right," Parker promised and she slid over and took the wheel as Boyd got out. Her hand was on the ignition key.

"That's it. Just step right over here," Nick called. He was loving it. A showdown. Finally a little fun for Nickie.

The two men faced off.

"Nick, stop it. Right now," Arthur ordered.

But Nick wasn't going to stop it. Boyd could see that. Quickly sizing up the odds, Boyd was sure he was stronger. And faster. If he took advantage of the situation now .... he lunged forward and grabbed Nick's wrist. Boyd wrenched the gun away and slammed Nick's hand against the car with a metallic thud. Nick yelped. He punched Nick in the face, which put him on the ground a second later. Boyd stepped back, the gun now hanging safely down in his own hand.

Nick was winded but only for the instant. He aimed a vicious kick at Boyd with one boot. With no place to move, Boyd wasn't fast enough to get out of the way so his knee took the full brunt of the blow. Pain went rocketing up through his body and his leg buckled but the car was there and he fell against it. Nick was up again. This time he had a knife in his hand, pulled from his jacket pocket. Boyd saw it. He didn't wait. He just cocked the gun and let off a bullet. Straight into Nick's stomach it went, blood spurting just like a movie stunt squib. The knife fell harmlessly in the dirt at their feet as Nick looked down at himself. He put a finger into the hole. He was laughing. Grinning and laughing. Marvelous. He was shot. Really shot.

Arthur had put out a protective arm in front of Beth, but she pushed him off. In the instant, she walked over to Nick. Looking down at him, she said, "You really are useless." Arthur was not pleased.

"Step away, Beth" he ordered. That was the voice of a commander, not civilian request, and she stepped back.

"That's enough," Arthur said to Boyd. "It's over."

Nick had folded onto the grass. He was smiling but the smile was thinning out.

"You can leave now." Arthur reached down and picked up the knife, closed it and put it in his pocket. "Take that thing." indicating the gun, "with you. I've changed my mind, of course, he said looking at Maggie, who was staring out the open window with a dropped jaw. He told her, "Your contract is at an end. I hope you enjoyed it all, my dear, because in all likelihood, things will never be that wonderful again. All the adulation, the big checks for big paintings ... it's over, you understand. All over. What happens in our little paradise, stays in our little paradise. All of it. If you get my meaning."

Maggie said nothing but gaped at Arthur wide-eyed. She looked at Nick, now laying on the ground, his breathing labored.

"Get out now" Arthur demanded. He turned his back on the car and bent over Nick's body. "Beth, come ...we have work to do."

Maggie opened the door and pushed over. Boyd hobbled in. He quickly stored the gun in the glove compartment and strapped on his seat belt. Parker gunned the motor. Stomping her foot all the way to the floor, the engine cranked up noisily. Dirt was flying from the back wheels as the car peeled off down the road. The sudden forward motion of the car pressed them to the seat. She only let up when they reached the exit onto the highway and slowed down, checking for the traffic streaming by.

Looking over her shoulder through the rear view mirror, she assured herself that no one was chasing them. Gauging the traffic flow, she found an opening and quickly entered the outside lane. Driving as fast as she dared, she was willing the car to blend with the busy lanes already crowded with traffic, with the many hundreds of humans in automobiles going to the city pouring by her. If this was any kind of protection, even if unnecessary, she wanted it. They all wanted it.

Boyd was sitting stiffly looking straight out the window. He had never shot another person. Now that the moment was over, he knew he didn't feel quite well. Also his knee was throbbing angrily. He remembered he didn't even like going after squirrels and rabbits when he was a kid. While other kids enthusiastically grabbed BB guns for small animal target practice, he stayed behind and read books or kept himself busy ... but that was then. This was now.

CHAPTER THREE

Watching the taillights in front, matching the speed around her, Parker kept her eyes on the road. After a bit Boyd said aloud that it was unlikely that Arthur would follow them, even if he had considered it before. Whatever their plans, it had apparently not included fist fighting, knives or gunplay. That's not how they worked their scheme, he said. No one from Fleetwater would be coming to see them. He wouldn't be chased for shooting Nick or hounded if he'd killed the man after all. "We'll find a spot and get rid of the gun. I don't want it."

The girls agreed. They didn't want it either.

A few miles later Boyd said he wouldn't be surprised if Fleetwater simply closed down at the end of season and didn't open up – ever again. Or maybe that was wishful thinking. At least he was pretty sure the unexpected shooting had changed the game plan in some way.

No one before had ever given up the limelight, apparently. It might be taken away, but no one walked away, he allowed. Except Maggie. She had done that.

Boyd looked at her proudly. His usual attitude was live and let live. Right now he needed to calm down. The death of one of ours was no barrier to their success. However, the potential death of one of their side was a major dampener. That was why he had shot Nick. Boyd hadn't planned on letting Nick get even as close as he had done, so when he did, seeing Nick had ignored Arthur's order, using the gun was not a problem. Nick was not under control. But the bullet had stopped the drama from playing out. It proved to Boyd that these people weren't real fighters. The loss of even a single combatant, even a petty player ... that had stopped them.

Their main method was persuasion. Preying on the desire of people like Maggie to have the breakthrough they weren't otherwise able to achieve. Even Annette, who had been a huge success, was being duped. Because Arthur was offering her more. Somehow Arthur arranged it so it seemed as though he could do something for her no one else could or would. Their campaigns on behalf of an artist were quite formidable in fact ... all the artist had to do was create. Show up and create. Present the work and ...

For who? Who was doing all the buying? His knee was still hurt but he shut that out because he wanted to think. Obviously Fleetwater had a lively crowd of art enthusiasts. Moreover, there were day-trippers in abundance. Any way you looked at it, the artists in Fleetwater were thriving until ... and that shut Boyd up. He finally understood.

Maggie wasn't talking. She was just sitting there, squeezed in the middle of the seat, still shocked into silence. Still coming to grips with Nick being shot and worried about Annette, who was back there, sick. She might die. It would be up to the three of them to get her to pry her out of there and into a hospital.

"That Beth," Parker growled. "What if she goes back to work at the public library again? Trolling for artists, no doubt. I don't know how we could stop her. Do you really think we'll wake up ugly and old next week?"

Boyd said he thought not. "I suppose nothing's impossible. But I don't believe there's a time warp in Fleetwater. Time goes by in Fleetwater just like it does everywhere else. Arthur just said that to upset us."

"Well, it worked. And we are stupid humans, in a way. Didn't you notice that nothing ever really went wrong with one of their shows? I know Maggie doesn't like to think about it, but disappointments are pretty natural. One has to learn how to handle these things and move on. That takes strength. We all face barriers. Look at what Arthur is offering. Kind of an artist's dream, wouldn't you say?"

Maggie would say yes. Except that it had been a war after all. At least nine years long. And there had been a gift horse. She remembered the dream now. The gigantic horse – just like the one designed by Leonardo Da Vinci. A magnificent creature. Almost alive. It came bearing everything she had ever wanted, and just as soon as she took it inside her fortress ... well, she had been a fool. A stupid human. That's what Arthur had called them.

"Sometimes when you are so focused on a goal, nothing else matters. I didn't notice it either," Boyd admitted. "Even when there little signs, I ignored them. Please, Maggs, don't be too hard on yourself. We all wanted it to be perfect. I'm no different." He gave a dry laugh and went quiet.

Some miles down the road Boyd reached over and opened up the glove compartment. He looked at the gun.. He shut the compartment door again. "I see how they get you. They just do everything for you. You can own someone by getting them to fight you or ..."

"Give them everything they want." That was Maggie.

It was so.

No one spoke again for another while.

Parker took her eyes off the road an instant and looked at the engagement ring on her finger. What would Tony say about all this? How she would ever be able explain any of it, if she even wanted to?

In the meantime, Boyd's attention had shifted to wondering if Gelman had been a party to this charade. Keeping away from Maggie's opening. Did it even matter now? Who else was involved? He looked at Maggie. At regular intervals the highway lights would flash across the car illuminating her profile. She was just staring straight ahead. He had to say something to her.

"I'm sorry I wasn't there for the opening. I don't know if I exactly realized Gelman was trying to keep me there deliberately, but this morning his 'just one more thing' was the last straw." He paused. "I'm not leaving you," he said to Maggie. "I want to be with you." There. He had said it. Finally.

She swallowed over a lump in her throat. "I know." She was glad to hear it. As bad as things were right now, she was glad to hear it. There was something else on her mind. .

"I ought to tell you what Arthur said to me, back there, when I got out of the car. The thing is, you really did figure it out. What he said was: 'All you have to do is paint. We'll do the rest. We can give you everything you need ... everything. He meant it. He really can. That's the hardest part. If you're an artist like me, and you've struggled and struggled and doors don't open – not by manipulation – but just because you can't get them open ... he could. He could have had me without any of that. I would have gone to Fleetwater if he had just asked me. And even if I had known, I might ..." she stopped. But it was there and she needed to say it ..."I might have gone anyway, thinking I won't be like the rest. Thinking I'm stronger. Thinking I could leave. I could always walk away ..." Tears were spurting from here eyes. "Oh, nuts. When you want it that bad? I'm a liar. I would have stayed. 'Til the bitter end. Like that crazy actress in "Sunset Blvd". One more close-up. Just one more. I would have ended up dead. No one would have been able to pry me out of there." She stopped. Swallowing hard over the lump that now lay like a stone, she kept going. "Parker, she knew. In some way. She knows me so well. Talk about a major flaw. In every letter she wrote to me, in every way she could, she warned me ... all my life she's been warning me. There is a price for being feted and cosseted, for having every whim fulfilled. I didn't want to listen. That's all. I just didn't want to listen. I would have paid the price."

Parker took one hand off the steering wheel and squeezed Maggie's arm.

"I'm okay now. It's over. I'm back to reality."

Boyd rolled down the car window to let in some air.

Maggie spoke again. "Boyd is right. Beth Barrett won't be coming back to the library if she knows we are on the lookout for her. She'll have to find another way to recruit."

"Do you think he really could have *made* us stay?" Parker asked. The whole experience was like being inside an episode of "Twilight Zone." She didn't want to talk about it anymore and yet ... better to ask every weird question. Get it all out of her system, if she could.

"Us, maybe, but not you," Boyd said.

"Me?"

"Yes. I was thinking about it. Please don't be offended but you aren't an artist. Even you say so. You weren't trying to belong in Fleetwater. We were growing roots back there. There are people who come and stay. I think they can't get away. Something holds certain people there. Artists and certain others. The rest: they are just 'extras'. Like in the movies."

"I'm no saint, I assure you. You should only know. Maggs here, she knows. And me: having Richard for a father? That's like starving to death at a table loaded with good food."

Boyd looked at her puzzled.

"I'll explain it to you sometime, if you're interested. But really. It's not that big a deal now. I couldn't have said that to you last year. A lot has happened. Sometimes it's hard to see the forest for the trees."

"Amen," said Maggie very softly. "Amen."

Boyd would ask. A long time later, and Parker would tell him her story.

Maggie leaned forward and peered through the windshield. "I'm glad there's so much traffic. I sure wouldn't want this road all to myself." She sat back. The warmth of Boyd's arm on her shoulder was comforting. It was heavy. Heavy and warm. A happy weight.

"I don't know if we'll ever know the whole truth. I don't think I want know. I know enough as it is. We're never going back. I don't think we'll be seeing any of them again. Anyway, you see how it works. The way they seduce a person. Very smart really. But you, Parker, were never a part of *this.*" She didn't feel like talking anymore.

"Maggie probably told you, I got to Fleetwater eight years ago. Look at me. I'm out in the sun for days on end, year in and year out and I still don't have a wrinkle. I'm twenty-eight now. Now that I think about it, I should at least have some laugh lines around the eyes. They like to joke about how living in Fleetwater keeps you young. Maybe it wasn't a joke. It keeps you young – up to a point ... and then ..." but he didn't finish because Annette was still back there, and she was sick.

"About the burn marks," Maggie said softly, cautiously. "They're fresh."

Boyd looked at her. She was right. "Yeah. That pasture. It's a worry. But we're not going back. Of course you both know, no one would believe us. It's too outrageous."

"Too bad," said Parker. "Anyway, I think we got the picture. And Arthur, good old Arthur said just enough to confirm our suspicions. I've had enough."

"Me, too," conceded Maggie and she put her hand in Boyd's.

"Yeah. Enough is enough."

Suddenly Boyd told Parker to find a way to pull over. She hit the right-hand signal and moved over two lanes ... carefully. Finally they were driving next to the shoulder of the road. She watched for a lay-by. It took a few miles to find it but she found her slot and signaled. Having made her move, she pulled over and stopped the car.

"Okay," said Boyd. "Everyone out of the car. Right now. Start looking around the car. In your pockets. In your suitcase, Maggie. In your purses and backpacks. Look for anything that belongs in Fleetwater. I mean anything. Excluding my pants and underwear, you hussies," he joked. Anything to lighten the moment.

He didn't give them time to argue or question. Hurriedly opening up the trunk, he found his favorite all-purpose brush. Taking it out, he began to work the sand and dirt off the tires. Using a 5-gallon tank marked "sea water" he flushed the tires. After that, he didn't want to touch it again and threw the brush into the trash barrel. Emptying the last of the salt water on the ground, the plastic tank was crushed and also dumped into the roadside barrel.

"Okay, the trunk is clear. Maggie? Look everywhere. You, too, Parker."

It took half a minute to find and empty the chocolate cruller crumbs from Maggie's jacket pocket. A careful search under the front seat uncovered a Gus' paper bag with one cruller still uneaten (the one for Evan, finally) and an unused postcard of Gus himself holding his ubiquitous tray of fresh pastry. Into the barrel it went, albeit reluctantly. Another thorough search located a piece of Dentyne gum in the pocket of Parker's coat, beneath her mittens, purchased from the dispenser at Homer's. They scoped out every place in the car. Boyd reached in and took the gun out of the glove compartment. Taking a rag he wiped it clean. "This has got to be done," and he dropped that into the trash barrel, too.

Looking down at his feet, he growled. "My work boots! Well, I'll need new footwear, too. Everything I own is from Fleetwater ..."

"Except your car," Parker reminded.

"Everything but that. See how Fleetwater holds onto you? We'll change our tune when everything is gone."

"Too bad about your pants," said Parker with a grin, "but it's too cold. We'll just have to take you shopping with us. You haven't lived until you've been shopping with us." The girls were grinning. It felt better already.

"So we really need to leave it <u>all</u> behind. No moaning how good things were, what Arthur can do to us, how bad Beth was. Even that rat, Nick. It's over, right?" Parker asked.

"Right," Maggie agreed. "Boyd's got it right. Everything belonging to Fleetwater stays in Fleetwater. Even Arthur understood that – and that's the last time I mention Arthur, okay?" She looked at them both. "Okay?"

Boyd and Parker nodded. But Maggie was already thinking about Moses, floating in a basket. Befriended by the Pharaoh. Better to have left Moses in the river. See what happened? I'll bet that Pharaoh was sorry ... "Let me say this just once: I'm sorry about Oscar. I think he was a good guy. Maybe he was a part of the trap ... but in the end ..." It was hard to imagine: Oscar alone, standing in the middle of that strip of ocean bed while two mountains of miraculously parted water hovered high into the sky. They wouldn't stay that way very long. He's going to be drowned, along with all the Pharaoh's army ...

Parker gave her a hug. "I'm glad you said that about Oscar. I thought he was okay, too. But listen. There's something I read somewhere ... I didn't understand it before. I do now: How does it go? Oh, yes. 'There is no hope for the satisfied man.' "

Boyd understood. To him, Fleetwater had finally become the home he never had. He had been very satisfied. He thought he didn't need to hold onto a certain reserve and hope that his life would turn out well, that he could have a home at last, because he had finally let down his guard a little and he had been comfortable. He did feel settled and safe ... and then he met Maggie. Nothing of his life in Fleetwater compared with his future, once he met her. It hadn't occurred to him but until he met her, he didn't really have a future. Just a 'now' – a very acceptable, rather moderate, modest 'now'. He'd been so hungry for a stable life, he'd missed the fact that he was slowly smothering. Sinking into agreement. But with Maggie. Well, that was a vista that kept opening up – wider and wider still. Oh, he wanted to be with her. That he knew without a doubt. Even if none of this insane drama had happened to them. He let go of Maggie's hand which she had been gripping it for some time and from his pocked he extracted a little black velvet box.

He wanted to tell her: anywhere Maggie was, was home. He didn't know if he should say it yet. "I understand how those people owned us both. I was an easy mark, no matter what it was that brought me to Fleetwater. And remember, no one is looking for me. I have no family. As for Parker? She would be with Tony in Italy and you would be busy with your career. See? You were so successful, she didn't need to be looking after you anymore. So there you are, Maggie. After awhile your visits home would be fewer and fewer ... you know how it is. Your Nonie is getting old. You're a grownup now. Your parents won't insist on your coming to visit. Maybe you'd outlive your parents ... or maybe not. But either way, it would all be over. Do you understand? Your parents would never guess anything was wrong. People get sick, don't they? I mean, it's a tragedy but ... you would get sick ... and ... they really did have it all worked out." It was monstrous.

Finally he was shaking. He had been strong for years and years ... and now, he was shaking. Now he realized how close he had come to losing everything that mattered to him.

The girls nodded. They stood in a tight huddle. The wind from cars rushing by would buffet them. Passing traffic was making the ground rumble. It was late now. In fact, they had passed the darkest part of the night. Morning would be coming.

Boyd had worked it out. "When you think about it: they <u>are</u> mad for art. Any kind of art. It's all just close enough to the nuttiness of the real art world so that no one coming in from the outside would guess. It's like they feed off artists. They trap artists there and ... well, that's all. They just live there. Every whim, every desire, every goal. What could possibly be the matter with that! Arthur gave you everything. What is there to complain about? You can own a person by just giving them everything they want."

It was true. Isn't that what every artist wanted? Just to be able to create and not think about anything else. Maggie hardwired to making paintings and nothing else. Like she was a goose laying golden eggs. What kind of life was that? It looked good at first because the urge to create was so tremendous but ... what about friends, what about love ... a home and the other stuff? What about the rest of life?

Maggie had forgotten all about that in her drive to have a career.

"And then I met you," Maggie said to Boyd. She put her head against his shoulder.

"And then you met me."

There was a moment of silence. "All right, boys and girls. It's time to blow this joint," Parker cracked and she got back into the car, turned on the motor and the heater. Outside, Boyd and Maggie were still standing close. It was true. Now that he had said it, faced it all, he was right. The longer they were away from Fleetwater and the greater the distance, the less he felt the connection. Getting rid of everything that tied them to the place was vital.

As for Maggie, she wondered if she would even remember any of this after awhile. Is that how it happened? Maybe some other memory would replace the truth and she wouldn't know any better, she wouldn't question it. Maybe. Maybe not. There was no way to know until ... Maggie climbed back into the car. The door was still open. Finally Boyd got in, too. It turned out that having all three of them squished into the front seat was comforting. They had exorcised their demons. Now for a quiet ride home the rest of the way.

"Remember: don't wonder about any of it," Boyd said. "It's over. That's the point. We don't have to wonder. We don't have to care. Maybe we won't forget, but we're free now. Whatever they were going to 'make happen for us', we can do it ourselves. We're capable. That's the main point."

Boyd rubbed his eyes. He had gotten up early to make the drive back to Fleetwater. It had been a hell of a day. He meant to take his own advice and stop thinking ... and yet ... it came to him that he had deliberately broken twice with places he had settled in and now he was doing it again. He had to admit to himself that he, too, had liked living in Fleetwater. It had suited him. Work was plentiful, he and Maggie were having a good life ... the fact was, he had been played, too, as Arthur had made clear. It was brutal knowledge. Well, they were clever fellows, Arthur and his gang. Clever enough. They had gotten what they wanted for a long time. Now the lies were exposed. Now it was over. The game – whatever it was they were doing... hope you liked it while it lasted, Arthur. Goodbye and good riddance.

CHAPTER FOUR

Back on the road again, the traffic was beginning to slow down. A lot of people were going home.

Maggie asked, "Do you think that if Arthur finds out James has tried to reach Oscar, that'll put Oscar in danger?"

"It might, but Oscar's a very smart guy. He can take care of himself. I don't think he's quite the pushover Arthur thinks he is. You see, that's part of it. Arthur underestimates people. Oscar will be okay," Boyd explained. Anyway, he hoped so.

Parker looked at Maggie. She didn't want to admit that not coming home to see Maggie might have gotten her killed. How would she have lived with that? She had made a promise and not kept it. All the reasons in the world didn't cut it. She and Maggie were supposed to grow to be old ladies together, doddering into the café at Rockefeller Center and slurping their hot chocolates. They would talk about this later.

She asked Boyd, "Was there ever a time when you thought maybe Gelman was deliberately keeping you on the job?"

"Yes. When I agreed to miss the opening. It was just the most fleeting thought. So tiny ... so tiny ... I called Maggs and explained it ... and she was so understanding. It was the easiest thing in the world. The money was so good ..."

Parker rolled up the window again. It was too noisy and cold outside. They still had a ways to go before they reached the city. There was a little time for each to do some thinking, some considering. The last, final bits.

For Maggie it meant realizing the whole past two years really had been a lie. Even if her patrons, as she liked to call them, did like her work, there was so much else about the whole matter that had been manipulated and troubling. It was too too bad. Rats. And double rats. Fleetwater had been her idea of paradise and now it was just a bad place where she might have died young. She shivered at the thought. Now that the adrenaline rush was over and she was calming down a little, she wondered aloud, "How am I going to explain this to Mom and Dad?"

Boyd answered. "Maybe you won't have to. Or we'll think of something."

"Right. We've decided we're not going to call the police," Parker asked. "Too bad. It'd be nice to know they were locked up"

"We can't prove anything. None of it," Maggie replied. "We'd just sound crazy. Can't you hear it now? You see, Officer, there are these bad people. What happens is this: if you're an artist, like me, they will give you just about anything you want ... all you have to do is ... oh sure, little missy. It sounds bad. Really vicious. Let's go arrest them right now. "

Parker sniggered.

"You could stifle that, you know," but she laughed, too.

"No, you should laugh," Parker noted. "Because we're ridiculous."

"It's amazing how many people would give anything to have what we just gave up," Boyd remarked.

Maggie agreed. "Yes, there are. Artists who would give anything. Artists who already have. Like Annette."

That was a sobering thought. They would absolutely have to do something about Annette. It would be tricky. Parker understood. "We'll help you," she said to Maggie. "One way or another. If she can't understand, if she won't come back, at least we know we did everything we could."

"We will do something, Maggs," Boyd said. "Somehow we'll do it." He hoped it was true.

"It's freaky. They had me in their sights the whole time. And you. Just enough of the artist in everything you do ... think about it. A pedestrian person wouldn't attract their attention. When I think of how easy I made it for them. What a sitting duck. I'm going to have to begin all over again," she said ruefully. "Back in the Manhattan Pond I'm one very small minnow. Isn't that funny?" (But she wasn't laughing.) "I was so important in Fleetwater. Amazing how good that feels. Now it's hello to being just about back where I started – back to "Maggie Who? " Maggie moaned silently.

"Maybe not," Parker said. "You know a lot now that you didn't know before. What's to stop you from making more paintings? What about write-ups, reviews. You can't be a complete non-entity after the ruckus you raised."

Maggie shrugged. "Maybe. Oh, I don't know. Suppose all that new work was just part of being there ..."

"No. You had your breakthrough at our apartment. Remember? *Who has the first drawing?*"

"You do! I forgot!"

"Yeah, well, I didn't. Not only that, but it's totally safe because I took it to Italy with me!"

"Oh, if you weren't driving I would kiss you!"

"You can kiss me as a substitute," Boyd volunteered and Parker heard the rustle of the coats moving together.

Parker took a quick peep. She caught Boyd's eye for just an instant. In that unspoken moment, they both knew: when you marry the girl, you get the family, the friends, the whole nine yards and it was okay because Boyd was okay with Parker.

A horn blared. Someone didn't like the way Parker moved over one lane. "Honk all you want. It doesn't matter. I love you all anyway!" she crowed. In fact they were very close to the city now and drivers were jockeying for their various exits. In spite of all the motion, there was tremendous comfort to be had in the sea of cars, pairs of red tail lights in the hundreds or thousands, and the closer they came to the city, the better Parker felt.

After finding their off-ramp, Parker broke the silence. "Listen, Maggie. I don't believe all that enthusiasm was fake. I think your paintings are wonderful. And unique. If you can sell in Fleetwater, you can sell other places, too. Don't let Arthur's poison get into your system. He needed you. You don't need him to be an artist. You were an artist long before he came along."

Exiting the Queens Mid-town Tunnel, Parker took a familiar, if hurried, left turn into a side street and parked by a small supermarket.

"What's the matter?" Maggie asked.

"There's something we haven't talked about," Parker said, looking a bit serious.

Maggie shook her head. "I don't know what you mean. We're home. We're safe. Everything I painted or drew is back there in Fleetwater ... except the original "Red Toaster" ... I mean, really the only thing that came with is ... is Boyd ... and ..."

Parker shook her head. "No. Actually, there is one more little thing." And here she looked expectantly at Maggie. But Maggie didn't get it. "Boyd? A little help here ..."

Rats, Parker cursed. I'm going to have to be the baddie here. "Okay, children. Let me help you." Pregnant pause. "Money? The money. You know. The moola ... the gelt ... the francs, pesos, dinero ..."

Maggie looked puzzled.

"Oh." from Boyd. He looked at Maggie and waited another few seconds. "Our ill-gotten gain."

"What ...?" Maggie yelped. "What do you mean?! Ill-gotten? I slaved for every penny of that!! Oh, god. I earned it! I mean ... it's ... so ... much ... oh ... oh ... uh-oh ... noooooo," she wailed. "My money! Boyd! You can't be serious! Oh my god, it's so much money!!"

"Well, Maggs. It's up to you. You'll decide."

"But ... but ... it's ... it's ... gazillions. It's ... it's mega-zillions." She stopped.

Boyd and Parker shrugged. It wasn't their decision to make. Boyd had the same problem. His bank account was in Fleetwater. Luckily he had made some money years ago, before he got to Fleetwater that was invested elsewhere, but it wasn't much. His little fortune, as he called it, had mostly been earned working in Fleetwater ... like Maggie's. "I don't know. I have the same problem you have. Well, actually, I already made my decision.. I don't care what happens to my money in Fleetwater. They can keep it."

"Suppose the money from that Japanese publishing house was part of their scheme. I spent a bunch of it ... oh, hell and damnation. Whatever I earned before I went, that's the real deal. Right?"

"I'm not telling you what to think. I can't," Boyd said. "Maggs, listen. It'll be alright. But I was thinking the same thing Parker was. We'll see. At least, if we're broke, we're going to be broke together. Right? So, these will be our salad days ... every couple has them." And he stopped.

That was the cue Parker needed. She opened the car door. " 'Scuze me, I need to stretch. We must have been sitting in there since at least The Middle Ages."

Boyd and Maggie were alone. In front of them, through the car window they could see a man in a white apron, a big coat and earmuffs was on the sidewalk, moving crates of vegetables.

"You people want something?" he called.

"Not them. Me. I'll be in. Just stretching. We just got off the road," Parker volunteered."

"Okay," he said and walked through the doorway carrying a basket of apples.

Parker leaned into the car. "At least you can eat your salad in a very nice, actually very posh apartment. _Since the family apartment is mine_ – all mine. Did I forget to tell you?! Good old Emily. She finally came through. La-di-dah! So, except for the yearly taxes and ... blah, blah, blah ... it's also yours. Randall and Cook are still there, so it's a really posh set up. Dudley is, so I hear from Mrs. P, making goo-goo eyes at the girl in 3-C. You know, the nice girl from The Bronx? The one who works for an insurance firm. Wait until Barton finds Dudley isn't going to be a virgin anymore. He's going to flip his wig. In the meantime, we do not want to interrupt their budding romance ... so we can bequeath our place to Dudley. Mrs. P will look after him. She can handle Barton, if anyone can." With that Parker stepped back and continued chuckling aloud to herself.

After another minute she poked her head back into the car and said, "Okay. Time to make it official, Power Tool Boy, pul-eeze. Tell our Maggie that you love her to bits, that you will never leave her, kiss her. The suspense is killing me. We need a happy ending. I mean, what with the gunplay and throwing away the best chocolate cruller ever, etc. etc. etc. ... I'm so effing tired," Parker said with a wry grin. "Just do it!" She turned around and smiled – first to herself because she was sure the two lovebirds must be kissing by now because finally, finally the sun was coming up. It was a new day.

She was really feeling good. After all, exactly what could Arthur do to them? So Maggs doesn't show in his gallery anymore. Big fat phooey. Who cares? What kind of weirdo are you, Arthur, huh? Come on. Let's strip you to your skivvies and show us your alien body parts? Pu-leeze. You can't do anything bad to us! You ... you ... snake! (It was the worst epithet she could think of.) Hey! Arthur: you don't want to see Richard get angry! Now that is something to behold. And Evan? He was in the army. We have our own Special Forces. We have resources. You don't dare mess with us. Or William! Or my Tony!! Or Vincent! So, there!

Sunlight was streaking through the spaces between the buildings. It was beautiful. It made her feel very brave. Just as Maggie had been holding onto the idea that the only place she could make good was in Fleetwater, Parker knew she had been holding onto something, too, and it was time to let go. It was time. She just never found the exact right moment to do it. Well, moments happen when they happen. So she said it. Because it really was time: wherever you are, goodbye, Fred. Thanks for everything. I love you a lot. God bless.

Looking around, it seemed that everything was sparkling more brightly than usual. That made her very glad. She went into the little grocery store to do a quick shop.

Inside the car Boyd was telling Maggie, "I was going to ask you last night – well, that was before I got back to Fleetwater and ... you know, all the rest of it ... I mean, who has time to plan a future when they're busy escaping ..."

Parker opened the door and interrupted. "Geez, are you not done yet? Okay, five minutes more and that's it. I know how romantic this is and all that, but guys! We need to keep going!" She closed the car door again with a bang and went back into the grocery shop.

"Hi. I gotta buy some more stuff. My two friends ..." and she nodded in the direction of the car, "they're in love and I hope he's popping the question because I'm hungry. We've been on the road half the night. I need some sleep."

The grocer looked at her with mild surprise. "I have some nice Golden Delicious apples here," he offered.

"Sure. Of course. Apples. Great. Love them. One a day keeps the doctor away – oh, boy. I'm blithering here. All right. That bag of apples ... and," she looked around ... "Oh, you have fresh donuts!"

"My wife makes them. We always sell out. You're lucky. By 8 o'clock there won't be any left.'

"Fantastic. Give me 6 and I'll get a quart of milk." Parker paid up and carried her bag back to the car.

"Okay in there? I hope you two have figured it out because I'm tired. I want to sleep in my own bed. Come on. Shove over. Love you, kiss kiss, will you? I do ... let's go home! Pul-eee-zzz!"

Boyd and Maggie laughed. They were kissing again while Parker started the car. She waved at the grocer and called through the window, "Young love! Isn't it wonderful? Have a great day!"

The sound of smooching lasted a minute or so, while Parker looked over her shoulder, found the coast clear and got them back onto the main street again.

"So, listen, Power Tool Boy," Parker wise-cracked. "Is it good?

Maggie was nodding and grinning and holding out her hand. "See?"

"Hey, I have to watch the road ... oh, look at that. Oh, my. What a good fellow are you! Maggie say something!"

But Maggie couldn't. She was just beaming. She was just too happy to talk.

"She's fine. She gets tongue-tied like that when she's very happy. We're fine. You just drive."

"Yippee!" Parker shouted out the window. They were just passing the far end of Central Park when Maggie started to laugh, really laugh. It was too funny. After a little bit, the laughing wound down.

"I need to sleep," Maggie said and let her head roll onto Boyd's shoulder.

They were just passing 60th Street when Parker realized just how quiet everything was. Looking over, she saw that Boyd and Maggie were both sound asleep.

Boyd was right. There comes a time to close the book on tragedy. That was why she had said goodbye to Fred back there, outside the grocery store.

"Good-bye, Fred," she said again in the smallest of whispers.. "Wherever you are ..." at which instant a highly antagonized cabbie interrupted with an enormous blaring of his horn.

"Hey, lady ..." he hollered through his window. "What's the matter with you?!? Are you completely blind? Maybe I should get into your car and help you drive?"

She rolled down the window a few turns. "I love you, too," she hollered back. It didn't matter. It was lovely. Cabbies who yell and bang on their horns ... "Thank you, God!" she yelled out the window. "Yahoo!"

"What happened?" mumbled Maggie, waking up.

"Nothing. We're home. That's all. We made it. We made it!"

Maggie looked over and saw a couple of tears rolling down Parker's cheek.

"Hey, what's this? Are you okay?"

Parker nodded. "I'm fine. Really. I'll tell you later ... it's a good thing, really."

"Okay," and Maggie sagged back on the seat and closed her eyes again. It was good. They were home.

PART FOUR:

Fleetwater Revisited

CHAPTER ONE

"I shall be telling this with a sigh
Somewhere ages and ages hence:
Two roads diverged in a wood, and
I took the one less traveled by,
And that has made all the difference.
                    - "The Road Not Taken" by Robert Frost"

Arthur read the card once more. Pretty good poetry, he supposed. He looked at the envelope again. No return address. Humph. It didn't matter. Lots of people send cards to him at the gallery.

He met so many, he really couldn't keep up. Taking a whiff – his tongue darted out for an instant ... it wasn't a scent he recognized. But it was Christmas, he noted, so it would have to be something genuinely humanoid. Of course, Mindar didn't quite celebrate these kinds of holidays,. but here since we are here, we always make sure to put up whatever trappings the holiday require: hearts for Valentine's Day, pumpkins for Halloween, etcetera. He had Oscar hang wreaths and even some clumps of mistletoe. Swags of wiry silver and gold ribbon were tied into big bows. Maybe decorating a tree wasn't completely and utterly ridiculous. Maybe. It could be fun, in a barbaric sort of way. Anyway, the transport had just dropped several new arrivals. Babies. Strictly babies, so to speak. We'll have to teach them everything about being human. Such a lot of work.

Reed and Pinky used to be so good at that. They were so enthusiastic. But they were gone. The Council had approved their departure even as Beth had laughed at the idea but Oscar thought it might be interesting. Anyway, the two youngsters had actually gone on a road trip. Off to see America. They departed right after Maggie's big breakout show. Put everything possible in storage and rented out their posh little cottage to some day-trippers they met at a potluck dinner during a fundraiser for the newly inaugurated library. "Just be sure you clean up," Beth had warned but Pinky and Reed planned to have the last laugh. Lined up in the trunk of their car were half a dozen Dust Busters, and several large boxes of those big green biodegradable bags with the drawstring tops. They would drop their bagged up sheddings into an obscure dumpster. No one would ever know the difference. And off they went. They knew all about the Southwest. Thousands of miles of desert. It wasn't Mindar, but it would do in a pinch.

Arthur sighed. At least Nick was gone. Good riddance. The council would handle him. Punishment? That was so passé. They'd just put him to work-work-work. He probably had just enough credits to re-establish himself, not that Arthur cared. What a mess he had made. Getting shot. The man shuddered. Nick The Would-Be Hood would not be missed.

What Arthur didn't like, however, was the way things were changing. Little by little. It couldn't be helped, he supposed. It had started with James. That was years back.

Or perhaps that didn't count. Then Maggie. Maggie Malone. Our star. Took Boyd with her. Too bad. He was a very good carpenter. Very professional. But strictly human. Totally expendable. So that didn't count either. Reed and Pinky? Huh. They'd be back eventually.

He stood in his private office at the gallery. Upstairs he could hear two carpenters laying the second floor. Pound, pound, pound. Hammers going at it. Now, that was a good sound. Le Prochaine Vague. The Next Wave. His second gallery. It was coming along very nicely. They might be ready by Christmas after all. Luckily Annette was feeling better. All the attention she was getting was doing wonders for her shaky health. That meant she might be good for another six months or a year. Longer even. It would be well worth the effort. Those lovely landscapes. He did so enjoy them.

Looking at the wall directly before him, on it and centered, behind his desk, was a small painting. It the only self-portrait Maggie Malone had painted. She had given it to him as a gift, after the triumph of her participation in that first group show. She was standing with her back to the viewer but looking over her shoulder with a look of calm determination. In one hand a set of paintbrushes. Exiting her shoulder blades, coming through a red t-shirt, was a set of baby angel wings.

"You thought you owned me." That's what she had said to him as they stood by the car the night she left.

"I own you now," he had replied. He continued to look at the painting.

She had differed. *"No. I shared my gift with you. And I'm taking it back."*

"I gave you everything you ever wanted," he had said, keeping his anger under control. Now he repeated himself aloud in the quiet of his office. "I gave you everything you ever wanted. Why would you give that up?" *He refused even now to let her get the upper hand in this battle of wills.*

Standing there in the dark that night, he had wondered that she had the nerve to talk to him this way. *"I gave you everything you ever wanted, too, Arthur."*

She couldn't have the upper hand. He wouldn't permit it. If only Nick hadn't pulled that gun and ... oh, dear. What a mess. Of course she left.

It's a good thing Nick went back to Mindar alive. It would have cost Arthur a pretty penny, losing a crewmember. There would have been an inquiry. So much for Beth's having vetted the perfect work party for this project. Her first mistake was James. His departure was pure treason. They managed to report it to the Council in a way that erased all suspicion. Just an unfortunate loss. Better in the long run for them than James getting killed or hurt ... the inevitable reports to the police, hospitals, dear me ... things in all the papers. You know, doctors open us up and ... oops. Some of the parts are ... wrong. All that 'Extra! Extra! Read all about it! Be the first to see the photographs.' There'd be James, in some mid-town hospital room with a candid snap of his sallow face ... an alien living amongst us and all that ... getting interviewed ... anyway. Frank Scully's "Behind the Flying Saucers" was bad enough. At least Project Blue Book had been squelched ... but its release had horrified Arthur at the time. All that worry for nothing. There was nothing on the news. They were safe. No one believed a word of it.

So, Nick had been successfully replaced. At least the new boy showed no slightest hint of romantic admiration for physical violence. Bart, the dear boy, liked riding bicycles in his spare time. How charming. And healthy. How innocuous.

Arthur considered the goal of this whole expedition. That artists tended to die young was surely a small price to pay for so much in return, for so much adulation. In the long run he supposed the people on this planet simply didn't know a good thing when they had it.

As for Maggie Malone, it wasn't true he had liked her art more than anyone else's. It simply wasn't true. That's what he told himself: it wasn't true.

Vig hanish dal:
Gif-manen: yel vahn hareth shar aarctin.
Gif-maneneth: shar-shen aarctin-ben.
Never forget:.
The Definition of a critic: one who accepts easily and
with enthusiasm.
The Definition of criticism: eager interest.

Well, that's the way we do it on Mindar.

The translation wasn't quite perfect. But close. Close enough.

Never forget. *Vig hanish dal.* Ah. Just thinking in Minda made him feel better. Maybe his protestation wasn't quite true. He had liked Maggie's paintings. It was just some flair, she had, perhaps. A little bit of the iconoclast in those unsaintly images. The smooth passages of color, the freedom of joining creature parts and objects. It was amusing. That was all. And perhaps a bit of unsuspected irony. He was sure she knew nothing about who Arthur and his crew really were. Looking at the back of his hand, it looked smooth, but he could feel the smallest itch. Tugging on his ear covering, he knew he would need to shed very soon. Maybe Beth and he could make a day of it. Go off to some cabin in the woods and ... a little outdoorsy slither would be nice. Maybe hanging from a tree limb? He laughed. The thought of the two of them hanging from some tree limb all entwined. It made the gills behind his knees flutter. Lovely. Just lovely.

He regarded the painting on the wall. In it she was smiling. Looking at the viewer with something approaching a Mona Lisa smile. It did capture one's attention. One didn't want to let go.

A hand knocked at his door and Beth entered.

Well, it was about time. Arthur already knew what he was going to do. He lifted the portrait of Maggie off the wall. He realized it was with a modicum of reluctance. Not an emotion a citizen of Mindar would normally ever feel. You had to be human in some way. He wouldn't miss these nuances once they were home again. They were distracting. Even if one doesn't forget, one shouldn't dwell on the past. One might get stuck there. He took the painting off the wall and leaned in against his desk facing inward. Checking his wristwatch, he was reminded that he had duties to attend to.

"Tell Bart to get rid of it, will you?"

"Of course." She tucked her hand through his arm and squeezed. He smiled at her and gave her hand a pat.

Arthur had many factors to consider. If he wasn't careful, she would surpass him. Beth – his Beth, bless her skin – was very ambitious. Her reports to the Council were always very impressive. He was very pleased with the way she had managed to handle that little kerfuffle about Nick. On the other hand, it would be a sin and a shame to let her get the upper hand. Yes, they would have a little get-away and he would reaffirm who ruled their nest.

For her part, Beth had two tiny secrets. She liked secrets. They were very erotic. She'd just been to lunch with Morgan Milstern. He was a very dynamic creature, regaling her with some wonderful stories, interesting ideas, and when his napkin slipped off his lap, it was no mistake that his hand had rubbed her foot. It had certainly given that erogenous zone a flutter.

The other secret was quite something else: all the wild couplings with Arthur had finally done the trick. She was carrying a small clutch of eggs. There was no doubt that some would hatch. Motherhood was imminent. Today would be the day she shared the news with Arthur. Either he wanted to go home to Mindar and make a nest with her or she'd give Morgan that opportunity. If neither wanted her, Beth was packing up and leaving anyway. She'd had enough of Earth and Earthlings. However it played out was fine with her.

Beth and Arthur left the office, making sure to lock up when they walked out. Viola, their very human cleaning lady, had almost walked in on them once. That would have been bad. There would be no explaining what she saw. So now Arthur locked up with extra care and vigilance.

But there was someone new in the gallery. Arthur was as eager as ever when it came to new artists, new potential.

Beth decided she would tell Arthur the news later on. It could wait.

CHAPTER TWO

Arthur spied Fiona Doolittle, patted Beth's hand, and with a nod, let go and walked to the front. This new girl was blonde and very pretty. A sculptress, Oscar had reported. She had been in to check them out several times in the past couple of days. Arthur thought her quite a good candidate. Already twenty-eight years old, she was a more seasoned individual than some of the desperate, younger Earthlings he had represented. She was someone they definitely could do something wonderful for.

In that same instant Arthur began to imagine himself wrapping his arms around her. So malleable. So blonde and ... yummy. Arthur liked a little flesh on a woman. Too bad she could never stream or flow. Of course Beth was still exciting. She had – not just the knack – but the temperament for flowing in a way that humans would never understand ... still, there was something about Fiona. Just thinking about coupling with a human ... oh, my. It would be ... unique. He looked around. Was anyone looking while his thoughts betrayed him? But no, Beth was already talking to a customer at the far side of the room.

His fantasy continued: winning Fiona would be too too delicious. Her comfort requirements were so small. Earthlings asked so little. The expenditure was so ... ah, he sighed ... cost-effective. His masters would be enchanted again. He had already found out that her entire family consisted of a distant uncle and an aging mother. Better yet – the remarkable Fiona Doolittle sculpted marble puppies! The most adorable puppies. He could already imagine the roar of the crowd when he presented his newest bright light.

Everyone will love her. Everyone will love me. And all because of lovely Fiona Doolittle. Sculptress. Earthling.

"Welcome to our gallery, my dear."

Fiona turned around, her blond curls bouncing.

"I understand you're a sculptress ... did you happen to bring your portfolio? I have a few minutes and I'd love to see it."

"No, I didn't. I was just visiting." Fiona didn't like when people fawned and this man was definitely fawning. She turned back to eye the dull little landscapes of Annette Rousseau, their headliner. She certainly didn't want to be represented by a gallery with such a lack of taste. Downstairs was another artist of no particular light. Just noisy abstracts. How they got sold was a wonder. Of course, she had heard rumors that these people really knew how to cater to an artist. Still, she had her standards. But here was this dreadful man again, accompanying her to the door. He was sticking to her like glue. She really wanted to get away. She put her hand to the door. Oscar stopped her momentarily. She acquiesced, staying long enough to have a brief chat. This other fellow was much more acceptable. Finally she was out the door and heading down the stairs.

"Do come back," Arthur called unctuously.

When she was partway down the path, she looked back. He was still there. Actually waving. Twiddling his fingers. How gauche. Fiona gave one of her best fake smiles. It would be a cold day in hell before the likes of him ever got near the likes of her a second time. She already had a good offer from a mail order company who advertised in women's magazines. She would find a studio to reproduce her work. This visit had definitely helped her to decide to accept that other offer.

As for Arthur, he liked it little. He could tell she wasn't interested in his representation. The little fool. Still, his hopes had been raised and dashed. It was too cruel. He had really liked the idea of a limited edition of her adorable marble puppies. He was disappointed when she left. That singular hope of coupling with a female human had just gone by the boards. Maybe he should stick with Beth after all. Arthur became lost in the litany swarming in his mind.

It wasn't as if Oscar could read Arthur's mind but he was sure Arthur was having thoughts he shouldn't. Oscar shook his head silently at Arthur and shrugged. The gallery had customers. There was no time to discuss what happened with Fiona. There would be others. There were always others. Earth was full of artists just looking for a helping hand, a little support, someone to make a fuss ... he'd better go upstairs and see how the carpenters were coming along.

Arthur watched Oscar head upstairs. His thoughts segued again to the last time he had talked with Maggie. It all came back to him unbidden. "Artists are clamoring for the life you are throwing away." He wanted her to know, to fully grasp, to be pierced by her decision, to feel the consummate loss caused by her wrong-headedness.

Standing by the pasture railing, he had at first been certain she would change her mind and stay, or at least come back, having once thought everything through. It might have happened ... until stupid Nick had pulled a gun. Stupid stupid man. Well, that had been the clincher. Maggie would not be back. Not after that dramatic little denouement.

He knew he'd been over this territory before. The problem was: it haunted him.

Arthur looked around and realized Oscar was nowhere to be seen. Where did he go? Oh yes, Upstairs. Still, lately there were moments when that man was making himself just a bit irritating. Ah, there he was, the miscreant.

So it was. The miscreant was now standing outside the gallery, by the white fence over which abundant swags of large red late winter roses were draped. He was looking up at the night sky. Naturally he heard Arthur calling but he ignored the summons and started walking down the street. Overhead a comet flashed across the inky darkness. He was sure Arthur had called a third time, but perversely, and not in keeping with his usual nature, Oscar kept going anyway.

Arriving at Maggie's old studio, the lock was hanging open because no one was using the place just now. He went inside. Snapping on the light switch, he looked around. It wasn't as though there was much to look at. Mrs. Aubrey was very efficient. After Maggie left, Gus had the place was stripped clean and disinfected, which Oscar thought was a little extreme. Anyway, now the studio looked just as though Maggie had never been there, which wasn't true. He missed her. And Boyd, too. He had liked

Boyd. He even liked Parker although, of course, she wasn't a real member of their community the way Boyd and Maggie were.

It had pleased him to watch Maggie and Boyd making themselves into a couple. He had approved. Maggie and Boyd would make a very nice couple. Certainly by now they were nesting. Eventually they would have an egg … well, a baby, just to be species-correct. Oscar thought about what it would be like to have someone … it had been so long. But no. There was simply no one in Fleetwater he could imagine wanting to nest with, Mrs. Aubrey's not too subtle aspirations notwithstanding. She might be age-appropriate and even species-correct but … no. They were not compatible in the least. Still she hovered. He couldn't stop her from hoping.

He noticed that Arthur and Beth never spoke about Maggie. Well, that was to be expected. They never spoke about any of their past artists – some few of whom were literally *past*. Oscar thought about Maggie's painting, the one which still hung behind Arthur's desk. Oscar had made it his business to slip in once in a while and look at it. For him it was a great comfort. Beth didn't think so. She liked to wrinkle her nose at it as though it gave off a bad smell. To Oscar, it had indicated a conflict for Arthur. Therefore, it was a reason to hang onto some wisp of hope that Arthur might actually have a shred of decency still remaining in his nature. Why else was he keeping it? This evening he understood Arthur to say that Brad had been told to remove the painting. Cut it up for scrap. It sickened Oscar. It told him that there was no hope for Arthur. One couldn't shed that.

Oscar turned to other thoughts. For example, here he was alone. Well, he was used to it. But if he ever felt a bit 'under the weather' so to speak, he would come here to Maggie's old place. Gus would eventually rent it out – again and again. But Oscar was glad it was empty now, especially considering he had felt the beginnings of an itch behind his left knee. Being fastidious, he never delayed shedding the way some Mindarians did. They were getting lazy. The way some people delayed doing their laundry. But not him. Hadn't he detected just this morning the smallest iota of that familiar musty smell?

Taking hold of his right ear covering, he made to pull it off. They were expensive little things and one had to be careful not to spoil them. He gave a tug and ... ow! Ouch! ... Ouch? What was going on? The ear covering absolutely wouldn't come off!

He took hold of the other covering and pulled a bit harder than was really necessary. Maybe the coverings had gotten stuck? Of course there was no such thing. He stopped struggling. He knew when something was useless. Anyway the itch had stopped. Also the familiar musky smell had vanished.

Something had happened. The last time he shed, it had been difficult. He had never had problems before. But this time ... apparently there would be no 'this time'. He knew he hadn't been mistaken in the minute signs of needing to shed. But the ear coverings were ... (and he felt around the back of his ears) ... well, they weren't coverings anymore. It seems they had been ... absorbed. The significance was monumental. He wasn't afraid but ... he needed to think. To consider. Obviously he didn't need the indoor solitude. He would go. Oscar knew he could always come back another time – to visit Maggie's studio, this is.

Walking to the door, he took one last look around, snapped off the light, pulled the door ajar and went into the alley. Outside the comet shower was still performing. It was a magnificent display. It was during just such a phenomena as this that landings were so easily attained. He remembered his very well.

Looking up he counted three, four ... no, six slashing exuberances entering the atmosphere, etching momentary golden scratches through the sky. He checked his wristwatch. It was time to go back. Arthur would be very put out if he stayed away any longer. Just at that moment, another feeling that Oscar hadn't yet identified, announced itself again. This was something not to be ignored either. It was wending its determined way through his mind and in unexpected consequence of its intrusive demand at that moment, he didn't care what irritated Arthur, even if the other was in charge of this expedition.

Which made him consider one of the few things Arthur did which Oscar quite approved of wholeheartedly – gathering the crew together to do a Recitation. It was wonderfully healing. He knew The Recitation by heart, of course. There wasn't a Mindarian in Fleetwater – or in their Home Quadrant, for that matter – who didn't know it. It was part of their life, wherever they were sent. When sung (it was actually part of an old folk tune) or spoken, it always had the power to move:

Vig hanish dal
Vig hanish dal:

Gif-manen: yel vahn hareth shar aarctin.
Gif-maneneth: shar-shen aarctin-ben.
Never forget:
The Definition of a critic: one who accepts easily and
with enthusiasm.
The Definition of criticism: eager interest.

So different here on Earth, of course. He read newspapers. He knew the scene was very different indeed. It was very interesting that the words 'critic' and 'criticism' were such opposing concepts here. Well, when one had little or no aesthetics of any kind, he supposed it made sense. It was more than a little amusing how the cream of Fleetwater scrambled through a gallery on an opening night stripping the place like locusts – wildly in heat and on the lookout for something with the least bit of art, artifice, design ... well, you name it. Because aesthetics was everything. It was the food of the soul, was it not? How could one live without it? How had he managed on Mindar? How would it be, living like that again?

He looked up. The wonderful inky night filled his eyes. Overhead the sky was alive with comets punctuating the darkness. He simply didn't want to go back to the gallery yet. He would stay right where he was and savor it, Arthur's desires to the contrary..

So he said to himself: this, too, is beauty. This, nature's bounty, the creation of the wider expanses, is art. It didn't matter who the artist was, but it pleased Oscar no end to consider that this artist – some called it God – he didn't care about the name – came and went as he pleased. Whenever he pleased. That fellow could not be bought, couldn't be catered to nor provided any earthly possession. Nothing Arthur could use to entice.

Never stated exactly in the terms we think of on Mindar, Oscar didn't think that calling the humans' Creator an artist was a misstatement.

When he thought about it, Fleetwater's galleries simply served the more earthbound. Generally they were a little more vulnerable to Arthur's high-powered act. Except that this one, this God, was one artist Arthur could never lay a possessive hand, or bore into his center, discover his secret desires. This artist was above all that. Always. And he was eternal. How about that, Arthur. Hmm?

It occurred to Oscar that all this independent action and these thoughts he was entertaining were quite heady and totally unusual in one as steady of temperament and loyal as he. Meanwhile, high overhead more celestial arrows were racing across the heavens.

He settled his hands in his pockets and walked on. Feeling one hand touch something – a small piece of card – he took it out to examine. It was the card Maggie had slipped into his hand the night she had left.

CHAPTER THREE

Oscar read the card. There had been so much going on that difficult night, he didn't have time to read it, after which he forgot all about it. There had been so much to do. Nick had to be carried back to his room. Gus was called. He was their medical staff. He was rightfully angry and made no bones about it. Mrs. Aubrey did the nursing and when Nick was well again, he was shipped out. Not stuffed in a transport locker deprived of food and water as both Elizabeth and Gus would have enjoyed more, but without any special privileges, except to be surgically stripped of the humanoid body he'd been using. At least he had a suitcase full of "Cahiers du Cinema". He would read and re-read them until they fell apart or he lost his fascination with reading.

Then there was Gus. Oscar thought Arthur would actually burst a blood vessel when he found out what Gus was up to. Decided to domesticate with a humanoid? Was he joking? Gus was not. In careful increments, Gus had explained to Veronica who – or what – he really was, originally, that is. And that he had been humanoid for quite a long time now. Why she liked him, he really didn't fully understand. All he knew was she liked him enough to be his mate. They were going to make a nest. Arthur was really quite vituperative. His remarks about what the potential offspring of their union might be was expressed in very cruel language. Arthur had quite a command of the

English language. So much so that Gus realized Arthur was enjoying himself.

"I can always get a vasectomy," Gus countered.

"Who's going to perform it? Are you going to do it to yourself? This is madness."

"We are going to mate. If it's a true Mindarian or a hybrid, we can ship it to Mindar. I think she'll be okay with that. If it's a human child, we'll raise it."

The blasphemy of it all was absolutely staggering, but Gus seemed so matter of fact, Arthur just nodded his head in agreement and laughed. Which angered Gus quite thoroughly..

"As long it never interferes with our work, for as long as we're here."

"It never will."

"Fine."

Oscar just stood still by a back wall of the office listening to this. He did nothing, said nothing.

"I have all the right equipment," Gus snarled. "I know how to use it. I read the manual. I've been practicing."

Beth, also in this meeting, laughed out loud. It was the funniest thing she had ever heard. What he said must have been hilarious because Oscar thought Beth never laughed.

"Never mind. I know how it works. It's pretty good actually. I'm getting used to it.

Beth laughed again. "All this practice you're doing ... you know what humans think of that?"

"You can just shut up. It was research. I wasn't going to couple with Veronica and disappoint her. Now that would have been stupid. Don't you think?"

Beth stopped laughing. It might be a point in his favor. Gus had always been a practical man.

But Arthur was still purpling with emotion. "You would give up ... writhing ... for *that?*"

"I know it's not a snake ball. I thought about it. Talk about crazed couplings ... I remember. I wasn't any stay-at-home. I just realized I wouldn't miss it. Haven't been to one of those shindigs in decades anyway. And these things ..." and Gus patted himself on the arm, "they run better if it's one partner at a time anyway."

A snort from Beth told him her view of all this. "As if we're the monogamous type."

"One ... steady ... partner," Gus said emphatically. "That's how it works. Not random couplings. We're not all sex-crazed." His words hung in the air.

Beth and Arthur looked at each other, at\Oscar and back around again. "Actually we are," Arthur said.

"Well, I don't care what you two think, uh – no offense, Oscar. I realize you have to put with this. I wrote it up already. And sent the report. Told the medical liaison on Mindar that, basically, I've been here too long. I was one of the first to ship. I don't want to go back. That's all. I'm not bugging out – like James. I'm no traitor. But I'm doing this and if you bother her or me – let's just say, I can break either of you in half – like dry twigs. Are we clear?"

Beth stopped sniggering.

Arthur become conciliatory. "My boy, my boy. If you want the Earth Girl, why not? Hmm? She's lovely. And really quite young. I think you are very lucky. Now, you go back to your shop and stop worrying. We'll give you a lovely wedding. We'll have it here at the Gallery and make an occasion of it. All right?"

"Damn straight it's all right," and with that Gus walked out the front door making sure he slammed it loud enough to remind all of them of his physical strength.

"On Mindar ... well, you didn't know him, Beth. But I did. He attained quite a length."

"South Port slitherer, you think?"

"South Port all the way. Mission Control made a very good choice. Until now."

"But he's marrying that silly little Veronica," replied Beth by way of objection.

"I think she may be less silly than we think, if she cares for Gus. She'll be a fine addition to the group, just as she is. It'll be fine."

So, Gus was getting married to a human girl, and Beth was standing there with her own clutch of eggs forming. Arthur knew nothing about it. That's when she realized she couldn't tell him. Knowing him now, quite thoroughly, she knew her days on Earth were limited. Next flitter to land had to take her home. As she was. She had enough credits to sort it all out. By laying in stasis, the eggs would – should – hold. If not, there were always more. The idea of so many little Arthurs wriggling after her was not appealing. The irony of that was she had no idea what her offspring would be: reptile, humanoid, hybrid. She'd been here quite a long time, too. Well, hybrids were incredibly valuable. On Mindar. Because she could not deliver them here. Absolutely not. Those wild trysts with Mr. Debonair over there glaring out the window after Gus had been a mistake. Because now here she was. Holding the bag. How did two different reproductive systems manage to hook up anyway? There was precedent. But it wasn't supposed to happen while on Mission. And another thing: while Beth had been straightening the coat closet earlier in the day, she had found a card in Oscar's coat pocket. Taking it out, she had to admit she was shocked. James. She had sniffed it. Oh, yes. The scent had faded but there was no mistaking it. That was his scent. Let Arthur stay here and rut with anyone he cared to. Beth was getting out. To top it all off, Beth had put the card back in Oscar's coat pocket.

CHAPTER FOUR

Astray wind visited. It rattled doors and windows, tugged at the trees and moved on.

Oscar had to get somewhere and think. He had to calm his thoughts and think. He looked at the card again. James was living in Copper Springs? It was so close. James had been there the whole time. Walking further down the road, he headed for the pasture. No one would guess his whereabouts very quickly. They didn't want any unnecessary attention on the pasture. That was their portal. It had to be protected.

James alive! He held the card in his hand and let the understanding sink in. Oscar now realized his ear coverings weren't just stuck. He now possessed a totally authentic pair of human ears. Gus hadn't said so, but Oscar would bet he, too, was morphing into humanoid. Probably all done by now, too. And there were other signs. All the emotional drama. On Mindar this kind of display was simply unheard of. Look at Nick. Not that Oscar had found anything admirable in his character, but on Mindar he would have been your usual layabout, looking for a good time, happy to service any female who was lusting. He served a purpose and no one cared. Society took no notice. Here his fixations bordered on madness. And murder? On Mindar? There was nothing in the day-to-day living that would cause such behavior. They had plenty of everything.

Ah. Everything but art. Somehow, that aspect of life had lost its place. It was just this fringe group that cared. Which was the purpose of the Mission. To sate their needs. They had done well. But Oscar always knew there were dangers. Arthur wouldn't listen. Beth couldn't care less ... but Oscar knew. You manage to mingle to races, however alien, and if there was a way for them to find common ground, they would. That was Gus and Veronica. And, really, wasn't he in the throes of this himself? How long before Mindar meant nothing? He didn't know. But it would be soon. He had thought about assimilation but never quite believed it would happen to him ... and yet ... isn't that really what he wanted? To be human. To live as humans do.

If James had sent this card through Maggie, it was a message. Surely it meant that James would be willing to provide a safe haven for him, should he need one. Leaving was treason, of course. No doubt of that. But Arthur and Beth were betraying their Project Orders. They had changed the plan nearly 25 years ago when they decided to trap Maggie instead of just openly inviting her. He could never figure that out. When it should have been reported, Beth and Arthur very carefully omitted this information. They had managed to do a very efficient hatchet job on Maggie's departure. That had been laid at Nick's door. Nick would be paying for that little failure for a long time.

The more Oscar thought about it, the more he knew that deep in his heart staying here permanently was exactly what he wanted. He didn't want to be a part of this exploitation of artists any longer. He surely didn't want humans dying on his account. It wasn't right. Arthur didn't

430

care. Dead artists were of no matter to him. Supply and demand. That was his concern.

Oscar looked at the card again. It was incredible. Here was this lifeline – reaching out to him in the dark. When had such a thing happened before? He remembered how deeply he had been touched when Maggie had offered him a ride that night. He had felt so sad, so beaten down, he couldn't even think about reaching back ... but now, this message from James. No one else had ever been as kind to him until Maggie came – not since James had left. Well, Boyd had been decent to Oscar, that was true. Not deeply a friend, but decent. What about Maggie's friend, Parker? She, too, had been truly civil. The comparison was aching to be noticed ... look, it said! We humans, we have compassion. We care.

Mindarians cared, too. About different things, in a different way. Oscar liked being kind. He liked helping. He did not like the idea that Annette would sicken again. Arthur was so anxious for her replacement, it was driving him batty again. Too bad that Doolittle girl had gone off. Arthur had been very hopeful. But it couldn't be helped. It couldn't be helped.

He was certain that things had begun to go off the rails when they cooked up their scheme about Maggie. They wouldn't try anything like that again. Of course, the Mindarians living in Fleetwater didn't care one way or the other, most of them anyway. High-flyers like the Heilbroners or maybe Morgan Milstern might have an inkling, but not the others. They don't know the difference. They are ... philistines, nearly. You could slap a price tag on a slab of brick and call it art and the Fleetwater barbarians would be tripping over each other to own it. He had heard on the grapevine that some of the older members were getting ready to go home. Time to get all those human parts out. Time to get back to their own reality. There were plenty of new arrivals scheduled so, what was the matter with Arthur? Why couldn't he just get on with it in a way that didn't mean such a bad ending for the artists? That had been bothering Oscar for a long time. Something about Arthur's thinking was very faulty.

What Oscar wanted was to dwell again on the experience of the kindness, the friendship ... and that rare sweetness ... that humans had in such abundance. He felt himself being embraced again by that essence. It never faded. No matter how many times he revisited those moments, they were always fully intact. It filled him and he was gladdened.

He put James' card back in his pocket.

Thinking back on what he had studied before coming here, to Earth, that is, he remembered reading about all the conflicts humans indulged in. It seemed easy enough to be critical. What with all those wars and dead, what was the problem if a few artists died for a good cause. At least their art wouldn't go to waste. That was a good thing, yes? Well, it had sounded right ... before James left that is Before Nick tried to shoot Boyd. Before a lot of things.

Exploring the concept, he invaded the depths of it with his whole being. It didn't want to go away. He didn't want to let go. It had no equivalent in Minda, on Mindar, for Mindarians. There was no need. Everything there was so decided. All was provided. One did the thing one was born to do and the rest ... all provided. Of course it taken a long time to arrange society in that way, but once done, why go back? Why bother.

Here, on Earth, so far away ... he was beginning to understand it. A whole feast of ideas that had no firm place in his thoughts until now. It fascinated him. Almost as though another being was talking to him from inside himself. Oscar was trembling.

"Rebel," it whispered to him. *"You can do it."*

Just as those of Mindar needed art, so he wanted this: to rebel. A thing he had never done before, never considered it. But he wanted it. How he wanted it.

There wasn't even a word for the concept in his language. Imagine that.

Taking the card out of his pocket again, he realized his body was beginning to heat up. It was cold outside and yet ... oh, it was happening again. Right now! He could feel it.

What to do? What to do?

A hail of comets was flooding the sky – so Oscar decided to sing. It was an uncharacteristic as anything could be. But he needed to. He really did. The melody was quite subtle. Probably a little off-key to human ears, to Oscar it sounded beautiful. And reverential. Maybe it would be the last time he could sing it. Maybe it should be. Loyalty divided was no kind of loyalty at all.

"Vig hanish dal ... Shar-shen aarctin-ben".

Imagine him being one of those who accepts easily and with enthusiasm.

He'd never tried it before. He was not a critic. He had been born an organizer. Now he was being something new. A door was opening – a door to a new world.

Oscar put his hand to this door of a new world and pushed. It opened so easily. As easily as the petals of a rose gave way in his hand. Of course, now that the door was open, what next? So he looked. There was a path. He would go down that path ... to where? ... a place he had dreamed of and never before admitted dreaming about ... but it was as though his feet had accepted the invitation and now he couldn't have stopped his feet even if he tried.

So Oscar went to that place in the dream that was real. Step by step.

Looking behind, he understood perfectly how it was that Maggie had not treated him like a sad drone. Parker, too – her gift was respect. From Boyd – simple decency.

We do it that way on Mindar, too. In our own way. None of this hysteria, this madness which Arthur needs, revels in.

Oscar considered his race. They didn't know how to handle emotion anymore. It twisted them. To Arthur: everyone here was merely for his use – like so much tissue paper – one good blown and thrown away. As for Nick, he resented anything that walked and breathed. On Mindar this situation would never have happened. A few days at the Juno Sanitation Waste would have cooked any such nonsense right out of them. On Earth, it mattered greatly.

Which brought him to James. It seemed to Oscar that there had been some kind of understanding between them. And James had sent his card to Oscar through Maggie. He had done that deliberately – three months ago. Of course, that didn't signify because Mindarians weren't known for their speed, but there was nothing wrong with their memories. Therefore, James had not forgotten Oscar after all this time. He had taken the risk by giving his card to Maggie.

Did Oscar dare? Did he really dare? James understood. He was Mindarian, whatever change his body had gone through. It takes planning to rebel. One had to arrange carefully to escape successfully. Overhead, expressing their full agreement, the dark night was alive with flaming arrows of comet life.

Climbing over the familiar rails of the fence, he walked to the very center of the pasture. The sky above him was extraordinary. Oscar felt very very alive. And hopeful. This new feeling was filling him up; it was exceeding his essence; it was spreading out. It was covering the pasture. It didn't want to stop. He remembered another Recitation – one in particular, one less often re-stated. It was so very lovely, it deserved to be heard. Certainly this night of comets would appreciate it. Certainly they would give testimony to this emotion blooming inside him. He was so happy he had not forgotten.

So he opened his heart and sang the well-remembered, exquisitely beautiful phrase of notes out loud while comets high overhead traced the darkness in fiery affirmation.

Vig hanish dal: Gif-manen en dicht-la fahlen.
Never forget the definition of a true friend.

PART FIVE:

Manhattan One More Time
(Eighteen months later.)

CHAPTER ONE

Boyd was waiting by the apartment door.

"Come on, Maggs. It's a beautiful day outside. Let's go get some of it ..."

"I'm coming ... I'm coming ... "

He turned around, put down the house keys on the front hall desk and let the door close. Walking down the hallway, he stopped at their bedroom door and watched with amusement while his wife hopped around, one leg inside a pair of jeans, her hands grappling with a sneaker. She began to fall, but the bed was there to catch her.

"What?" she asked.

"You. Hopping around like a one-legged frog. Best show in town."

She was now untying the lace of the shoe.

He took a few steps in. Getting down on his knees, he took the sneaker out of her hand, and with a quick shake, straightened out her pants legs. "Leg," he said. She presented her leg. "Stand." They both stood up. He pulled up her jeans and buttoned her.

"I can button myself."

"Of course you can." He kissed her. "Outside it's about 68 glorious degrees. Sky is totally blue. It is one freaking great day and we are going out there to get some of it." He walked to her bureau and out of a drawer pulled a dark green sweater with a rolled collar. They had found it together in a sale bin on their first trip to The Village last spring. "Wear this," he said handing it to her. She dutifully pulled on the sweater. He sighed. "I'll just have to wait until tonight to see 'the girls'."

Maggie laughed. "I can't believe my shy guy from Maine now calls my breasts 'the girls'.

"I'm still shy."

"Right."

"If I wasn't, they would have names by now," he said laughing.

That set Maggie to laughing, too.

"So now you are dressed. Here, sit." He patted the bed.

"I can put on my own shoes. I'm not sick. Just pregnant. And barely that."

"I know. But this way, I have a legitimate reason to feed my obsession about your feet.

You didn't know I liked feet so much."

"I do now.'

"Sit."

Maggie sat.

"Foot."

She sighed.

"Foot?"

"Okay."

Boyd slipped on a sneaker and tied it up.

"Maybe you should have been a shoe salesman because, I gotta say, there is something about the way you put on a shoe. I think any shoe store you worked in would have no trouble,

today's troubling economic climate notwithstanding. Is that what they taught you in Orphan School?"

Boyd laughed. "There's no such thing as 'Orphan School'. And thank you, but I will not be working as a shoe salesman anytime soon. I have a day job. At night and on the weekends I have a second job looking after this barely pregnant young woman. She won't eat her vegetables if I don't cook them."

Maggie smiled. "I see. This ... uh ... young woman is very lucky to have you.".

"She sure is. Foot ..."

She presented her other foot. Now being fully dressed, the usual few minutes of romantic, wrestling ensued, requiring the recently made bed to be messed up again.

"Okay, here's the deal," Maggie said cheerfully. "If you stop kissing me, I'll put on some lipstick while you straighten the bed and we can really go."

"First off, nothing – especially a lousy deal like that – would make me stop kissing you and secondly, we don't have to make the beds. It's the weekend so no one is here to see it and besides that, Randall and Cook think the amount of work they do here is puny enough as it is. Let's leave them their self-respect."

But as Maggie was lying on top of Boyd while he issued this heartfelt request and she was laughing, that meant she was bouncing up and down on him in a rather erotic way, so the heartfelt request went ignored by both. A little later, Boyd turned his head and seeing the bright blue sky beckoning, rolled his wife over and kissing her soundly said, "Okay, you win."

"Naturally," she said and climbed off. "I love you," she called over her shoulder as she ambled into the bathroom to put on the promised lipstick.

441

Boyd was heading to the door when he heard Maggie's feet returning, going further into the apartment. He turned and followed her to the den as she looked in.

"Sure doesn't look like the same room anymore."

"No. Kind of reminds me of your shed ... except for the high class mahogany shelves,

the rolling library ladder, the ... uh .. gold leaf detail on the ..."

"Okay, buster," she laughed while punching him lightly on the shoulder. "We get it." She paused in front of the easel. On it was a painting. A rather large painting, as it happened. The subject was a very formal portrait of a baby rhino in full profile. "So, what do you think?"

"I think the Honorable Ambassador of South Africa is going to have his socks blown off when he sees it. The director of the Hluhluwe-Umfolozi Reserve – and I hope I have pronounced that right – is going to also be blown away. It's spectacular."

"But don't you think it's very derivative of Jamie Wyeth's pig painting?"

"You don't paint anything like Jamie Wyeth. True?"

She nodded. That was true.

"Are you happy with it?" he asked.

Maggie looked at Boyd. "Yes, I have to admit it. I'm pretty damned happy about it.

"I say: sign it, call the Ambassador and let him know the painting is now drying and give him a day and time when he can pick it up."

"You're right." She walked over to the painting and said, "Tonight, you get signed. We are going out."

Leaving her workroom, they walked down the hall where Boyd picked up the house keys from the hall table. Two minutes later they were waiting in the agreeable quiet by the elevator.

"What made you decide we should accept Richard's offer to take this apartment for a wedding present?" she asked Boyd.

"Honestly?" he asked.

She nodded.

"Well, he is a fairly selfish man, but he's not a monster. Besides that, he's changed. What he couldn't confront – the relationship with Parker – he can better deal with as a grandparent. He is putty in little Rocco's pudgy hands. It's a miracle."

"Yes, that is a most amazing sight." She paused to contemplate the image of Richard and Rocco together as she had last seen them, sharing a dish of ice cream in the kitchen of this very apartment at Christmastime. "First off, I didn't know for sure if Richard knew where his own kitchen was located."

Boyd laughed. He had to agree with her. Richard Feldman was one seriously formal man.

"Second, I didn't know if he recognized the existence of ice cream. Like, it was peasant food."

"I know what you mean," Boyd said.

"Well, kids are messy and as far as I knew, nothing on God's earth would ever induce Richard to allow a single follicle of hair to be out of place, in himself or anyone else, if he could help it."

"You mean, he's a control freak."

"Yes. Completely ..."

443

"And yet ..."

"And yet, we all saw it. Rocco was on his lap and they were sharing a dish of chocolate ice cream ... I have to give the man credit for not wearing full set of washable overalls. He actually had a smear on his chin. It was almost scary."

"Listen ... did it ever to occur to you ... to any of you ... that man might have a reason for the way he behaves?"

"No. His parents were filthy rich. They could give him everything. Are you kidding?"

"Richard Feldman was a most unhappy little boy," said an interrupting voice.

Boyd and Maggie turned to see Mrs. Heffernan standing beside them, perfectly turned out in a two-piece black wool pant suit with scarlet wool scarf, hat and gloves.

"You knew Richard, Mrs. H?"

"He lived here all his life. And I have lived here all my life." The older woman threw a glance back down the hall towards Maggie and Boyd's apartment door. "He had a frog. He liked that frog a great deal. It broke his heart to leave it behind when his parents sent him away to boarding school. He gave me the frog. I took very good care of it."

"I'm sure you did. I didn't know you had much to do with the Feldmans."

"I don't now. The Richard I knew as a little boy bears no resemblance to the man he became, not the least of which is that he decided he didn't care to recognize my existence after he went away. I thought it was very bad of him, especially as I was looking after his frog."

Maggie and Boyd were speechless.

"I saw Richard walking with his grandson at Christmas. I believe the child's name is Rocco. He walked over and offered me his hand just as though the last almost-fifty years had not passed. I have to admit I wasn't sure I wanted to accept his apology ... but I did. I thought it was the right thing to do. Sending away a child – *an American child* – to school at such a young age. I think the shock alone nearly killed him."

"I had no idea," Maggie said, shaking her head.

"No, no one does. He had the most selfish parents a child ever had the misfortune to be born to and they unloaded him as fast as they could. Quite despicable. But he turned out well, considering. Married Emily – lovely woman, so devoted – and of course, Parker is a lovely young woman. And now she has that nice young Italian man for a husband and Rocco."

Maggie stared at Mrs. Heffernan. "But Mrs. Heffernan, Richard pretty much did to Parker what his parents did to him. He was terrible to her. You know that, right?"

"No, I don't. He didn't send Parker away. He broke that mold. It must have been very difficult for him."

"No, he just ignored her and ..."

The older woman ignored Maggie and kept going. "How he managed, after what he went through, to keep Parker as close by as he did must have been very difficult. You have no idea what it takes to break the stranglehold of aberration."

Now Maggie's mouth dropped open. And Boyd's as well.

The whole story left her speechless.

"He'll be fine now," said Mrs. Heffernan. "We've had tea. And talked. But to change the subject, I understand you are keeping the apartment. Wonderful places, these apartments are. I'd spend my last cent before I'd give mine up."

"I do love it but I also sort of miss the little cave Parker and I had down on 23rd Street. Still, we're doing okay, Boyd and I. It's not like we have an income to match this place. So, it's just a gift."

"Do what you can to hold onto the place. I can assure you it's worth every penny – the lack of salary notwithstanding."

"Very sound advice, Mrs. Heffernan. I was just telling Maggie the same thing."

"You should listen to your husband. He sounds very wise."

Maggie gasped but Boyd took her hand and squeezed it. He also gave her a tiny shake of his head.

"He is," she finally answered, feeling Mrs. Heffernan's gaze boring into her.

Ding. The elevator had arrived.

"Finally," (meaning the elevator) "I shall have to speak to Frederick, the Concierge. We've spent half the day here waiting."

This was a gross exaggeration, of course, but it came with the territory, living in such an elegant building. They all stepped inside and moved back to let the doors close.

Once they reached the lobby, Mrs. Heffernan said, "Mignon and I are going out to take advantage of the lovely weather.."

"Mignon?" asked Maggie

They all heard a tiny, high, "Grrfffff!"

Out of Mrs. Heffernan's shoulder bag popped a small head. Mignon. Her Yorkie.

"Good morning to you, Mignon," said Boyd with due formality.

Mignon extended her head a little more, her bright button eyes alive with interest.

"I didn't know dogs were allowed," said Maggie.

"They aren't," said Mrs. Heffernan frostily.

"Oh," said Maggie.

"I've lived in this building since I moved in here with my parents, right after World War II. I don't care what the rules say. I've owned Yorkies all my life and I certainly do not plan to live out the rest of my days without one."

Maggie was thinking about her Grandma Nonie and all those years of rescued greyhounds. "Absolutely not. Unthinkable. We are on your side."

"All the way," and Boyd said this with such conviction, the woman relaxed a fraction. "I heard that Lacey Algernon ..."

Boyd turned to Maggie and whispered, "She's in 404"

"... reported you."

Mrs. Heffernan's back was now quite stiff. "She did. Wrote a complaint to the Condo Board."

Boyd told her, "Well, we're on your side."

The older woman didn't answer.

Boyd continued. "The Andersons don't care. I know because I asked. They're going to write a letter to the Board saying they have no objection. And you have our vote. I think we can sort out whatever it is that has Lacey's knickers in a twist."

"I must be honest with you. I'm afraid that on several occasions Mignon has mistook Ms. Algernon's welcome mat for ... a different kind of grass."

Maggie laughed. She just couldn't stifle that.

Mrs. Heffernan ignored Maggie and went on. "If she would just wash the mat and disinfect it so it doesn't have that inviting odor, Mignon would not be tempted."

"Of course," said Boyd. "Makes sense to me."

Mrs. Heffernan looked at Boyd hard, but it was the kind of scrutiny he was very good at handling. "Thank you, young man."

Ding. The elevator door opened again and out walked Lacey Algernon, a stringy, middle-aged woman in a long, skinny, dark brown sweater worn over dark jeans and Ugg boots. Her hair was up in a knot held with chopsticks, its usual arrangement.

"Good morning, Ms. Algernon. We were just having a little chat with our other neighbor. You know Mrs. Heffernan," said Boyd diplomatically.

"Not really. She knew my parents probably." Obviously no love lost between these two, Maggie noted.

"Yes, I did have that good fortune. We used to walk in the Annual Easter Parade. Everyone on the 4th floor did. Beginning in 1949. We made it a tradition ... until Leona and Eldridge passed, that is."

Lacey Algernon glared. There was silence and then "Grffffff!"

Mignon was not to be excluded from whatever was going on and it didn't matter to the little creature that all was not well amongst the humans.

"I'll be going," said the unrelenting Ms. Algernon.

448

They watched her leave.

Boyd turned to Mrs. Heffernan. "I still think we can work it out. Okay?"

Boyd had grasped the situation. Mrs. Heffernan was not the kind of woman to ask for help. But she would accept it, if offered.

"That would be very nice of you. We have to go now. Mignon must have her exercise."

"Phew," said Maggie as they watched Mrs. Heffernan take Mignon out of her shoulder bag, place the tiny creature on the street and run to the end of the long lead, where she piddled daintily at a tree trunk. Elsewise on the street, New Yorkers were indeed taking advantage of an early spring day.

"Maggie, don't."

"Don't what?"

"Don't get all in a dander about Lacey Algernon. I knew about that letter. I went to the office last week and read Richard's file. He reported Mrs. H, too. I don't think she knows that. Anyway, it was a few years ago. It's like there's a "Before Rocco" and an "After Rocco". The man has improved. I had to know what he's been up to so we would have some ammunition to mend the fences with."

"Even if they aren't ours."

"That's right. Living in a place like this is like living in a small village ... we'll be fine." He patted her hand, which was now looped through his. "We'll do it. We'll mend them all. That's another reason I think it was a good idea to take the place. First off, it's an incredible wedding present. Secondly, your cave is pretty much no longer yours. You cannot dispossess Dudley. He's got a girlfriend."

"He what?"

"Yup. According to Barbara, he's got a girlfriend. *Mrs. P's niece!*"

"Holy Moses. Mrs. P's niece is a very sweet girl. I met her a couple of time. Tell me, how does Barbara know about this?"

"Because your mother went over there with food and Mrs. P was there at the door ahead of her, just about to knock, with cookies."

Maggie threw back her head and began to laugh.

"Oh, that is funny. That is too, too funny."

"Yes, indeed. Jewish mother meets Greek mother both bearing gifts ..."

"Gift horses," Maggie said still laughing.

"Well, how else are they going to find out what's happening with Dudley. They have to keep Barton happy ... true?" Boyd asked.

"Absolutely," she said, her voice softening.

"I love you, I love your whole family. I love ... being a part of a family."

"I know. Everyone loves you."

"It's just luck."

"No, it's not. You're a lovely man."

Which seemed a good moment to kiss, so they did.

"You did not see that, Frederick," Maggie said to the doorman.

"Of course, I did, Mrs. MacArthur. Nice to see young people being in love."

"Okay, you saw it."

"I certainly did." He pulled open the door to let an earnest-looking young man in running clothes inside.

"Well, we're off. See you later, Frederick," said Boyd and taking Maggie by the arm, they walked to the street corner where they waited for the light to change.

CHAPTER TWO

Maggie and Boyd were standing side by side looking. "So you really think the March Hare looks like Arthur?" Boyd asked.

"Hmm. No, not really. It's kind the spirit of the thing – that wild-eyed look. It doesn't have to be literal. I mean, this is literal, but it doesn't have to be."

"I see. And the Cheshire Cat? Who does he remind you of?" he asked.

They both answered in unison: "Beth. Definitely," and both laughed.

"Let's sit on a mushroom," she said, patting the one nearest to the March Hare. Boyd sat down. Maggie put an arm around his neck and settled herself on his lap. "This is so nice," she said as she snuggled her head against his arm. "Someday, in the not too too distant future, our baby will be crawling all over this."

"How about a little art history?" Boyd asked.

Maggie was a fountain of art knowledge. He liked hearing her share it with him.

"Why not?" She paused a moment. "This sculpture was created by Spanish-born, French-trained sculptor Jose de Creeft. He lived from 1900 to 1982. He was a modern guy, our Jose."

"Very nicely done," Boyd said, giving her tummy a pat.

She looked down. There was barely even a baby bump.

"Just saying hello." He leaned over and whispered, "Hello, whoever you are. Welcome to the family."

Maggie smiled. "Might not be an artist, you know."

"That's fine with me. He – or she – isn't going to be an orphan. That's mostly what I care about."

"I forgot to tell you but now you've reminded me. I had a call from Dudley the other morning."

"How is he ... and his new girlfriend?"

"I did not ask about that. Having all those women watching him is sufficient pressure to break stronger men. No, he was asking about my first "Toaster" painting. Parker brought it back and hung it up. She didn't want to take it to Italy the last time she was here. After all, it's hers to do with as she wishes. Dudley wants to buy it. What do you think about that?"

"It's Parker's to sell."

"Since Parker is in Italy, I called her and ask how much she wants for it."

"What did she say?"

"She said somewhere between: 'You should get as much as you can for it and I paid you $100, so all I want is what I paid for it.' Oh, Boyd. That is a lot of leeway. I'm sort of stuck. I don't want Barton to get wind of this little transaction."

"You'll figure it out." He jiggled his legs and Maggie jiggled along with him.

She paused smiling. "The truth is, it's been months since I've done any of my new type of work. I don't know if there's any more of it left in me. I'm really glad that I can do animal art. It's where I started, after all. Maybe that new stuff, it was one fire – just one – and now it's all burned out." She looked at him. "What do you think?"

"The better question is what do you think?"

Maggie paused again. "Two answers. If a certain flow of work has run its course, so be it. I've been reading up. Renoir's style changed a lot over the course of his career. And Matisse – same situation. I don't see that this is something totally unusual. Secondly: I had seven paintings planned and I only did six. Number 7 is still there, waiting. I'm beginning to feel the pressure to do something about it. This discussion about the Toaster painting has kind of kicked up some dust. You know?"

Boyd did and he allowed as much.

They lapsed into quiet. Pretty soon Maggie found she was watching two mothers pushing baby carriages down the pathway towards them. Suddenly she was staring hard at something.

CHAPTER THREE

Just behind the two mothers was another couple, also pushing a baby carriage. Physically the man was on the burly side and the woman with him was obviously younger, slim, with long dark hair. They were two people Maggie would have recognized anywhere, even out of their usual element.

Boyd looked where Maggie was looking. She slipped off Boyd's lap and stood up. He got up as well and stepped in front of Maggie. They both waited.

From about eight feet away, Gus and Veronica slowed to a stop.

"That's close enough, Gus."

"There isn't going to be a shoot-out, Boyd, but I understand your concern." He looked around. "I would like to close the gap a little. I don't think everyone wants to hear our business." He smiled pleasantly as a little girl skipped by him towards the sculpture and began climbing up the mushrooms. A man, probably her father, followed her and came to stand near by while she settled herself in Alice's lap.

"It's kind of lumpy there, sweet pea."

"I know, Daddy. Your lap is better," she answered, which made the man smile. He put his hands in his pocket, obviously ready to wait.

Gus walked a few feet closer, still pushing the baby carriage. "Why don't we all talk over here. Let that little girl and her Daddy have their fun. Shall we?" He looked at Boyd and Maggie. Boyd looked stony-faced. Maggie shrugged. It seemed like she was willing for Boyd to be in charge of this showdown, if that's what it was.

"Fine," Boyd answered grudgingly.

They all stepped to one side and out of earshot of the constant flow of children coming up to the statue to climb on.

:"Okay, Gus. We're here. All nice and civilized. What do you want?"

"Pretty civilized considering," he commented. "Better than I expected even. You've got class, Boyd. You always did."

"I'm feeling pretty harsh, actually. What I'd like to do is punch you in the nose. And considering that I nearly killed Nick, you really don't want to mess with me."

Gus replied quietly, "I don't blame you for wanting to take a poke at me. We were friends. Supposed to be, anyway.'

"You got that right." Boyd took a breath. "I still don't know for sure how involved you were with that whole deranged stalking thing ... I guess we can agree to call it that ... I know for sure Beth was up to her eyeballs in it. And Arthur." Boyd paused. "So now, what the hell do you want? What are you doing here? Stalking us again?"

"Well, I'll answer your second question first. I live in this neighborhood. This is America and people can still live where they want, if they can meet the rent, that is. Secondly, I've been looking for you. I had nothing to do with stalking Maggie. I can tell you that. Veronica here can back me up on that. I just ran my shop. Okay?"

Boyd shrugged. He looked at Veronica, then at Gus. It was obvious that Veronica was going to let Gus do all the talking.

"I've been looking to talk with you two. Back in Fleetwater I heard Parker and Maggie talking, you know, about Parker's parents having an apartment on the Upper West Side and how they decided not to close it down. So I figured Parker was living in it with her boyfriend ..."

"Husband," Maggie said with hostility. "Tony is her husband."

"Fine. Husband. Tony. Her nice fellah from Italy ... anyway, I figured she'd be living here with her *husband*, but that meant you and Maggie wouldn't be far away. Because you're all really close. Friendships like that are hard to break."

"Not that you'd know anything about that, Gus," said Boyd.

Gus did not reply but he did feel Veronica take hold of his hand. It was the back-up he needed. He could do this alone, but it was so much better with Veronica here. He sighed.

"I have to admit I deserve that."

"Good. Now, if we're done ..."

Gus held up his free hand. "No, we're not done." Shit, Boyd was not making this easy. Well, no reason he should, he thought to himself. He doesn't know what I know.

Boyd crossed his arms over his chest. "Well?"

Not much of an invitation but probably the best I'll get.

"I need to tell you some things. Some of it's for you, Boyd, and some of it's for Maggie. I'm pretty sure you will want to hear what I have to say. So, if you will cut me some slack, I'd appreciate it, because, contrary to what you are thinking, I am not just a bad guy. I'm what you call ... 'a practical guy'. Or I was. Unattached, no home to speak of – which you do know something about, Boyd – and I made certain choices ..." Here he held up his hand as if to stave off any objections Boyd might make "... and while they didn't start out to be bad choices, they did get out of hand. Now, I'm not a regretful type of person, either. Maybe not a great intellect, but not stupid. I've seen how things went. They went down badly in the end."

He paused, watching Boyd's face. Okay, he thought. I've got my foot in the door.

"Not all the details are important," and here Boyd made a kind of disbelieving snort ... "but there is some stuff to tell you. To begin: James Fugard was one of our group – originally, that is. I know you met James. He's my friend, too."

Maggie gasped.

"But hold on, Maggie. Just hold on. He got out. He left a long time ago. He didn't like what Beth and Arthur had in mind – which, yes, was tracking you. You are a very good artist, you know. Really. Even a guy like me could see that. In fact, you were the best artist Arthur ever found. If he had just been up front with you ... I mean, all he had to do was just come up to town here and just give you his card. But no, Arthur just couldn't play it straight. James told him it was wrong. That he wouldn't be a part of it. And since James couldn't stop it, he left. As for Nick, who was definitely a bit ... ah, anti-social, shall we say ... he was a bad choice of personnel we were stuck with because he was James' replacement and we were in a hurry and we needed the manpower ..."

Maggie interrupted. "It was Oscar who saved Parker when Nick tried to push her into the traffic ... she finally told us what happened."

Gus winced. "I heard about that. I thought Oscar would just about kill Nick for that caper. That kid was so stupid ..." and he shook his head. "So, to make a long story short, what started out as 'just keeping tabs' on one of the best young artists in the city, got completely out of control."

"Because of Beth and Arthur," Boyd said.

"Right. Strictly because of Beth and Arthur. Being the kind of flawed characters they are," said Gus.

"What about Annette Rousseau?" Maggie asked.

"Well, Arthur gave her this big build-up, this big show ... she got sick. That was completely unexpected."

"And yet Arthur was building a second story onto the gallery to give her another show and run the risk of her getting sick all over again?"

"The answer to that is yes, but as to exactly why she got sick, we really weren't sure."

"Maybe you are just a bunch of bad people and being around bad people like that could actually help make a person sick. How about that?" Maggie's voice was very cold and hard.

"Well, I can't say we thought about it like that."

"I think you better spit this out, Gus," Veronica said, prompting her husband.

"All right. It's like somehow the way Arthur completely blankets an artist's life seems to take energy from them."

461

"You mean, they just keep taking until the artist is drained, even getting sick," Maggie said, finishing the thought.

"Yeah. It's not like I'm some kind of social scientist. But it is what I thought."

"And yet, knowing this, you continued."

"Yes. I'm not making any excuses."

"Good, because we would walk away," said Boyd.

"And you'd be right to. So. Where were we? Oh, yeah. James quit the group. Oscar threatened Nick. After that he was pretty much protecting you all the rest of the time you were in New York because Nick worked at the library with Beth, so me and Arthur couldn't be keeping tabs on him all the time."

"What about Oscar?" Maggie asked. "Was he a part of this scheme?"

"Well, that's a loaded question. He and James were pretty good friends, but like I said, Oscar stayed, in part, at least, so he could look after you. Protect you. That's the truth. Oscar really liked you, really liked your work. He objected to the scheme, but he wasn't in on the decision-making, but once he found out, he had his say. You wouldn't know this but he worked for Arthur for a very long time. Almost all of us are orphans. Literally. It's almost kind of funny, how many orphans are mixed up in this thing. Oscar was apprenticed to Arthur when he was a young man and he had a very big bill to work off. Very big. It got to the point where it looked like he would never do enough to get out from under so when Arthur got this ... uh, job ... running the gallery, Oscar decided to make the most of the opportunity. He paid off his bond. Finally he was making real money for a change. He was being paid pretty well. He worked hard. He likes people. He really liked you, Maggie. So, mainly, he stayed for you. I don't even know if he realized it, but I did."

Maggie nodded. She was glad. That was some of the best news to be gleaned from that most distressing period of her life.

"So, he stayed to protect Maggie," Boyd said.

"That's how it looks to me."

"What about you?" Boyd asked.

"Fair question." He looked at his watch. "You got another fifteen minutes and I think I can wrap this up."

"Maggie?" Boyd asked.

She nodded.

"Go on," Boyd said.

Still not friendly, but what else was I expecting? Gus thought. It's not like I can tell them everything. That would be way too much. So, let me get on with what I came to do.

"Well, this is all a little complicated but here goes. I was one of the originals of our group. I helped settle modern Fleetwater, if you want to know. I did a lot of work. Like I opened my own shop, did all that baking ... it was a lot of work. Plus – and please do not freak out – I was the treasurer for the gallery corporation." Here Gus took a pause while that bit of intelligence sank in.

"You were in charge of the money?" Maggie asked.

"Yup. All the money. Banked by me. I'm the only signatory on the accounts – for mad reasons best known only to Arthur. He did it that way in case anything went wrong; he had no money of his own. I mean, he had his

463

salary, which was substantial. We were all salaried, but the bulk of the money earned from sales and commissions — it's all in my name."

No one spoke. Maggie and Boyd looked at each other in astonishment, and then back at Gus. This whole time, no one had given Veronica a thought, but now Maggie looked at the young woman.

"That means Gus has all my money?" Maggie asked Veronica.

"Gus has all of your money. We put it into various interest-bearing instruments. When the stock market got wonky near the end of the year before, we pulled the money out, just about in time. We lost maybe five percent. But it went into safer investments and we built it back up so there's more now than when we started."

Maggie nodded. It's not like she was angry with Veronica.

"So?" Maggie asked with a kind dead neutrality in her voice.

"So we also have all your paintings — all the unsold work that is — and some of the pieces that were sold, too, which is kind of weird but when Fleetwater closed down there was no time for certain people to pick up the art work. So we took them. We didn't want to leave anything behind, just in case we could find you. The land had a radioactive seepage thing. Apparently there was trouble there before and it was supposed to long time over but it wasn't. Government officials came in, banged up signs and told us to pack up and leave. People just took whatever they thought they wanted and left the rest behind. That was it. They packed up their belongings and left. All those beautiful houses. Such a shame. And galleries. But as it turned out, not everyone was totally careful about the art work, so we went through all the homes of the gallery customers we could get into ..."

"... and helped yourself," Maggie said wryly.

"That's about the size of it," Veronica explained. "We took a Geiger counter with us. We were wearing Hot Papa suits for a week. I was a little freaked out. The first thing we did was to recover your work – anything of yours we could. We noticed some other good pieces, also left behind, so we took those, too. We had to leave pretty fast. No going back. Fleetwater was my home, you know. I mean, I was born there. My parents were both kind of old when they had me, so I lived with my aunt once I got into high school and worked at Gus's to help pay the bills."

"You have all my paintings?" Maggie asked Gus.

"Almost all. Arthur cleared out. He had to. The seepage ... we were warned. No – ordered – to leave ASAP. He took all the gallery records, but from what I saw, I think we got anything of yours that was left behind. I'm pretty sure of that. Because it was very distinctive. I mean, no one is doing anything like what you're doing." Gus paused. He had hoped a little admiration would soften her attitude toward him. No so far, from the looks of things, but he still had a few minutes on the clock.

"I had to leave my notebooks in my room," Maggie said.

"I packed up your room," said Veronica.

"... you did that? For me? ... why? Why would you do that for me?"

"Because you were actually pretty nice to me and you were definitely nice to Gus and I didn't know why you left everything behind. I wasn't in on the situation at that point. I felt packing it all up was the right thing to do. We got it all. In storage."

Maggie shuddered. All that work she thought was gone. She could almost weep with relief.

"You don't have to worry. I know how to pack. We've been paying for first class space at a mini-storage in Midtown the whole time. I don't know much about the price of paintings but I know good paintings when I see them, so they've been wrapped professionally, corner protectors and all. Everything standing up right on specially built shelving. We got a specialist over there to install some free-standing units to pull any water out of the air."

"Well, uh ... Maggs, that sounds good," Boyd offered.

She nodded. She didn't know what to feel, in fact.

"Let's talk about money, shall we?" Gus asked in a brisk, pleasant way.

"Sure, Gus. Let's talk about money. Why not." It didn't sound friendly or pleasant coming from Boyd like that.

"Honey?" Gus said, turning to Veronica and she handed him a padded envelope.

Gus reached inside it.

First he pulled out a key. "This is to the storage locker. I wrote down the address and everything, the specialist I worked with, everything. It's all here." He took a sheet of paper out of the envelope and handed it to Maggie. "You are expected, by the way. Probably they think you are overdue because your name is on the locker and they keep wondering when you are going to show up. They saw the

466

paintings. Loved them. Especially "The Red Toaster". Gus smiled. For the first time.

"Okay. Now, these here are copies of all the quarterly statements of the investing we did with your money from the sales of your artwork. Like I said, we lost a little when the market took a dive, but Veronica here turns out to have a head for this stuff, so we made it all back. It took us about six months and we've been rolling it over ever since." He handed Maggie a check which, when she took hold of it and read how much the check was for – an even $300,000.00, in fact – she nearly folded at the knees. She grabbed onto Boyd's shoulder.

"For Boyd here, the last job you did, which you never got to collect on, which was a put-up job to keep you out of our hair, but which you did the work on, fair and square, I just did a fast calculation and made it for $10,000.00. Hope that's okay with you."

Veronica searched through some papers, found the check for Boyd and handed it over.

Gus noticed that Boyd didn't even look at it. He certainly had to admire that. Boyd knew how to be cool.

"Even though we certainly spent money, we made money. I also had my shop, which did really well. I was proud of that shop, even if I did sort of act like I wasn't. I said I didn't used to be too smart. But I got Veronica now. She keeps me in line." Here again Gus smiled.

It was just enough to remind Maggie of how much she had liked her life in Fleetwater and what had been lost through greed ... and well, even if she had stayed and nothing had been wrong with Arthur and Beth, there was still the matter of the radioactive seepage. So Fleetwater

467

was a doomed town all the while. She might have even got sick, too, if she had stayed. And Boyd. That might in fact be the real reason artists would get sick from time to time. Other people would come and go, but being near the seat of the seepage, it wasn't safe. So now the whole thing was freaking her out. Now she was pregnant. She was imagining what radioactive seepage could do to a fetus ... but Gus was still talking.

"So there was a serious pile of cash in the account, and some interest-bearing investments with real, well-established institutions. Arthur wanted to keep it all in Fleetwater so I lied and told him what he wanted to hear, but he never looked at the books." Gus shook his head. "His laxity is our gain, because Arthur has gone home and he will not be coming back. Guaranteed. He was a pretty rich guy from the get-go. Stupid in certain ways but money seemed to find him. Go figure. Which means, he could try and find me and ask for his share, but I think he knows he doesn't deserve it. Really. Once he started interfering with your life, Maggie, from the way I see things, he forfeited his share of this ..." and he pointed at the envelope which Veronica was still holding.

"What about Beth?" Boyd asked.

"Pretty much the same. She was rich when she signed on. She just got richer because she spent very little money on herself over the years she was with the team. And she worked at the library, too, don't forget. For which she got paid. She was a real librarian. That was no fake.

Knew how to research, our Bethie did. But, again, I'm the judge and jury on this. I did have a long conference call with our home office some time ago. They didn't have all the details for a very long time. I had to fill them in. It got very noisy there for awhile. I made certain proposals to handle the situation, all of which they agreed to, except one and I talked them into agreement with that. See, I decided I didn't want to be recalled. I've had enough of being 'in the field'. (Gus really hoped he was successfully diverting Boyd and Maggie from asking about the parts he really couldn't tell them about. Luckily, he seemed to be having his way so far.) "They finally saw it my way. I can tell you this, Maggie: they would never have agreed to having you stalked. It's not their way. So, the disbursement of this is all up to me." At this, Gus smiled again. Even bigger than the first two times.

What is he up to? Boyd wondered. He looked at Maggie but he could see she wasn't wondering anything. She was evidently still trying to deal with the check she was holding. A cashier's check, he noted, dated recently, too.

"I made arrangements to pay Annette Rousseau's hospital bills, compensation for her house and studio – the one over on Spice Road – and some more besides. She moved to Nantucket Island and set up a studio there. Last time I saw her, I told her I wished her the best. I think she'll be fine. I think it was the seepage that got to her."

"Good for Annette," Maggie murmured.

"So, let's see: that's your art sales money, Boyd's money, told you about Annette. Is that all of it, honey?" Gus asked Veronica.

"You know it isn't," she said looking at Boyd and Maggie.

"You're right. I am beginning to have some fun though. Putting this stuff where it will do the most good. I have to admit, I am enjoying it. Okay. So, last but not least. Okay, not last. Parker. This is compensation for her being in the battle zone. It's a check for $5,000.00. It's just money. It isn't much. But Nick scared the be-jesus out of her, trying to push her into the traffic. That's so wrong I can't believe it. Of course $5,000 is just a number, like I said, but it's what we decided. Also, I know she's married to a rich fellah – it still seemed like a good amount. You give it to her, Maggie." He handed Maggie the check for Parker. "And there's still 10 million dollars left."

Maggie and Boyd were both stunned.

Gus paused to let that sink in. He was beginning to feel a whole lot better. Even if Boyd wasn't smiling yet. But he could tell he'd made an impact on Maggie. That's what comes of having a family, Gus thought. It takes more to break down a guy who was raised the way Boyd was raised. He waited but neither spoke, so he got on with it.

"I know it's a lot of money, but New York is an expensive city to live in. I have expenses, too. I mean, I am a capable guy and I have a very capable wife, so here's what we decided. Notice I said "we". Because I had Veronica's input on this. It had to be okay with her. That was first and foremost for me. You two still want to hear the rest of this, what I have to say?"

Maggie looked at Boyd. He shrugged. Maggie answered for him, "I'm listening."

Gus knew that would have to do.

"I know where Oscar is. He's fine, he's safe and he's ... well, recovering from what 20-odd years of associating with or being ordered about by Beth and Arthur will do to an honest person.

"Actually, he's living with James, who still has a house in Copper Springs. I figure you have his address but I have a copy of it here on this sheet, just in case, and they both hope you will both call and come visit, by the way. Oscar had his own bank account but I figured he earned himself a bonus. Honestly, he could have left, having completed his bond with Arthur, but he stayed to protect you, Maggie. That was about 10 years of protection. No kidding. So, I sent Oscar a check for $500,000.00. I don't know what the hell he will do with that much money, but what the hell, it's only money. And same thing for James. He's got his own money, he's done good in the stock market but hey, we all seem to live a long time these days so, I sent him a check for half a million, too. Feeling like goddamn Santa Claus here, if you don't mind my saying so. So, now, with one thing and another, there's eight million left. Which is still a lot but it has to last a long time, because I can't see myself falling over eight million again any time soon.

Maggie had to smile. Gus was something else. The man had a certain style, and she couldn't fault it. She could feel Boyd holding her hand. She gave it a squeeze. He paused a second or two and squeezed it in answer.

"There is that matter of what we – what our group did to you, Maggie. I'm real sorry about that, kiddo. I don't know when I ever said I was sorry to anyone about anything. Veronica will tell you. I don't apologize. I just try to do what I can and keep going. But that stalking thing: that was insane. Strictly for the birds. So, I made out two checks ... because I really still couldn't figure out what was right."

Maggie looked at Boyd as if to say, he can't do this to me. It's not fair. That was when Boyd smiled.

Gus showed both checks to her. Her hand quivered. No pressure here, she thought. She picked the check she wanted and folded that up, too, and put it in her pocket.

"Good choice, Maggie," said Gus. Veronica nodded. "Hope that clears my account with you."

"It does," she replied.

"Great. And by the way, Boyd, old man, forgot to tell you, all your stuff is in the storage locker, too. All your clothes and tools. Veronica did the packing, so I know it was done right. Everything smoothed out, you know. Folded nice."

The sound of a very small baby waking up from a nap called out. All four looked in the direction of the carriage.

"Oh," said Gus. "You thought this was some kind of a stage prop, I'll bet. Oh no. Come take a look." He turned back the lightweight flannel cover and there inside was a beautiful baby girl looking bright and quite interested. She had Veronica's straight black hair and a pair of very large blue eyes.

"This is our daughter, Sophie Maude Stander. She's seven months old ..."

"Tomorrow. Sophie will be seven months old tomorrow," said Veronica.

"She's beautiful, Veronica. Look, Boyd, she's beautiful."

Boyd looked in. It was true. The little girl was quite a beauty. Perfectly formed head, rosebud mouth, big blue eyes and a head full of straight black hair adorably tied up in a little fountain-like spray on top.

"She gets her coloring from her mother," said Gus, bursting with pride.

"She is beautiful, Gus," Maggie said.

Boyd knew he had to say something nice. Anything else would be pure meanness. Gus was certainly trying. Doing everything he could to square the mess that Arthur and Beth had made.

"She's very beautiful, Gus," he said meaning it."

"Well, thanks for that. I appreciate it. Me and Veronica. So, I think we're done here. Honey, give them the envelope. No sense carrying all that paperwork loose in your hand."

Veronica handed Boyd the envelope. He loaded everything Gus had previously handed him inside and closed it. "I don't know who you bank with but if that money went back to that bank for safekeeping, they'd be thrilled. 'Course I told them not to hold their breath, it wasn't my call."

Boyd laughed. "It is the same bank we use. No irony there."

Gus and Veronica both nodded. "Well, the way we see it, Veronica and me, everyone wins who should and the people who forfeited their share deserved the penalty. I, uh, I put my contact info on the sheet, too. I'm not hiding. And hey, when Sophie has her first birthday party, maybe you folks will come. You think?"

It was hard for Boyd to answer but it was obvious Gus had now done everything he could to make up the damage, so he thought it would be wrong to shun the man. Like he said, he didn't apologize, he just fixed what he could and kept going.

"Sure. Why not?" Boyd replied, warming up a little. "Uh, listen ... I don't guess you know, but Maggie and I are married."

"Thanks but I did know. Your mother put a notice in the paper."

"I'm pregnant, too," Maggie said, just a little bit shyly.

"Congratulations. It's great. Either way, boy or girl, our kids can be friends."

Boyd nodded. He stuck out his hand. Gus took it and they shook.

"You got big ones, son, to want to shake my hand. Even with the pay-off ... it could have gone either way."

"Well, Gus, I think you really stepped up to the plate. Taking responsibility for all the people in this misguided scheme. You get points for that. You did a lot of work to make this all come out right."

"Yeah, it was a lot of work, but I have Veronica. This young woman saved my life. Hell, she saved my soul. There. I've said. I love her to bits. We're happy. So, you and me: we're good?"

Boyd had to admit it. "We're good."

"Maggie, you, too?"

It was hard not to warm to Gus. He had changed in some subtle ways and some which were not so subtle. He was still Gus – an interesting piece of work. She thought Gus and Veronica were good together. She liked that. Seeing people get together and be happy.

"Yes. We're good. I'm glad for you, Gus. About the money? Phew, I really don't know what to say. I'm still

stunned about that. And my artwork and my notebooks –
even more stunned. It'll take me awhile to recover. I'll be
on the phone with Parker for a week – maybe we'll just
stay on the phone, sleep on the phone, have our meals on
the phone ..."

"She means maybe I'll have to send her to Italy for a
week or two and save the phone money. It'll be cheaper."
Boyd was smiling.

Gus had always liked the two of them together; he had
just felt pressured by Arthur to demean their relationship.
Now he was free of that influence. It had been a long
unburdening – peeling off Arthur's influences. At least
Beth had been disdainful, which mean she was easier to
dismiss. But Arthur's sticky, heated emotions had been
harder to scrape away. It was like something would
happen and Gus would notice – oh, that's how I really felt
– not Arthur. Me. It was always revelatory.

"Be seeing you. Maybe soon. I take the train down to
Copper Springs about once every two weeks. You and
Maggie can come along."

"We'd like that, I'm sure. Maggs?"

Maggie nodded. They both waved Gus and Veronica
goodbye as they turned the baby carriage around and
headed back up the path. She was still stunned. Boyd took
her by the hand and walked her out of the park. Left to
herself, Maggie would probably have still been standing
there at dusk. All she could think was: surely this was not
another gift horse. The checks had to be real.

As it proved on the following day, they were entirely
real. Of course they had to call Parker in Italy and make a
visit to see Evan and Barbara, too. Naturally they raced to

the storage facility. Everything was as Veronica and Gus had described it. Seeing all that artwork again really made a difference to Maggie. Moreover, she told Boyd, he should build her a big canvas because she planned to start work on #7. Maggie ended up going to Italy for a week but ended up staying a month which was fine with everyone, during which time Boyd sold the Toaster painting to Dudley for a modest sum. Everything that followed that was just as Boyd had predicted – Maggie was off and running again as an artist.

Just as they left the Park, mostly all she was up to was hanging onto Boyd's hand all the way home.

"I keep remembering all these conversations I had with Parker. About wanting ... everything. You know. The whole big winning package as an artist. She was always warning me about certain types. I didn't listen. I wouldn't. I just didn't believe her."

"Now you do."

"Yes. But I also understand that it's not everyone. That would be the wrong conclusion to jump to. Because that might have meant refusing to talk to Gus and we needed to be able to listen. You have to know the difference. That's the trick, "she said just as they reached the door to their building.

"Did you have a good day?" Frederick asked cheerfully.

"You should only know, Frederick. Completely unbelievable."

"Well, you are good people, so you must have deserved it."

"You are good people for saying so," Boyd replied as Frederick opened the door.

They walked into the lobby still holding hands.

Frederick smiled at the young couple as they walked towards the elevator. Nice people. They deserve the best, he thought.

Back in Central Park, standing by Jose de Creeft's sculpture, Gus and Veronica had returned, wanting to stay outside a little longer. It was fun to watch the children climbing all over the sculpture.

"Our little girl will be climbing that one of these days," said Veronica.

"She will," Gus agreed as Veronica leaned in and uncovered a sleeping Sophie.

"She's perfect, Gus."

"She is, isn't she? No webs, no gills, nothing. She's ... totally human. God in heaven, she's beautiful ..." He stopped. Looking at Veronica, he considered this beautiful young human who had agreed to be his mate. How had he been so lucky? What had he done – really done – to deserve her? "You really took a chance with me. I know that. You know that. I mean, Sophie could have turned out ... a lot of different ways."

"Maybe not," said Veronica. She looked at her husband. "It's not all luck, you know. It's not. You're human now, Gus. Just like me. Human through and through. Okay, maybe the tiniest bit of Mindar is still there, but in all the important ways, you are just as human as I am."

He took Veronica in his arms and held her close. "I say that I am the luckiest man alive. I got a second chance and I took it. Well, I told you, I wanted the whole donut," and that made both of them laugh out loud.

"Hey, Veronica," said Gus, as his wife was tucking the blanket around little Sophie again for the walk back to their apartment, "I thought I heard Maggie say something about a ... a ... what was it? A gift horse? I must have missed that one in school. What's a gift horse?"

"It's when someone leaves you a gift and you take it but it turns out the enemy was hiding inside the gift, so now you've let the enemy inside your gates."

"Really. What a hell of thing that is."

"Yeah. The Greeks did it a long time ago. That's how they won a war. Famous story."

Gus nodded.

Anyone standing nearby would have heard their happy voices blending with the twilight as they walked away down the path both holding onto the handle of the baby carriage, heading out towards the street.

The early spring day had been a gift to the people of New York City for having borne the previous months of bitter winter cold and the crazed wind known as the Montreal Express that had harried their footsteps. The wide swath of blue which had filled the sky flawlessly for hours was now darkening. Several well-known constellations managed to wink into view. A new moon began its slow ascent just as Venus arrived to elegantly place herself at the tip of that milky-golden sliver.

The day that had been eased itself into a setting sun gilding the edges of everything it touched. People looked out their windows and were glad for the beauty. The world was too much with them for these citizens not to understand there would be other battles other times. Right now it was enough for them to know that spring had arrived once more. For today, at least, there was no named or unnamed enemy possessing a heart filled with deceit seeking to bring them down. For today, at least, there was no gift horse waiting patiently at the gates of their city to beguile the weak. Today, this fortress they called home, was safe.

Acknowledgement

The author wishes to deeply thank Erin Imhoff for her careful editing of this book as well as her continued, unbridled enthusiasm for my fiction. Also, many thanks to fellow writer, Brooke Babineau. He kept me at it until it was right.

Thank you for reading.
Please review this book. Reviews help others find
Absolutely Amazing eBooks and inspire us to keep
providing these marvelous tales.

If you would like to be put on our email list to receive
updates on new releases, contests, and promotions, please
go to AbsolutelyAmazingEbooks.com and sign up.

ABOUT THE AUTHOR

Formal education finally concluded with a BFA in painting from the Massachusetts College of Art. Leslie is a published poet: in magazines, anthologies, in her own chapbooks, on the Internet. She has participated in well over 150 open mic readings in Boston, New York, Miami and Tampa, Florida, Los Angeles and Paris, France.

While still a visual artist and poet, Leslie's short stories "Mischief" and "A Christmas Fare" were broadcast live on cable radio in Los Angeles. 10 years ago she became de facto leader of a writers' workshop now in its 22nd consecutive year.

Leslie has turned her passion for writing also into a day job; she is now freelancing as a book editor and writing coach. Her clients range from an exuberant 23-yr old with a flair for sci-fi to a 42-yr old writing young adult stories to a 78-year old finally getting to live the dream of writing a memoir.

In 2011 her short story "The Storm of the Century" appeared in a Sleeping Cat Books anthology and "Out West A-Ways" was included Angie Merriman's anthology, "Intertwine". In 2012, British mystery writer, Neal James, made her Guest Author twice on his website with "The Emperor's Gate" and "In Lewis Carroll Country". The publication of her novel, "The Gift Horse," marks her debut as she joins the swell of new writers bringing their work to the public.